I0819192

LOVE
Lost

The Tails from the Alpha Art Gallery Series

Love Bites

Love Sucks

Love Lies

Love Binds

Love Lost

LOVE LOST

CYNTHIA
ST. AUBIN

TOR PUBLISHING GROUP
NEW YORK

This is a work of fiction. All of the names, characters, organizations, places, and events portrayed in this work are either products of the author's imagination or used fictitiously.

LOVE LOST

A Tor Book
Published by Tom Doherty Associates / Tor Publishing Group
120 Broadway
New York, NY 10271

www.torpublishinggroup.com

EU Representative: Macmillan Publishers Ireland Ltd, 1st Floor, The Liffey Trust Centre, 117–126 Sheriff Street Upper, Dublin 1, D01 YC43

The Library of Congress Cataloging-in-Publication Data is available upon request.

ISBN 978-1-250-40720-7 (trade paperback)
ISBN 978-1-250-40721-4 (ebook)

First Tor Paperback Edition: 2026

Printed in the United States of America

10 9 8 7 6 5 4 3 2 1

For my mother, **Barbara**,

who made me a reader and always told the best—if not always strictly age-appropriate—bedtime stories.

I love you, Maaaahm.

LOVE
Lost

Prologue

I'm melting.

The skin on the top of my feet bubbles up as the scalding ooze I'm standing in climbs my ankles, cementing me in place.

Pain sizzles along my nerves as I pull against it, all too aware that if I lose my balance I'll fall face-first into the molten pool spreading around me. Like quicksand but thicker, hot as lava and eerily viscous, burning, *burning* as it creeps from my ankles toward my knees. Panic sets in, my heart pounding in my chest, a drumbeat echoing in my ears.

I can't move.

And the more I struggle, the faster I sink.

My breath comes in short, harsh gasps, each one carrying the sickly reek of charred flesh.

It's licking up my naked thighs now, reducing the nerve-dense gather of flesh between them to a bolt of agony that temporarily fills my vision with a brief, blinding flash. Perversely, I glance down to watch the glowing sludge fill the knot at my navel. The place where once life had flowed into me, seared forever shut.

My throat is raw, shredded from the ragged scream tearing from my vocal cords.

No one can hear me.

No one is coming.

I can't die like this.

Oh, but you can, a silky, feminine voice answers from somewhere in the ether. *And you will.*

1

The evil sludge climbs my ribs like a ladder, brushing the bottoms of my breasts as gently as a lover before the fatty tissue begins to pop and hiss.

I summon every ounce of strength left in my trembling limbs, galvanized by the hideously surreal sound. My arms are still free, and I swing them hard. My fists connect with something solid. My fingers claw at the invisible force that held me captive even as the ooze rises to kiss my elbow with flame.

It's at my collarbones now, my neck.

My chin.

I feel my lower lip swell as the flesh begins to blister. In the split second before my taste buds are seared away, I taste death.

I taste burning.

I taste . . . *cheese*?

The thought barely has time to register before my scream chokes to a gurgle as the substance fills my throat.

My head jerks backward, fighting to keep my nostrils above the scorching surge.

My lungs fill for the last time, sucking in a pungent aroma triggering a memory within the brain that hasn't yet boiled inside my skull.

Gruyère? Emmenthaler?

Then pain vacuums this last thought away. Darkness closes in around me. My eyelids are gone. My forehead. My hair.

The small spark of life causes my lungs to work like a bellows, still attempting to deflate the now oxygen-depleted breath.

But I am sealed.

Surrounded. Suffocating.

Dying.

My arm spasms, and in my mind's eye, I can see the naked bone drive into the solid object with the furious final swell of my life force.

"Fuck!" The muffled word cuts through the muck.

Just like that, the nightmare shattered like glass, pieces of it still embedded in my mind as I blinked gritty eyes in the pitch dark.

Disoriented, I blinked rapidly, gulping deep breaths of clean, cool air.

And on one of them rode a current of a scent that lit up the overdeveloped olfactory bulb of my shifter brain like the Rockefeller Center yuletide tree.

Warm, sleep-salty skin still carrying traces of starch from a shirt collar. Silky hair tinged with pillowcase fabric softener. Hints of cedar, and scotch, and salvation.

Mark Abernathy.

My mate. My love. My—dear sweet Jesus, was that a *bruise*?

Being somewhat of a late bloomer when it came to the actual *shifting* part of being a shifter, it took me a beat to click over to the far more finely tuned night vision of my canid nature.

When I did, the bedroom bloomed around me in a far subtler palette of muted butter yellow, acid greens, and dusky violets despite the total blackout curtains Abernathy favored.

With the arrival of each detail of the master bedroom in our château-style mountain chalet home, my panic began to ebb.

Four walls adorned with ornately framed paintings that probably belonged in museums. The bookshelves bearing first-edition classics—many of them signed—that would likely sell for enough to buy a small island.

Our oversize antique four-poster bed, and Abernathy in it, his muscular torso bare from the waist up, biceps bunching as he massaged the deep magenta spot on his jaw.

"Oh, babe," I said, quickly peeling away the sweat-soaked covers to slide over to him. "Are you okay?"

He nodded, his crown of dark hair sleep-rumpled, his hooded eyes fluorescing emerald in my grayscale night vision. "Fine."

He wasn't, but I knew he would be, rapid healing one of the more useful upsides to sharing your corporeal being with a supernatural wolf entity.

"I was doing sleep karate again, wasn't I?"

"A little." A loud pop emitted from the hinge of his jaw as it locked back into place. "The dream?"

"The" dream.

As if there had only ever been one.

And "dream."

Such a totally innocuous term for the horrific slideshow of demise that played on loop in my subconscious since officially mating with Abernathy.

Indeed, my scattered squirrel brain had basically been like a game show contestant, where the grand prize was a nightly front-row seat to my own funeral.

There was the one where I was buried alive by a vengeful girl ghost, the weight of the dirt crushing my chest and worms slithering into my mouth as I scream soundlessly.

Or the one where I'm being burned at the stake by an angry mob of werecats. Nothing like the smell of your own charred flesh mingling with burning catnip blunts to spice up that REM sleep.

Or the unique ASMR that was being mauled by a pack of berserkers: the torn-fabric sound of my muscles ripping from my bones and the satisfying crunch of my nose cartilage disappearing into a slavering maw.

And who could forget being run down by a demon donkey

pulling a cart of whiskey casks, my ribs splintering with every turn of the wheels?

I shivered as the memory of its unholy bray echoed in my ears.

Yes, my nightly repose had been a veritable cornucopia of gruesomely violent endings.

But drowning in Satan's own fondue? That there took the shit biscuit.

I mean, it would have been heaven if not for the whole melted-flesh-and-suffocation thing, but—

"Hanna?" Abernathy asked after what must have been an extensive silence.

"Yep." I sighed. "I had the dream."

"Must've been pretty bad," he said, thumbing the already-receding bruise.

"The worst," I admitted.

Abernathy lifted his arm in invitation for me to slide under it. "Come here."

Which, of course, I did.

He was big, and warm, and wonderfully solid; the weight of his arm around my shoulders felt like an anchor to the earth and every good, safe thing in it.

"Want to tell me about it?" he asked.

The heat of his body enveloped me like a blanket, slowly coaxing my tension-knotted muscles of my neck and shoulders to relax.

But still, I shook my head. Poring over the still-fresh and excruciating details felt like about as much fun as a lizard shifter hot tub party.

Sidenote: If you've never been to one, I 10/10 do not recommend.

"You should try to get some sleep." Abernathy scooped his arm behind my back and down to my waist, rolling me into the little spoon position against his broad torso. "Tuck on in here."

"Actually," I said, patting the heavy hand resting on my hip, "I think I'm going to go check on the cats."

True, this was 100 percent an excuse, but not an altogether unreasonable one. My dreams tended to spook them into varying arrays of problematic behavior.

Gilbert, the portly elder statesman of my feline life partners: anxious-pooping on any surface, most likely to be discovered by a bare foot.

Stewie, the tabico agent of chaos: wanton destruction of any unattended expensive and/or necessary object.

Stella, the tuxedo cat vendetta specialist: disgorging partially digested kibble into Abernathy's handmade Italian loafers.

My insistence that this was Stella's way of urging Abernathy to explore the exciting new terrain of vegan leather was never enthusiastically received.

He nuzzled my neck and pressed a kiss to my hair.

"They're fine," he mumbled in a voice already thickening with drowsiness.

I felt a sizzle of envy.

I'd personally witnessed Abernathy sleep through a barroom brawl between a banshee and a bodah (think bogeyman but with more skin folds and a really bad attitude) above a Dublin shifter pub / Airbnb.

Hell, not even my occasional passive-aggressive hausfrau Saturday-morning revenge cleaning could rouse him.

I rolled over in the circle of his arms, pushing a stray lock of dark hair from his perma-furrowed brow. "Then how about this," I said. "You're going to dissolve into epiglottis-rattling snores in about zero point two seconds, and I don't feel like lying here listening to it, twitchy with adrenaline and marinating in the nameless dread still lingering at the edges of my consciousness until my alarm goes off and cattle-prods me toward a shower."

Abernathy opened his mouth, but I started speaking the same second he did, making his next sentence come out in perfect unison.

"I'll cattle-prod you toward a shower."

He arched a dark brow at me. "So I snore, *and* I'm predictable. Remind me why you're still with me?"

"Because werewolves mate for life?" I teased, propping myself on an elbow.

His brow furrowed deeper in mock-worry. "Is that the only reason?"

It's one of those questions that's never truly casual, even when, like now, it's being asked with a playful edge.

"Also because I'm madly in love with you and pretty much have been since I set foot in your disaster zone of an office?"

I smiled, remembering how the old wooden staircase in the Victorian-era redbrick building had creaked as I'd climbed toward his office for my interview. Each step felt like a lifetime, my heart banging like a bongo when I'd overheard him threatening someone on the other end of the phone.

Of course, if I'd known then what I know now—namely, that Abernathy had caught my scent before I'd even exited Buckminster, my '67 Mustang—I wouldn't have bothered trying to sneak away.

But, oh, to see him again for the first time.

To taste the tingle of trepidation I'd felt registering Abernathy's towering six-foot-six frame looming in the doorway. To sample even a single sip of the delicious shiver that had slithered down my spine under his penetrating gaze. To feel the hairs on the back of my neck lift at the first rumble of that peat smoke–and–coffee ground voice in my ear.

Okay, so technically, the first time I'd heard his voice, it had been through a Walmart burner phone I'd had to purchase when my shitweasel of an ex had cut my cell off postdivorce. Even though I'd been curled in a ball below my coffee table with a bag of peanut butter M&M's and a bottle of Gentleman Jack, it still featured as a positive memory.

"Better," Abernathy said in the present. "But it still doesn't solve our problem."

"Which one?" I snorted.

I instantly wished I hadn't. Because it's the kind of thing you can only joke about when none of those problems have teeth—literally *and* figuratively, in this case—and the growing legion of ours most definitely did.

"The one where you end up anxiously prowling the house inventing elaborate projects that involve feeding and/or housing the local woodland creatures and I end up in bed without you."

"It's like you know me," I said.

"Oh, I know you," Abernathy and I said in unison.

One corner of his mouth curled into a sleepy smile. "And you, apparently, know me."

"Like the back of my hand," I said.

Abernathy's irises melted from emeralds to yellow topaz, deepening to the glowing amber that marked either anger . . . or arousal. The latter, I happily discovered as he captured the hand I'd held up as a visual aid and guided it beneath the covers.

"*Sir*," I said, affecting an overblown Southern belle accent as I hooked a leg over his hip in invitation. "That's no cattle prod."

We melted into a tangle of seeking lips and grasping hands. The pace was slow, almost lazy, but no less intense for its unhurried unfolding. By the time he slid into me, I was writhing beneath him, too far gone for teasing.

And as he filled me, I imagined the darkness being driven out. Going away.

Going. Going. But never gone.

Lingering in the misty distance. Watching. Waiting.

2

If there are depots on the way to hell, I'm pretty sure Costco on a Saturday morning is one of them.

However bad the labyrinth of big-box bulk consumerism had been on the few occasions I'd had to embark on such a feckless venture when I was fully human, the chaotic scene confronting me now was a bajillion times worse.

Because: sensory overload multiplied by shifter.

The sounds, for one. Crashing carts. Whining wheels. Checkout stand swipes and beeps. Cardboard rasping against skin. All of this peppered with the staccato shrieks of small humans and the insectile hum of large ones having hundreds of the most mundane conversations possible all at once.

But even worse: smells.

As much as I adore a mood-enhancing Polish sausage or bougie Hot Pocket Parmesan chicken bake, when combined with the reek of at least thirty-eight humid dirty diapers of varying strained vegetable and liquified protein bouquets, it's not exactly Chanel N°5.

I flicked a look at Abernathy, this particular scent being somewhat of a trigger for him after a very regrettable evening babysitting River and Olivia, my niece and nephew, when they were still inclined to colonic pyrotechnics.

The fact that they were out of diapers and roughly equivalent to third graders now had done little to relieve the psychic carnage.

Or at least, this was the reason Abernathy had cited when

declining my brother Steve and sister-in-law Shayla's last several dinner invitations.

"Remind me why we're here again?" Abernathy's jaw flexed in my peripheral vision as we assessed the gridlock of aisle 37—Frozen Foods: Dinners, Snacks & Appetizers.

Samples of the last being the reason for the unyielding clot of humans preventing me from accessing the next item on my extensive list.

"*I'm* here to panic-purchase backup booze and nibbly bits for the gallery show tomorrow evening because the new caterer I hired to take care of the refreshments *still* hasn't called me back, and the idea of there being no food when people show up makes me want to vomit. You're here because I asked you to come with me when there was still enough postcoital dopamine and oxytocin left in your brain to make driving the sixty miles to Westminster to fight the family hordes for mid-level chardonnay and charcuterie trays seem like a good idea."

My enhanced sensitivity to the biochemical signature of his simmering rage notwithstanding, I was just delighted that Abernathy had agreed to come at all, prone as he had been to remaining welded to our overstuffed leather sofa or closeted in his study as of late.

"Right." A slow, measured inhale inflated the deep expanse of his chest.

A cart bursting with an impressive assortment of household staples (disinfectant wipes, Swiffer pads, paper towels, detergent pods) and organic toddler snacks (applesauce pouches, banana-yogurt bites, sweet potato puffs) pulled up alongside ours. The strawberry-blond woman steering it pawed through a diaper bag with one hand and pulled out a pouch of travel wipes before tearing open a yet-unpaid-for box of gluten-free cheddar cheese bunny crackers. Tucking one pack next to the infant fastened to the cart caddy, she handed two more to the elementary school–aged boy and preschool-aged girl trailing her like satellites.

"Phone." She held out her hand to the boy, who completely ignored her, his pale-lash-fringed green eyes fixed on the smudgy screen.

"Braxton, that's *one*," she warned in a voice that suggested it was probably closer to twenty-seven.

The boy heaved a put-upon sigh and plopped the expensive device onto her palm. Huffing a breath onto the screen, the woman wiped it on her yoga pants and dropped it into her purse.

Then she stroked the buttery cheek of the curly carrot-topped infant, who gave her a gummy grin and cooed.

A sound so goddamn adorable that it felt like I'd been punched in the heart and ovaries simultaneously.

Every time I thought I'd made peace with my broken lady bits, some innocuous encounter like this happened and woke the familiar pang.

Tears filmed my eyes.

Naturally, Momma chose that exact moment to look my way.

"She's beautiful," I said, blinking furiously.

"Thanks," she said, adjusting the harness as the baby began to squirm. "Unfortunately, she's going to start screeching like a hyena if I don't finish shopping and feed her in the next fifteen minutes."

We exchanged a sympathetic *these bitches* look at the trio of latte-sipping lululemon ladies who, after being just *shocked* to run into each other, had apparently decided to review their respective families' every milestone smack in front of the bacon-wrapped scallops.

Ever galvanized by someone else's discomfort more than my own, I nudged my way closer.

"Excuse us," I said, attempting to get their attention.

"Fourth grade? Already?" one of them said, her iced coffee to her glossy lips. "How did you grow up so fast?" she asked, aiming the question at the only one of their combined brood who wasn't pinging off the fogged doors of the refrigerated cases like a sticky pinball. The small, bespectacled girl shrugged.

"Pardon me," I tried again. "If we could just squeeze by you—"

"Now is she still on the waiting list for Montessori this fall or—"

"We *could* just turn around and go back the way we came," Abernathy suggested.

"And bypass the samples?" I clutched the list to my chest in exaggerated horror. "Perish the thought!"

Judging by the lines bracketing his downturned lips, most of his thoughts were presently dedicated to regretting every life choice that had led him to the present moment.

"Ladies." Abernathy's deep, resonant voice seemed to turn the volume down by at least two notches in our immediate area. The tight smiles all three women turned our way abruptly melted as their eyes rose to Abernathy's face, then retraced their steps downward. Even dressed in jeans, boots, and a button-up shirt rolled to the elbows, he passed for a suburbanite about as well as a bomb passed for a bagel.

"Mind if we sneak by?" he asked.

"Not at all," purred the one closest to me, batting her Bambiesque lash extensions.

I resisted the urge to step on her perfectly pedicured toes as I passed.

I was more than used to watching other women eye-hump my mate, animal magnetism being one of the lycanthropic side effects he had zero control over.

But still.

No sooner had we steered our double-wide grocery cart through the narrow path they cleared than we ran into the next knot of bodies.

I could literally *feel* Abernathy's blood pressure rising.

"Two seconds," I promised, holding up two fingers as I glanced back at him.

Leveraging skills learned from my exceedingly brief foray into roller derby, I waded into the fray.

I emerged moments later, triumphantly carrying a frost-kissed box of bacon-wrapped scallop skewers and two fluted paper cups holding wedges of spinach-artichoke mini-quiche. "Behold!" I declared, presenting them to Abernathy. "The spoils of battle."

His nostrils flared briefly before the bridge of his nose accordioned with disgust.

"Pass," he said.

"Oh, I wasn't offering," I said, well aware of his carnivorous leanings. "These are for me. You're just a convenient decoy that makes my appetizer avarice more socially acceptable." Despite the sour look this earned me from Abernathy, I couldn't help but feel my oma would have been proud. A veteran of what she had referred to as "the free buffet," my sassy Bavarian-born grandmother would frequently use her age as carte blanche when finessing the sample pushers who attempted to discourage her from scoring seconds.

"Vhat are you going to do, tackle an eighty-year-old voman for taking a second crab cake?"

The crystal-clear memory of her familiar voice arrived with a sneaky sidecar of grief that only augmented the lingering ache in my chest.

When I was growing up, my mother and I had frequently butted heads on everything from the proper color of pantyhose (no one's, and I mean *no one's*, legs are actually "smoky taupe") to the correct cycle for washing whites. (Trick question: Everyone knows you dump the whole hamper in, put that shit on hot, and pray.)

But Oma?

We just . . . *got* each other.

Since her untimely passing, I'd been surrounded by any number of beings who were older than I was, but rarely wiser.

Except for Allan.

That thought, I mentally donkey-kicked into the stratosphere before it even had time to tickle my tear ducts.

Not today, Hades.

"Worth all that effort?" Abernathy asked as I popped the first bite into my mouth and chewed.

"You bet your biceps," I said, savoring the second bite of silky egg and buttery pastry. "And look!" I held up one of the weensy recyclable spoons tucked into each cup. "Adorable *and* environmentally friendly."

I leaned across the cart to drop the tiny utensils into my purse pocket, and Abernathy's eyes softened, the corner of his mouth twitching upward as he brushed a flake of pastry from my chin.

"I like to use them for ice cream," I explained, leading us around the corner at last. "Makes it last longer."

"Since whe—" The word dissolved into a pained grunt, then morphed into a deep-throated snarl that sent ice water spilling down my spine.

I whirled in time to see Abernathy's eyes flash yellow as he glared at "Braxton, that's one," who had hijacked his mother's cart and rammed it into Abernathy's ankle.

"Braxton," she scolded, still finishing tucking the baby into a chest sling as she jogged over. "Apologize to the man."

The kid only stared at Abernathy, his mouth frozen in a cheese dust–ringed *O*.

"It's fine." I laced my fingers through the cart and propelled Abernathy forward. "No harm done."

Yet.

"Did you see that?" I heard the kid whisper in our wake. "His eyes were literally like Waffle's."

"Braxton," his mother clucked. "*Literally* means *actually*. As in, we've *literally* talked about not using that word. And there's *literally* no way the man's eyes were *actually* yellow."

"But they *were*," Braxton insisted.

"Braxton, that's *two*."

The bites of quiche curdled in my stomach as their voices dissolved into the sound stew.

It's common knowledge within pretty much every sector of the supernatural world that engaging in any behavior around humans that might even *hint* at the existence of a paranormal realm is a big no-no. Suspecting that *now* might not be the optimum time to remind Abernathy of this, I tried a different tactic.

"Happy now?" I said through the side of my mouth. "You literally have eyes like Waffle."

"At least I can see where the fuck I'm going with them," he muttered.

"He was like six," I pointed out.

"Which is why his mother shouldn't let him drive a giant metal cart around a crowded grocery store."

What I *didn't* say was, "Or maybe his finance bro of a father could have offered to watch the kids instead of playing golf with his khaki shorts–wearing cronies so she could shop in peace for the house she probably does 97 percent of the work to run."

Not because I wasn't thinking it.

But because I sensed that this addition would likely only amplify the hot waves of irritation I felt rolling off him.

"You know," I said, lightly placing a hand on Abernathy's arm. "It's just a hop, skip, and a jump from that kind of thinking to *get off my lawn*. Just because you're turning four hundred and thirty-two in a couple of weeks doesn't mean you have to—"

"Don't remind me." Abernathy lengthened his stride.

The ache lodged behind my sternum deepened into a throb.

Abernathy had always been a broody bastard, but lately, there was something . . . darker, heavier about his moods.

My attempts to decipher the cause were met with the stony resistance that had driven me batshit crazy in the earliest days of our acquaintance.

If the overwhelming responsibilities of becoming the alpha had one upside, it was significantly reduced time and/or energy to obsess about anything not directly related to the survival (or lack thereof) of the shifter kingdom.

"What do we have left to get?" Abernathy asked, longingly eyeing the main thoroughfare leading toward the registers.

My vision blurred once more as I glanced down at my list. "Um, a dessert tray," I said. "Over by the bakery."

I let him get a few steps ahead of me as we wound through the brazen display of carbs. Crusty artisan loaves, flaky curls of croissants, mammoth muffins.

And *cake*.

I lingered before the refrigerated case, my taste buds contracting at the sight of the snowy blankets of white icing harboring what I knew would be layers of melt-in-your-mouth vanilla sponge sandwiching a fluffy strawberry mousse. I could practically taste the sweetness of the fat frosting balloons still cold from the fridge, dissolving like a truffle on my coffee-warmed tongue.

After all, Abernathy *did* have a birthday coming up, and the way I figured it, pretty much any birthday after four centuries should totally qualify as a milestone.

Milestones pretty much *required* parties, and parties *definitely* required cake.

Glancing up to see Abernathy approaching the butcher section, I snuck my phone out of my jeans pocket and quickly tapped out a text.

Down to help me with a secret mission involving a certain someone's four hundred and thirty-second birthday?

To my delight, the answer pinged back almost immediately.

Maker of merriment, rouser of rabbles, and sherpa of shindigs at your service!!

Splendid! I typed back. *Chat about it tonight?*

Indubitably!

For the first time in longer than I could remember, I felt a small spark of anticipation. With any luck, this covert convivial gathering would be just the thing to drag Abernathy out of his funk.

Smiling to myself, I tucked my phone back in my pocket and aimed myself toward the meat section.

Only to find Abernathy staring straight at me.

Though I wasn't doing a single thing wrong, my latent ancestral religious guilt and cursed ginger genetics triggered the involuntary feet-to-forehead flush that had been the bane of my existence since puberty.

Cheeks glowing an atomic cherry, I hastily snatched up one of the plastic-domed trays of assorted mini-desserts and made a beeline for my now-scowling mate.

I'd gotten as far as the bubbling live lobster pound when an abrupt aberration in the ongoing auditory assault caught my attention.

Children.

A sudden and inexplicable chorus of small, excited voices.

Inexplicable, that is, until I glanced up to a sight that made me stop in my tracks.

Furries.

As in, adults wearing exceedingly detailed full-body character-based animal costumes for the purposes of social belonging and/or sexual gratification.

Three of them in total, arrayed like comic book–esque conceptions of werewolves. Elongated snouts. Pointy ears. Broad shoulders. Thick necks.

And flannel.

Each wolf wearing a different color of Buffalo check cloth, mid-transformation semi-shredded Carhartt-style work pants, and battered work boots.

Having binge-watched several seasons of *My Strange Addiction* during the bleak depression phase of my divorce from Dave the Shitweasel, I was familiar with the concept of a "Fursona" and wondered if their backstories might involve some kind of lupine lumberjack scenario.

I *also* wondered what possible reason three lupine lumberjacks could have to prance through a Costco on a Saturday morning.

Like the proverbial deer in the headlights, I remained rooted to the spot, silently willing them to hang a right. A left. A diagonal.

Basically, any direction at all that would carry them away from my general vicinity.

No such luck.

On oversize foam and fur feet tipped with comically large black talons, they shuffled in my direction.

I cut my eyes to Abernathy, who was watching the proceedings with something bordering on amusement.

Which, weirdly, is progress.

Once upon a time, he'd already have hung the largest wolf from a meat hook by its own jaunty red bandanna, demanding that it state its business with me or be disemboweled.

Hot? You betcha.

Effective PR strategy for an alpha? Not so much.

As such, I'd politely requested that my mate extend me the great courtesy of allowing me to attempt to resolve potential conflicts *before* pendant viscera became part of the equation when my life wasn't in immediate danger.

And it wasn't.

As I would, Abernathy would doubtless have caught the gust of stale pizza, energy drinks, and adrenaline sweat common to the chemosensory profile known as *Gamer* venting itself through the screened eyeholes of the furries' suits.

So why did his failure to send humans flying like bowling pins as he mowed his way down the aisle to get to my side feel like the emotional equivalent of an atomic wedgie?

Time took on an odd *Twilight Zone* quality as the red flannel–wearing wolf who appeared to be leading the motley crew stopped right in front of me and *kneeled.* Its companions followed suit. Forearms braced on knees, furry fabricated heads bowed deferentially.

"Please tell me this is some sort of weird flash mob," I said, feeling my armpits dampen.

"Your Majesty," the wolf intoned in a reverent voice. "We have come to offer our service."

A film of sweat bloomed between my fingertips and the dessert tray.

"Look, I super appreciate the sentiment, but I'm pretty sure I haven't joined any secret societies lately. Or sworn any blood oaths. Or, you know, done anything I can think of that would necessitate people dressing up like anthropomorphic Muppets to subjugate themselves to me in the seafood section of a wholesale retail store."

By mechanisms I had zero hope of understanding, the wolf's ears drooped slightly. "You do not accept our fealty?"

"Nope," I said, repositioning my dessert assortment within my sweaty palms. "Hard pass on the fealty."

"Then what of our protection?"

"Your protection?" I repeated.

"We are sworn to protect the alpha," the wolf declared solemnly.

At this word, every single hair—including the fine blond ones my sugar wax kit hadn't quite managed to yank from their Westley à la Dread Pirate Roberts configuration on my upper lip—lifted from my skin.

While *alpha* was still commonly misused by misguided males in everything from terrible dating profiles to alt-right rallies, hearing it spoken *to me* in this context implied all sorts of things I didn't particularly like.

"Sworn to whom?" I demanded. "Protect the alpha from *what*?"

As if on cue, a throaty but distinctly human *arroooooooo* rose over the murmur of the shoppers, who, gratefully, seemed more concerned with doing their weekly restock than watching . . . whatever the hell this was.

Until now.

Carts froze. Conversations ceased. And heads whipped my way as several technicolor bodies barreled into view.

Oh, yes indeedy, friends and neighbors.

More furries.

These ones, a technicolor woodland assortment like something out of a fucked-up fable.

A scarlet-red steampunk-styled fox. An electric-blue rabbit in a jaunty vest and bow tie. And was that a purple . . . dog? Coyote? Whatever it was, it wore an ascot and a monocle.

My would-be subjects shot to their feet (paws?), placing themselves between me and the approaching entourage.

"We meet again, *Vargr*." The fox's voice sounded neither masculine nor feminine, whether warped by whatever materials comprised the costume's head or intentionally altered to align with a character.

"*Again?*" I hadn't meant to ask this aloud, but the idea that I might have inadvertently strayed into an ongoing but completely unrelated RPG furry feud brought a measure of relief.

The red flannel–wearing lumberjack wolf stepped forward, pointing an impressively attenuated claw at the fox. "You have overstepped your borders, trickster. The alpha is our kind, not yours."

"Um, guys," I said, "and I mean that in a strictly gender-neutral sense because I can't really tell what's going on in there." I motioned toward the new arrivals. "The only *kind* I am is kind of in a hurry to get the hell out of here. So if you could—"

"Stand down, pretender!" The fox's voice cracked like a whip, raising gooseflesh on my skin.

"You dare call *Vargr* a pretender?" Green Flannel wolf nudged closer to his leader.

"We do not wish to engage in violence today." The fox's black leather-gloved paw hovered near the studded belt at its waist. Above that, twin mounds of either foam or flesh pushed out against the lapels of the black leather vest covering her Atomic Fireball–colored pelt.

"Then you surrender?" Red Flannel wolf asked.

Leave now. You are not safe.

I was so stunned by the resonant power of the words that it took me a full *one Louisiana*—because who the fuck counts using a state *not* famous for beignets—to realize that I'd heard them not with my ears but *inside my mind.*

The realization slammed into me as a wave of nausea rocked me back onto my heels.

Then several things happened at all once.

"Never!" The fox leaped at the wolf with an eardrum-piercing shriek, the momentum sending them tumbling into the display of coffee cakes and danishes. The other furries jumped into the fray, rainbow tufts of fur and cinnamon streusel crumbs flying.

"Tear its tails off!"

Hearing the violent suggestion spoken in a child's voice, I turned to see Braxton standing rapt at the edge of the fray, analyzing the action like a boxing coach.

"Braxton, that's six!" his mother said, wheeling over in her cart.

"But that's how you kill one," the boy said, pointing a sticky finger toward the scarlet fox, whose multiple tails were currently clamped in one of the wolves' maws. "You've gotta—"

"You want to go to the bounce house after this or not?" his mother snapped, parking a hand on her hip.

Braxton heaved a snotty, put-upon sigh. "*Fine.*"

"You okay?" Abernathy was suddenly at my side, the need to wreak very real havoc on these very fake shifters writ large on his features.

Luckily, his need to exit this fresh hell proved even more compelling.

"I'm fine," I said, already pointing the cart in the opposite direction. "Quick. While everyone's distracted. Let's get to the register!"

We fast-walked toward the front of the store, reaching a completely empty lane just as the security guards arrived to break up the action.

"Vanquish the *Vargr*!" the fox growled as I slid the dessert tray onto the conveyor belt. "Freki will be avenged!"

Vargr. Freki.

Wolves from Norse mythology.

I dared a last bewildered glance over my shoulder.

In that moment, I wasn't certain what I found more disturbing.

The red fox's cryptic psychic warning right before the battle, or the realization that every single one of the raspberry-jam-and-icing-smeared combatants would have had to display a Costco membership card to get in.

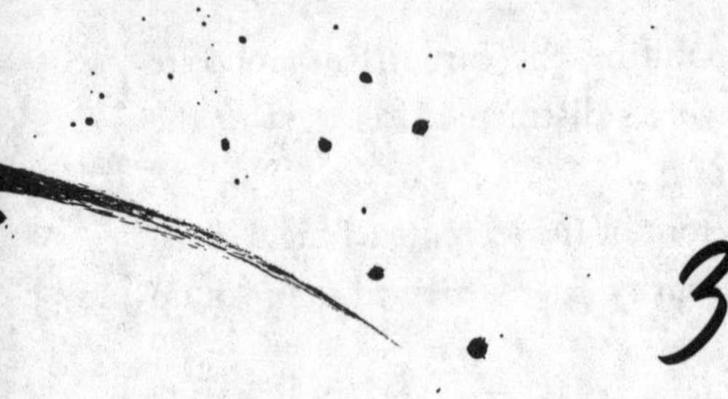

3

A heavy summer rain pounded the skylights, giving the second-floor loft overlooking the Crossing's gallery an eerie underwater quality.

Beyond the railing, where my desk was parked outside Abernathy's office, the main display space was empty.

Hours from now, it would, hopefully, be filled with patrons ready to part with a small portion of their disposable income in exchange for one of the pieces on offer by our resident artists or occasional locals who submitted their work.

But for now, it was blessedly silent.

Like Abernathy's office.

I'd come in early for this very reason.

A chance to work through the most pressing items on my never-ending to-do list without the distractions and interruptions that frequently accompanied the Crossing operating at full tilt.

That had been the plan, anyway.

Instead, I sat glaring at the rainbow spinny wheel of death on my gratuitously oversize monitor with nary a box checked, an untouched grilled gouda and honey crisp apple panini languishing at my elbow.

"Come on," I crooned, half holding my breath and willing the IRS.gov page to load. "Come on, baby, you can do it."

If, perchance, the page timed out, I would lose all my progress on the seemingly endless form I'd been laboring over for the last four hours.

And if that happened, I'd have to leap from the landing outside Abernathy's office and launch myself in front of the next oncoming low-emissions bus.

Only, in the tiny mountain tourist hamlet / former mining hub that was Georgetown, Colorado, that could take at least half an hour. And even then, the hybrid engine topped out at a minor-maiming twenty-five miles an hour.

Why, why, *why* hadn't I just clicked the goddamn Save My Progress button?

Because you leaped tits-first down a real estate rabbit hole, stalking cabins for sale in the Pacific Northwest, when you saw that price-drop notification on your saved searches? the little voice in my head unhelpfully chirped.

Though annoying as shit, the little voice was technically correct.

Lately, escapism via Redfin had become one of my favorite pastimes.

When the daily balancing act of being a mate / gallery assistant / official alpha of the entire shifter kingdom reduced my soul to a withered husk of sadness and resentment, I would serenely swipe through pictures of remote living spaces surrounded by acres of forest and dream about running away.

I wouldn't need much.

Just a modest little cottage big enough for one woman, three cats, a sizable collection of art history books, and a lifetime of simmering feminine rage.

The catio and cheese pantry, I could build on later. Right after the chipmunk condo and the—

"Hungry like the woooolf!"

From the caddy on my desk, a slightly mechanized rendition of Duran Duran's '80s new-wave synth pop classic announced an incoming call on the cell phone I reserved specifically for official shifter business.

When I saw the name flashing on the screen, I felt my face slide a good three inches down my skull.

Thumbing the red button to send the call to voicemail, I glanced back at the computer screen, where the rainbow circle still turned its mocking cartwheel.

I placed a gentle hand on the monitor's alarmingly warm titanium side.

"Look, I know I always have eighty-seven browser windows open and I haven't updated you since the last time you arm-twisted me into an involuntary reboot, but can't you cut me a break?" I asked, patting the MacBook with all the tenderness I could muster.

Like the Ferris wheel of hell's own circus, the rainbow button still spun.

"You're absolutely right," I said. "I did choose your Super Retina XDR display thinking we'd spend our days admiring high-resolution scans of paintings and maybe the occasional email or QuickBooks interface, but times change. It's not like I *knew* I'd need you to google things like 'length of time to bleed out from tusk disembowelment' and 'remedies for ancient Celtic blood curses.'"

Was it my imagination, or was the wheel actually spinning *slower* now?

"Believe me, no one wishes more than I do that being the alpha of the shifter kingdom would excuse us both from the plethora of bullshit administrative overhead required to exist in the human realm. Especially filing quarterly business taxes."

Which, I had recently discovered, Abernathy hadn't done in about a century.

Given the utter wreck his paperwork had been when I'd started in his dubious employ, this wasn't exactly shocking, but providing the smegma-sucking IRS leeches (I say this with the deepest possible affection) any reason to shine a flashlight up the Crossing's collective asshole was about the last thing we needed.

No sooner did my phone chirp to announce a voicemail when it began to ring again.

With the same goddamn name lighting up the screen.

Heaving an epic sigh, I swiped to answer it, not even bothering with a greeting. "Listen, now's not a good—"

"Alpha Harvey, we have a situation." The voice was male, but high-pitched and wheedling, resembling nothing so much as a disgruntled hog. Which made sense, seeing as he was a boar shifter.

I pinched the bridge of my nose, willing the tension headache I could feel forming to go away. "Hank, for the eleven thousandth time, please don't call me that—"

"There's been another incursion on our western border," he blustered on. "A pack of coyote shifters is attempting to claim some of our hunting grounds outside of Baton Rouge."

I stifled a groan. Boar shifters were notoriously territorial and aggressive, but Hank and his pack had made the Roman legions look like the Ladies Auxiliary club. As he rattled on, I couldn't help but think back to my college days driving through the Deep South to get to my hometown of Abilene, Texas. Never in a million years would I have guessed the flashing eyes I kept seeing in my peripheral vision might actually belong to unholy pig-men straight out of ancient folklore rather than three days of zero sleep and the metric shit ton of caffeine required to slingshot me through finals.

"Hank, I understand that you're upset, but—"

"This is the third incursion this month," he interrupted, the words strangely scratchy and distorted. "If it happens again, I can't promise there won't be consequences."

I couldn't have heard his swallow more clearly if it had been accompanied by an Adam's apple–bobbing cartoon bubble *gulp*.

"Hank, are you *eating* while you talk to me?" I asked.

A rattling noise abruptly ceased.

"I'm on patrol," he said with not a lick of remorse. "We only get a five-minute lunch break." For most boar shifters, this would be long enough to shove a seven-course meal down their neck and knit a napkin to wipe their mouths with.

If either knitting or wiping their mouths was a thing for Hank and his ilk.

My left eyelid began to tic as my personal cell phone began to ring.

The caterer whose ghosting me had resulted in yesterday's panicked dash into Westminster and the resulting Bizarro World cosplay combat.

"Hank, I really need to go," I said.

"But the incursions—"

"Look, I'll reach out to the coyote shifter liaison within the hour. You think you can try to keep things from escalating until then?"

"I'll do my best, Alpha."

I hung up one cell phone but fumbled the other with stress-slick fingers as I scrambled to answer it. I watched as, in slow motion, it bounced off the corner of my desk, squirted through the railing, and clattered to the hardwood gallery floor.

I didn't even have to peek to know it was pulverized, because buying a new case for it was still somewhere in the triple digits of the List.

Turning my attention back to my monitor, I felt a burp of joy to see that the rainbow wheel had vanished.

Until I saw the reason why.

The page had timed out.

My chin wobbled. My vision blurred. My throat clenched like a fist.

Despite knowing I couldn't even afford the energy required to manufacture tears, I folded forward onto my desk. Forehead buried in the crook of one arm, the sobs silently shook my rib cage before the grief finally forced its way up my throat in the key of dying cat.

I was still locked in that pathetically defeated posture when the sound of a polite but distinctly masculine cleared throat stabbed me with a jolt of adrenaline.

As a shifter—even a relative rookie like me—being caught off guard is kind of a rare occurrence. What with the ability to hear a rat break wind in Brooklyn and practically catch a whiff of the whole-grain mustard and sauerkraut shreds that gave him a case of the butt trumpets in the first place, chances are, if it's alive, we know it's coming.

So, when something *not alive* sneaks up on you?

That right there is what I call a very bad thing.

Because the list of *not-alive* things that can both A) ambulate and B) clear their throats is short, and at the tippety top of it are, as you may have guessed, vampires.

A word—okay, a bunch of words—about vampires for those who are fortunate enough not to know fact from fiction.

Fact: They drink blood (duh). And when they've done the blood-drinking thing relatively recently, that blood pretty much behaves in their bodies the way it does in a mortal meatsuit. This includes such phenomena as blushing, bleeding, and even maintaining a pulse . . . until their unnatural cells eventually absorb the life elixir, and it's back to being cold, pale—and very cranky, I might add—creepers bent on satisfying their infernal cravings.

Fiction: They can't go out in daylight. Turns out, most vampires adopt a circadian rhythm like the infamous Club Kids of the early '90s and for surprisingly similar reasons. Technically, they *could* rise earlier than sunset, but why bother when you're too fabulous to need to work and your favorite haunts open only after dusk?

Fact(s): Not only do vampires not have a smell—which, for the record, is just completely fucking weird—but also, they can pretty much pirouette through a roomful of nitroglycerine-baited mousetraps without making a single sound. And this is to say *nothing* of the fact that they're cruelly, unfairly gorgeous, fully equipped with mesmeric powers, and, last but definitely not least, immortal.

To review, we're talking unnaturally beautiful, hypnotically powerful, unscented ballerina-meets-ninja-level bloodlust-addled serial murderers who can't die.

So as you might *also* have guessed, being snuck up on by one of these motherfuckers is usually a very, *very* bad thing.

Unless that vampire happens to be former detective, former sneaky link, former complicated situationship James Morrison.

My heart stuttered at the sight of him through the curtain of my tear-dampened red hair, my mind swinging wildly between annoyance and relief. Annoyance that he'd found me face down in a pool of snot and tears. Relief that he was probably the only vampire in existence who didn't want to make earrings out of my spleen.

Slowly, and with as much decorum as I could scrape together given the circumstances, I sat up, dabbed my eyes and nose with a napkin from the lunch I didn't even get to taste, and rotated in my chair to face him.

Despite his relatively recent and dramatic transformation from human to vampire and homicide detective to paranormal private investigator, he still wore the exact same unofficial uniform that had been such an iconic part of his previous identities: rumpled khakis, a white button-up shirt, a pre-loosened necktie, and a beige Dick Tracy–style trench coat.

If the outfit induced an intense surge of nostalgic fondness, what lay beneath it made the muscles behind my belly button snap to attention.

His lean frame, once merely toned, was now cut in diamond-precise angles, each curve and contour in perfect flexion as he stood at attention.

His hair, still the color of brown sugar fudge, glowed with deep gold filaments made even more vibrant against his luminously pale skin. His rough-hewn features were finer now, as if a master sculptor had happened along and decided to make a masterpiece out of the rough draft of mortal clay.

Once hazel, his eyes now swirled with an otherworldly mélange of colors, ranging from the deepest blue to the most passionate crimson, shifting like the tides of the ocean pulled by his mood rather than the moon.

And judging by the stoplight-red irises burning like embers beneath the dark fringe of his lashes, that mood was *pissed*.

"James," I said, the *m* blunted into a *b* by my tear-swollen sinuses. "What are you doing here?"

"Where is he?" he demanded, his knuckles marble white as his powerful hands bunched into fists. "What did he do?"

Déjà motherfucking vu.

It had been in exactly this same spot on my second day as Abernathy's newly minted gallery assistant that then-Detective Morrison had shown up to ask the same questions about the same man.

Or at least a being whom I had quite naturally *assumed* was a man.

Then, Morrison had been investigating the death of Abernathy's lady friend who had apparently misplaced her throat.

Now, I wasn't sure if it was my tears or some other unrelated topic prompting his (borrowed) blood-boiling rage.

With the ongoing dong-measuring contest between Abernathy and Morrison, you just never knew.

"He's at home," I insisted. "So whatever it is you think he did, he probably didn't. Unless it involves a remote control and/or an artisanal meat platter."

My stomach growled its protest at the thought.

"What did he do *to you*?" The deadly calm of his voice chilled the air around me, the pointed tips of his fangs just visible above his bottom lip as he spoke.

"Nothing," I said, hugging my arms tightly around my torso as I stood. "It's just been a shitty day, okay?" I shuffled over to the file cabinet, giving him my back as I opened one of the drawers and pretended to browse among the manila folders. "What are you doing here, anyway? I thought you couldn't enter a building without an official invite."

He cleared his throat again, maintaining a respectful distance until I glanced over my shoulder. So as not to startle me again, I realized with crushing certainty.

A small smirk tugged at the corner of his mouth as he reached into the pocket of his trench coat and produced a thick, creamy postcard I recognized instantly.

An invitation to tomorrow evening's gallery show.

"*Fuck*," I huffed. "I forgot you're still on my mailing list."

I reached for the file folder labeled *Caterers* and winced as I sheared the pad of my thumb on its inexplicably sharp edge. A bright red seam of blood instantly welled up in the cut.

The sound Morrison made, I'd heard before, but in much, much different contexts.

Plural.

Like the time when he'd bent me over the back of my couch in my postdivorce/pre-mating studio apartment and buried himself practically to the base of my spine.

Morrison's pupils widened, spreading until the entire surface of his eyes were black as ink.

I was paralyzed, afraid to so much as to twitch an eyelash lest it drive him into a predatory frenzy.

Like the time he'd accidentally killed me in the dungeon of an Irish castle.

Told you it was complicated.

Morrison held very, very still for an extended beat. Slowly, and with the care one might take when handling a spun-glass spider-web, he fastened cold fingers on my wrist.

Those obsidian eyes stayed fixed on mine as he gently guided my wounded thumb into my own mouth.

The second my lips closed over it, the thunderheads in his eyes began to clear.

"Shitty *how*?" he asked, returning to my earlier statement.

My cue to pretend that what had just happened . . . hadn't.

"I . . . uh, dropped my phone," I said around my thumb.

"You dropped your phone," he repeated as if trying to sift the syllables for an answer that made sense.

I nodded as I made my way over to my desk in search of the tin of impressionist Band-Aids I kept in the drawer above my emotional support snacks. The sooner I could put a few layers of gauze and plastic between Morrison's infernal bloodlust and my salt-and sugar-laden life-juice, the better.

"And *that's* why you were sobbing at your desk?"

"I wasn't *sobbing*." I carefully body-blocked his vantage while I quickly tore open and bound the damp digit with a strip of Monet's *Water Lilies*, mentally reciting the provenance to myself to prove I still could.

Giverny, France, 1914–27, thank you very much.

"You were sobbing."

"Okay, fine. I dropped my phone, and I probably haven't backed it up to the cloud in about a year, so I probably lost a ton of pictures, including the ones I'm supposed to upload to make the program for the gallery show, which I can't print because I completely forgot to grab paper while I was at Costco being accosted by furries while I attempted to purchase some goddamn cheese puffs because I've been ghosted by the fucking caterer who apparently can't leave a voicemail to save his life and the one time he actually called me back, I'm stuck on the phone with a boar shifter with hairy shoulders who thinks he's G.I. Joe." I laughed, the sound only slightly manic. "Also my vampire ex-boyfriend just snuck into my gallery and scared the shit out of me mid-meltdown."

Morrison's pupils lightened to the amber shade of burnt sugar. "Boyfriend?"

I blinked at him. "Of everything I just said, that was the part you focused on?"

"No, it's just . . ." He shrugged. "I never knew that you thought of us as official."

"I would love to review how this changes the material reality of your everyday life, but for the purposes of this conversation, let's just say you're welcome." I plopped back down in my desk chair and reached for the remnants of my Dirty Earl latte from the Dusty Dahlia tearoom down the street. "Now how about you tell me what you're really doing here, because I know for a fact that it's not to attend the gallery show."

"May I?" Morrison indicated one of the leather club chairs parked next to the end table by Abernathy's door.

Uh-oh. For Morrison, sitting was the conversational equivalent of a crash helmet.

"Sure."

In movements too swift for me to see while not intentionally dialed into Shiftervision, Morrison removed his coat, scooted the chair over to my desk, and sat down.

Only once the coat was no longer within the field of his scent-suppressing undead mosquito powers field did the scents rising from the rain-damp trench slung over the railing bloom to life.

"You were at the coffee shop," I said, picking up on the familiar bouquet.

When he was alive, he'd often camped out there while reviewing the details of whatever case he'd been working on. A tradition he'd apparently elected to continue despite the fact that if he were to ingest the hot black brew now, it would result in a bout of *Exorcist*-level projectile vomiting.

"Old habits," he said with a chagrined smile. "That's actually part of what I wanted to talk to you about."

"Coffee?" I asked.

"Cryptids." He cleared his throat. "More specifically, about Dan."

"*T. rex* cardigan–wearing paleontologist Dan?" I asked.

"It's an *Elasmosaurus platyurus* from his dissertation about Nessie's rumored cousin Dobhar-chú, and yes. That Dan."

"Mmmmkaaay," I said, utterly unable to think of a single topic of conversation that an undead paranormal private investigator and the aging hipster who had bought out Jitters and changed the name to Sasquatch Sips could have to discuss. Much less a topic they had to discuss that might potentially affect me.

"As you know, cryptozoology is a hobby of his—"

"You mean cryptid conspiracy theories," I corrected. Long before he'd purchased the old coffee shop and rebranded it with the iconic lumbering Big Foot silhouette, Dan's specialty had been holding court at the Dusty Dahlia's circular booth, peddling half-baked theories about Georgetown's paranormal population to his devoted acolytes.

Emphasis on the *baked*.

"Semantics aside," Morrison continued, "he wants to hire me to investigate the disappearance of the local population of Sasquatch."

"*What* local population of Sasquatch?" I asked, plucking my tube of lip balm from the adorable organizing tray I'd paid entirely too much for after a night spent doomscrolling #CleanTok videos.

"Exactly," he said.

"What I mean is, I make it my business to be aware of all the nonhuman populations not just in the world at large but also in the greater Georgetown area especially, and my sources have yet to include any mention of any—what would you call a group of Sasquatch, anyway?"

"A stench?" Morrison suggested.

A bubble of warmth bloomed in my middle at the familiar

twist of Morrison's snark. It had always been one of my favorite things about him.

"Right," I said. "Anyway, since becoming alpha, I haven't seen hide nor hair of a local Sasquatch population or received any intel that might even suggest their existence. My advice would be, take a retainer if you're hard up for cash, but you're going to end up chasing your tail."

The faintest hint of a smile crinkled the corners of Morrison's hooded eyes, and my cheeks heated out of reflex.

Because in reality, only one of us occasionally had a tail, and on one of said occasions, Morrison had bitten my furry flank to help save Abernathy's life.

"I didn't actually come to ask for your advice." Morrison thumbed a shortbread crumb from the corner of my desk and flicked it into the wastebasket.

My cheeks heated. "No?"

"I came because of *why* Dan said the Sasquatch were disappearing."

"Oh, uh-huh." I reached for Clancy, my silver flying pig letter opener, and began slicing into the stack of envelopes that had been sitting in my matching incoming mail tray for at least a fortnight.

"Dan says that they left to join the cryptid uprising."

The winking blade froze mid-slice. "Cryptid uprising?"

Morrison nodded. "He said that the cryptid community is gathering to plan for a revolt."

"Against *what*?" I asked.

Thunder rumbled the stained glass skylight overhead. "Against you."

4

For a moment, the gallery felt like an airless pocket out of space and time.

"Against me?"

Morrison's long fingers threaded together to cup his kneecap. "Not you specifically, thank God."

Thank God.

I wondered if such phrases were still an unconscious part of his vocabulary, or if he actually still believed.

"Dan seemed pretty vague on the actual details," Morrison continued, "but he did mention that a recent change in the power structure of the shifter community was at fault."

"I see," I said, itching to open my snack drawer for a cognition-enhancing mini-Snickers.

As a rule, I made an effort not to eat in front of Morrison, knowing that vampires never lose the craving for their favorite mortal pleasures, even if they lost their ability to see/feel/smell/hear/taste them.

Which would make me cranky AF too, TBH.

"Even *if* there had been a cryptid community in Georgetown—and I'm not at all convinced that there was because I'm *quite* certain I would have smelled that shit both literally and figuratively—and they indeed fucked off to join some kind of uprising, which, again, I haven't heard a single whisper of despite being up to my ass crack in reports from every corner of the nonhuman kingdom—why would I be remotely interested in *Dan's* theories about why it was happening?"

Morrison's silence seemed to stretch even more now that it was no longer segmented by breaths. "Because Dan is convinced that Georgetown is ground zero and is telling every damn tourist that wanders into his shop for a chupacabra cappuccino."

My shifter business cell was ringing again, a different number this time but equally exasperating. I quickly sent it to voicemail.

"Listen, I've already got about a million problems on my plate and roughly the same number of things to do before the gallery show tonight, so as much as I wish I had time to help you chase theories about the fascinating world of paranormal politics, we're going to need to wrap this up immediately, if not sooner."

Morrison's shoe blocked my chair's rollers before I'd even had a chance to push back from my desk. His irises caught fire, a mesmerizing corona of yellowish orange dancing around the bottomless black wells of his irises.

"I worked Denver homicide for twelve years before moving to Georgetown, and in that time, I was personally responsible for solving one hundred and eleven homicides. Nearly three times as many as any other detective in my precinct and twice the national average. I don't *chase theories*. I hunt *facts*."

Thunder rumbled overhead, a glorious bass boom that amplified the pounding of my heart.

"The *fact* is," Morrison continued, "whether or not there's any credence to his theory about the local cryptid population, Dan is correct about there being a werewolf pack in town. And having seen what humans are capable of doing to members of their own species, the *fact* is that I don't even want to think about what they might be capable of doing to nonhumans. The *fact* is that you are one of those nonhumans now, so I'm here to warn you to watch your shit and to ask your permission to investigate whether there's any truth to Dan's theory about the cryptid uprising."

My throat rasped on a dry swallow. "Dan is your client. Why would you need my permission?"

"I don't," he said, and the implication hit me like an arrow to the heart.

He didn't *need* my permission. He *wanted* my permission. To take action on my behalf.

"You really think there's something to this?" I asked.

"Why is it that cryptids are the only supernatural creatures routinely identified in sightings?" he asked, bolstering his case.

"Almost like they *want* to be seen," I said idly.

"Exactly," he said. "Why would they want to catch the attention of humans? What's the endgame?"

The same anxiety I'd felt yesterday when the wolf furry had referred to me as the alpha returned to my stomach in a hard, cold knot.

With the help of a good hour of trash TV and several whiskey sours, I'd managed to convince myself that it had been an isolated incident. Completely unrelated to either the actual shifter kingdom or my governance of it. That the random voice in my head had been nothing more than suggestion brought on by the truly bizarre encounter.

But now, with Morrison's unnatural eyes lasering a hole in my flimsy self-generated defenses, it all had the whiff of bottom-shelf denial at best, top-shelf delusion at worst.

"Okay," I said. "Permission granted."

The tips of his fangs dimpled his lower lip as he shot me the same cocky grin that had leveled me on the morning we first met. When, on my way to my interview with Abernathy, I'd rear-ended his hideous gold tooth of a Crown Victoria and promptly burst into tears. Unemployed, uninsured, terrified he'd call the cops, not yet knowing he was one.

Not yet knowing so many things.

Not yet seeing what a complicated tapestry would be woven by the intersection of our two threads.

Morrison glanced down at the Seiko watch strapped to his wrist. A crushingly endearing human habit for an immortal who no longer had any reckoning with time.

In the next blink, he was standing at the top of the stairs leading down to the gallery.

"I know you're all hot to get started and you don't technically feel things like *wet* and *chilly*," I said, rising from my desk chair and reaching toward the railing, "but you're at least going to need your coat."

"It's 5:47," Morrison said, the significance of that particular number failing to ring any bells of recognition.

"And?"

Morrison's sable brows lowered. "Doesn't your gallery show start at seven?"

A jolt of adrenaline forked like lightning along my nerves, followed by a cold dread. I'd been so totally subsumed by my administrative purgatory and Morrison's subsequent interruption that I'd lost all track of time.

"Motherfucking shitbiscuits!" I said. "I haven't even gotten out the food tables yet. And the programs—"

Morrison whooshed past me to the storage closet on the landing in a sky-blue and khaki blur, the air-sucking vacuum he created sending a breeze across my tear-stiffened cheeks.

That fast, the food tables were unfolded right where they always were in the corner of the main gallery. The crisp white tablecloths still creased from the linen closet as he fanned them out.

"You have a steamer?" He glanced upward to where I still stood on the second-floor landing, mouth open, eyes peeled wide as duck eggs.

The full array of supernatural powers had been paraded through my life in all their splendor.

I'd just never seen their splendor applied to *this*.

"K-kitchen cupboard." I coughed and reached for the last of my watery tea latte.

The scent of steam-heated cotton and starch was already tickling my nostrils before the cup had been returned to its damp coaster. The squeak of the steamer's rubber cord being wound tickled my ears before I'd even finished swiping the mascara sludge from beneath my puffy lids.

"Paper?" he asked.

"Please."

He held up his hand for his coat, which I tossed over the railing, and he was gone.

By the time he returned from the Paper Patch print and copy center fifteen minutes later—it would have been sooner had he not been bound by the illusion of human physics once the soles of his oxfords hit Rose Street—I had repaired my makeup, twisted the red squall of my hair into a half-assed chignon, and changed into the body-hugging little black dress that was my standard uniform for our monthly art-hocking events.

"Special delivery," he said, slinging several bags down on my desk.

Bags as dry as his hair, face, and coat were soaked.

I pawed through them, perplexed by the extra bulk.

Morrison had bought the paper, yes. But beneath it, I also found Visine. Peanut butter M&M's. A bottle of Gentleman Jack.

And beneath that, I found my phone.

The same phone that had swan-dived from the landing to the gallery floor. He must have picked it up sometime during his ministrations downstairs.

I blinked up at him, awestruck.

"Receipt's in the bag if you don't like the case," Morrison said, running a hand through his wet hair.

I'd been so astonished by the pristine screen that I'd barely even noticed the slight extra bulk around its edges.

I flipped it over, running a thumb over the buttery leather case in the same mossy green that matched all my desk accessories.

"How did you—"

"Cell phone CPR, right next to the Paper Patch."

"But replacing the screen usually takes at least an hour," I said, having had occasion to bring many patients there when Abernathy was still a technology neophyte and prone to bouts of device-gnawing frustration.

"I have an understanding with the kid who runs it," Morrison said, shrugging out of his dripping jacket. "I've gone through a few phone screens since . . ." He trailed off.

Since.

Since the night I helped you rescue Abernathy from the undead despot Emperor Nero's house of horrors.

Since the night I became a vampire.

Since the night I died for you.

"Thank you," I said. "For everything."

Morrison shrugged. *No big deal.* "Don't suppose you have a hair dryer hidden in there." He tugged at the front of his shirt, sodden in a pattern that looked odd until I received a sudden flash of Morrison hurrying down the street in the driving rain, the bags bulging beneath the lapels of his trench coat.

"Please." I swallowed against the growing ache in my throat and pulled out the drawer above the emotional support snacks. "Have you *seen* my hair?"

I handed the mini-dryer over and turned my attention to the programs, grateful I'd at least had the foresight—or low-level humming panic—to lay out the text blocking of descriptions and prices during this morning's post-nightmare, predawn stretch.

With any luck, inserting the pictures of the paintings and pottery would only take me until the very second that the first guest arrived instead of having to hurriedly march around handing them to patrons already tipsy with prosecco.

The dryer clicked off, and Morrison bent to put it back in the drawer from whence it came. "May I?" He gestured toward the notepad on the corner of my desk containing the tornado of chicken scratch documenting what per-show tasks yet remained.

"If you can read it," I said, eyes glued to the monitor screen.

Morrison was silent for a protracted moment. "Can I ask you something?"

"Hmmm?" I was on a roll now, approaching a Zen-like state of copy/paste nirvana.

"Why not just hire someone to run the gallery? With everything else you have going on, it seems like it would be one of the easier items to hand off."

My fingers halted on the sleek keyboard. My eyes remained fixed on the screen, refocusing on my reflection superimposed against the somber color field painting of moody purples and velvet blues.

"Because art is the last part connecting who I am, with who I used to be. If that makes any sense." My gaze drifted from my reflection to Morrison's, nothing but a watercolor smear of sky and sand over my shoulder in the early-evening gloom.

The pale thumbprint disk of his face nodded.

"It does."

—

Where the shit *was* he?

The question looped in my head like a mantra as I darted around the gallery like a caffeinated squirrel greeting patrons, refilling champagne flutes, refreshing the appetizer tables, and desperately trying not to panic.

Trying, and failing.

Twenty-two minutes after seven, and no Abernathy.

No call from Abernathy.

No text from Abernathy.

Against the innocuous symphony of polite conversation and Spotify's vibey "Art Gallery Chill Mix," my mind spun out ever-more graphic scenarios.

The Phantom engulfed by a fiery inferno after Abernathy had pushed the old engine too hard coming down the canyon.

The Phantom in a twisted heap at the bottom of a rocky ravine after Abernathy had taken a curve of the windy mountain road too fast.

The Phantom's windshield crushed in by the massive brown bulk of a bull elk, antlers pinioning Abernathy to the driver's seat. His blood-soaked fingertips barely able to brush the phone.

I *really* needed to stop falling asleep to HBO tragedy porn.

"Pardon me," I murmured, sidestepping a woman who seemed to be piling an entire wheel of Brie on one measly black pepper water cracker. "I'd try one of the hazelnut-cranberry crisps," I whispered, setting out a fresh tray of goat cheese tartlets. "The buckwheat's stabler gluten structure holds up better."

I winked at her as I scanned the food table. *More melon and prosciutto purses.*

I slipped into the small kitchen that had been added to the gallery during my tenure and opened the stainless steel fridge—the only full-size appliance I'd insisted on in the limited space.

Because: priorities.

"Come to Momma," I said, sneaking one of the salty-sweet delicacies from beneath the cling wrap and popping it into my mouth as I took a step back to let the fridge door swing closed.

The unexpected sight of a man standing behind it made my

limbs jerk as if yanked by marionette strings, sending the tray and its delicious contents flying.

It's kind of one of the more irritating side effects of being a shifter: Even your startle responses are extra.

As if my already unwieldy limbs needed any help in that arena.

The fact that recognition dawned while the chunks of ripe melon wrapped in delicate slices of dry-cured pork yet somersaulted in the air did nothing to slow my body's immediate fight impulse.

"*Steve*," I gasped, clutching my chest. "Jesus."

If you put Machine Gun Kelly, a golden retriever, and a space alien in one of those teleporting pod things from the 1980s Jeff Goldblum sci-fi-horror classic *The Fly*, my brother Steven Franke is what would step out in a tide of billowing special effects smoke on the other side.

But with his skeletal structure and internal organs on the inside and stuff.

His underwear, on the other hand? It depended on the moon cycle, really.

"Sorry, Han," he said, picking a ribbon of prosciutto from his black tuxedo T-shirt and popping it in his mouth. "I just came to tell you that we're out of goat cheese tartlets."

Steve and I crouched and began scooping up the ruined meat-purses.

"But I *just* put a tray of those out there."

Steve's green eyes, a shade slightly more emerald than my own, skated down to his red Chuck Taylor high-tops. "About that . . ."

A reedy, high-pitched squeal of a laugh sliced through the ambient noise outside the kitchen door, sending a road flare of dread through my middle.

Even though I'd only ever heard it via my phone's speaker, I knew it instantly.

Hank.

Hank, the boar shifter.

Hank, the boar shifter whose request for a coyote shifter liaison I had completely forgotten about.

Hank, the boar shifter whose request for a fox shifter liaison I had completely forgotten about, and who now stood at the refreshment table in full hunting camo, doing a remarkable impression of Slimer at the room service cart.

Even through the frosted surface of the kitchen door's plastic porthole, I could see expressions of polite horror on the faces of the surrounding patrons as they watched him stuffing handfuls of mini Brie en croûte into the pockets of his sleeveless tactical vest.

"Um, potentially unrelated note, but someone blew up the bathroom, and there's a line of people waiting outside the door."

"This can't be happening," I said, resting my forehead against the door. "How did he even get here?"

Steve scuffed at a dark smudge on the linoleum floor with the sole of his sneaker. "My guess is the prop plane currently parked in the field behind Sasquatch Sips might have something to do with it."

"Fuck." I thumped my forehead against the door. "Fuck, fuck, *fuck*."

Steve cleared his throat. "Kirkpatrick offered to ask him to move it, but—"

"Wait." I clutched at the painted-on lapels of my brother's tuxedo T-shirt. "*Kirkpatrick* is here?"

Steve nodded, the silver studs and rings punched through his eyebrow and nose winking in the overhead light.

Once one of the gallery's resident artists, Scott Kirkpatrick and I had somewhat of a colorful history.

And by *colorful*, I mean that he was a tumbling, tumbling dickweed whose misanthropic antics made my life a living hell right up until he painted the gallery walls with the brains of an octogenarian were-lady on the verge of relieving me of my heart.

The misanthropy had lessened somewhat after he'd shacked up with a fellow shifter and settled down in the Denver suburbs to raise a pack of ginger-haired rug rats who had proved to be an extremely effective birth control until I discovered that my lady bits were broken anyhow.

"He hasn't set foot in the gallery in nearly two years, and now he just shows up and starts acting like he's still part of the pack?" Squatting near the door, I began furiously scraping up the ruined appetizers.

Steve's protuberant Adam's apple bobbed above his many leather necklaces. "Actually, he—"

The kitchen's swinging door exploded inward, launching Steve and the tray forward into a utility shelf.

"You have to hide me." A dark-haired woman body-blocked the door closed behind her, her chest heaving on panted breaths. "They're driving me *crazy*."

"Excuse me," I began, getting to my feet to frog-march her back out of *my* kitchen. "But this area is—holy *shit*. Helena?"

Saying her name proved the proper catalyst to ignite the engine of recognition.

Kirkpatrick's wife had traded her pleather pants and dominatrix boots for a casual cocktail dress and sensible heels, but it was she, all right. Same ink-black hair, now shaped into the expensive layers favored by mountain town MILFs. Same pale blue eyes, but artfully smudged with a brunch-worthy beige instead of the always-perfect winged liner I'd low-key coveted. Her perfect pout, now a regular old shimmery nude instead of their former bloodred, pressed into a flat line as something impacted the other side of the door.

"*Moooom!* Are you in there?"

"You brought your kids to my gallery show?" I asked.

Helena shoved a tart into her mouth from the pile that I had only just noticed was clutched in her hands. "You try finding a babysitter for *one* pup," she said, pastry flakes and goat cheese crumbs falling from her lips and fingers. "Let alone a pack of six."

"*Six?*" I gaped, trying to make the math work in my head.

"Didn't you know?" Helena asked in a flat voice that barely rose to a question at the end. "Twins run in my family."

In fact, I did not.

Steve, just getting to his feet, rubbed his knobby knees below the pleated edge of the kilt he'd worn as part of his gallery show ensemble.

"Are you hurt?" I asked, resting a hand on his shoulder.

"Nah," he said. "Just rubbing the cheese in."

Now, I've wound up with cheese on my general person as much as the next turophile—a few shreds in my bra at the end of the night, a fine thread of melted mozzarella peeled from my chin when washing my face before bed—but never on any of these occasions had it ever occurred to me to *rub it in*.

My face must have said something to this effect, because Steve pointed to the pinkish patch on one knee.

"Got a touch of the eczema," he said gravely. "Goat's milk is way therapeutic, you know."

"*Moooooooom?*" The sound was accompanied by several pairs of small—probably sticky—hands impacting the door.

"It never stops," Helena said, eyes glazing over with tears as she pushed another tart between her lips. "Never. Fucking. Stops. That's why he's here—to ask for his studio back, you know. Because he says he can't work at home anymore. That he can't *create* with all the racket."

Steve and I traded a knowing look.

In the early days of my employment at the Crossing, Steve had been the target of Kirkpatrick's never-ending noise complaints. Then, the Jazzercise VHS tapes Steve favored to get the creative juices flowing had been the most hotly contested issue.

"Meanwhile, do I get to create anything?" Helena asked no one in particular.

"No?" Steve guessed.

Slap-slap-slap. "Maaaaaahmm!!"

"*No.* I sure the fuck don't. Unless you count grocery lists and lunch boxes and snacks that look like goddamn caterpillars as *creating*," Helena said.

"Actually," I said, "I do."

Our eyes met then, and in hers, I saw something I recognized all too well.

Exhaustion.

Bone-deep, soul-emptying weariness.

"Tell you what. Why don't you take these," I said, holding up another tray of the tartlets, "and this," I said, retrieving a bottle of cabernet sauvignon from the stainless steel counter, "and go have some alone time in Abernathy's office. Steve and I will keep an eye on the kids for a bit."

"Thanks," she said, "but now that they know I'm in here, they won't give up until they get in. Do you have any idea how many bathroom doors we've had to replace?"

Steve and I shared another fond glance. Like my niece and nephew, most shifter offspring tended to develop at a remarkable rate. Trouble was, this applied not only to their height and weight percentile but also any latent powers they might possess.

Fortunately, their visits to the gallery had prompted me to replace pretty much every surface below waist height with something that contained the word *reinforced*.

"You're in luck," I said.

Walking over to the small closet that doubled as a pantry, I pushed on the back wall of shelves to reveal a narrow passageway. "I had the construction crew put in a back staircase to Abernathy's office when they installed the kitchen."

Because you never knew when some embittered witch/warlock/vampire/werewolf with a grudge might decide to avenge their tragically fallen kin.

<cough> Theo Van Gogh <cough>

"You can head up there and hang out for as long as you want," I said. "We'll keep an eye on the kids."

Tears spilled over Helena's lids and trailed down her cheeks. "You would do that?"

Under normal circumstances, the answer would not only be *no* but *hell no.*

But, I realized, having had Morrison's help with the final preparations for this evening, I *could.* I had sufficient bandwidth to offer her a small, temporary channel that might sustain her for even a little bit longer.

"You bet," I said.

Steve pushed a palm against the door Helena had been leaning on and nodded his readiness to keep her prowling pack at bay.

Helena barreled past me, grabbing the wine and tarts and shearing a grateful kiss onto my cheekbone as she disappeared up the narrow stairs.

I secured the secret door behind her and closed and locked the pantry.

"Okay. You handle the kiddos. I'll get rid of Hank and have a little chat with Kirkpatrick."

"10-4." Steve raised his hand in salute. "But if that pigeon-livered porcine pisspot gives my sister any guff, Johnny Danger will feed him a fresh fistful of comeuppance on an extra-crunchy crostata," he said, cracking his knuckles like an old-timey gangster. "Seriously, though. You ever bit down on one of those puppies wrong? Little bastards will shred the shit out of your soft palate."

"For sure," I said, not quite suppressing a giggle. "And I'll be sure to let Hank know."

"I was actually talking about Kirkpatrick," Steve said, "but . . . yeah. Him too. They don't even *want* to catch these hands."

"Totally," I agreed, my desperation to evict Hank from the gallery gathering strength by the second.

Steve exited first, and I watched in awe as, Pied Piper–like, he led the jostling crowd of ginger-haired Kirkpatricklets toward his studio.

Once they were fully out of sight, I took a deep breath, fixed a confident smile on my face, and pushed forward.

I'd made it two whole steps when my sensible pumps came to a screeching halt as the bottom dropped out of my stomach.

There, at the food table, was Hank the wereboar.

But he was no longer filling his bulging pockets with appetizers.

He was talking to none other than shifter-suspicious Dan Davis.

The action around me slowed, and time took on the pulled-taffy quality I associated with moments that had changed my life instantly and forever.

Backlit by the gallery's track lighting, the individual filaments of Hank's shoulder hair glowed as he chopped a meaty hand at the air several feet above the sweat-stained crown of his mesh trucker's hat.

"Hairy sumbitch was at *least* 'at tall. And the *smell*." He flapped his engine grease–afflicted fingers near his nose. "Like a box of smashed assholes."

Dan's dark eyes widened. "This happened in your kitchen?"

"Hell naw." Hank lifted a silver can in a foam koozie to his lips and slurped. "On my back porch."

"Oh." Dan's forehead creased. "But you said you were on your way to the fridge?"

"'at's right. The fridge *is* on my back porch. I was standin' there in nothin' but mah diggers on account of I'd just finished givin' the wife a ride on the ol' boudin Bentley, and let me tell you, I was hungry enough to reach up a hog's ass and pull out a ham sandwich right up until I saw the pair on that 'squatch. Like a sack of furry footballs. No wonder he was bowlegged as a barrel rider." He waggled his wiry eyebrows, giving Dan an elbow nudge as the cardigan-wearing coffee connoisseur did a full-on sauvignon blanc spit take.

This, at last, proved the solvent I needed to liberate my sluggish limbs.

"Hank!" I called, throwing my arms wide as I sailed over to them. "It's been a minute!"

"Alpha Harvey." Hank grinned, his yellowed teeth splitting the wild thicket of his beard. The scent of cheap beer and ball sweat wafted off him like a particularly prurient cologne.

"*Alpha* Harvey?" Dan repeated, his dark eyes flicking between Hank and me with an unsettling intensity.

I attempted a dismissive laugh that landed closer to manic. "Just a little nickname my old friend here gave me in grad school."

"Graaad school . . ." Dan pronounced the syllables as if stretching them to fit the lumbering oaf before him.

Granted, it wasn't my finest fib, but desperate times and all that. "Yes, sir," I said, looping an arm through Hank's.

"Me and *Beta* Beauchamp here go *way* back."

"Now wait just a minute, yo—*ouch*!" Hank grunted as I covertly tweezed a crispy clump of his prodigious armpit hair between my thumb and index finger and pulled.

Sidenote: If you ever find yourself on the wrong side of a boar shifter—and I sincerely hope that you don't—I highly recommend follicular force as a persuasion tactic.

Just trust me.

You do *not* want to know how I know.

"Would you mind terribly if I borrowed my friend for a moment?" I asked. "We have *so* much catching up to do."

"Not at all." Dan's voice was a little too solicitously smooth. "I was just about to have a look around, anyway."

Our mirrored smiles displayed more starch than sincerity.

"Please do."

Rather than try to steer Hank's bulk, I waited until Dan sauntered off, then whirled on my unwelcome guest.

"I'm not going to ask you what you're doing here," I said, folding my arms over my chest. "I'm not going to explain to you how inappropriate it is. I'm not even going to *begin* to attempt to drive into your thick skull how completely the sight of you fills my every fiber with infernal, all-consuming rage."

"But—"

"What I *am* going to do is tell you that if you and your corroded crop duster aren't out of Clear Creek County before I finish one of the delicious goat cheese tartlets that I *still* haven't had the chance to eat a single one of, I'm going to be topping the next one with *couillon* cracklins. Got it?"

His small, piggy eyes flashed green. "Got it."

"Good." I turned on my heel. "And, Hank?" I called over my shoulder.

"Yes'm?"

"I chew fast."

One unpleasant task down, I located Kirkpatrick at the back of the gallery, head bent in conversation with a sleek, muscular Latinx woman of the David Bowie–esque androgenous masc variety.

In a journal entry I'd written back when I was still making a half-assed attempt at therapy following the spectacular demise of my first marriage, I'd once described Kirkpatrick as the love child of Yosemite Sam and Porky Pig.

Now that he'd added a bushy beard to the equation, I'd swap Yosemite Sam for Gimli, son of Glóin.

"Hello, Scott," I said. "Got a minute?"

His small, squinty eyes narrowed, even as his porcine nostrils flared above his bushy red mustache. His round, ruddy face deepened to an even more intense shade of Tex Avery cartoon smashed-thumb red.

He'd come hoping to speak with Abernathy.

"Excuse us for a moment?" I asked the woman.

"No problem," she said, giving me a smile that made my stomach do a mini-flip.

"Super," I said. Threading my arm through Kirkpatrick's, I guided him through the gallery toward the attached oddities shop.

"So," I said when I was sure we were out of the human hearing range. "I hear you're looking to resume your previous studio space?"

"Where did you hear that?" he asked.

"From your wife." I opened the door to the darkened space housing the Crossing's collection of unusual items and used Kirkpatrick's arm to steer him through it. "Who practically barricaded herself in the kitchen."

His padded shoulders deflated a fraction. "I told her we shouldn't have brought the kids."

"You did?" I asked.

"Yes," he insisted, clearly encouraged by my interest in his side of the story. "I said that she deserved a night out. Just the two of us. Like it used to be."

"I see," I said. "And your idea of a night out was to come to the gallery where you used to have a studio to ask for a space free from the interruptions that she endures on a daily basis?"

"Well, you see—"

"But I'm sure since the activity you chose was primarily beneficial to *you*, you had plans to take her somewhere *she* might really like afterward?"

"Actually, I—"

"And your incredibly thoughtful plan would have worked perfectly, had the childcare you *surely* arranged so Helena didn't have to bear the weight of that responsibility too hadn't canceled at the last minute, thereby making it necessary for you to bring the aforementioned children?"

"No, but I—"

"Because I can't think of a single other reason that you would be standing there, calmly talking to patrons despite not having a single work of art in the show, while Steven Franke, whose life you made a living hell with your incessantly petty and pointless complaints, is entertaining *your* children in *his* studio while *I'm* standing *here* talking to *you* instead of selling the paintings patrons are actually interested in buying?"

Kirkpatrick's mustache twitched as his mouth opened and closed in rapid succession.

I folded my arms across my chest and leaned in, letting my full height loom over him.

Sidenote: If you get the chance to loom, do it. 10/10 totally recommend.

"I'll make you a deal," I said. "Come to next month's show. Bring Helena. And *only* Helena. If she looks at least 77 percent happier than she does now, I'll not only give you your studio back, I'll personally oversee the installation of soundproofing on every wall. Deal?"

"Seventy-seven percent is a very specific number. How will I—"

"*Deal?*" I bayonetted my hand toward his sternum.

His freckled lids and translucent lashes lowered in the world's slowest blink. "Deal," he said.

We clasped hands and shook, Kirkpatrick hissing in a sharp breath when his knuckles crunched satisfyingly beneath my grip.

"Oops." I released his hand and gave him a sunny smile. "Sometimes I just don't know my own strength."

I could tell by the salty-sweet umami hit of glutamate in his body chemistry that he'd taken my meaning.

Kirkpatrick cleared his throat. "Well, I'd better get back."

"*Because?*" I arched an eyebrow, refolding my arms.

"Becaaause . . ." His eyes ping-ponged inside the frames of his gold wire-rimmed glasses. "I was just about to take my kids out for ice cream at the Dairy Dream?"

"What a lovely idea," I said, giving the scruff of his thick neck a squeeze. "You have fun. And don't hurry back."

I waited until he was gone and the oddities shop door closed to deflate over the credenza I had turned into a counter on my first day in Abernathy's employ.

Alpha or no, bravado is most definitely *not* my default setting.

The calming shot of Gentleman Jack I'd pregamed before the show had long ago worn off, and my nerves were as thin and brittle as spun sugar.

I needed to get back, but facing the crowd without Abernathy in it felt like a recreational stroll in front of a firing squad. Particularly with Dan among their ranks.

The thought tightened the hot wire of unease that had taken up residence in my middle.

Though I knew it had the potential to double down on my worry, I pulled my phone out of my bra, silently praying I'd find at least one notification when I flipped it face up.

Nada. Zip. Zilch.

On a heavy sigh, I peeled myself off the counter and shuffled back toward the gallery through the narrow hallway flanked by artists' studios.

Seeing light spilling from Steve's cracked door, I slowed as I passed, assuming he might have forgotten to close up after the feral pack of ginger mini-shifters had departed.

I had assumed incorrectly.

Through the narrow slice revealed by the door, I saw Steve. Standing with arms folded, his mouth slanting in a boyish grin.

What, or should I say *who*, he was smiling at, I smelled before I saw.

A pretentious bouquet of wool, craft beer, and light perspiration breaking through ammonium-free tapioca-and-shea-butter deodorant. But something else too. An odd, earthy scent I remembered but couldn't quite place. Garbanzo bean? Lentil? Mingled with the spotlight-stealing note of coffee, it was hard to tell.

Coffee.

Alarm bells already jangled in my head as I took a step to peer further into the crack.

My perpetually guileless, often too-trusting shifter brother had been cornered by Dan Davis.

5

Even before I'd known Steve was my brother, I had fallen hopelessly in love with his work. Steve specialized in portraits.

Animal portraits, to be exact.

Animal portraits where his subjects wore human clothing, carefully styled to reflect something of their personality/story/spirit.

His oeuvre ranged from playfully whimsical to achingly tender and never failed to make me feel like someone had flamenco danced over my heart.

In baseball cleats.

But the painting Steve and Dan were currently examining produced an altogether different reaction.

Cold, tight fear.

"Tell me," Dan was saying in his sonorous, I-really-ought-to-have-a-podcast voice. "What exactly inspired you to combine the wolf's head with a human body in this piece?"

I couldn't have leaped forward any faster had my ass been zapped with an industrial-strength cattle prod.

"Dan!" I said, pushing the door wide. "I'm so glad you stuck around." I cupped his elbow, covertly swiping my palm sweat on the corduroy patch of his Mr. Rogers–meets–philosophy grad student sweater. "I meant to tell you earlier that I'm so glad you could finally make it."

Given the exceptionally small pool of Georgetown's year-round population, he'd been on the invitee list since always pretty much, but tonight marked the first time he'd ever actually attended.

An occurrence that struck me as downright foreboding after Morrison's earlier visit.

"Miss Harvey," he said, eyes flicking to mine behind the thick lenses of his black-framed glasses. "Always a pleasure."

"I was just giving Dan-O here a peek behind the curtain," Steve said, wiggling his fingers. "Not that I'm comparing myself to the Wizard of Oz or anything, because I personally find everything about the idea of petitioning a giant disembodied floating head for gifts wildly disturbing." Steve shuddered.

"Bro, you ever see *Return to Oz*?" Dan asked.

"*Dude*," Steve replied, shaking his head. "How the hell did they ever get away with calling that absolute dystopian hellscape a *kids'* movie? I mean—"

"The Wheelers!" they said in unison.

The casing of ice that had surrounded my heart began to melt incrementally when they slapped an awkward high five.

"Wow." Dan tugged his glasses from his face and polished the lenses with an actual by-God handkerchief. "Your work makes so much more sense within that framework."

A thoughtful crease appeared between Steve's fine dark blond brows. "How so?"

Slipping his glasses back on, Dan strolled over to a painting of a raccoon in a three-piece suit propped against a stack of canvases on Steve's supply cabinet. "Take this one, for example. There's a darkness to it. A malice."

"Malice?" Steve chuckled, walking to stand beside Dan before I could catch his eye. "Nah, man. I just thought it would be hilarious to see a trash panda in Armani."

"You don't give yourself enough credit," Dan said, a smile crinkling the corners of his eyes. "What you've created is a beautiful Heideggerian metaphor for life in post-postmodern society."

Two round red spots appeared on his sharp cheekbones. "I did?"

"Absolutely," Dan said. "At first glance, it's all harmless whimsy.

Artfully rendered details in an ironic composition." He gestured to the raccoon's paws neatly clasped against the suit jacket. "But the longer you look at it, the more you realize that beneath the fancy fabric, it's still an animal. And not just any animal—a disease-ridden, invasive species living off the refuse of humanity."

"I—I guess I can see that." Steve shifted on the rubber soles of his Chucks.

"And then there's symbolic visual heritage of the raccoon itself. By the nature of its very physiognomy, it wears a mask, thus its rich historical associations with disguise." Dan paused, turning to look at Steve. "Trickery."

The tips of Steve's ears glowed a beet red.

"It almost makes me wonder"—Dan's eyes narrowed as he leaned closer to the canvas—"if there isn't something deeper going on here? Something *confessional*?"

A single bead of sweat crawled down my ribs. As much as I wanted to wade in and tell Dan where to shove his theories, a sudden burst of defensiveness on my part would do little to diffuse the crackling tension.

"Actually," Steve began, "there is—"

"Dan the Man!" The sound of the familiar but completely unexpected voice made me whip around.

"Detective Morrison." Dan brightened, clearly as surprised as I was to see him standing in the doorway to Steve's studio.

Relief rushed over me like a summer tide. I hadn't expected him back after he'd finished helping me fold and staple the catalogs, hot as he was to get started on his Sasquatch search.

Judging by the healthy glow in his face, he'd found sustenance instead.

A fact I tried not to think overly hard about, given what that sustenance was.

"I see you've discovered one of Georgetown's hidden gems," Morrison said, clapping Steve on the shoulder. "Amazing, aren't they?"

"Yes, well." Dan repolished his glasses, preening under Morrison's attention. "I was immediately drawn to them."

"Doesn't surprise me in the least, man of taste that you are," Morrison said, really pouring on the infernal charm now. "You're thinking what I'm thinking, aren't you?"

Dan's eyes took on the laminated shine of dollar-store marbles. He was 100 percent *not* thinking what Morrison was thinking, but he obviously wanted to be. "Absolutely," he said.

"I knew it." Morrison glanced around Steve's studio. "So how many are you thinking? Five? Seven?"

"Seven? Oh, man, I wish," Dan said, thinking he'd caught on. "But with my research library, I don't think I'd have room in my bungalow for more than one."

Morrison's chuckle was rich and warm. If it could have smoked a corncob pipe, it would have. "Not for your bungalow, for the coffee shop."

"Of course!" Dan's chuckle, on the other hand, was pure sweater vest. "These are *so* rad that I thought about it too, but . . ." Dan shook his head, the very picture of chagrin. "I'm really trying to stick to the Sasquatch theme."

"Exactly," Morrison said. "Which is why commissioning custom portraits of Sasquatch would be so amazing."

"Well, of course they would," Dan said, finally catching up to Morrison's point. "I just wasn't sure if that's something Steve would be interested in doing."

"Ummm, *yeah*, I would," Steve said. "If I can get one to sit for me."

For a horrifying beat, Dan looked at my brother, and my brother looked at me, and I looked at Dan, the three of us perilously close to cementing this as an admission.

Until Morrison lightly punched Steve's arm and laughed like he was part of an inside joke. Steve picked up the cue, and Dan joined in, and my lungs finally consented to admit breath.

No doubt about it. Morrison was *good*.

"Well, I'm sure we've kept Steve and Hanna long enough," Morrison said, nudging Dan with an elbow. "I was about to grab a beer. You want to join me?"

"Love to," Dan said.

My blood pressure lowered by several points with every step they took toward the studio door.

But my hypertensive de-escalation proved premature.

Before they could reach the threshold, Dan pulled a Columbo, stopping to thump his forehead as if he'd forgotten something.

"The gallery's owner doesn't happen to be around, does he? I owe him a long-overdue introduction."

Sand filled the column of my throat.

"I'm afraid not," I said, locking eyes with Morrison over Dan's shoulder. "But I'll be sure to tell him you stopped by."

"Will he be at the gallery this week?" Dan asked. "Seems like I haven't seen him around town much lately."

This seemingly casual statement introduced not one but two alarming concepts.

That Dan was taking note of Abernathy's presence or absence within the local community.

That Abernathy's insistence on the latter lately had been the cause of concern.

"You know how these philanthropic types are." Morrison was back on his bro bullshit, his tone like an affectionate eye roll. "Famously reclusive."

"Philanthropic?" Dan glanced at him over his shoulder.

"You're shitting me, right?" Morrison asked. "The Curb Conservancy, the Benevolent Order of the Antelope, the Georgetown Civic Coalition, the Front Range Historical Society . . ." Morrison trailed off as if the entire list was simply too long to recite. "I daresay Mark Abernathy has done more for Georgetown than ol' George Griffith himself."

Dan gave a derisive snort. "If by 'contribution' you mean depleting the mountain majesty of its precious metals."

My fist was itching to deplete Dan's mouth of some precious metals.

"How about John Tesh?"

A question that I suspect was destined to be met with a similar silence in any gathering.

"*A Romantic Christmas*?" Steve prompted.

Crickets.

"It's only the most heartwarming seasonal pop offering since Wham!'s 1986 après-ski standard 'Last Christmas.'"

More crickets.

"Oh, come *on*." The rubber sole of his sneaker tapped impatiently on the studio's paint-spattered wood floor. "You *have* to have seen that video. The artfully frosted mullets, the tinsel fights, the smoldering looks across a glass-topped yuppie ski chalet dining room table?"

"Nope," I said, "but I worked at the gift-wrapping hut in the Mall of Abilene as a teenager and heard it so many times that I thought about stabbing myself in the ear with the ribbon-curling scissors eight times a day, if that counts."

"Totally counts," Steve said.

"Point is," Morrison cut in, "Abernathy's done more for Georgetown than George Griffith *and* John Tesh. And I'm sure next time he's at the gallery, Hanna would be happy to give you a buzz."

"Absolutely," I said with perhaps a shade too much enthusiasm.

"I'll look forward to it," Dan said. "Always a pleasure to converse with a man of such *sterling* qualities."

I couldn't decide if the extra emphasis on *sterling* was an ode to the town's origins, or something much, much worse.

Still, the delicious irony of a werewolf choosing a tiny mountain town originally founded by offshoots of the Colorado silver boom to establish a pack was never lost on me.

A rebel at heart, my Abernathy.

"*Sterling* might be overstating it a bit."

Dan's eyes widened in surprise at the resonant rumble of the voice from the hallway, and for a moment, it seemed as though he might choke on his own tongue.

We all turned to see Abernathy standing there behind Morrison, looking slightly disheveled but no less imposing in his dark—if rumpled—suit.

My heart leaped at the sight of him even through my momentary confusion as to why I hadn't picked up on his scent.

Morrison stood between us, the undead equivalent of a Febreze odor neutralizer.

"Mark," Morrison said, sounding genuinely delighted or doing a damn good impression of it. "Impeccable timing, as always."

A flicker of understanding passed between them, and I instantly knew that Abernathy must've heard at least part of Morrison's glowing recommendation.

"Pleasure to meet you officially," Abernathy replied, fixing his gaze on Dan as he offered his hand.

"Likewise," Dan said.

And that was about *all* he said. Seeing Abernathy at a distance around town was one thing. Having all six feet, six inches of him close enough to pound your head down your neck like a tent stake was quite another.

Despite my lingering irritation with his earlier ghosting, watching his physical form in action produced a delicate flutter in my middle.

"Dan and I were about to grab a drink," Morrison said. "Would you care to join us?"

"Actually," Dan said, before Abernathy could answer, "I didn't realize how late it had gotten. I need to get running along myself. The Guild awaits. Pleasure speaking with you all. And I'll be in touch about those portraits."

Steve's sneakers squeaked as he clicked his heels together and saluted Dan.

When Dan had departed, Steve excused himself as well, citing his urgent need to check the provisions at the food table. As much as I appreciated it, I also knew it was primarily motivated to escape the miasma of masculine discontent filling the hallway like acrid smoke.

Abernathy and Morrison's ongoing mutual dislike persisted despite the tenuous truce that existed between them mostly for my benefit.

So, arriving at the gallery to find Morrison not only in it but also extolling the virtues its absent host had to be as disorienting for Abernathy as it had been for me. Especially since I hadn't had the chance to bring him up to speed on the afternoon's unfoldings.

"Thanks," Abernathy said. "For . . . whatever the fuck that was."

Morrison's eyes flared a sunset-worthy reddish gold. "I didn't do it for you."

Abernathy's hands curled into fists at his sides, the ponderous crease in his forehead deepening to Mariana Trench level.

Not. Good.

In days past, Abernathy had been a *tear throats first, ask questions later* kinda guy. Under my constant haranguing, this had been modified to an *ask at least one question before the throat tearing* approach, but I couldn't think of a single interrogative that wouldn't result in wanton bloodshed between them.

The one werewolf-vampire brawl I had witnessed was enough to last me a lifetime.

And not just because the werewolf-vampire combo in question had been Abernathy and Oscar Wilde.

"Unless this fight ends with a scenario where I can convince the two of you to kiss and make up," I quipped, trying to lighten the mood, "my vote is that we call it a day and go find a snack."

"Fine by me." Morrison finally broke eye contact with Abernathy, turning on his heel and disappearing into the crowd. Abernathy looked after him for a moment before turning to me.

I readied myself for the explanation that was surely forthcoming, mentally puffing a bellows at the coals of the Big Mad I'd been stoking all evening.

Abernathy only looked at me as if *he* were the one owed an explanation.

And I was *not* about to fall for that recycled nugget of reverse psychology, boys and badasses.

"Where were you?" I asked. "What happened?"

"You didn't get my messages?"

"*What* messages?"

"Hanna, I've been trying to call you all night. I left at least half a dozen voice messages and sent at least as many texts."

A profound sense of disorientation blasted through me. "Umm, no," I said. "You sure didn't."

His dark head cocked, he reached into the pocket of his suit coat and pulled out his phone. He thumbed it open and turned it to face me.

Sure enough, the call log displayed row after row of my name in Unanswered Outgoing Call bold black type.

Fuck a duck (tenderly and only after acquiring consent).

I reached down the neckline of my shirt to retrieve my phone from my bra. "But that doesn't make any sense."

Until it did.

Either in its adrenaline junkie jump off the second-floor balcony or the fiddly operation required to fix it, my phone had ended up both in Airplane Mode *and* Do Not Disturb. And between the brand-new pretty protective case and the gallery show's manic distraction, I'd been too thick to notice it.

Wouldn't you know it, once I'd restored everything to its usual settings, the numbers on the small red notification bubbles began to miraculously multiply.

I'd missed calls not only from Abernathy but also from Morrison, Steve, even my mother.

"I'm so sorry," I said. "I dropped my phone earlier and I was rushing to get things done, and then the gallery show started and Kirkpatrick and Helena showed up with their six children—which like get *off* her, dude—and she took all the goat cheese tartlets and barricaded herself in the kitchen and proceeded to have a nervous breakdown, so I gave her a bottle of wine and sent her up the secret stairs to your office, which I hope is okay, and—"

Abernathy gently put a finger to my lips.

"It's okay," he said. "It's all okay. But there's something I need to tell you."

Those words alone were enough to make the bottom drop out of my stomach. "What?" I asked. "What is it?"

"The reason I'm so late is because I couldn't leave the house."

"Oh, Mark." Reaching up to place a hand on his chest, I felt the steady thump of his heart through the layers of cotton and wool. "Because your upcoming birthday is causing you to question your own mortality, and the inevitability of death makes socializing with gallery patrons feel like a completely pointless and exhausting exercise in futility?"

Abernathy's lips flattened into a tight line as his eyes narrowed. "Because your mother showed up at our front door."

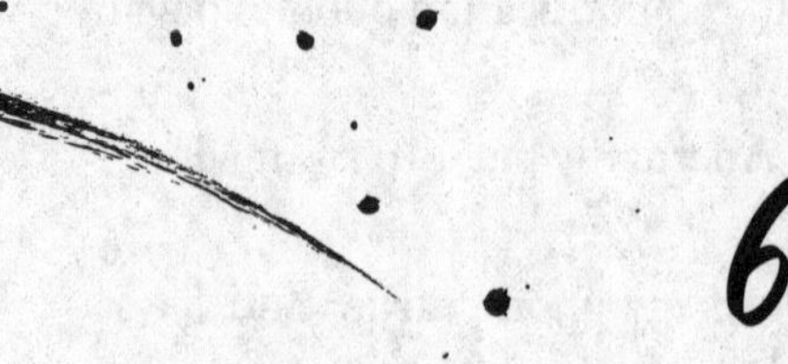

6

The Crossing's familiar scent of linseed oil and turpentine filled me with sweet relief as I flipped on the lights, in desperate need of this small ritual.

My head still spun, my nerves crackling from the four cups of coffee I'd slurped down during the exceedingly awkward breakfast I'd shared with Abernathy . . . and my mother.

Awkward because, among other things, my mother seemed to have absolutely no memory of Abernathy despite his formative role in our family's history.

No memory of his having protected our family for generations.

No memory of his having driven her home from the UCLA hospital after she gave birth to a baby boy who had almost died in the process.

No memory that Abernathy's plan to protect the first son born in my family's alpha line had gone disastrously awry, resulting in my father's death.

Of course, my mother had never informed *me* of any of these things growing up, but after having learned about them from Abernathy, I'd assumed that her reasons for keeping our bizarre heritage under wraps had more to do with wanting me to lead a relatively normal life until the time came for me to know than willful deception.

But watching her amnesiac performance of an average, everyday, meddlesome mother-in-law over breakfast, I was beginning to wonder if that was actually the case.

Thus the aforementioned "other things."

The highlight reel, in no particular order:

Abernathy's resonant snore during the painfully long pre-omelet prayer wherein my mother outlined her gratitude for the various breakfast foods before petitioning the creator of the universe to bless my womb with "abundant fruit" that I "might know the joys of motherhood," followed by with at least five false windups before she finally dropped the supplication sloop's Amen anchor.

Abernathy crushing a glass in his hand when my mother pointed out how much better looking he was than "the last one."

Abernathy nearly aspirating a bite of bacon when my mother casually mentioned that she wasn't sure exactly how long she'd be staying.

And last but certainly not least, Abernathy doing a full-on scalding-coffee spit take when my mother—while knitting something that looked remarkably like a baby bootie—expressed her hope that he "wasn't one of those young men that got a preemptive vasectomy," because she just *knew* our kids would be beautiful.

An extra knife twist to the gut, unintentional though it was.

I had assured her that Abernathy's plumbing was fully functional, as much to curry favor with her as to bolster Abernathy, whose mood my mother's arrival had done little to improve.

I'd given him a free pass for the day, loudly lamenting that we hadn't known she was coming; otherwise, we'd have canceled the absolutely mandatory arrangements that necessitated our presence elsewhere for the next ten hours.

The grateful look Abernathy had shot me made it instantly worth it.

My mother's nose had already begun its inevitable ascent toward the ceiling when I suggested she might like to reorganize my pantry since we both knew how absolutely terrible I was at maintaining an orderly store of dry goods and sundries.

This had proved to be the magic sauce, my ticket to freedom.

For at least the next ten hours.

Now, standing at my desk, I ran face-first into a brand-new wrinkle.

Steve.

Steve, my brother.

Steve, my brother, who my mom presumably still believed I was unaware of, and who she thought had died in the tragic car non-accident that had killed my father.

Since learning of our sibling status, we'd decided it best to minimize the danger to my mother—and the world at large—by limiting the information available to her. A tactic that had proved necessary even before I'd learned that we were both descendants of an ancient alpha bloodline believed to have the capacity to restore peace and plenty to the shifter kingdom.

Sure, Steve and I had talked about her and our late father. Looked at pictures.

But until this very moment, I hadn't even thought about how he'd feel once he found out that she was *in town.*

Luckily, the note on my desk in Steve's unmistakable scrawl afforded me the opportunity to find out.

Hey, seeeester! Ran to Sasquatch Sips for much-needed caffeinated elixirs / custom portrait discovery sesh. Come on over if you want to talk about Abernathy's impending surprise soiree! XOXO, Steve

The coffee puddling in my stomach turned to acid.

If the idea of setting foot in Sasquatch Sips gave me heartburn, the idea of Steve sitting there unsupervised while Dan batted seemingly innocuous discovery questions at him made me feel like I'd downed a lava smoothie.

Either way, I needed the chance to get my brother up to speed on both emerging situations before his sweet-natured, guileless heart inadvertently exposed the Crossing's vulnerable underbelly.

With a heavy sigh, I grabbed the bag I'd barely set down, turned on my heel, locked up, and headed back out.

Main Street, with its intertwining cobblestone paths and ancient oaks standing guard between old-fashioned wrought iron lampposts, was part of the nostalgic charm that had beckoned me after my divorce. History nerd that I am, I found comfort in the primly painted Victorian houses with their flower-draped balconies and white picket fences, in the old brick buildings adorned with elaborately painted hanging signs.

Three blocks down from the Crossing, a brand-new one shaped like the iconic lumbering silhouette of a Sasquatch swung in the fragrant summer-morning air.

The delicious aroma of freshly brewed coffee clocked me square in the face as I pushed through the door of Sasquatch Sips as the bell above the door jingled—ominously, I swear to you—my arrival.

I spotted Steve wedged into a corner booth, sketch pad balanced on his knobby knees as he sat longways on the red vinyl bench.

A graveyard of sugar packets and bramble of gnawed-on red plastic stirring sticks littered the table's surface, scattered among the tawny coffee rings left by a cup refilled many times over.

Steve didn't notice me until I cleared my throat.

Twice.

"Oh, hey!" He glanced up from the pad, tucking a pencil dented with teeth marks behind his ear. "You got my note."

"Sure did," I said as I slid into the seat across from him.

Steve swung his legs off the bench and swiveled to face me, signaling to the server.

I felt the synaptic snap of recognition as she approached, identifying her as the androgynously elven-featured femdom Kirkpatrick had been talking to before I'd marched him off for a lecture. Today, her manic pixie cut was partially obscured by a knit beanie perfectly perched on the back of her skull. Paired with a sleeveless T-shirt that revealed the muscled length of two tattoo-sleeved arms, fashionably shredded jeans, and brown leather riding boots, she gave off a rockstar-esque mystique.

"Welcome to 'Squatch Sips," she said. "What can I brew for you?"

I glanced at Steve, whose relatively recent obsession with the art of coffee making made him my go-to guru for all things java-related. "Thoughts?"

Steve leaned forward, thoughtfully stroking the patch of blond stubble on his chin. "Hmmmm. What indeed? Any recommendations, Vada?"

"Vada?" I repeated. "That's an unusual name."

She shrugged. "My parents smashed at a drive-in showing of *My Girl*."

"Ahh," I said, not sure what else to say.

"Vada here is a Caffeine Connoisseur," Steve chimed in. "An Espresso Enthusiast. A Mocha Maniac. A Cup o' Joe Devotee. A—"

"A person who really fucking loves coffee," she interrupted. "What's your thing?"

"My thing?"

Vada shifted her weight and tucked a thumb in her apron's waist strap. "Cold brew, espresso, drip coffee, French press—"

"Let's assume I don't have a thing and you just bring me the very best coffee I've ever had in my life."

A dimple flashed in her cheek as she smirked at me. "Can do. Another for you?" she asked Steve, lifting the empty hourglass-shaped carafe from the table.

"Why not?" Steve said, leaning back on the bench. "I'm feeling saucy."

"So will your trousers if you've already had a whole one of those," I pointed out, all too familiar with coffee's peristaltic priming powers where my brother's digestion was concerned.

"Good point. How about a 'squatch-slurp-size Nutty Yeti instead?"

I raised an eyebrow at him.

"Okay, okay. Goblin-gulp-size."

I folded my arms.

"Fine—sprite sip, then."

"Coming right up," Vada said.

"So." Steve clapped his hands and briskly scrubbed his palms. "Ready to get this Abernathy shindig sorted?"

"Actually," I said, forcing a dry swallow. "There's kind of something else I need to talk to you about first."

Steve rearranged his limbs, leaning his elbows on the table in his more formal and disarmingly mantis-like *I'm listening* posture.

How to begin . . .

"So, um, you know how you're my brother?"

"Indeed," he said.

"And you know how that means we have the same parents?"

"Quite so." Why careful attention on Steve's part was frequently accompanied by a British accent was just another of the mysteries of his psychological matrix.

"And remember how one of those parents is still alive?"

"*Deffo.*" A new Anglo-slang nugget, this.

"Well, the one that's still alive is, um, currently alive much nearer than was previously the case."

"As in, somewhere in colorful Colorado?" he asked.

I plucked a napkin from the chrome dispenser and used it to brush the raw sugar granules scattered over the table's surface into my palm. "As in . . . at my house."

"My mom is *here*?" Steve's voice cracked, making him sound like a disarmingly prepubescent version of himself I dearly wished I would have known.

So began the unraveling.

On the walk over, I'd mentally rehearsed my pitch for what I'd decided to be the best course of action. Send my mother packing back to Texas as swiftly as humanly possible and convince Steve to put off meeting her until we'd had time to schedule a visit specifically for that purpose.

But one glance at the hopeful look in his guileless green eyes, and I *knew*.

I knew he'd have to see her.

And for him to see her, we'd have to tell her.

About the accident. Abernathy. Alpha stuff. All of it.

"Yep," I said. "She got in last night. That's why Abernathy was so late to the gallery show."

"Whoa," Steve breathed, running a hand through his blond hair. "This is . . . this is like, *whoa*. Have you told her about—" He gestured vaguely at himself, then at me.

"Not yet. That's actually what I wanted to—"

"Sergeant Steve!" Dan breezed over to our booth, leaning in to give my brother a hearty clap on the shoulder. "How's that Guatemalan single-origin treating you?"

"Lieutenant Dan!" Steve grinned. "It was like a movie premiere in my mouth and my tongue was the red carpet. You're an artist and scholar, my friend."

Two round red spots appeared below the thick frames of Dan's Buddy Holly glasses.

"Always happy to please a fellow coffee connoisseur," he said with a wink. "Let me know if you're ready for another round. I've got a new Kenyan roast I think you'll love."

Steve shot me a pleading look.

"Your shorts." I shrugged.

"That sounds splendid," Steve said.

"Vee," Dan called to the counter. "Eighty-six whatever she ordered and bring them a Pegacorn Press of the Kenyan."

I bit down on the need to protest, reminding myself that

establishing and/or maintaining a good rapport with Dan would probably help more than it hurt, given the current climate.

"Get a whiff of this wizardry." Dan reached into the pocket of his apron and came back with a glass test tube of coffee beans. Pulling out the cork stopper, he handed it to Steve.

Steve waved it below his flaring nostrils, and I swear I saw his eyes roll back in his head for a split second before his lids fell closed.

Even from across the table, I could see—or smell, rather—why.

"Black currant," Steve whispered rapturously. "Red wine. Caramel. And is that a hint of . . . Ribena?"

"Wow," Dan said, nodding his approval. "You're goo—"

"Picked on a south-facing slope still wet with morning dew by a gentleman who takes lemon and enough sugar in his morning tangawizi tea to give him the 'beetus despite comparatively low national averages."

Noting Dan's narrowed gaze, I lightly nudged Steve's shin under the table with the toe of my sneaker.

His eyelids snapped open. "At least, that's . . . uh, what I imagine." He handed the tube back to Dan, who gave it a sniff himself before sliding it back into the holster containing a row of several other tubes tucked behind the front pocket of his apron.

"Yes, well, wait 'til you wrap your lips around this stuff," he said, taking the hand off the French press and two fresh mugs from Vada and setting them down on the table between us. "It'll knock your socks off."

"Thanks, LD," Steve said, sliding one of the mugs across to me and decanting the burnt-sugar-colored brew.

"Hey! Is that a sketch for one of my portraits?" Dan asked, catching a glimpse of the pad Steve had propped against the window so he could pour.

"Affirmative," Steve said.

"May I?" Dan held out a hand.

"*Por supuesto.*" Steve passed the pad over his lap and filled his own cup, letting his beaky nose linger over the rim until I gave his shin another nudge. "But it's still a work in progress."

"This is, uh . . . really good," Dan said, his brow furrowed. "Really good."

"*Danke*," Steve said. "Like I said, it's just a rough sketch. It still needs—"

"A much more delineated supraorbital torus," Dan said. "To protect his highly developed tapetum lucidum from the concentrated UV rays when he wanders from dense forest into a clearing."

Both Steve and I stared at him through the veils of steam rising from our cups.

"At least, that's what I imagine." Dan's stubble-flecked Adam's apple bobbed above the collar of a T-shirt suggesting that we SAVE A HORSE, RIDE A PACHYCEPHALOSAURUS. I couldn't help but notice the three fingerprint-shaped spots where Dan's sweat had wrinkled the thick, creamy paper.

Interesting.

"10-4, big buddy." Steve picked up his pencil and began notching marks near the Sasquatch's formidable brow.

"Well," Dan said, thumbing his apron ties. "Better get back to the galley. You still good for Thursday?"

Steve shot him an uneven grin. "Does the Tin Man have a metal meat wand?"

They executed a complicated handshake that would have passed for the final stage of a Three Stooges slap fight.

I waited until Dan disappeared behind the swinging door behind the lunch counter before allowing my anxiety to seep out in the form of a question.

"What's Thursday?" I asked.

"Hmm?" Steve asked, absentmindedly flicking graphite strokes onto the pad. "Oh. Dan invited me to pledge their guild."

"Guild?"

"For gaming." Steve lifted the mug, his lips pursed to puff away the steam. "Dan and his crew are currently working their way through another play of *Skyrim*, which happens to be one of my all-time favorites." He took a dainty sip against the cup's rim as I'd seen self-proclaimed wine snobs do. "Gods, that's so, so . . . juicy."

Glancing at the lethally dark brew in my cup, I noted that there was neither a metal-capped sugar dispenser nor miniscule drums of half-and-half in sight.

Because this was 1000 percent the kind of establishment where such accoutrements would be tantamount to an insult to the craft.

Picking up my own cup, I took a sip and tasted . . . coffee. "Oh, wow," I said, acutely aware of Steve's eager gaze.

"Right? It's so fruit forward." Steve slurped again. "But acidic enough not to be cloying."

"Uh . . . totally," I said. "That's just what I thought."

Quite against my will, I realized that this must be what people who disavowed blue cheese must feel like when I attempted to extol the innumerable virtues of *Penicillium roqueforti*.

"So who all is in this guild?" I asked.

"Dan, Vada, a couple of the other baristas, and some of his postdoctoral colleagues."

"That's great." Quashing a new connection was the last thing I wanted to do on the heels of Steve's loss of and subsequent grief over his dear dragon-shifter friend and former gaming buddy, Hayden. But the big-sister part of me couldn't let it go without at least communicating a word of caution.

Sidenote: Shut up, I can so be cautious.

"Listen, Steve, I'm really glad you and Dan have so much in common, but—"

"—acts like he should get a medal just for taking the girls to ballet. Like it's my job and he's doing me this *huge* favor by 'helping me.'"

The woman speaking made air quotes with her fingers as she slid into the booth behind Steve, her friend taking the opposite side.

"But?" Steve prompted.

"But . . ." I hesitated, trying to think of a way to say what needed to be said without tipping the women off to what we were really talking about. "The, uh, thing about group quests is everyone might start out with the same goal, but as time goes on and things get more challenging, there can be jealousies. Resentments. Especially if one member of the group has, uh, *superior abilities*." I lifted my brows and angled a look at him to make sure he took my meaning.

"Like *The Fellowship of the Ring*?"

"Yes!" I said. "Well, kind of."

"—does one sink of dishes and spends the rest of the night pouting because that holey T-shirt I've begged him to throw out is the only thing getting moist."

Steve and I both shuddered in unison.

"Anyway, what I mean is, in the beginning of the Fellowship, everyone probably really did want to help Frodo get the one ring back to Mount Doom, but the more time everyone spent together, the more comfortable they got. And the more comfortable they got, the more their true colors came through, and before you know it, Frodo and Sam were CGI spider bait."

"But that wasn't the fellowship's fault," Steve argued. "Granted, Boromir was pretty much a walking red flag since the council meeting at Rivendell, but it was Sméagol who lured them into Shelob's lair."

"Right," I agreed. "But if Boromir hadn't been on his bullshit, the Fellowship might not have broken, thereby leaving Frodo vulnerable to Gollum's nefarious—though at times strangely adorable—machinations. Get what I'm saying?"

"I think so?" Steve tore a strip from a coffee-stained napkin and began twisting it into a rope. "Are we still talking about the Guild?"

I placed my hand over his to stop his fidgeting. "I know things have been hard for you since Hayden . . . passed." The word seemed vastly inadequate to describe the mind-meltingly awesome sight of a dragon exploding into a brand-new galaxy of stars, but I'd yet to come up with a better one. "What the two of you had was comfortable and familiar because you both were so much *alike*. And when you're used to having a friend like that, it can be easy to forget that not everyone can be trusted with the weight of your truth. Does that make sense?"

Steve nodded slowly. "I'm picking up what you're putting down."

"Good," I said, desperately hoping this was true.

"Speaking of scorched rings . . ." Steve's chunky silver rings clinked on the table as he fanned his hands on the surface to push himself up. "I'm just going to nip to the little lads' room. Back in a tick."

I deflated against the back of the booth, already exhausted though the clock had yet to strike 10:00 A.M.

I was debating the merits of slipping into Abernathy's office for a power nap once I got back to the gallery when my phone buzzed inside my purse.

Please don't be Mom, please don't be Mom, please don't be Mom, I silently prayed as I fished it out.

It was not Mom, but the directness of the text made my heart pick up to a jog all the same.

Where are you?

At Dan's coffee shop with Steve, I quickly typed back. *Why?*

Stay there.

I really hated it when my questions were answered by a command.

Blowing out a breath, I forced myself to dig my shifter business cell out of my purse and scrolled through my email while I waited.

One of my first acts as the official alpha had been to have each flavor of shifter designate a liaison whose unenviable task it was to keep me apprised of the various developments within their respective sector.

The delegates varied vastly in qualifications and temperament, the turnover was constant, and the reports they sent every Monday morning about as fun to get through as a recreational flaying, but it had still proved a reliable early warning system for potential conflicts.

Only, this week, there weren't any.

No epistolary discourses from the always-offended owl shifters.

No curmudgeonly crocodile constituent complaints.

No passive-aggressive skunk citizen missives.

I flicked through the messages, each as concise and sterile as the last. No unusual activity, no reports of any shifters stepping out of line or causing trouble. Nothing that seemed particularly urgent at all.

I frowned, a prickling sensation of unease skimming down my spine.

Something was most definitely *off.*

"This seat taken?" Morrison stood next to the bench Steve had vacated, already managing to look rumpled despite having changed into a completely different outfit since the night before.

Confusion crowded out my startle reflex. I glanced toward the front door, having neither seen it open nor heard the bell. "Is it just me, or are you a thousand percent sneakier now that you're undead?"

"Came in the employee entrance." Morrison shot me a grin. "Dan felt strangely compelled to give me a key." He twirled the key ring on his long, pale finger before shoving it in the pocket of his trench coat.

I shook my head. "It's a good thing I'm immune to your glamouring."

"Yes," he said, his smile slipping from its moorings. "It is."

I took a sip of the coffee to wash down the rock that had mysteriously lodged itself in my throat. "So what's up? Why the urgent text?"

Morrison's lips parted, but closed again as one of the women at the booth behind us rose to saunter to the bathroom, stealing a prolonged look at Morrison on the way.

"I have some information about the . . . uh . . . situation we discussed yesterday prior to the show."

My heart knocked even harder against my ribs. "Perhaps we should discuss this back at the gallery?" I said, cutting my eyes toward the coffee counter, where Vada was excavating a wedge of pie.

"Actually," he said, "I think here is just the right place to talk about it. Better if certain people don't get the idea that you have any reason to avoid their establishment."

As if on cue, Dan's bespectacled face appeared in the round porthole of the kitchen door seconds before it swung open. "Detective Morrison. How's it going?"

"Like a freight train, Dan," Morrison said, sliding into the same jovial bluster he'd employed last night. "Like a freight train."

Dan slid a tray of iced sugar cookies onto the counter and lifted the glass dome to begin stacking them on a vintage cake stand. "What can I get you?"

"Don't suppose you have any of that Colombian roast left?"

The corners of Dan's mouth curled into a simpering grin. "It just so happens that I keep a special stock of it in my office for just such an occasion. Drip or French press?"

"As long as it pours into my thermos, I don't especially care."

"Roger that," Dan said, disappearing back into the kitchen.

"You realize pouring out perfectly good coffee is a Permanent Record–worthy offense, right?" I sipped the rapidly cooling brew and scooted over to make room on my bench as Steve approached.

"Who says I pour it out?" Morrison nodded to Steve as he scooted in next to me, trailing a waft of urinal cake and hand soap.

"Pour what out?" Steve asked.

"Coffee," I said.

Steve gasped and clutched his heart. "You wouldn't."

"I *don't.*" Morrison leaned to one side and pulled Steve's sketch pad out from under his thigh.

"Ope, sorry about that." Steve reached for it, but Morrison didn't seem to notice, his eyes turning a burnished gold as he studied the drawing.

I cleared my throat as Dan emerged from the kitchen with a tall metal thermos, and Morrison's eyes quickly flashed back to a human iris–approximating hazel by the time he reached our table.

He presented the thermos to Morrison with all the pomp of a master sommelier, unscrewing the lid to release its heavenly breath. "This is—"

"Hacienda El Roble," Steve whispered in a tone of hushed reverence. Eyes closed, his head listed gently from side to side as if to collect the individual notes straight from the air. "Stone fruit. Pear. Hazelnut. Fudge."

The shadow of abject misery that haunted Morrison's face scooped my chest hollow.

In his former human life, Morrison had been just as much of a foodie as I am. Maybe more so, if such a thing was possible. Confined now to an eternal shell whose only sensory experiences could be conveyed through blood, his ache for the mundane pleasures of the flesh was devastatingly palpable.

"And very balanced despite the high caffeine content," Dan said. "But for peak cognitive enhancement. May I recommend that you drink half before a nap of exactly twenty-two minutes?"

"A nap?" I chuckled. "Doesn't that kind of defeat the point of coffee?"

Dan, Steve, and Morrison all looked at me like I'd just yanked a rope ladder out of my nose. Which, with my Bavarian heritage and waning estrogen, was less of a stretch than I would have liked to admit.

"You would think so," Dan said. "But coffee primarily promotes wakefulness because the caffeine antagonizes the effects of endogenous adenosine, which in turn facilitates dopaminergic neurotransmission by stimulating dopamine release. By taking a nap directly after you drink coffee, you reduce the available quantity of free adenosine in the brain, thereby maximizing the brain's dopaminergic neurotransmission once the caffeine begins its work as an adrenal agonist."

"Uh, yeah." Steve nodded. "What he said."

"Thanks," I said, snatching the thermos and capping it. "Could we go ahead and get the check when you have a moment?"

Dan's self-satisfied smile wilted. "Of course." His corduroys whistled an indignant *vttt-vttt-vttt* as he shuffled off toward the register.

"Talk fast," I said to Morrison.

"It's true." Morrison handed the pad to Steve. "All of it."

Shock dropped a noise-dampening blanket over the whole scene, populating the café with an eerie pin-drop silence. "All of it?" I asked.

"All of it," he repeated.

"All of what?" In the time it had taken me to process these three simple words, Steve had unscrewed the cap of Morrison's thermos and had poured himself a cup.

I summarized everything Morrison had shared with me just as quickly, dropping my voice even lower when I got to the part about Dan having hired Morrison to investigate the disappearance of the Sasquatch.

"Being hunted by a vengeful were-senior or getting framed for a vampire massacre is one thing, but alienating the entire cryptid community?" Steve exhaled a melancholy whistle and shook his head. "That's impressive."

"It's not like I did it on purpose." I screwed the lid back on Morrison's thermos before Steve could refill his mug. "I don't even know what I did to alienate them in the first place."

Morrison shifted in his seat. "It's more what you *didn't* do."

"What do you mean?" I asked. "What didn't I do?"

A muscle in Morrison's jaw flexed. "From the information I've been able to gather, it seems that you neglected to observe certain social customs that were put in place by a previous alpha."

"But there hasn't even *been* a previous alpha in centuries," I whisper-hissed. "Half the actual shifter community didn't actually believe that the alpha existed. Hell, a good third of them still randomly send me bags of chocolate dicks or care packages that I'm 99 percent sure are actually cursed."

"Be that as it may, there was indeed an agreement, and now that the agreement has been breached, they're technically within their rights to lodge a formal challenge to your rule."

"An agreement with *whom*?" I asked.

Morrison's hair caught strands of gold from the pendant light as he leaned forward and rested his forearms on the table. "Does the name *Freki* ring any bells?"

In fact, it did.

And an alarmingly recent one at that.

Freki will be avenged!

As much as my mind's superb engine of rationalization wanted to sweep this convergence far from the bucket of my dwindling fucks, time and many, many painful experiences had taught me the folly of that particular suboptimal coping mechanism.

"So a local community of Sasquatch up and moved out of the area to join a cryptid uprising whose chief aim is to challenge my rule because they're salty that I somehow breached an agreement that I didn't even know existed, but that was apparently sworn to by a previous alpha I've never heard of."

"Basically, yes," Morrison said.

Reaching for my coffee cup, I took another swallow of the now tepid brew. "I don't suppose you know the terms of the agreement I've allegedly breached."

"Not exactly," Morrison said. "But I have a pretty good idea of who would." He cut his eyes to Dan, who was speaking animatedly to a man wearing a trucker hat and T-shirt emblazoned with the word CHUPACABRA in the iconic Coca-Cola swirly scripted font.

Morrison slid out of the booth and strolled over to the counter. His body language was a masterclass of masculine manipulation. All good-cop cool and beta male buddy-comedy deference.

He was back in surprisingly short order, his expression grave.

"What?" I asked, already steeling myself for the worst. "What is it?"

Morrison matched the tips of his fingers together. "You were supposed to have invited their duly appointed representative to brunch."

I felt my eyebrows accordion toward the center of my forehead. "That's it?"

"Yep," Morrison said.

"The reason that an entire population of ancient and mysterious beings has decided to revolt against me is because I didn't invite them over for quiche and mimosas?"

Morrison shrugged. "Turns out, Sasquatch are pretty easily offended."

Steve snorted. "I could have told you that."

"Well, I wish someone had." The quip came out harsher than I'd meant it to, stinging me with instant regret when the smile abruptly evaporated from my brother's face.

It wasn't until I heard the audible gurgle from Steve's

midsection and noticed the fine film of sweat on his upper lip that I twigged to the real reason for his suddenly stricken look.

"You okay?" I asked.

"Begging your pardon, but I seem to be brewing a batch of keister kombucha." And with that, Steve levered out of the booth and duckwalked toward the restrooms.

"That's one thing about being human I don't miss," Morrison said, shaking his head.

"How *does* that work, exactly?" I asked, realizing I was exactly today years old when I'd actually paused to think about how blood was processed by a vampire's digestive system. If digesting was even a thing for them.

The pale skin around Morrison's lips turned an even chalkier white. "I'd prefer to stick to the topic at hand if at all possible."

I leaned back against the booth and crossed my arms over my chest.

"I literally scrubbed partially digested onion ring chunks out of your hair when I found you face down in a puddle of your own vomit on my doorstep, and *now* you're shy about your biological functions?"

Now it was my turn to receive a nudge under the table.

"Compliments of the house." Vada breezed up to the table and dealt out three plates with fat wedges of cheesecake swathed in dark, glossy berry compote. "And the check whenever you're ready."

"Actually," I said, already reaching for my wallet. "Can I just give this to you now?"

"You bet."

"And would I be the worst if I asked for to-go containers for these?"

A shadow so brief I wasn't even sure I'd seen it flickered across her features. "Not at all."

Her lithe limbs looked oddly tense as she walked away.

"You know what the last thing I ever ate was?" Morrison's eyes stole the jewellike hue from the berries, darkening as he stared at the plate in front of him.

Winding my memory back to the night he'd insisted on helping me storm Emperor Nero's château of horrors, I found only a sketchy action movie montage of Morrison's town house, the two of us the plucky protagonists arming ourselves against the Big Bad.

"I don't."

He gave a bitter chuckle. "A goddamn protein bar."

Steve's return at precisely that moment felt as welcome as springtime—if not exactly scented like it.

"That was a close one." He plopped down next to me, looking like he'd run a 5K in Hades. "Oof," he said, dubiously eyeing the desserts. "I throw dairy into this mix, and I'll have the Havana mudslides for sure."

"Vada is getting us to-go containers," I said. "About the Sas—"

"*Sauron?*" Steve tipped his leopard-print beanie toward the counter where Dan was not so subtly bar-mopping his way toward us.

"Right," I said. "So now that we know *Sauron* is miffed because Frodo hasn't yet—"

"Wait, I thought *I* was Frodo." Steve picked up a piece of the graham cracker crust from his plate and popped it into his mouth.

"Fine," I huffed. "I'll be Aragorn, then. Just someone please answer my question."

"No *way.*" Vada was back, a stack of recyclable cardboard clamshells clasped in one hand and the small leather folder with the check in the other. "You guys do *LOTR* RPGs too?"

"Does the scarecrow shart straw?" Apparently, last night's discussion with Dan had set my brother on a *Wizard of Oz* theme.

"You've *got* to join my game sometime," Vada said. "We're down three players and—"

"We'd love to," I cut in, desperate to get rid of her so we could finish our discussion. "How about I check the calendar when I'm back at the gallery and we can compare notes next time I stop by?"

Which would be never.

"Better yet," she said, handing the containers to Morrison and flipping open the folder. "I'll just jot my cell on here and you can text me."

The smile she gave me was just shy enough to tweak my antennae.

Since when have you attracted anything but covert narcissists and mildly unhinged men with wildly unhealthy coping skills?

Also never.

"Will do," I said, hating myself for the blush I could feel creeping up my neck. I signed the check, left a nice—but not *too* nice—tip, took a picture of Vada's number, and started boxing up the cheesecake. "Can we please return to the topic at hand so I can get back to the gallery and start my day?"

"The maternal unit or Sauron?" Steve asked.

Fuck.

I'd managed to forget about that little wrinkle entirely.

"Maternal unit?" Morrison asked.

I exhaled a sigh that felt dragged from the base of my spine and gave him the TLDR version.

Afterward, Morrison stared at the vintage Formica-flecked tabletop for a long time, his face grave. When at last he lifted his eyes to mine, the pain in them stole my breath. "You've got to tell her."

I slid one of the containers of cheesecake across to him for appearance's sake. "I don't think you understand what you're saying. This woman is physiologically incapable of keeping a secret. She'll blab to her church lady bingo friends at the first opportunity, and the next thing you know, there will be a mob of Lindas and Karens with torches and pitchforks camped on the gallery steps."

Morrison pushed Steve's shrapnel of napkin shreds into a tidy pile. "She went your entire life and never mentioned to you that you were descended from a line of ancient alpha wolf shifters."

A topic of some consternation to this day.

"He has a point." Steve shrugged.

Annoyingly, he usually did.

"Either way, she deserves a chance to know her son."

Long ago, Morrison had shared with me about his ex-wife having had a late-term miscarriage with their baby daughter. An event that had preceded his descent into a deep depression and his wife's subsequent departure from their marriage with the assistance of a fire-breathing sideshow performer.

A double loss I suspected that he was conflating with my mother's loss of her husband and infant son.

"Okay," I said. "I need to think about the best way to do it, but okay. That just leaves what to do about Sauron."

Steve gasped, and for a moment, I expected him to sprint toward the bathrooms again.

"Hear me out." He swiveled to face me on the bench, his eyes bright with excitement. "What if, uh—Aragorn invited Sauron to Arwen's super surprise shindig? You know, like a peace offering?"

Morrison snorted. "If Abernathy is Arwen, then I'm friggin' Galadriel."

"Well, obviously, if we were basing the substitutive nomenclature on physiognomy instead of romantic attachments—" Steve began.

"Guys." I slapped the table with the flat of my palm, making the silverware jump. "Can we please focus here?"

"Sorry," Steve said. "I just don't get to use words like *substitutive nomenclature* very often since the twins came. First it was *Peppa Pig* and *Bluey*, and now it's *Five Nights at Freddy's*."

My heart gave a painful squeeze. I was all too aware of the accelerated passage of time where my niece and nephew were concerned, and alpha business had kept me away from them for way too long.

"Purely hypothetically speaking, if Aragorn agreed to this absolutely insane plan, and I'm not saying that he does, what makes you think Sauron would actually come?" I asked. "Isn't he on his way to . . . wherever this cryptid convention is supposed to be taking place?"

"Vegas," Morrison said.

Because of course it was.

"If he's already on his way to Vegas, what makes you think he'd come back for this?"

"Only because it's a known fact that Sauron—and his kind—can't resist a party," Steve said.

"And you know this *how*?" I asked.

"Reddit," Steve and Morrison said in unison.

"Reddit?"

"*Oh* yeah," Steve said. "It's the one-stop shop for sightings, theories, lore, you name it."

"If I build it, he will come," Morrison said decisively.

"And probably do a keg stand," Steve added. "Plus, who wouldn't want a Sasquatch at their birthday party?"

Abernathy, that's who. *Especially* if the threat of keg stands was imminent.

My purse was vibrating again, and I didn't even have to look to know whose name I would find on the screen.

Mom.

I know it sounds improbable, but I'd swear under oath that the universe had somehow instilled her with the power to warp my phone's ringtone to a discordant key. To amplify a text notification to a pins-and-needles buzz.

"Okay, fine." I sighed, feeling the weight of responsibility once again settling on my shoulders. "How do you propose we extend this invitation?"

"Leave it to me." Morrison tightened the cap that doubled as a cup back on his thermos. "Just text me the details and I'll make it happen."

Such was my gratitude—and also my exhaustion—that I had no interest in asking how.

"Splendid," Steve said, clapping his hands together decisively. "Operation Sasquatch Surprise is a go."

We rose and gathered our things, Morrison excusing himself for a pressing engagement.

Steve and I walked back to the gallery together, the air thick with perfume from the seasonal blooms spilling over the cement planters lining either side of Main Street.

"So what of Operation Madre?" Steve asked, slowing for a crosswalk. "How do we want to do this?"

His question raised another one that hadn't occurred to me until that precise moment.

If my mother genuinely didn't remember Abernathy, what *did* she remember about the circumstances of my father's death? And of the son she lost?

"Let me do a little recon when I get home tonight," I said, shifting my paper bag of cheesecake to my non-purse-bearing arm. Already, the dense desserts were causing the raffia handle to press little ridges into my arm. "Test the waters."

"Roger that," Steve said. "Shayla has her green witches' group at our pad tonight, so I'm on kiddo duty, but just give me a shout if you need anything."

What I needed was a newsletter, apparently.

"Green witches?"

The pedestrian signal blinked to the iconic ambulating figure, and we stepped off the curb and into the crosswalk.

"It started as a Facebook group for ladies who are super into plants, but they've started doing in-person meetups. Last time it was our turn to host, Ollie ate someone's monstera albo, so tonight is kind of make-or-break, if you know what I mean."

I knew all too well.

"I do indeed," I said. "In fact, if you want to take off early this afternoon—"

The screech of tires tore away the rest of my sentence, the roar of a big engine rattling my rib cage.

I glanced down the street to see the wide chrome grille of Morrison's gold Crown Victoria barreling toward us like a freight train.

Under normal circumstances, my reflexes would have vaulted me out of its path before the image had finished forming on my retinas. But seeing Morrison's anguished face behind the wheel, my legs froze solid, welding me to the spot.

It veered at the last second, coming to a halt with a hideous mechanical squeal and an oily plume of blue burnt-rubber smoke. Morrison launched himself out of the vehicle before it had finished moving. I felt a jerk and a brief flash of pain on my wrist and the bag tore away, landing at my feet.

"What the—"

"Poisoned," Morrison said. "The coffee too."

As if on cue, Steve's stomach rumbled its complaint. Beads of sweat stood out on a forehead that had gone bone white. Greenish spots had appeared at the downturned corners of his mouth.

"Oh dear." Clutching his middle, Steve folded in half and retched a jet of rich, brown vomit onto Morrison's shoes before collapsing to the asphalt.

7

My arms burned as Morrison and I lugged Steve up the gallery steps, my brother's head lolling against my shoulder. Steve's limp, clammy arm flopped unnervingly out of my grasp, and I nearly dropped him in my haste to catch it.

Why the hell was he so heavy?

"Watch his head," I grunted, my voice trembling with the effort of holding back tears.

Terror clawed my gut at the feeling of his cold, damp skin against mine.

Please, *please* let him be okay.

"Get the door," Morrison said, his voice strained as he shouldered the lion's share of Steve's deadweight. His struggle only intensified my panic as I fumbled for my key ring.

I was so relieved when the key slid home that it took me a moment to comprehend why the dead bolt refused to tumble open.

Because it was already unlocked.

A tremor of fear rippled through me, half expecting to find further horror awaiting me on the other side of the door. But when my sweaty palm managed to turn the knob and I hip-checked it open, the first thing I saw was Abernathy.

Halfway up the stairs to his office, his keys still looped around one finger, his leather satchel slung across his chest.

He'd only just arrived.

Relief washed over me like a tidal wave as he thundered down the stairs, anger darkening his face as he focused on Morrison.

"What happened?" he demanded. "What's wrong?"

Somehow, both questions sounded like *What did you do?*

"We think he's been poisoned," I said. "Help us get him to your office."

Abernathy's face went white, but he didn't hesitate. As gently as if Steve were made of glass, Mark lifted him into his arms and maneuvered my brother's unconscious body up the two flights of stairs.

I followed his long strides, Morrison on my heels until we reached the landing and I hurried past him to open Abernathy's office door.

Locked.

"For fuck's sake." I pawed through my purse once more, annoyed to discover that the keys had already migrated back to the bottom.

"Take mine." Abernathy extended his index finger, Steve braced on his forearm.

This time, I got the key into the lock on the first attempt. The bolt tumbled open with a satisfying *thunk*.

"All right, buddy, let's get you onto the couch." Abernathy shouldered through the doorway and froze. "What the *fuck*?"

I nearly crashed into his broad back in my haste to see what had elicited this reaction.

There, stretched out on Mark's couch, was Helena. Her shoes were kicked off haphazardly on the floor next to an empty bottle of wine, flakes of pastry dusting her dark hair and chest, a soft snore rising from her lightly parted lips.

Sleeping Beauty after a bakery raid.

Quickly walking back through my memory, I scoured for any detail about Helena's having left after the gallery show last night, but came up empty. Pretty much everything after "Your mother showed up at our front door" was a complete and total blur.

I strode over to the couch and gently shook her shoulder. "Helena. Wake up."

"Fuck off," she mumbled, burying her face in the leather couch's arm. "Already a member."

"*Helena*," I said shaking a little harder this time.

"Back off. *My* breast milk—"

"Here," Abernathy said, draping Steve over Morrison's shoulder. "Hold this."

Morrison grunted, but remained upright.

"Helena." Abernathy's booming voice cracked through the office like a whip. "Up. Now."

Helena stirred, rolling over and curling an arm around Abernathy's thigh before snuggling her cheek against it like a contented cat. Eyes still closed, a wicked grin spread across her face. "Oh *yes*," she purred. "That's it. Just like that."

The office door burst open just then, and Scott Kirkpatrick stumbled in, looking even more disheveled than his wife. His eyes were bloodshot and wild, his curly ginger hair sticking up in whorls and tufts. Mysterious smudges marred his rumpled khakis and a plaid shirt whose buttons were a couple of holes off from lining up.

His darting gaze landed on Helena, who was practically welded to Mark's leg.

"What in blue blazes is going on here?" Scott thundered, face reddening.

"Mmmm, *Freki*." Helena's arms tightened around Abernathy's thigh.

Every nerve in my body sizzled to attention as I locked eyes with Morrison. "Did you hear that?"

"I most certainly did." Kirkpatrick's barrel chest puffed out by another inch. "I entrust my wife to your care and you lure her into some sort of *freaky*, sick, twisted sex game."

"That's not what she said—"

"And you," Kirkpatrick said, stabbing a stubby finger at his lasciviously lounging wife. "How *could* you? I've been worried sick while I'm home alone caring for our pups, up to my elbows in macaroni and Pull-Ups, and you're out in the streets doing gods know what with this mouth-breathing meathead and a woman you once described as Little Orphan Annie's codependent cat lady cousin. Have your morals truly stooped so low?"

"Now, wait just a minute," I said. "You're the one who didn't even come looking for your wife until practically noon, and it sounds to me like you're only bitching because you had to do everything that Helena normally takes care of without your help. Absolutely nothing other than your wife getting a full night of obviously much-needed rest happened here last night, so can you kindly help us get her ass off this couch so we can take care of Steve?"

"Steve?" Confused, Kirkpatrick followed my gaze. Seeing Morrison, his eyes widened in panic, all previous anger vanishing from his ruddy face. "Oh God. Hold on."

With speed and strength surprising for one of his size, Kirkpatrick scooped his wife up newlywed-style and dumped her into Abernathy's office chair.

Mark helped Morrison lay Steve on the couch, the two men in my life handling my brother with a tenderness that made my heart ache.

Scott immediately rushed to Steve's side, propping a throw pillow beneath his head.

"What happened? Who did this to you?" He clutched Steve's limp hand, eyes fierce behind their wire-rimmed glasses.

A lump formed in my throat. The depth of his feelings for my brother were written plainly across his face.

Steve's eyes fluttered open, and he gave me a weak smile. "Told you he loves me."

As it so often had when anything remotely pleasant was said about him, Kirkpatrick's emotional dial snapped back to its default asshat setting. "I most certainly do not," he sputtered. "I was just . . . concerned."

I nudged Kirkpatrick out of the way to kneel beside my brother, smoothing his sweat-soaked hair from his forehead as he blinked up at me.

"Did I . . . did I soil myself?"

I barked a laugh, surprised by how quickly relief flooded through me. "No, you didn't," I reassured him, tears prickling at the corners of my eyes.

"Thank God," Steve mumbled, attempting a smile that looked more like a grimace. "Last thing I remember, I was about to pull an Old Faithful from both ends."

"You're good," I said, patting his knee. "No gut geysers to speak of. You just rest here. I'm going to call Shayla."

"*No.*" Steve tried to sit up, then winced. "If you do that, she'll cancel tonight. I really don't want her to do that. Please. Just let me power down and I'll be fine. I promise."

Having had occasion to witness Steve pull his healing nap trick when he'd had his throat mostly torn out, I was relatively confident that he'd be able to clear a headache and any lingering intestinal distress.

"Okay," I said, guiding him back onto the pillows. "Take it easy."

We were far from out of the woods, but the fact that he was both conscious and cracking jokes seemed like an overall positive sign.

"All right," Abernathy said. "Let's give him some space."

"That means you," I said, ushering Kirkpatrick and his wife toward the door.

"But I don't wanna go," Helena whined. "I like it here. Maybe I could help out around the gallery. Like a part-time gig?" She clutched Abernathy's hand, her ice-blue eyes pleading as she looked up at him.

"You'd need to discuss that with Hanna," he said, the flicker of a grin haunting one corner of his lips.

Oh, how my love for him doth bloom.

"I'll think about it," I said, mostly because I suspected it would be the faster way to get rid of her.

"You won't be sorry." She rose and threw her arms around me, enveloping me in the strange bouquet of expensive perfume, goat cheese, and cabernet sweat.

"I'll be in touch," I said, handing Kirkpatrick her purse.

"Now," Abernathy said when they were gone. "Who would like to tell me why Steve looks like an asparagus stalk and you smell like coffee and shame?"

Morrison and I exchanged a look.

"When do I not?" I asked, attempting to lighten the mood. Abernathy wasn't going to like what I had to tell him about Morrison having stopped by before the gallery show yesterday to inform me of the potential cryptid uprising any more than he was going to like the revelation that I'd failed to mention it to him in the maternal kerfuffle that last night and this morning had turned into. That I'd ended up having coffee with—okay, *near*—Morrison this morning was just going to be the cherry on the shitbiscuit Blizzard.

"Well, what had happened was—" I began.

"It's my fault," Morrison said. "I was at the coffee shop this morning because I've been gathering intel on local cryptid populations for a private client."

Why he didn't yet want to reveal that Dan had been the initiator of said investigation, I wasn't certain, but decided to let Morrison play out his hand.

Abernathy folded his arms across his broad chest and seated himself on the corner of his desk. "*What* intel?"

"That there's been a mass migration of the local Sasquatch population as part of the ongoing unrest within the cryptid community."

"And how exactly did you become aware of this unrest?" By the careful way Abernathy asked, I wasn't entirely convinced that this was news to him.

"Reddit," I said as if this information hadn't been newly lodged in my brain.

"Correct," Morrison said, following my lead. "One of the most frequent contributors to the Creepiest Cryptids of Georgetown feeds is one *E. Pidendrosaurus*, whose user profile lists his profession as javaphile. Having made the staggering leap that this was likely Dan Davis, I've been conducting undercover surveillance at his shop, where I was informed of the simmering resentment that a certain influential Sasquatch feels at having never been officially acknowledged by the new alpha as per the terms of the previously negotiated agreement, which I'm sure you're aware of. Just as I'm sure you're aware of all ongoing operations in the shifter community since you labored so tirelessly to install Hanna in this oh-so-vital but indescribably difficult role. In fact, I don't even know why I'm telling you, as you're doubtless already monitoring the ongoing situation as well as tracking potential threats to Hanna's rule so that you can effectively neutralize them while minimizing her discomfort."

The air in the room thickened like cooling tar, refusing to fill my lungs.

I would run out of appendages counting all the times I'd seen Morrison and Abernathy square off, but there was something different about this time. Something . . . elemental. Primeval. Uncivilized.

Also, kinda hot.

"That explains what *you* were doing at a venue you suspected of being a gathering place for cryptid sympathizers." Abernathy's voice was as flat and calm as a frozen lake, and just as deceptively dangerous. "It doesn't explain what Hanna and Steven were doing there."

"Steve was already there when I got here this morning," I blurted. "He asked me to meet him there. I needed to talk to him about Mom, anyway, and I thought that, after last night, showing up there might give Dan less of a reason to suspect us."

"Last night?" Abernathy asked.

"Dan randomly popping up at the gallery show," I said. "Nosing around Steve's studio, then asking about you."

"I take it you were made aware of the cryptid situation *before* the gallery show, then?" I heard the first crystalline cracks fissuring Abernathy's words.

"Yes," I said. "Morrison stopped by as a courtesy."

The prominent vein that doubled as a spectrometer for the relative magnitude of my regrettable life choices rose and beat beneath the smooth skin of Abernathy's kingly brow. "Detective Morrison has always been *very* courteous where you're concerned."

"One of us should be," Morrison muttered.

A deliciously dizzying but decidedly inconvenient wave of warmth flooded through me as the unmistakable musk of androstadiene surged in Abernathy's bloodstream.

Thousands of years of evolution and still, the heady energetic/olfactory double shot of *Eau de I'll Kick Your Ass* had the power to trigger an involuntary lady boner.

And if my body could emulsify wolf wafts and vampire vapors into a cocktail that juiced my limping libido, couldn't my mind wrangle the men responsible into a mildly civil cognitive concord?

I 100 percent intended to find out.

As I had so many times before, I stationed myself between them. "Tell him about the brunch," I said, spearing Morrison with a pleading look.

"Brunch?" The furrow between Abernathy's brows temporarily canceled out the vein.

Progress, I decided.

"In the course of my investigation, I came across certain . . .

materials that documented an existing agreement between the former shifter kingdom's alpha and the appointed representative of the cryptid community."

I studied Abernathy as he listened to Morrison, panning his features the way prospectors had once sifted the murky waters of Clear Creek, eyes peeled for any lambent spark of gold.

Or in my case, recognition.

"*What* former alpha?"

"That's exactly what I said!" I looked at Abernathy for an extended beat before snagging gazes with Morrison. "Isn't it? Isn't that exactly what I said?"

"That's exactly what she said."

The little bubble of warmth behind my rib cage expanded at Morrison's use of the third-person article. He was technically addressing Abernathy.

More progress.

"Okay, but cinch your sock garters, because this shit gets even weirder." I took a step closer to Abernathy while gesturing at Morrison. "Tell him," I said. "Tell him the name of the alpha who signed the agreement."

"Freki," Morrison said.

"*Freki!*" I widened my eyes at Abernathy in preparation for his recognition.

"Freki," I repeated, suddenly feeling like an amateur magician whose hocus-pocus over a top hat had failed to produce the rabbit. "You know, *Freki* like the name that the steampunk fox furry yelled when she roundhoused the lumberjack wolf into the apple streusel at Costco yesterday? Freki like Helena was mumbling as part of her sex dream just now?"

Abernathy pushed himself from the corner of the desk. "I don't wear sock garters."

"Of course not." I forced my mouth into a starched smile despite wanting to grab Abernathy by the scruff of his neck and shake him until his perfect, impossibly white teeth rattled out of his perfect, impossibly handsome head.

"This agreement," Abernathy said, beginning to pace the length of his bookshelves. "What do we know about it?"

We.

Promising.

Morrison cleared his throat. "It basically states that the cryptid community will agree to recognize the alpha shifter's authority so long as a formal invitation has been extended to the recognized leader of the Sasquatch species so long as they choose to self-govern in this manner."

"I see." Abernathy pivoted on the heel of his loafer and retraced his path. "Where does the brunch thing come in?"

Seating himself on the arm of the couch, Morrison picked a hot pink petal from the cuff of his pants. "That was an addendum after the fact, signed off on by both parties."

Abernathy paused mid-step. "Signed? Meaning there's a paper copy?"

A beat passed. "Yes."

"You've *seen* it?"

Another beat. "Yes."

"Well?" Abernathy swept a hand out in invitation.

"Well what?"

"Where is it?"

Morrison folded his hands in his lap. "In a secure location."

"When can *we* see it?" I asked.

Departing from his perch, Morrison wandered over to the windows overlooking Main Street. "I'm afraid that's not possible."

"Because?" I asked, preempting Abernathy.

"Because it would mean compromising my client's confidentiality." Morrison turned around to face us, his jaw set in an implacable angle.

"How are we supposed to verify its authenticity?" Abernathy asked.

The floorboards squeaked as Morrison took a step toward Abernathy's desk. "I guess you're just going to have to trust me."

"Trust you?" Abernathy scoffed. "When you show up here telling me that my brother-in-law apparently got poisoned on your watch?"

As if sensing the shift in attention, Steve stirred on the couch, his hands beginning to sleep-paddle above his chest in an endearingly canine fashion.

Meanwhile, I was trying to remember what even were knees.

Brother-in-law?

Since the painfully awkward conversation earlyish on in our official acquaintance that resulted in my having made a missile of my Steve Madden peep-toe pump, Abernathy and I had strenuously avoided any discussions even grazing the topic of nuptials.

So had our mating relegated the other M-word to the realm of foregone conclusion?

Or had Abernathy said it for Morrison's benefit? The implied legal status simply the common-law coverture equivalent of scent marking.

"If it hadn't been for me, Steve *and* Hanna could have ended up like *this*." Morrison reached into his suit jacket and tossed a handful of brown flakes at Abernathy's feet.

I wasn't sure exactly what I was looking at until I saw the withered black stem poking out of Morrison's coat.

I plucked what remained of the withered rose from his pocket, turning it in my fingers. "Ended up like this *how*?"

Morrison retrieved his phone from his back pocket and swiped the screen several times before turning it to face me.

Bountiful roses, obscenely, boastfully crimson in their showy late-summer glory.

"That's what the rosebush looked like *before*."

"Before . . . ?"

"Before I poured the coffee into their soil."

I stared at the image on the screen, the edges of the blooms blurring slightly as the full picture came into focus.

Not the roses.

The immortal responsible for their existence.

James Morrison was a vampire who pretended to drink coffee even when investigating cases that had nothing to do with the coffee shop.

James Morrison was a vampire who pretended to drink coffee even when investigating cases that had nothing to do with the coffee shop, and took the specialty brew he couldn't drink to water roses with instead.

James Morrison was a vampire who pretended to drink coffee when investigating cases that had nothing to with a coffee shop, and used the specialty brew he couldn't drink to water roses instead . . . and *took pictures* of the roses he watered.

My heart gave a painful squeeze whose origins I couldn't afford to think about at that particular moment.

"If it was your coffee that was poisoned, how do you know *you* weren't the target?" Abernathy asked, sounding like he didn't exactly hate this idea.

"Because it wasn't just the coffee."

This point of basic logic that my mind sailed clean over caught me for a moment. Morrison had come screeching to a halt in front of us and slapped the cheesecakes out of our hands.

"How did you—" I began.

"Brutus." Morrison flicked a glance my way. "The bulldog who lives next door to the house with the rosebushes. I gave him some of the cheesecake."

I gasped. "Is he . . ."

"No," Morrison said, a small crease tugging at one corner of his lips. "But his owner is going to need a power washer and a priest to undo what he did to the patio."

"It had to be Dan, right?" I chewed my cuticle as I gazed down at Steve, whose color had thankfully begun to return to something like normal. "First he sniffs around the gallery show last night, then he basically wedges himself up your and Steve's ass this morning. Maybe he *knows*."

Morrison shook his head. "No way he'd tell me what he's told me if he suspected that I'm a . . . a—you know."

"Undead bloodsucking fiend?" Abernathy helpfully suggested, earning him an acid look from Morrison.

Sensing another shift in the cabin pressure, I relaunched my unification campaign.

"Let's not forget how he ended up that way, shall we?" I asked, keeping my tone as light as possible. "Before he was an undead bloodsucking fiend, he was the guy who helped me storm Nero's house of horrors when *you* had been poisoned."

I squeezed Abernathy's forearm with one hand and poked Morrison's biceps through his trench coat, not exactly hating the little frisson of electricity that arced between the contact points.

Like, *at all*.

Abernathy broke the circuit, massaging his temple as if to loosen the early grips of a tension headache.

"Maybe the coffee being poisoned doesn't have anything to do with your being a vampire. Maybe Dan just doesn't like the idea of an investigator lurking around his coffee shop."

We took a moment to let that settle in.

"Has Dan ever told you *why* he's so invested in cryptid conspiracy theories?" I asked, idly thumbing the scattered papers on Abernathy's desk back into a pile.

"I got it," Abernathy said, hovering behind my shoulder.

"I mean, it does seem kind of odd to me. Single gamer guy in his thirties with a dual PhD in paleontology and mythology, living alone in a tourist town where there isn't even a college. Seems low-key sus is all I'm saying."

"Just leave those," Mark said, reaching for a folder as I slid it back into its appointed (by me) cubby.

"And what's with the bumper stickers? I like a pithy decal as much as the next person, but MY OTHER CAR IS A PLESIOSAUR?" I said, making air quotes with my fingers before turning my attention to the proliferation of pens littering the leather blotter. "What does that even mean?"

"*Don't.*" Abernathy's palm came down on the desk with enough force to make me jump.

I turned to the bookshelves as much to avoid Morrison's gaze as to blink the sudden sting from my eyes.

"Either way, my vote is that we get to the bottom of this Freki stuff pronto."

"Agreed," Morrison said.

I could literally *feel* Abernathy giving him a filthy look. "How?" he asked.

I turned to face him. "For starters, by talking to the Sasquatches' duly appointed representative to see what I can learn about the so-called alpha who entered into this ridiculous agreement in the first place."

Abernathy sank down into his office chair. "How do you propose to do that?"

"I'm so glad you asked." I beamed an overbright smile at my mate. "Because I sort of have a plan with exactly that end in mind."

The vein reappeared over Abernathy's dark brow. "Why do I have a feeling that I'm going to loathe this sort-of plan with every fiber of my being?"

"Because you have a real issue with pessimism and negativity?" I suggested.

"I prefer to call it *experience*," Abernathy said. "What's the plan?"

I took a deep breath and launched. "To invite the king of the Sasquatch to your birthday party next week."

"Out of the question," Abernathy said. "Absolutely no—what party?"

"The one that I may or may not have already invited several people to and that they've already booked flights to attend." I batted my eyelashes down at him.

Abernathy stared at me like I'd lost my mind. "You're kidding, right?"

"Wrong," I replied, matching his intense gaze. "It's the perfect opportunity to gather information and get a better understanding of what they want while in a casual and convivial setting." Despite an utter lack of salesmanship dashing my early dreams of becoming an infomercial host who evangelized all manner of time-saving kitchen devices, I thought it sounded reasonably convincing. "Besides," I challenged. "Do you have a better idea?"

A ragged gasp sliced through the room, effectively ending the conversation.

We all whirled toward the sound.

There, in the doorway to Abernathy's office, stood my mother.

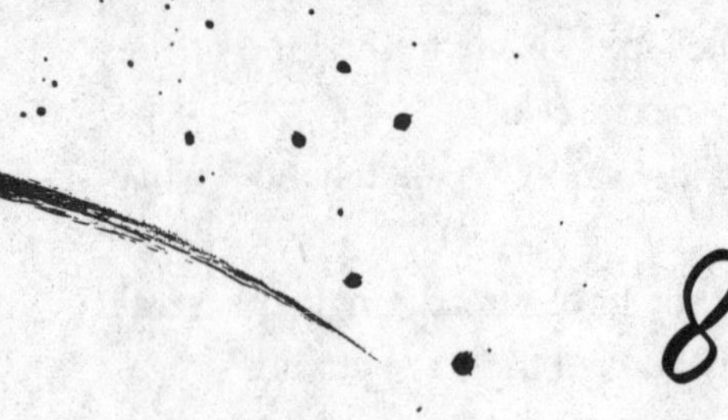

8

The familiar environs of Abernathy's office took on a distinctly Salvador Dalí–esque quality. Everyday familiar objects warped by unsettling circumstance. The polished wood desk with its antique black lacquer phone and feathered fountain pen suddenly felt like a stage set. The bookshelves I'd spent months organizing, a cheap canvas backdrop for the *Twilight Zone* episode I currently found myself trapped in.

Mom's hand hovered over her mouth, eyes frozen wide in shock.

"Mom, wait—"

But she was already bolting toward Steve, who was still sprawled out on the couch, snoring heavily. Her brimming eyes spilled over as she threw her arms around him, causing him to jolt awake with a high-pitched scream. In response, my mother let out a startled shriek, which in turn prompted another screech from Steve.

In the hushed stillness that followed the comedic duet, my mother pulled back, her swollen eyes glistening beneath the soft glow of the aged floor lamp.

"Am I dreaming?" she whispered, her voice choked with a raw emotion that hung in the stillness of the room like a tangible entity. Behind her, I watched helplessly as Steve blinked up at her in disoriented confusion, his face still pale.

Her arms rose slowly, trembling as she reached out to him.

My throat knotted as she cupped his chin, tracing his prominent cheekbones with the pads of her thumbs.

"Ma?" he choked out. His green eyes glistened with disbelief as they locked onto our mom's tear-streaked face.

"My baby!" she sobbed, clutching the hideous rhinestone cross necklace I'd noticed at breakfast. "My baby boy. You have no idea how hard I prayed for this."

I leaned against the doorframe, feeling a strange mixture of relief and trepidation as they hugged each other hard.

I hadn't had the chance to provide any context, or gauge what, if anything, she remembered about Steve's birth and my father's death.

Clearing my throat, I sat down on the arm of the couch. My mother whirled around, her eyes swimming anew.

"I can't believe you found him."

"*Found* him?" I shot a worried look at Abernathy.

"Can you ever forgive me?" she asked, turning to Steve.

"Forgive you?" Steve asked. "For what?"

Mom took Steve's hand in hers. "Putting you up for adoption."

"Adoption?" I repeated. "Mom, what are you talking about?"

She let out a watery exhale, glancing between us as she spoke.

"Your father had just left, and Hanna was only four years old. I was all alone, and I hadn't worked in over a decade. The only jobs I could find wouldn't even cover the cost of childcare. Giving you up was the hardest thing I've ever done, but I just thought it would be best for you. To grow up in a home with a mother and a father. A family."

I glanced at Abernathy, trying to communicate the depth of my confusion.

Strange constellations of words swirled in the cosmos of my mind.

Stroke. Dementia. Delusion.

"Mom," I said, fighting to keep my tone neutral. "Oma was living with us. And dad didn't leave. He—"

Abernathy stood behind his desk. "I'm sure your mom and

brother have a lot of catching up to do. Why don't we give them some privacy to chat?"

I snagged gazes with Steve over my mom's shoulder, seeing in them the assurance that he understood what Abernathy intended.

"Of course," I said, rising from the couch. "We'll be downstairs."

Abernathy, Morrison, and I trooped down the creaky gallery stairs, cutting a path across the main gallery space toward the kitchen. Proximity to food always proved to be a powerful blood pressure–reduction agent, but the room's sound-dampening qualities were just an added bonus.

"What the actual fuck?" I said as soon as the door swung closed. "First she doesn't remember who you are. Now my dad left her and she gave Steve up for adoption? I've heard of denial, but this shit is on a whole other level."

Abernathy's jaw flexed as he stared at the stainless steel counter.

"I mean, I don't know what's scarier," I said. "That this is some kind of passive-aggressive masterstroke of retributive fiction, or that she genuinely doesn't remember."

"I'm not thrilled about either option," Abernathy said. "Especially in light of our recent conversation. Keeping the pack's identity under wraps was hard enough *before* she arrived."

My pulse began to pound inside my ears.

"Of course, now that she knows about Steve, I doubt she's going to want to leave anytime soon," Mark added.

Sweat broke out on my back and face.

"And once she finds out about the grandkids, she might even decide she wants to move closer permanently."

Lunging toward the fridge, I opened the door to the freezer compartment and stuck my head inside. Once there, I pulled the cooling air deep inside my lungs, reaching for a frost-kissed box of calm-enhancing cream puffs.

"Guess we'll have to cancel the party," I heard Abernathy say behind me.

"Not possible," Morrison said. "The invitation has already been sent and accepted."

I glanced back at him through the cloud of freezer fog. "How the hell could you have invited Saur—what the hell is Daddy Sasquatch's name, anyway?"

"Morg," Morrison said.

"How the hell could you have invited Morg to the party *and* received his acceptance in the time it took for you to leave the coffee shop, discover the coffee was poisoned, and Grand Prix the Crown Vic down two blocks to slap a sack of cheesecake out of my hands?"

The last bit I was still mildly bitter about, potentially poisoned or no.

"Email," Morrison said.

"Email," I repeated. Because why wouldn't the king of the Sasquatch have email? "So he's definitely coming?"

"Said he would be there with bells on."

"Really?" I asked, feeling strangely flattered. "He said that?"

"Yes," Morrison said, "but in this case, he probably meant it literally. Sasquatch collect bells. Especially ones acquired from the homemade security systems rigged up by humans in their more . . . rural haunts."

"Right." I closed the freezer door and leaned back against it. "So now we just need to figure out what to do with my mom so she won't be traumatized by a jingly, hairy hominid and several assorted superhuman entities."

"I say we pawn her off on Steve for a couple of hours." Abernathy paused in his pacing to grab a glass from the cupboard and fill it at the sink.

"But then Steve would have to miss your birthday party," I pointed out.

"Birthday party," Abernathy muttered with a bitter snort. "As if I care who shows up to this fucking farce of a diplomatic pantomime that I never wanted in the first place."

Maybe it was the moon. Maybe it was my mother. Maybe it was the fallen cheesecake, or the Mars-Venus conjunction during a Mercury retrograde.

Whatever the case, I felt the familiar strangling tightness at the base of my throat. The unwelcome sting at the corners of my eyes. The pulpy ache dead center in my chest.

Because *I* cared.

I cared enough to help Toulouse-Lautrec look for flights and spring for first class. I cared enough to source primarily meat-based appetizers that included some of Abernathy's favorite rare game. I cared enough to stay up to the wee hours and sneak down to the basement to call around London booksellers looking for first editions to complete Abernathy's collections of Dickens, Poe, and Lovecraft. I cared enough to commission custom boxes to hold them because I knew of Abernathy's deep and abiding hatred for the texture of cardboard.

I bit the inside of my cheek hard enough to taste iron, but it was no use.

The first fat tear scalded its way down my cheek and fell to the countertop with a *plop* that might as well have been a snare drum.

"Nice job, you insensitive asshat." Morrison's eyes flashed a stoplight red as he leveled a withering glare at Abernathy. "You made her cry."

Abernathy's hands bunched into brick-like fists at his side. "What the hell are you still doing here, anyway? I don't see how any of this is any of your fucking business."

"I'm not surprised," Morrison said. "Considering how far your head is wedged up your own ass."

A low, rumbling growl ripped from Abernathy's chest.

Wickedly sharp fangs sprouted against Morrison's lower lip.

The close air of the kitchen took on that electric crackling quality that typically escalated into nothing good real fast.

"Guys, it's fine," I insisted, quickly swiping my cheek. "Really.

All this Mom stuff is just a little overwhelming. Let's just table this discussion until—"

The kitchen door swung violently inward, launching Morrison belly-first into the counter.

I *really* needed to remember to keep him from coming between me and any potential source of creatures whose sounds and smells would be absorbed by his life-canceling undead aura.

"How could you not have told me?" Mom stood in the doorway, storm clouds in her eyes and her hands on the hips of her oversize T-shirt adorned with frolicking Boston terriers that in no way resembled the two frog-mouthed demon spawn who had made my every visit a misery since college.

Steve hovered behind her, his cheeks glowing red and an apologetic frown on his face.

I swallowed hard. "About?"

"About the *real* reason you've been so distant ever since you started working at this gallery."

I cast a helpless glance between Abernathy and Morrison, both of whom looked like livestock in the headlights.

"Well," I began. "The situation was kind of complicated, and—"

"I just don't understand how you could be so selfish. So . . . cruel."

My mouth opened, but words failed to materialize.

"All this time I spent alone, ignored by my daughter, when I could have been part of—"

"A werewolf pack?" I blurted.

"My grandchildren's lives!" My mother threw her hands up in frustration, only to have her features abruptly rearrange to confusion. "Wait, what did you just say?"

"Nothing," I said. "I just meant that, uh, the reason I kept everything a secret is—"

"I asked her to," Steve blurted.

Our mother turned to face him, her expression softening faster than butter under a heat lamp. "You did?"

Steve nodded. "I . . . uh, wanted our reunion to be really special. I just wasn't sure what would be the best way to facilitate that."

"Oh, Steve," Mom gushed. "How very thoughtful of you."

Less than ten minutes in, and I was selfish and cruel while my newly discovered brother was thoughtful.

That, as the kids say, tracked.

"All right, let's all just take a deep breath," I said in an attempt to regain control of the situation. "Mom, I know you're excited to meet your grandkids—"

"River and Ollie," Mom squealed, clapping her hands together in delight. "What beautiful names! Did *Shayla* pick those out?" she asked in an obvious bid to demonstrate her knowledge of this recently acquired personal detail. "I just can't wait to meet her too. She sounds like such a special young lady."

"She definitely is," I said in a slightly less saccharine tone. "But right now, Steve, Abernathy, Morrison, and I have some important work do around the gallery. Why don't I get you a Lyft back to our house, and we can make plans this evening?"

"Of course," Mom sniffed. "I'd hate to be in the way." A comment surely designed to elicit the assurance that she *wasn't* in the way.

"You're not in the way at all, Ma," Steve said, squeezing her shoulder. "But the sooner I can get these custom pieces banged out, the sooner I can give you my full attention."

If this was bullshit, it was top-shelf special reserve, and our mom guzzled it down like ambrosia.

"There's nothing I would love more," Mom said, squeezing Steve's bracelet-studded forearm.

"Excellent," I said. "Wonderful. Splendid. If you want to wait for me in the foyer, I'll be right there to get you taken care of."

After another prolonged Hallmark movie–worthy look at Steve, Mom turned on her Croc and shuffled out to the gallery.

I sagged against the counter, suddenly feeling empty, tired, and about a thousand years old.

"What the hell do we do now?" I asked.

Steve's dimples flickered as his lips stretched into a slow smile. "I have an idea."

—

I stood in the kitchen, staring open-mouthed at the counter. It looked like a bomb had gone off at a farmers market.

And in the center of the sprawling chaos was my mother.

Standing on her tiptoes, pulling spices out of my cupboard, and making a pre-party coronary a very real possibility.

"What the hell, Mom? All I asked was for you to add baby carrots to the veggie trays."

"Oh, I know, sweetie. I was going to do that, but I was putting the ranch in actual serving bowls instead of the plastic containers you had it in and got some on the counter and I was trying to clean it off when I noticed the rest of the counter could really use a wipe down and I was looking for a clean sponge when I saw this box of baking soda under the sink and thought I could put it in your freezer to help with the smell but when I opened it I noticed that you had the cake in there uncovered and I didn't want the frosting to taste like fishy ice so I went to get some aluminum foil but you were almost out so I figured I'd just prop a mixing bowl over it instead but the biggest one you had was already in the fridge and needed a spoon to transfer the coleslaw out but all your big spoons were dirty so I thought I'd just use the same spoon that I had to transfer the ranch but then I remembered that when I'd licked it the ranch was pretty bland and since I know how important this party is, I thought I'd just tweak it a little bit because I'd hate for your guests to think Texans don't know their way around our unofficial state condiment." Mom tucked a silver threaded wisp of auburn hair back behind her ear and smiled at me. "Do you have garlic powder?"

"Oh, dear God," I said, blinking at the brutal biological mirror. "I'm going to die alone."

Not necessarily the ideal moment for a midlife mortality crisis, but here we were.

"Oh, sweetie." Mom patted my hand. "Onion powder would work too." She'd resumed pawing through the cabinet again. "Honestly, anything would probably be an improvement." Her patronizing chuckle made my already humid skin feel extra swampy.

I mentally counted back from ten, turning her to face me only when I could no longer feel my heartbeat in my eyeballs.

"Mom, we have party guests set to arrive in less than half an hour. I'm still not finished with the decorations, and if we don't get the food tables done in the next ten minutes, I'm not going to have time to change into my costume before people start showing up." I paused to allow this information to sink in. "Can you please, *please* just put the carrots on the tray?"

"Of course," she replied absentmindedly, picking up the bag of baby carrots only to wander over to the balloon station where Steve was operating the helium tank. "Is this a rental?"

"Indubitably," Steve said in a high-pitched, munchkin-esque voice that made it obvious that he'd been sampling his own wares.

"Mother!" I snapped, my patience wearing thin.

"Ope, sorry," she mumbled, returning to the cutting board. She picked up the knife, stared at it as if it were an alien object, and then placed it back down. "You know, I've always wondered how they make those little guys, anyway. Do you think they shave them down?"

I shot Steve an exasperated look. He widened his eyes, his

mouth forming a silent *wow* at the precise second that our doorbell rang.

Glancing at the digital readout on the microwave, I felt a cramp of dread.

None of the guests were supposed to show for twenty minutes yet.

"I'll get it," I said, my voice hitching slightly in my tightening throat. Leaving Hurricane Helga behind, I wove my way through the domestic disaster zone toward the front door.

It swung open with a gentle creak, revealing an empty porch.

"Weird," I said.

But no sooner had I closed it than another chime rang through the foyer. Digging my phone from my pocket, I checked the Ring app. It, too, revealed nary a shade.

The phone buzzed in my hand as I stared at the screen, the name in the notification giving me a little pop of joy.

Abernathy, who was hiding out at a biker bar halfway down the canyon, waiting for my signal to show up and act surprised.

The fuck is going on with the doorbell?

Luddite that he'd been when we met, his adoption of advanced automated security measures still caught me by surprise.

Not sure, I quickly typed back. *Hoping it's just a misfire rather than an unidentified creature that can ring a doorbell without a corporeal body.*

Three dots appeared and disappeared several times.

Doing okay?

If by "okay" you mean ready to lock my mother in the pantry and make myself a whiskey milkshake, then yes, totally okay.

Save some for our after-party.

His words generated a rush of warmth in my middle. It was easily the most directly provocative thing he'd said to me in months, and the fact that he'd attempted a joke even though he'd been violently opposed to everything about this idea seemed like a not-terrible sign.

You'd better believe it, Buster, I typed back.

The door chimed again, and I wrenched it open before the musical cadence of notes had finished tolling through the speaker.

A peculiar mixture of disbelief and wonderment doused the adrenaline that had my fists already balling at my side.

There, bathed in the glow from the porch light, stood a unicorn.

And not just any unicorn.

Wallis the unicorn.

Pearlescent horn, sweeping golden mane, shimmering snow-white coat, and pale eyes that held galaxies within them.

Though our previous interactions had given me cause to threaten him with bodily harm on occasion, I couldn't help but be momentarily stunned by his ethereal grandeur.

Until he opened his mouth.

"Hey, hey there, sweet cheeks. Long time, no squeeze." He ducked his majestic head and clicked his velvety pink lips at me.

Looking past him to the circular drive holding only Steve's Volkswagen Bug, I saw no indication from whence he might have come.

"What—and I cannot emphasize this next part enough—the actual fuck are you doing here?"

"Sweating my sugarplums off on your front porch at the moment." His gilded tail swished side to side as if to ventilate the area in question. "You going to invite me in or what?"

"Or what," I said, folding my arms across my chest.

"Aww, come on, toots," he said, a pleading note in his voice. "You're really going to leave me standing out here after all we've been through together?"

"You mean the time you destroyed my apartment with a house party and pooped in my shower? Or are you referring to the occasion when you nearly ruined my brother's wedding?"

"Um, how about the time this wicked horn made fledgling

vampire shish kebabs at Nero's castle?" The rainbow flag of his tail swished at a horsefly on his snow-white flank.

"Please." I snorted. "You showed up at the tail end and spent more than half the time bragging to the lady vampires about your genitals."

"Whaaaa?" His eyes in exaggerated equine shock. "Naw. You must have misheard me."

"I believe the words *delicious donkey dong* were used."

Wallis's golden hooves shifted on the wooden slats. "Okay, what about the time I got rid of the Tommyknockers for you?"

"Tommyknockers?" I narrowed my eyes at him. "When did you ever get rid of Tommyknockers for me?"

"About two minutes ago," he said. "Little bastards were stacked eight high before I ran them off. One of them even manhandled the ham candle right into your petunias."

Leaning past the jamb, I glanced over at the wooden planter box hanging from the porch railing. Sure enough, a silvery substance like a slug trail dripped from one of the hot pink petals down onto the porch planks.

"Ugh." I grimaced. "That's disgusting."

"If you think *that's* disgusting, you definitely don't want to look behind your azalea bushes."

I let fly a choice assortment of words and mentally beseeched the heavens for patience.

"On the upside, Tommyknocker turds make excellent fertilizer," Wallis said. "That's probably why Morg sent them."

"Wait," I said. "You know Morg?"

"Duh," Wallis said. "Who do you think sent *me*?"

"Satan was going to be my first guess," I said.

Wallis bent his foreleg, lifting his knee to his chest. "Ouch, babe. Big ouch."

I indulged in an epic eye roll. "Why on earth would Morg have sent you?"

"I'm part of the gift too."

"*What* gift?" I asked.

"The customary Sasquatch birthday booty."

"I sincerely hope that you mean that in piratical terms," I said.

"Aye, wench." Wallis winked at me and cleared his throat. "On this the day of your natal emergence, may favorable winds blow, magnificent mead flow, and bountiful crops grow."

"Okaaay," I said.

"It's the traditional Sasquatch birthday blessing," he explained. "You're supposed to give a gift from each category. 'Squatch are big on the themes."

"I'm afraid to ask which category of the theme you're part of."

"Mead." Wallis tossed his head back toward his flank, where I noticed an ornate saddle with handcrafted baskets tethered to either side. "Morg's own elderberry brew in there."

"Thanks," I said, already inching the door closed. "But I've already got a fully stocked bar."

Wallis shoved his golden hoof between the door and the jamb. "I wouldn't do that if I were you," he said in a singsongy lilt that made me want to punch him right in the muzzle.

"*Not* doing things you would do if you were me is pretty much my life philosophy," I said.

"Would that include giving mortal insult to the acting ruler of the Sasquatch?" Wallis asked. "Because I know a woolly monarch who's going to be all kinds of offended if you reject his gifts."

I indulged in the heaviest of sighs. "Sasquatch hooch. I'm sure Abernathy is going to be thrilled."

"Sasquatch hooch served by a *unicorn*," Wallis corrected. "That shit there is a recipe for some magical merrymaking."

"Here's the deal," I said, stepping out onto the porch and closing the door behind me. "You circulate outdoors and on the deck *only*. You are not to speak one word to anyone during the entire party, and under no circumstances are you to eat any items containing glucose, fructose, or any other chemical compound approaching sugar. Got that?"

I suppressed an involuntary shudder at the sensory memory of a cotton candy–scented blast of glitter baptizing my face and hair right before I was set to walk down the aisle at Steve's wedding. And this was to say nothing of the vastly unsettling sound of a baby giggling that accompanied Wallis's colonic expulsions.

"Take it easy, baby," Wallis said. "Ol' Wallis is here to help."

"You'd better be," I said, lowering my voice. "Because you step one hoof out of line, and so help me, I'll have you made into sparkly glue sticks quicker than you can tail-swat a tick."

Wallis mimed zipping his lips with one raised foreleg.

"Good," I said. "You can go around the side of the house to the back deck. The gate's open."

Closing the door behind me, I did a round of mental yoga before I ventured back toward the kitchen.

"Who were you talking to out there?" Mom asked, tucking a stray silver-red tendril back into the complicated updo she had architected for this occasion.

"No one," I said. "Not one person."

Technically true.

"How are we coming on the balloon arch?" I asked Steve.

"Almost finished," he reported. Noting the presence of a small herd of balloon animals on the dining room table, I couldn't help but smile.

But it abruptly evaporated from my face as soon as I turned and saw the food table. I could only blink, my throat suddenly dry. The rooms around us melted away as my mind was consumed by the fresh hell before me.

An alarming corona of red hazed the edges of my vision, pulsing in time with the beating of my heart. My skin prickled as if little ball bearings had appeared below my dermis, crawling over the surface of my muscles.

It was a feeling I recognized but had only ever experienced one other time.

My one and only involuntary transformation.

"Mom?" I asked, attempting to keep my voice even.

"Yes, sweetie?"

"Did you reorganize all the food trays?"

"Oh, just a little bit. Having everything in big groups just looked so . . . blah. This way, everything looks more festive!"

She'd pieced out the entire contents of the antipasto platter, mixing the olives in with the cherry tomatoes, the marinated artichoke hearts in with the celery sticks.

"It looks like crudités confetti."

Crudités confetti that was *still* sans carrots.

"I'm afraid your sister never did have an eye for design," Mom said to Steve conspiratorially as she set down the tray of brioche rolls and mini-biscuits that she'd arranged into a wreath pattern complete with radish roses with basil greenery. "I'm glad at least one of my children inherited my artistic sensibilities."

"Nonsense," Steve said, his tone jocular enough to make the contradiction seem like banter. "Hanna simply favors a more carefully curated minimalist approach designed to elicit a culinary aesthetic equilibrium."

"If you say so," Mom said, moving on to the dessert table. But her blithe acknowledgment did nothing to quell the tempest growing within me.

Steve glanced my way, and I gave him a tight-lipped grin of gratitude.

"Say," he said, dropping an arm around Mom's shoulders. "Why don't you go ahead and get changed. I can help Hanna get finished up here now that I'm done with the balloons."

"Are you sure?" she asked, gazing up at my brother adoringly. "This table still needs a lot of work before it's company ready."

"Positive," Steve said. "You go ahead and scoot."

"But—"

"*Upstairs*," I said.

Okay, I didn't *said* so much as *growl from the carnivorous bowels of the ancient beast that made its den somewhere in my soul.*

And it wasn't the first time.

Discovering that werewolves could speak while in four-legged form had been startling enough. Discovering that *I* could summon a voice that sounded like an unholy host of Satan's minions whether I happened to be human or canine had been a first-class mindfuck.

"Oh dear," my mother said, pressing a hand slick with lotion against the cheek I'd spent the better part of an hour and three YouTube tutorials contouring. "Are you getting sick?"

The corona of red around my vision intensified, obliterating my peripheral view. I felt an uncomfortable heat bubbling beneath my skin, my mind teetering on the edge of control.

"I'll whip her up my famous saltwater swish," Steve said, steering our mother toward the back staircase by the laundry room.

I waited until I heard the door to the second-floor guest room close before sliding down the wall into a crouch against the kitchen cupboards.

"I'm sorry," I said. "She just knows exactly how to push my buttons."

"Well, yeah," Steve said, crouching down beside me. "She installed them."

"I feel like such an asshole complaining to you about it."

"Why's that?" Steve asked.

He had never offered many details about the host family Abernathy had placed him with after rescuing him from the non-accident that had claimed my father's life, and I had never pressed the subject. But now, with the woman who made us both bustling loudly above our heads, the words would no longer consent to stay buried.

"Because at least I grew up knowing who my mother actually was." I looked over at him, overcome by a sudden surge of gratitude. "Believing you were an orphan with no family couldn't have made things easier for you."

"True," Steve said. "But then, I might not have developed into the paragon of masculinity and canny wiles that you see before you."

His Chucks squeaked on the wooden floor as he pushed himself up and planted his feet wide, hands on his hips to strike the action figure–like Front Lat Spread bodybuilding pose.

"Excellent point," I said.

Steve offered me a hand and tugged me to my feet. Together, we made quick work of restoring the trays to their former non-salad-like groupings, pulling the plastic wrap off the hummus and ranch boats just as the doorbell rang again.

My phone buzzed in my apron pocket a split second later.

This time, I opened my Ring app *before* I answered it.

What I saw defied all logic.

Three figures loomed ominously, their winged silhouettes dominating the grayscale footage from the doorbell camera. The glow of the porch light rendered their reflective eyes incandescent on my phone's smudged screen. They belonged on hillbilly horror podcasts and lurid urban legend TikToks. Not on my front porch while spinach and Parmesan puff pastry turnovers baked in my state-of-the-art Wolf convection oven.

"No *way*," Steve said, peeking over my shoulder.

"Way." Wallis's voice filtered through the open kitchen window. "They're part of the—"

"The gift," I finished for him. "Yeah. I know."

Removing my apron, I handed it to Steve and released my hair from its messy bun at my nape.

"Here goes nothin'." I sighed, making my way to the door.

The mothmen looked like nothing so much as the live-action

version of He-Man figures. Roughly human-scaled heads, but equipped with the iconic curled proboscis where the nose should be and capped with two feathery antennae. Muscular torsos beneath a fine pelt of mushroom buff–colored fur. Equally defined human arms and legs—the latter gratefully concealed in an array of cargo pants.

But their *wings*.

Their wings were a brocade of earth-toned iridescence and shadow, shimmers crawling like liquid moonlight over the glistening scales. It was a spectacle that both repulsed and dazzled, their grotesque beauty mesmerizing.

"Welcome!" I said when I'd recovered my breath. "I'm so happy you could make it!"

They said nothing, only exchanged a glance betwixt themselves and nodded.

"Won't you come in?" Stepping to the side to clear the path for them, I gestured toward the living room. Their wings folded neatly against their broad backs as they stepped across the threshold, an air of regality mixed with a hint of formality evident in their body language.

"Dear God!" The sound of my mother's voice ringing out from the base of the stairs froze me in my tracks. For a moment that seemed to stretch into eternity, I held my breath. "Would you just *look* at those costumes!"

Steve and I exchanged a triumphant look.

His plan had seemed like absolute lunacy when he'd first described it.

That if we had at least some of the guests dress up in costumes, the presence of at least one follicularly fecund quasi-humanoid might not seem so odd.

But that had been before the interlopers from the Lepidoptera kingdom had joined the party.

Now that our mother—attired as a mildly MILF-y butterfly—was circling them with abject admiration on her makeup-caked features, I felt the iron band around my lungs beginning to loosen.

"Speaking of," Steve said sotto voce. "Maybe we should change into our shindig attire before everyone else arrives?"

"Good idea," I said. "Just, uh, make yourselves at home. I'll be back in a jiff."

Scampering upstairs, I frantically shimmied into the full-body black pleather catsuit I'd ordered off Amazon, praying to several lesser-known deities as I coaxed the clingy fabric up over my thighs and hips.

"Don't even start, okay?" I said to Gilbert, who paused in his spring cleaning of his börthole to narrow his golden eyes at me from the vantage point of our extra-tall four-poster bed.

By some miracle of physics or Lycra, I wrestled the bodice over my torso and zipped it closed.

"There," I said, giving Gilbert a triumphant look. "And you didn't think it would fit."

My senior feline life partner flicked his tail, his ear rotating to the rubbery squeaks I made as I shuffled over to my vanity. There, I fastened a silver-studded belt with a long faux-fur swishy tail at my waist and slid the headband with a pair of pointy cat ears atop my head. Uncapping my liquid eyeliner, I flicked black whiskers onto each cheek and drew an inverted black triangle on the tip of my nose.

"I just need to put on my boots and we're off to the races," I informed Gilbert, who had moved on to the furry caverns between his toes.

It was then that I ran into the fatal flaw in my brilliant plan.

With the built-in corset cinching my pastry-pooch up to my neck, I didn't exactly *bend* at the middle.

Which made zipping up my thigh-high boots a problem.

Easing down on the edge of the bed, I stretched my gangly

arms to their maximum extension and swung the wicked-looking boot toward my extended foot. Five minutes later, the only thing I'd managed to put on was an extra film of sweat between my clammy skin and the catsuit.

I lay face down on the bed, panting when my phone buzzed in concert with the door chimes.

Shit.

Slithering down to my knees, I retrieved the boots and knee-walked to the bedpost to haul myself upward again.

"Coming!" I called, the *wick wick wick* announcing my presence as I shuffled down the hall toward the main stairs.

But when I reached the landing, I saw that my mother had beat me to it.

There, in the open doorway, was Morg.

9

I wasn't sure exactly what I'd been expecting.

Actually, that's a lie.

I knew *exactly* what I had been expecting.

Some variation on the classic movie *Sasquatch.* Chewbacca with a bad barber, basically.

But the creature standing in my foyer wasn't it.

At least as tall as Abernathy and just as solidly built, but with a regal bearing that seemed altogether more dignified. Lordly, even. An effect that his jaunty brocade waistcoat, bow tie, and gold pocket watch only served to enhance.

Even sans pants.

I would have liked a good five minutes or so to stand there, studying him from the seclusion of the reading nook on the upstairs landing, but with Mom as the self-appointed one-woman welcoming committee, this was not to be.

"Well, there she is now!" She swept an arm toward the staircase, commanding Morg's gaze along with it.

We locked eyes, and I gripped the railing as the most intense wave of déjà vu I'd ever experienced in my life swept over me.

Which, for the record, is *absolutely* saying something.

Morg smiled up at me, his warm earth-brown eyes crinkling kindly at the corners.

Odd, I thought, considering the whole reason for inviting him hinged on his not being especially fond of me at the present moment.

“Hanna, you have *got* to come get a look at his costume,” Mom said, resting a hand on his forearm. “It’s just the most fabulous thing I’ve ever seen.”

I couldn’t be certain if the *whoosh* from my lungs was air that had broken free from the stranglehold of my corset, or an exhale of relief.

Until that moment, I hadn’t been convinced Steve’s plan would actually work.

Just because Mom seemed to have forgotten everything about the shifter kingdom and our family’s history as part of it didn’t necessarily mean she would be naïve enough to assume that any paranormal creature she was presented with had to be wearing a costume.

Even if the other life-forms she believed to be strictly human were wearing them as well.

Now that Mom seemed to be cooperating with at least this part of the plan, my legs consented to become flesh and bone rather than concrete.

Gripping the railing for dear life, I began my descent.

The joints of my catsuit conspicuously creaked as I tried to saunter down the stairs with grace and dignity but instead lurched my way to the bottom like a marionette operated by a drunken puppeteer.

When I at last reached the ground floor, I let my boots fall to the area rug, fully intending to have Shayla help me get them on as soon as she arrived. Which I dearly hoped would be any minute now.

“Hello there,” I said, fixing a warm but polite smile on my face. “I’m so thrilled you could come—” My lips were already pressing into the voiced bilabial nasal buzz of an *M* for *Morg* when two facts suffered a head-on collision in my cortex.

One: I had absolutely no idea what his official title was.

Two: Both Morrison *and* Wallis had made a point of telling me how easily offended Sasquatch were.

Panicked, I seized upon the first title I could think of that shared the same letter and cringed the second it tumbled from my mouth.

"M-majesty."

"Majesty, eh?" Mom echoed, elbowing Morg's burly ribs. "Are you supposed to be some kind of prince?"

"Alpha Harvey," Morg said, his voice surprisingly refined. My cold, clammy hand disappeared in his large, leathery warm one. He raised it to his lips, planting a gentle kiss on my knuckles. The tenderness of the gesture caught me off guard.

As did the scent enveloping me.

It was like nothing I had experienced before.

Or . . . was it?

The bouquet evoked images of ancient trees stretching toward the sky, their trunks coated in velvety mosses. Flashes of damp undergrowth carpeted in fallen leaves that crunched underfoot, now turning to humus and releasing their earthy breath. Vignettes of fungi in varying stages of decay and rebirth, the crisp tang of berries and wildflowers. A primordial woodland, absent of human touch, the raw purity of nature in its fullest bloom.

Sidenote: If ever I have time for a side hustle, I am *totally* making a candle of this.

"Wait, were our costume characters supposed to have titles?" Mom asked. "Because you didn't tell me we were supposed to have titles. Can I be *Lady* Zoey Zephyrwing?"

"Sure, Mom," I said.

Looking into Morg's eyes, the very last ounce of trepidation I'd had about my mother encountering him—or any other paranormal creature—instantly evaporated.

"It's a true honor, Lady Zephyrwing," he said, executing a bow without managing to look pretentious. "Did you enjoy my gifts?" Morg asked, a hint of mischief lighting his eyes as he glanced at me.

"Very much," I stammered, searching for a diplomatic response. "It's been such a unique treat to learn more about your rich traditions."

Morg threw his head back and laughed heartily, his booming voice echoing through the foyer, causing me to wince slightly. "Alpha Harvey, you have a talent for diplomacy. I appreciate your honesty."

"Gifts?" Mom asked. "I'm confused."

"We have His Majesty to thank for the libations being purveyed by the noble steed out on yon deck," I said.

"Please, call me Morg," he said.

"Only if you call me Hanna."

"I'd be delighted."

"Wait, *you* brought the unicorn with the cute little wine baskets?" Mom asked with a flirtatious flutter of her oversize fake eyelashes. "That was just the most thoughtful gift."

"Would you care to accompany me to sample some?" Morg offered her his arm.

"I'd love to!" My mother's enthusiasm was borderline alarming. She linked her arm through Morg's and practically skipped alongside him, leaving me to question whether I had landed in an alternate reality.

Such was my relief at how well this was already going that I didn't even feel inclined to stop her.

"Knock, knock!" The front door swung open and Shayla sailed in, a sight as welcome as Christmas morning. Her hip-hugging maxi skirt of seafoam green embellished with clusters of pearls and iridescent sequined scales caught the light with every movement as she made her way over to me. Combined with the iconic purple seashell bra, it made for a killer mermaid outfit.

"Babe!" Steve emerged from the downstairs guest bathroom behind me, his face transformed into a circa 1960s–style wolfman by the use of fun fur and foam latex prosthetics. "You look *hot*," he said, causing her fins to flare as he spun her in a circle.

Even just hearing the word seemed to drag a fresh wave of sweat to the surface of my skin.

"Aren't we the most meta?" Shayla asked, tossing the cobalt-blue waves of her hair over one shoulder.

"The most," I agreed, trying to shake the feeling of unease that scalded the pit of my stomach.

"Hey," Shayla asked, green eyes darkening with concern. "You okay?"

As if on cue, Mom laughed far too loudly at something Morg had said, eliciting an involuntary cringe.

"Actually," I whispered, leaning in closer. "I need your help. Mom has been dying to meet you. Can you maybe keep an eye on her and make sure she doesn't do anything too embarrassing like sexually harass the duly appointed leader of the local cryptid community?"

"On it," Shayla replied with a wink and a sardonic grin.

"Steve, you up for DJ duty?" I asked.

"Roger that." Steve clicked the heels of his paint-spattered work boots together and saluted. Moments later, the mellow strains of the perfect party mix began piping through the house's speaker system.

Progress.

Taking advantage of the sudden lull, I squeaked over to the bar and poured myself a shot of whiskey. It went down like smoky silk, pulling a channel of fire in its wake.

On the one hand, I felt my nerves begin to loosen their white-knuckled grip on the adrenaline tear-assing around my blood-stream. On the other, I felt my body's internal thermostat get cranked up by several degrees.

I was about ready to peel the cursed suit off, run around stark naked, and declare myself a sphynx when the doorbell rang.

Only as I crossed the cathedral-ceilinged living room to answer it did I remember that I'd completely forgotten to ask Shayla about helping me with my boots.

Just as well.

With my luck, I'd probably beef it on one of the many Persian rugs and knock my caps out on the imported Norwegian wood floors.

Pausing to reheat my hostess smile, I swung the door open.

Who I saw standing there wasn't quite as surprising as a unicorn or a mothman, but it wasn't necessarily far off.

"Scott," I said. "And Helena. Hi."

"Is this the party house?" Helena asked in a voice just furry enough to suggest that she'd done some hardcore pregaming.

The approximately ten thousand balloons, streamers, and paper lanterns would have made an answer of *no* somewhat untenable, so I just nodded.

"Sorry," I said, stepping back to grant them entry. "I didn't expect to see you here." Mostly because I hadn't invited them.

But someone clearly had, unless it was their habit to haunt random mountain châteaus dressed as the OnlyFans version of the Wicked Witch of the West and one of her flying monkeys.

"Scotty!" Steve said, throwing his arms wide. "You made it!"

Question answered.

"Here," Helena said, shoving a foil-wrapped aluminum pan at me as Steve and Kirkpatrick executed an extensive round of shoulder-slapping and bro-hugging. "We brought these."

I peeked beneath the foil as they both made a beeline for the bar.

Jell-O shots. Reeking of carcinogenic dyes, bottom-shelf booze, and palette-pounding artificial fruit flavors.

I handed them to Steve. "Please tell me they left the Lollipop Guild at home."

"*Our* home, specifically." Sticking a hand beneath the foil,

Steve pulled out a small plastic cup filled with cobalt-blue goo and squeezed it to pop the top off. "Shayla and I went in on a babysitter."

I folded my arms and angled a look at him.

"Look, he and Helena are going through a hard time, and I thought if they could maybe get out on the town, have the chance to reconnect, they might be able to find some of that magic sauce again."

Helena squealed as Kirkpatrick used the curled tip of his gray tail to lift up the hem of her thigh-high black miniskirt.

"All I know is, if any of his magic sauce gets on my furniture, you are *so* paying to have it steam cleaned," I said.

"Deal." Steve wobbled the shot's contents past the daggerlike teeth of his latex maw, his bushy artificial eyebrows lifting as he *chewed*. "Whoa," he said. "Are those gummy bears?"

"Gummy *sharks*." Helena tipped about four fingers of a twelve-year scotch into a rocks glass and took a greedy gulp. "I got the recipe out of the Halloween edition of the Martha Stewart magazine. I made them for Trapper and Trekk's kindergarten class party, and they just *loved* them."

"Sans the Rothschild, I hope." My nose wrinkled as I lifted a sacrament of moss-green sludge to my lips.

Helena gave me a slitted side-eye. "Do you honestly think I'd give alcohol to a class full of five-year-olds?"

A couple of years ago, I wouldn't have put it past her to give cyanide cupcakes to a group of Girl Scouts if they came between her and her morning latte.

"Well, we've all grown, haven't we?" I responded, taking the shot at once, my tongue wrestling with the wobbly alien of a gummy shark. The sharp sting of cheap vodka was followed by an unusually sweet taste that reminded me of watermelon bubble gum. "On a related topic, there was something I wanted to ask you about."

Her eyes narrowed as she took another thoughtful sip of her scotch. “Yeah?”

“The other morning, in Abernathy’s office, you said a name as you were waking up—”

“Look, nothing happened, okay?” Helena whispered as she grabbed my wrist. “Rayven is my yoga teacher, and I only do private lessons because he’s been helping me release stored trauma from my hips.”

“Rayven?”

Helena cleared her throat, her glassy eyes darting around the room. “That’s not the name I said?”

“No.”

“Oh.” She took another slug of the scotch. “Who was it, then?”

“Freki.”

A measure of her booze blush leached away. “I did?”

“Yep,” I said. “I was just wondering where you’d heard it.”

The puffed shoulders of her black peasant top jerked upward. “No clue.”

I took another shot, more in hopes of keeping her for a few more moments than out of any desire to participate in the party spirit.

“That was—” A racking cough seized my chest as I exhaled a cloud of high-octane fumes of lime-flavored paint thinner. “Wow.”

“Right?” Helena helped herself to one in solidarity. “Did I say anything else?” she asked not exactly casually.

I dropped the plastic cup into the trash. “You mentioned something about not wanting to join. And Pottery Barn.”

“Huh.” Helena’s eyes flicked toward her mate once too often. “Weird.”

“I don’t suppose you’ve had any random run-ins with furries lately?” I asked.

“Furries?” She listed toward me. “You mean like those sad,

pathetic losers who dress up in full-body animal costumes just so they can belong to an equally sad social scene?"

"Actually, it's a completely valid form of whimsical self-expression that connects with our bifurcated identity, but yes, there are full-body animal costumes."

"Whatever." She waved her pink-palmed, lime-green hand dismissively but gave no sign of answering my question.

"So did you?" I asked.

"Did I what?"

I fought a surge of exasperation. "See any furries?"

Her glossy black lips twisted into a comically intense frown. "Actually, now that you mention it. I *did* see some the other day."

My heart leaped into my throat. "You did?"

"Mm-hmm. I just can't remember *where*. Babe?" Helena called in a wheedling voice that made me feel a rogue stab of pity for Kirkpatrick. "Where did we see those anime-looking dog things the other day?"

Anime.

The word made my heart beat even harder.

Kirkpatrick scratched his artificially blackened brow, smearing the paint onto his freckled forehead. "It was on the way to the gallery, wasn't it?"

"That's right." She attempted to snap her fingers, seeming puzzled when she couldn't get the pads of her digits to align.

"Might want to take it a *little* slower," I said, plucking the already half-empty drink from her hand. "At least until Abernathy gets here."

This proved to be the magic word. A dreamy look smoothed out her sharp features.

"Where were they, exactly?" I asked. "How close to the gallery?"

"I don't know," Helena whined. "A block? Two blocks? All I know is, the kids threw a fucking fit about wanting to buy their stupid snow cones."

My mind was scrambling now, trying to force the disparate pieces into a picture that made sense.

"Snow cones?"

"Yeah." Helena picked at something beneath one of her daggerlike black nails. "They had one of those pop-up shop things."

"What did they look like?" I asked.

"What they always look like. Big round snowball in a pointy paper cup. Why does it matter, anyway?"

"Not the snow cones, the characters!" I hadn't realized I'd grabbed Helena's wrist until she yanked it back.

"Look, I'm real sorry you can't have kids, but I haven't been away from mine in fucking months, and talking about them is kind of the last thing I want to do tonight."

I could taste the sting of her words, harsher than the paint-thinner alcohol that still haunted my throat.

Helena's face softened slightly, realization dawning. "I'm sorry," she said. "I think I had one too many White Claws while I was getting ready."

"It's okay," I said mechanically. "I was just curious."

I waited until Kirkpatrick and Helena were reabsorbed in raiding the liquor cabinet before steering Steve out of their line of sight by the elbow.

"Did you mention to them about . . . you know?" I nudged my chin in the direction of the back door.

"Yes indeedy," my brother said. "They've solemnly sworn to be robustly rapacious representatives of the lycanthropic league." Squaring his narrow shoulders, he fluffed the artificial pelt sprouting from his flannel shirt.

"All the same," I said, adjusting his rolled sleeve so the tufts of fur he'd spirit-gummed to his forearm would lie flat, "would you mind just keeping an eye—and ear—on them?"

"Two of them," he said. "Or four, I guess, if we're counting eyes *and* ears. Speaking of . . ." He tucked a black claw–tipped hand into his lapel like Napoleon. "How do I look?"

Like an ill-tempered Ewok would have been accurate but exceptionally unkind.

"Like the life of the party," I said.

"Who wants shots?" Steve called, carrying the pan out toward the deck, where the other guests had already drifted.

The doorbell double-chimed and, too deflated to go back into the kitchen to screen the new arrival on my phone, I peeked through the peephole instead.

An empty porch greeted me, bathed in the fluorescent pool of LED light from the motion sensor that kicked on after dusk.

And dusk came early in our pocket of towering trees.

"That's a whole lotta nope," I said, deciding whoever had decided to ring and run could hide out there in the growing shadows while I fixed myself a scotch to rinse the taste of Helena's kiddie cocktail concoction from my mouth. Maybe by that time, they'd either give up or get a clue.

Padding toward the bar, I decanted an amber nimbus of the smoky liquid into a cut crystal rocks glass. I was already enjoying the first scorching sip and the tawny starburst view through the glass's bottom when a cascade of staccato knocks nearly made me fling the beverage across the room.

"That's it." I stomped toward the foyer as quickly as my pleather prison would let me, wrenching the door open with enough force to make the wreath of faded silk spring flowers that I'd been meaning to put away for months bounce. "If I catch you little fuckers shitting in my bushes, I'm going to—"

"Little fucker, *mais oui*. But I've not *fais une merde dans des buissons* since the *fin de siècle* New Year's Eve fête."

The moment I registered the speaker a good foot below my eyeline, I let out a yelp of pure, unadulterated joy. "Toulouse!"

I lunged forward to wrap him in a hug, reveling in the complex bouquet of his scent. Earthy, unguent linseed oil, crisp, cedary French-milled soap, spicy aftershave, all underscored by the black licorice tang of his favorite tipple—absinthe.

It was like an olfactory time capsule to a nineteenth-century Parisian café, and I couldn't get enough.

Sidenote: Side hustle craft candle idea #2.

"Mademoiselle Hanna!" he gasped. *"Je ne peux pas respirer!"*

In my excitement, I'd completely forgotten about the Shoulder of Death and its trachea-collapsing capacity.

"Sorry." Releasing him, I helped smooth his silk cravat and brushed a smudge of my face powder from his lapel.

Then, as now, Henri Marie Raymond de Toulouse-Lautrec-Monfa was fastidious. Every detail of his bespoke wardrobe impeccably coordinated and calibrated to fit his just-under-five-foot frame. His coarse features were oddly touching in contrast.

"I hope you will forgive me," he said, dark eyes cast downward in deference. "I received your note about the costumes, but I'm afraid it was too late for me to arrange something suitable."

"Don't you worry," I said. "You're perfect just as you are."

I wondered exactly how much of an asshole it made me that I'd already figured out that the only person in attendance who wouldn't know who and *what* he was would be my mother, and she would assume that his current getup *was* a costume.

"How did you get here?" I asked, scanning the driveway for the Hummer H2 Toulouse had been tooling around in when the unfortunate Vincent van Gogh Incident took place. "I didn't hear La Gouloue."

"Alas," he said. "Her name proved to be too accurate where fuel was concerned. I am trying to lower my carbon footprint. I booked a chauffeur service that utilizes a fleet of electric vehicles."

"Look at you, adapting to the times and stuff!" I stepped back from the door and waved him in. "Can I make you a drink?"

"*Merci*," he said, tapping the silver wolf's head on his gleaming, black-lacquered cane. "But I brought my own."

"But of course," I said. "Everyone's out on the deck if you want to pop out and say hello."

"*Everyone?*" he asked, giving me a pointed look beneath his dark, bushy brows. A reference to the *other* guest of honor my email had mentioned along with the last-minute costume theme.

"And then some," I said.

Toulouse nodded and unscrewed the silver wolf's head from his cane, lifting it to his lips for a quick sip. "I will be at my most charming."

"I don't doubt it for a second," I said. *So long as Steve's playlist didn't include anything that would inspire spontaneous karaoke.*

When he'd melted into the small but vibrant band of revelers on the back porch, I retrieved my phone and shot an *It's time* text to Abernathy.

On my way, came the instant reply.

I'd just helped myself to a celebratory daub of Cherni Vit cheese when a chance glance out the back door nearly made me choke on my artisanal cracked-pepper cracker.

My mother, tipsy and flushed, her tutu hiked up around her hips, and one sparkly tights-clad leg thrown over Morg's thigh as she ground her pelvis to the Ronettes' iconic classic, "Be My Baby."

Also known as the title track from *Dirty Dancing*—the movie that had pretty much been responsible for my adolescent sexual awakening.

Along with *Star Trek: The Next Generation*, that is.

PS: If the afterlife doesn't involve at least one ménage à trois with Jean-Luc Picard and Wesley Crusher, you can count me out.

"Shayla!" I hissed, trying to catch her attention over Steve's shoulder. "*Code blue.*"

"*Shit*," Shayla mouthed back. "*Sorry.*" The surge of her power made her irises flash an otherworldly teal for the briefest of moments before a small puddle miraculously appeared beneath the strappy high-heeled sandals my mother had borrowed from me.

Good ol' ordinary everyday physics took care of the rest.

Mom's arms pinwheeled out behind her as her single earthbound foot skated between Morg's legs. Steve was behind her in a wink, catching her beneath both armpits and turning the slip into a dip as he danced her away.

I exhaled a breath and shot the rest of my drink before weaving my way over to Wallis. "She's cut off. Got it?"

He exhaled a distinctly equine exasperated sigh that flapped his lips. At least he seemed to be observing the rules.

"*So* sorry about that," I said, sidling up to Morg. "My mother gets a little . . . overzealous at social gatherings."

"Not at all," Morg said. "My elderberry mead has been known to have that effect on the fairer sex." He held up an ornate glass goblet that had to have come with him or Wallis. The liquid within glowed a faint rose gold. As if it had stolen the last sips of sunset. "Have you sampled it yet?"

"I haven't," I said, though I suddenly wanted to. No. *Needed* to. With each swirling circuit around Morg's glass, the mead looked lusher, smelled more intoxicating.

"Allow me."

Morg extended the goblet toward me, his eyes twinkling under the ambient string lights. The glass was cool in my hand, intricately etched with runes that kissed my palm. I wrapped my fingers around the thick stem, feeling a rush of anticipation.

Inhaling deeply, I was seduced by a sweet, heady aroma that reminded me of dew-damp honeysuckle blossoms. As I brought it to my lips, it flooded my mouth and my senses with the flavor of summer. Of afternoons spent in the dappled shade of a cottonwood tree, the weight of a book in my hands, and the tickle of sun-warmed grass between my toes.

"Do you like it?" Morg's disembodied voice seemed to come from nowhere and everywhere at once.

"Very much," I said.

"Care for another sip?"

"Please."

The glass's cool rim met my lips once more. The second swallow somehow even silkier than the first.

Like a lullaby, the mead's taste comforted and lulled me, making my insides feel warm and liquidy. Butterflies fluttered in my stomach, but they weren't the usual I'm-about-to-make-a-fool-of-myself kind. They felt more like they'd been woven from moonlight and gossamer threads and sent to perform an ethereal ballet within the confines of my belly.

The world seemed to shimmer and pulse in rhythm with my heartbeat. The string lights overhead twinkling like distant stars against the black velvet curtain of the night sky.

"More?"

Morg's voice resonated like a forgotten melody, stirring emotions that ebbed and flowed like a tidal wave on the shores of my heart. A wild, almost primal yearning seized my senses.

"I . . ." I stuttered, the words seemingly caught in the wisps of sweet fog that had begun to cloud my mind. "I had something to ask you."

"I'm sure it will come to you." Morg surveyed me with an amused twinkle in his eye. "There's no hurry."

"No hurry," I repeated.

As the affirmation echoed on my tongue, the world around me blurred at the edges. The soft pulse of music that had been threading itself through the background of our conversation rose like a summer wind, humming melodies from half-remembered dreams. A sudden rush of silken fur brushed against my ankle, and I looked down, gasping in delight at the sight unfolding before me: mothmen, their wings iridescent in the glow of the moon, fluttering around me in enchanting spirals. Their eyes glimmered like dewdrops, a kaleidoscope of colors that inexplicably made me want to cry.

I stared in wonder at the border of quaking aspens at the edge of our sprawling yard, entranced by the heart-shaped leaves beating in the night's breeze like thousands of wings.

Why hadn't I ever realized everything was this . . . *beautiful*?

A strange sensation rippled through me, and it took me a moment to realize it was Steve, shaking my arm, his face all eyes and alarm.

"The Phantom!" he whispered. "I just heard it in the driveway."

Steve's words fell on me like a cold shower, yanking me back into the realm of the tangible.

The world began to sharpen around me once again, and with it, the realization that I was in very real danger of blowing Abernathy's fake surprise.

"Okay, people." I clapped my hands. "Everyone into the living room!"

"I'll get the lights!" Shayla said.

"I'll kill the music," Steve echoed.

I, on the other hand, dashed to the kitchen to fetch my prop: a triple-layer chocolate mousse cake with HAPPY BIRTHDAY ABERNATHY written in elegant white frosting.

"My precious," I whispered as I carefully removed the cake from the freezer and began hurriedly stabbing candles into the thick ganache.

"T-minus ten seconds," Steve stage-whispered.

I grabbed the lighter and quickly touched the flame to the wicks.

The room fell silent at the sound of footsteps on the front porch, anticipation hanging thick in the air as the dead bolt tumbled open.

I hurried around behind the sofa just as the door began to creak open.

"Surprise!" we all shouted in unison as Abernathy stepped through the doorway.

"Oh my God," he deadpanned, feigning shock with all the subtlety of a nearsighted rhinoceros. "I'm so surprised."

"Make a wish!" I lifted the cake, and in the faint golden glow of the candles, I met Abernathy's eyes.

His gaze moved over the colorful garlands of balloons and lingered on the party guests huddled near the room's only light source. An innocent little smile slowly spread across his lips before he pursed them and blew out a breath.

He looked so young.

The room dropped into a temporary darkness filled with raucous cheers, clapping, and the thunderous stomping of Wallis's hooves.

"What say we get some light in here?" Steve jogged to the kitchen to flip the main switch as I carried the cake to the kitchen table.

My mother's bloodcurdling scream ripped through the celebratory atmosphere like a scythe.

I turned with dawning horror, and the sight that met me was one that seared itself into my mind instantly and forever.

Morg, king of the Sasquatch, lying face down on my living room floor.

10

For a space of time that might have lasted for five seconds or five years, we all just stood there, frozen in shock.

"Is he . . . ?" Shayla began before her voice trailed off, unable to finish the sentence.

"He can't be," I said, crossing the living room to slide the still-flaming cake onto the food table. "Probably just had too much mead."

I approached the ponderously large, inert form, concentrating on the pin-striped fabric of his waistcoat for any signs of an in-drawn breath.

Nothing.

I swallowed hard, my mouth suddenly as dry as the Sahara as I bent to crouch next to him.

But my knees only made it to a ninety-degree angle before my momentum was arrested with a pained squeak. Aware of everyone's collective gaze, I straightened my legs and widened my stance, encouraged when I sank low enough to graze Morg's fur with my fingertips.

Before my catsuit promptly squeaked me to a halt yet again.

My thighs began to burn almost immediately, my bare feet planted at a pigeon-toed angle that thwarted my attempts to slide them farther apart or lever myself upward.

I was stuck.

"Uh . . . little help?" I asked, shooting a sheepish look toward Abernathy.

As my spectacularly shitty luck would have it, my mother was closer.

"I've got you, baby girl!" As Mom lunged forward and scooped her arms under my pits, one of her oversize iridescent fairy wings clipped the cake.

The gauzy organza ignited with a *whoomph* that briefly flashed orange in my peripheral vision.

"My wing!" Mom spun in a circle like a cat chasing its tail, spanking at the flames with the star-shaped tip of her wand, which promptly lit up like a match.

"My wand!" Mom swung the accidental torch like a battle mace, connecting with the cake and sending it sailing from the edge of the counter.

I watched as, in slow motion, the lovingly chosen confection plummeted toward the prone figure at my feet, candles first.

It hit Morg squarely mid-back, four layers of decadent devil's food sponge and Belgian chocolate mousse avalanching onto the kitchen floor.

A strange hissing sound made me look up, where I saw the mothmen closing in, miniature reflections of the flames dancing across the hundreds of tiny lenses in their oversize compound eyes.

"Oh no," I whispered. "No, no, no—"

They leaped toward us without warning, one of them knocking me onto my ass in his eagerness to get closer to my mother.

Abernathy bayed his rage, launching himself into the fray. He caught one of the mothmen by the wing and threw him over the kitchen island, sending up a blizzard of scales that invaded my eyes and nose.

The spark on the back of Morg's waistcoat flared into a blaze and quickly spread to his fur, fanned by their feverishly beating wings.

"Mark!" I choked. "No! The fire extinguisher!"

"I've got it!" Steve sprinted to the canister and wrenched it from the wall. One hand clutching the valve, he aimed the nozzle toward us and charged forward.

Only, with the latex wolf mask obscuring part of his vision, he failed to see the glob of icing smeared across his path.

His sneaker skated out from under him, and he went down in the splits, emitting a shrill screech and discharging a voluminous cloud that blasted Wallis from behind.

On a startled whinny, the unicorn charged through the kitchen, trampling over Morg's burning body and taking out the remaining mothmen like bowling pins before crashing into the food table.

"Get out of the way!" Abernathy snatched the fire extinguisher from Steve and, with a few quick bursts, he managed to put out both my mother and Morg's flaming fur. "Help me roll him over!"

Though Steve's hamstrings had been stretched to their absolute limit, he mustered the strength to push himself up from the floor. "Let's do it."

Steve grabbed an arm, Abernathy a leg, and began to heft Morg, whose enormous form was still partially smoking and smelling disturbingly of burnt hair and chocolate cake.

"Jesus," Steve grunted. "It's like he's got a lead liver or something."

A tapping sound came from the glass door leading to the deck. I glanced up to see Morrison standing in the open doorway.

"What's *he* doing here?" Abernathy wheezed, his face reddening.

Truthfully, I didn't know. He'd not been on the guest list for obvious reasons, and I most certainly hadn't expected him. Which begged the question how long he'd been out there, and for what reason.

The answers to the latter, I was afraid I already knew.

In case you needed me.

"You going to just stand there with your dick in your hand or make yourself useful?" Abernathy demanded, raking Morrison with a resentful scowl.

Despite their combined efforts, Steve and Abernathy had only managed to heft Morg's left side like a stroke-ridden Superman.

"I can't come in unless—"

"Won't you please join us?" I said hurriedly, breezing aside.

Morrison whizzed by me, a khaki blur.

Mom clutched my wrist. "Did you see that? He just—"

"On the count of heave. One . . . two . . . heave!"

With a grunt, the three of them wrenched Morg's bulk over. Wallis gave a startled neigh as the movement caused a minor seismic event that trembled through the kitchen floor and sent a wave of stomach-churning burnt hair and vomit wafting through the air.

Steve retched and doubled at the waist as Shayla rushed to his side.

It wasn't difficult to see why.

Morg's face was a catastrophic canvas of gore and sick, rivulets of blood running freely from his crushed nose to lips turned a sickly shade of plum purple. His warm brown eyes had gone cold, empty as they stared blankly at the ceiling.

"I'll do compressions, you do the breaths," Abernathy commanded, glaring at Morrison.

"I don't breathe, you ignorant fuckstick!" Morrison threw his arms up at Abernathy.

"What is he talking about?" Mom asked, her grip nearly grinding my wrist bones to dust at this point.

"Toulouse?" Abernathy had already started pumping the great barrel of Morg's chest as he glanced across the room.

The demimonde dweller vehemently shook his head. "*Mais non, mon ami.* My lungs, they have never been the same since the consumption."

"The consumption?" Mom repeated. "But—"

"Oh, for fuck's sake." I freed myself from my mother's grasp and swiped the mess from Morg's mouth with a bar towel. Only when I went to kneel beside him did I remember my sartorial setback.

"Let me!" Mom said, elbowing in. "I was a candy striper."

For all my irritation with her general nuisance, I couldn't deny that she'd always been at her best in a health crisis.

I snagged gazes with Abernathy, the unspoken question in my eyes. He nodded.

"Go ahead, Mom."

They worked together in syncopated cycles. After several minutes that seemed to stretch into eternity, Abernathy paused his compressions, hovering an ear above Morg's chest.

On a slow, deep exhale, he shook his head.

We all stood there in the aftermath, wide-eyed in shock.

"Do something!" I turned to Wallis, panic flooding my mouth with its acidic venom.

He blinked at me, eyes wide at this contradiction of my earlier commandments.

"Sweetie, have you lost your mind?"

I shrugged away the hand my mother placed on my shoulder and grabbed Wallis by the straps of his decorative bridle.

"You're a magical motherfucker, right? Isn't that what you're always saying? Fix. Him."

"I *can't*." Wallis bellowed and jerked his long face from my grip.

My mother screamed and leaped up onto a dining room chair. "The horse!" she said, pointing a soot-smeared finger at Wallis. "It's possessed of an evil spirit!"

"Not evil, per se," I said. "But a deeply annoying one."

"But it talked!" she insisted. "I heard it."

"And now it's going to fill the ice bucket with whiskey and

guzzle until its eyeballs float." Wallis trotted over toward the bar, curds of foam dripping from his flanks onto the frosting-and-ash-anointed floor.

Mom looked down at me from the chair, real concern etching her eyes. "Am I having a stroke? Because I feel like I might be having a stroke."

"No, Mom. You're not having a stroke."

"I don't understand."

"He's a *unicorn*," Helena's booze-loosened frame tilted against the kitchen island, a drink still clutched in her hand. Until that moment, I'd kind of forgotten she was still there. "Of course he can talk."

"Talk ain't all he can do." Wallis winked at my mother from above the ice bucket. "Fortunately for you, Wallis digs older women."

"Wallis is about to dig himself a grave if he doesn't *shut. Up*," I hissed between clenched teeth.

I felt a warm pressure on my lower back and glanced down to see Toulouse standing at my side, his lips folded into a regretful frown. "Mademoiselle, I'm afraid the jig, as they say, is up."

I met Abernathy's eyes, helplessly imploring him for some reassurance.

What I read in them made my heart sink.

"What is it?" Mom demanded, her voice taking on the nasal shrill that had preceded her Saturday-morning passive-aggressive cleaning binges. "What's going on?"

Holding up my hand, I helped her down from the chair.

"I literally can't think of a worse time to tell you this."

"Then don't." Mom's anxiety prickled like lightning across her face as she stared at me. But I knew that postponing this revelation wouldn't do either of us any favors.

Toulouse gave my hand a reassuring squeeze.

"Mom," I started hesitantly, "there are some things you need to know about me. About all of us." A lump formed in my throat as I tried to form the right words. "You know those totally age-inappropriate paranormal romance novels you used to let me read growing up?"

"Of course," she responded.

"Well, what if the kinds of creatures described in them weren't exactly . . . fictional?"

There was a long, pregnant pause as my words hung heavy in the hushed room.

"Are you saying that . . . that you're—"

"Yes, Mom," I rushed on, not wanting to lose my nerve. "I'm a werewolf."

Mom's look of wide-eyed astonishment melted into crumpled confusion, which then split on a burst of laughter. The laughter took a sharp turn into cackle country. Her shoulders shook as she slapped the counter, silent tears of mirth carrying muddy rivulets of mascara and glitter down her cheeks.

Steve and I exchanged a worried look.

"Oh, Hanna." She at last dragged in a watery gasp. "You really had me going there for a second."

"But, Mom—"

"Still, you didn't have to arrange this whole elaborate prank." She sniffed, dabbing at her eyes with a party napkin. "I know when I'm not wanted."

"Mom, no. That's not—"

"You and your brother obviously have a special connection, and then I show up and ruin the new family you've built for yourself."

"Actually, I—"

"I know things weren't always the easiest growing up, but I tried my best, Hanna. I really did." Mom lifted the sparkly pull-string bag of fairy dust she'd insisted on as part of her costume. "I'm just sorry I couldn't give you the love you needed to make you want to share this part of your life with me."

"Wow," Steve breathed. "You weren't kidding about the guilt Jedi thing."

I felt a small but definite stab of satisfaction that at least my brother saw it too. A dead Sasquatch in the middle of my dining room floor, and *still* my mother somehow managed to make this about her.

"I'll just pack my things and get out of your hair." She sighed, flouncing toward the back stairs.

"Mother, *stop*."

I hadn't meant to use the unholy demonic-sounding roar of my Angry Alpha voice, but it tore free from my vocal cords all the same.

She turned to face me slowly, every hair in her body looking like it stood on end. "Who taught you that?"

"No one," I said. "I'm a werewolf. So is Toulouse. Abernathy. So is your son."

Mom's gaze shifted over my shoulder where I presumed they found Steve by the way they softened.

"'Fraid so, Madre," he said.

Mom swallowed. "But . . . how?"

"The same way it's been happening for millennia," I said, taking a step toward her. "I came from an alpha bloodline. Just like Oma. Just like you."

Her elaborate bun wobbled atop her head as she shook it violently as if to fling away unwelcome thoughts.

"I had the choice to remain human, or mate with another werewolf and complete the transformation. I chose." Was it my imagination, or did Morrison turn an even chalkier white when I said this? "Once upon a time, you chose to remain human. You chose my dad, and the two of you knew what might happen if you gave birth to a boy, but you did it, anyway. You had Steve, only he was so sick that he spent the first few months of his life at UCLA."

Mom clasped her hands over her ears.

"When he was released, Dad was supposed to wait for Abernathy to escort them home, but he didn't. He didn't, and—"

"*Don't*," Mom wailed.

"And Dad was killed. Steve was hurt in the crash, and Abernathy finished his transformation and placed him with a family who could protect him the way Abernathy has been protecting our family for generations. Which you knew. You *knew*, and you never told me."

I knew this was neither the time nor the place, but the tempest within me had finally broken free, howling the one question that refused to be silent a second longer.

"Why didn't you tell me?"

Her red-rimmed eyes were a steely shade of gray blue when they lifted to mine, her voice quivering with barely contained emotion. "Because that world had already taken everything from me. I didn't want it to take my daughter too."

"And I thought *my* family was fucked up," Helena drawled, rattling the ice in her cup.

"Right?" Wallis echoed.

"I hate to intrude on this touching exploration of generational trauma, but there's a dead Sasquatch on your floor, and my guess is he's not going to smell any better an hour from now," Morrison said.

Indeed, the pong of burnt hair mingled with the scent of charred hors d'oeuvres still hung heavy on the air, sure to linger for days in the house and an eternity in my memory.

"Seems to me that we ought to A, figure out what the hell happened, and B, decide what we're going to do about it."

"*We?*" Abernathy asked.

Morrison pinned him with a pointed look. "You know any other homicide detectives willing to collect evidence that could potentially prove your innocence?"

Abernathy scowled, but stepped aside.

"First, I need everyone to back the fuck up and let me work."

No sooner had Morrison made his request than the doorbell chimes echoed through the foyer.

"Whoever it is," I said to Abernathy, "you have to get rid of them."

"I'll do it," Helena volunteered. "Scott and I are going to bounce, anyway. This party turned out to be a real fucking bummer."

But the door began to open before she had even reached it.

"Sorry I'm late." Crixus, the demigod, turned his back to us as he shrugged out of his motorcycle jacket and tossed it onto the coatrack. "I stopped at a Starbucks to grab one of those off-menu drinks I saw on TikTok, but the barista said that they were out of strawberry crème syrup, so the only way I was going to get a—holy *fuck*."

He froze in his tracks, a long, silver gift bag swinging from the wrist below the hand holding an iced coffee.

"Skittles Frappuccino?" my mom asked.

It was several beats before Crixus acknowledged the question. "What?"

"The off-menu drink you were trying to get. Was it a Skittles Frappuccino?"

"Uh, yeah, actually."

"Aren't those the best?" she gushed. "One of the ladies in my Bible study group turned me on to them on account of coffee is addictive and addiction is just one of the many tools of the Adversary. I'd rather taste the rainbow than the fiery fuel of temptation."

This from the woman who had not even half an hour ago been enthusiastically swilling homemade hooch and trying to dance the libidinous lambada with a total stranger.

"You can taste *my* rainbow—"

I clamped a hand over Wallis's whiskey-wet snout. "Not. Another. Word."

"*Morry*," he mumbled.

Crixus set the gift bag down on the entryway table and robotically marched over to us. "What the hell did you do to him?"

"*I* didn't do anything to him," I said. "One minute we were toasting Abernathy and yelling *surprise*, and the next minute he's lying face down on the dining room floor."

"Was that before or after he beat the shit out of himself and spontaneously combusted?" Crixus demanded.

I took a deep breath and launched into an abbreviated incident report of the evening's events.

"—and if it hadn't been for the mothmen flapping over like some kind of pyromaniac piranhas, none of this would have happened."

Crixus looked at me from beneath lowered brows. "*What* mothmen?"

"Those mothme—" But when I turned to point to the area where they'd congregated after being tossed by Abernathy and nearly trampled by Wallis, I found it empty.

"Well, shit." I glanced around at the remaining party guests. "Did anyone see where they went?"

I was met with a lot of sheepish looks and shifted feet.

"Great." I paced between the dining room table and kitchen island. "Just fucking fabulous."

"Hanna, just because you're upset doesn't mean you need to use profanity."

"Actually, Mother, that's exactly what it means."

"Mother?" Crixus repeated.

"Mom, Crixus the demigod. Crixus the demigod, my mom."

Mom's cheeks turned a rosy pink as she held out her hand. "How do you do?"

Crixus took it and squeezed. "I'll have to get back to you on that. Meanwhile, why the hell did you invite mothmen to a birthday party in the first place?"

"I didn't," I insisted. "Morg did. Just like Hornhead here." I hooked a thumb at Wallis.

"Hey," Wallis's voice echoed from the ice bucket. "That's no way to talk to your gift." Whether warped by the ice bucket or impaired by its high-octane contents, I picked up on a distinct slur.

"I'm about to march that gift straight off a canyon cliff, traditional Sasquatch birthday present or no."

"I can't believe I'm having to ask this again," Crixus said, "but what the hell are you talking about?"

"You know. May the mead flow and the winds blow and the crops grow or whatever." I looked to Abernathy for backup, but he appeared just as confused as Crixus.

"Hanna, there *is* no traditional Sasquatch birthday present."

I hugged my arms across my chest. "Then why the hell would Morg have sent the Tommyknockers?"

"Morg?" Crixus's smooth, tanned brow furrowed.

"You know, the dead hairy hominid on my area rug right there?"

Cold fingers of dread slid down my spine at the careful look Crixus leveled at me. "That can't be Morg."

My throat worked over a dry swallow. "Why not?"

"Because he's been missing for over a month," Crixus said.

"But I don't understand." I looked to Morrison. "I thought you said—"

"He wasn't missing," Morrison broke in. "He was in hiding."

"On the run, you mean," Crixus corrected.

Fine hairs lifted on the back of my neck. "On the run from *what*?"

"The Bureau of Supernatural Affairs wants him for questioning in connection with a series of suspicious deaths within the cryptid community."

My heart began to thump in my chest. "What?"

Crixus nodded.

"When Morg hired me to investigate—" Morrison continued.

"*Morg* is your client?" I stared at him in astonishment.

"*Was,*" Morrison said. "He was convinced he was being framed for attacks perpetrated by the shifter community. I knew that if he could just talk to you, he'd know that there's no way you could be involved."

"Wait," I said, the gears of my mind working so hard I expected smoke to come pouring out my ears. "Wait, wait, *wait.* So all that stuff about breaching the agreement with a former alpha?"

"True," he said. "But not the primary reason for the cryptid uprising."

"You *lied* to me?"

"What is it like?" Abernathy prowled close enough for me to feel his body heat through the rubbery coating of my catsuit.

"I thought if the two of you could talk and form an alliance, maybe we could get to the bottom of why someone is obviously trying to start a war between shifters and cryptids."

"The bottom line is, it doesn't matter what the hell the plan was because now I have a dead Sasquatch on my kitchen floor and there's no way the cryptid community isn't going to blame me for it."

"It's worse than that," Crixus said.

"Worse how?"

"The Bureau of Supernatural Affairs is hunting Morg in connection with a series of crimes in the cryptid community, and then he ends up dead at your house the night before they can bring him in to find out what he knows. What do *you* think they're going to assume?"

"That I took him out to keep him from implicating me," I said. In the desolate hollow of my heart, the final realization blew through like a lonesome tumbleweed. "So the entire cryptid community *and* the Bureau of Supernatural Affairs is going to come looking for me."

Seeing my despair, Abernathy stepped forward, his large form cutting an imposing figure against the room's macabre backdrop. His eyes locked onto mine, their deep-set intensity piercing through the layers of my shock and dread. "Hanna," he said, planting his hands on my shoulders. "We're going to get this figured out. You and me."

As much as I wanted to believe him, my stomach churned at the weight of the grim reality of my situation. Morg was dead, our attempt at a diplomatic mission in utter ruins, the cryptid community already believed that I'd broken faith with them and possibly targeted their beloved leaders, and the supernatural world's primary governing body would shortly believe I was responsible for offing a witness. A strange contingent of even stranger humans seemed to know way too much about my existence, and a strange rash of dyspeptic incidents had afflicted my brother as well as random gallery patrons.

"Poisoned," I whispered.

"What's that?" Crixus asked.

"What if Morg was poisoned?" I asked, glancing between Morrison and Abernathy. "You remember how weirdly heavy Steve was when we had to carry him up the stairs at the gallery?"

"What do you mean, *weirdly* heavy?" Steve asked, notching his narrow chin upward. "Through extensive weight training and the pioneering juicing efforts of one Jack LaLanne, I've added seven pounds of solid muscle to this frame, I'll have you know."

"We know, babe," Shayla said, patting his back.

"Do you know of any potions that would cause the drinker to become significantly heavier in addition to experiencing gastrointestinal pyrotechnics?" I asked Crixus.

"No," Crixus said. "But I know someone who would."

"And you," I said, turning to Wallis. "You said the mead was a gift from Morg?"

"Yeah. So?"

"Was he the one who actually put those particular bottles in your baskets?"

Wallis listed a little from side to side as he thought. "Actually . . . no."

"Where did you get them?"

"Well, I was supposed to meet Morg at the cabin where he was squatting near Lake Tahoe, but I was running a few hours late on account of I was still hungover from a very pleasant evening with this hot little filly I met down at the track the night before and—"

"*Where?*" I demanded.

"They were already in the basket when I picked it up. Morg left the saddle on the front porch, but I had to wait for a whole fucking hour before the caretaker showed up to strap it on my back."

"You can magic yourself from Reno to Georgetown, but you can't zap a drink saddle onto your own back?" Shayla asked.

"I also can't whistle, shuffle cards, or do a cartwheel," Wallis sneered. "You want to take some cheap shots about that, too, while you're at it?"

"This caretaker," I said. "What did he look like?"

"Like the centerfold for *Incels Illustrated*. Buddy Holly glasses, ironic hipster T-shirt. Gave me this whole lecture about how the sides were perfectly balanced so I should be extra careful that they didn't get jostled in transit."

Steve and I locked eyes. "Dan," we said in unison.

No wonder he'd been so specific with the details of Steve's portrait.

Motherfucker had *seen* a Sasquatch.

Motherfucker had also been at the coffee shop the day Steve was poisoned *and* the bathroom-busting gallery show.

"I'll rip that little cocksucker's intestines through his tear ducts," Morrison growled, obviously having arrived at similar conclusions.

"Not if you're taken into BSA custody," Crixus said, staring down into his phone.

"What do you mean?" I asked. "Didn't you say *I* was the suspect?"

He turned the screen around so I could see.

Noticing the block letter EMERGENCY BSA BULLETIN at the top, I scanned the contents until a phrase snagged my eye.

Hannelore Harvey and James Morrison wanted for questioning in connection with the disappearance of Morg Mirkin. Last sighted near the residence Harvey shares with Mark Abernathy.

My heartbeat kicked up to a thunderous gallop. "But if they know he was here, they could be on their way here now."

The unwelcome revelation crawled through my brain with the spiny feet of a thousand insects.

"What should I do?"

Crixus shook his head as he moved closer, his blue eyes filled with concern. "I don't know what you *should do*," he said. "But I'll tell you what I would do."

"What's that?" I asked.

"Disappear," Crixus said. "Go off-grid until I can get more information and try to smooth things over."

"Disappear?" I scoffed, glancing around at the mess our party had become. "I'm the fucking alpha of the entire shifter kingdom. Don't you think it would look even more suspicious if I just drop everything and go dark?"

"Not if Abernathy stays behind to run things and reinforce a different narrative," Crixus suggested. "You're off on one of those shroom ceremony retreats getting right with the Universe. A much-needed silent spiritual journey or whatever. Take your pick."

"Assuming you still have some pull with the parties that matter," Morrison added—not so subtle gauntlet lobbed at Abernathy's extinguisher foam-spattered feet.

I stole a sideways glance at my mate, whose stony silence was beginning to make my eyeballs itch. Never a good sign.

"Of course he does." I took a step in his direction, needing to feel we were unified if only by proximity. "But, provided that we agree this is the best option, where exactly am I supposed to go?"

My mother cleared her throat. "You and Morrison could always stay at my house."

I wasn't sure which aspect of her suggestion horrified me more: That she had made the assumption that Morrison and I would be hiding out together, or that she was suggesting we do this under her roof.

"I guess I could book an Airbnb somewhere remote," I mused aloud while resuming my pacing. "Or maybe sign up for a cruise to Alaska? I've always wanted to do that."

"Abilene is a pretty small town," Mom continued. "We don't even have stoplight cameras, which would make you harder to track. And you know I have that whole finished basement now, so sunlight wouldn't be a problem for your friend."

I nearly choked on my own tongue. "You didn't realize *I* was a werewolf, but you recognized Morrison was a vampire?"

"Well, *yeah*," she said. "You don't watch fifteen seasons of *Supernatural* without picking up some tips. Speaking of, has anyone ever told you that you bear a striking resemblance to Mr. Jared Padalecki?"

Mom twirled the singed tips of her synthetic wig and batted her lashes at Morrison.

Morrison was looking at me now, a familiar sharpness flashing in his unnaturally bright eyes like the fire in an opal.

"Your mother has a point," he said. "Her house probably *is* the last place anyone would look for us."

Us.

I held my breath, bracing myself for Abernathy's explosive

objection, my lungs and heart deflating simultaneously when it didn't come.

"If I know the bureau, I'd say you have about twenty minutes before someone with a long title and a short temper shows up to investigate. I'd pick a spot and get gone unless you plan on sticking around to explain this." As Crixus swept a hand over the scene, I received an involuntary flash of what it might look like through the eyes of one of the bureau's notoriously no-nonsense investigators.

My horror was born anew.

In the clammy clutch of all-consuming chaos, I did what I'd done so many times before.

I looked to Abernathy, my soul bleeding wishes that boiled down to one improbable hope.

Tell me I'm not going anywhere without you. Tell me I'm yours and I always will be. Tell me it's all going to be okay.

Command me to stay.

When he spoke, the words he chose felt like a sledgehammer to the chest.

"Go to your mother's. We can regroup from there."

"Maybe we should . . . think about this," I said, trying to sound decisive despite the howling hurricane inside me. "I can't just abandon my pack. Maybe, if I just talked to them. Explained some of the things that have been happening—"

"They'll just make a note that the cryptid dignitary who's been vehemently denouncing you via every available outlet wound up poisoned, trampled, and burned at a gathering of your pack was just a terrible accident?" Crixus asked.

"When you put it like *that*," I said.

"I think the Crixinator is right," Steve said. "Any way you slice it, you being here right now is maybe not the best idea."

"*Je suis d'accord*, mademoiselle," Toulouse added. "Go with Monsieur Crixus. We will handle this mess."

I knew they were right but couldn't help but feel rejected all the same.

"All right, fine," I said. "Let me just throw a few things in a bag. Mom, you have exactly five minutes to pack. Anything not in your suitcase or attached to your general person will have to stay behind until Abernathy can mail it to you."

I turned and aimed myself for the staircase, hoping the undignified chorus of squeaks and creaks that emanated from the catsuit at least covered the rogue sniffles fracturing my mask of calm.

Biting my bottom lip hard, I hauled my carry-on from the walk-in closet and opened it on the bed. When I returned from the bathroom with my hastily gathered armful of toiletries, I ran head-on into the one consequence I hadn't thought about.

My cats.

All three of them had assumed their appointed positions re: my imminent departure in accordance with their individual MOs.

Gilbert had flopped his bulk into the main compartment, while Stewie sniffed at the roller wheels and Stella batted at his tail from her makeshift cave below the open lid.

I would have to leave them behind.

The thought ripped the seams right out of my already fraying faith.

Silent sobs shook me as I sank back on the bed, my face buried in my hands.

As they had so many times during my epic unraveling post-divorce, my feline life coaches leaped into action. Gilbert, the size of a small dog with the soul of a cantankerous old man, dislodged himself from the carry-on and plopped into my lap—the feline equivalent of a weighted blanket. Stewie, attention-seeking middle child and an enthusiastic advocate of distraction therapy, sidled up next to me on the bed, headbutting my arm like a surprisingly pointy battering ram to demand pets. And

Stella, dark-corner-loving Wednesday Addams–like sensory specialist, parked herself on my chest, her sonorous purr rumbling away like an engine of love.

I buried my face in Stella's soft fur, filling my lungs with the olfactory equivalent of a beloved blankie. Warm, sweet, and lightly musky. I wrapped one hand around Gilbert's foot, mentally mapping his one pink toe bean on my palm as I scratched the strange ridge on Stewie's head with the other.

"I've g-got to g-go, guys," I said on hiccupping breaths. "But Daddy will take good care of you. And I'll ask Uncle Steve to come by too."

The idea brought a modicum of comfort despite the guilt I felt in taking Steve away from his busy young family.

Reluctantly dislodging the three furry bodies, I managed to drag myself upright and crossed to the walk-in closet to begin yanking clothes from the hangers. When I reached my favorite pair of buttery, well-worn jeans, I decided they made as good fugitive fashion as any.

Or would, if I could ever coax this cursed catsuit's stubborn zipper down my back.

"Help you with that?" Abernathy stood in the bedroom door, his arms folded across his chest and a bemused grin on his stoic face.

"Please," I said. Turning away from him, I leaned my chin toward my chest to allow him access.

Under his careful, confident touch, it glided down to the base of my spine with nary a whisper, the cool air on my back an instant relief. I peeled it the rest of the way down, knowing Abernathy heard the soggy slurp the legs made as I shucked them from my thighs.

Abernathy's grunt of approval hit me low in the gut. "Shame I don't have time to show you how much I loved your costume."

I gave a bitter snort as I pulled on my jeans. "I looked like a stuffed sausage."

I snuck a look at him in the mirror's reflection before I pulled a T-shirt over my head.

I'd given him the perfect setup, but no *I'd sure love to stuff my sausage* line was forthcoming.

Logically, I knew that his not being in a playful mood made perfect sense, but it seemed like yet another confirmation of the sea change between us all the same.

But instead of calling attention to it directly, I asked the series of loaded questions that often precede the departure of feminine domestic partners.

"Will you make sure Gilbert gets his meds with his breakfast?"

Translation: *Can I trust you to protect what I love?*

"Sure. Just text me the dosage again."

Translation: *As long as you carry the worry so I can do the work.*

"And make sure that Stella doesn't get trapped in the storage closet?"

Translation: *Do you understand how hard it is for me to be away from them?*

"I'll just keep them downstairs while you're gone."

Translation: *Harder than it needs to be.*

Zipping the suitcase closed, I lifted it down from the bed and parked it by the bedroom door.

"Let me get that." Abernathy reached for it, but I grabbed his hand instead.

"Wait," I said.

His concern was immediate and palpable. "If we don't get you out of here—"

"I know," I said. "But I can't go until I say this." I stepped closer, sandwiching his heavy, solid hand in both of mine. "I know you've been going through something that I don't understand lately. It's okay that you don't want to talk to me about it, but I do think you should talk to someone."

"Like who?"

"Crixus has been working with this therapist who's supposed to be amazing."

"Jesus Christ." Abernathy tried to wriggle free from my grasp, but I held on.

"Just hear me out," I begged. "She deals specifically with paranormal clients and even specializes in depression."

"I'm not depressed. I've just lived long enough to realize that no matter how hard or how long you try to fight for the highest possible good, and regardless of whether you finally achieve a goal that took you centuries to bring about, those efforts will inevitably be undone either by the merciless wheels of fate or the slow decay of time within a world that humans seem intent on destroying, anyway, so there really isn't a point to any of it."

The naked hurt in his eyes as he said this stole my breath.

Keeping my gaze on his, I lifted his hand to my mouth and kissed it before pressing it against my chest. I could feel my heart's thump against the hard knobs of his scarred knuckles.

"There's a point to this," I said. "There's a point to *us*."

His broad shoulders tensed under my touch, but he didn't resist me. Leaving his hand there, I slid mine beneath his arms and up his back, feeling the play of muscles beneath his cotton shirt. I felt him shudder, heard him drag in a ragged breath.

The corded muscles of his arms coiled around me, awkward at first, but softening into an enveloping embrace. I melted into him as our mouths met, surrendering to the bittersweet farewell. Pouring into our fusion every molecule of my love, longing, and a silent promise to return.

Mark broke the kiss before the heat building between us ignited into an inferno.

He pressed his forehead against mine, holding my face in his cupped hands.

"I'll be waiting," Abernathy said, his voice thick with emotion. "I'll *always* be waiting."

"But really, though," I said, thumbing tears from my face as he bent to get my bag. "Will you make an appointment while I'm gone?"

He heaved an exaggerated sigh as he released me. "Yes, I'll make an appointment."

"Thank you," I breathed, stepping back reluctantly. "Now I guess I'd better get out of here before the BSA comes knocking."

Downstairs, I gave Steve and Shayla quick hugs before marching up to Crixus. "Are you our ride?"

"Oh!" Mom, still dressed in her leotard and tutu, clapped her hands together. "Are we going on a road trip?"

"Not exactly," I said, kicking my carry-on and my mom's oversize suitcase into the center of what would be our circle.

"You're not an airline pilot?" Mom asked.

"Not so much," I said.

"Then how?" she asked.

Taking one of Crixus's hands in mine, I held the other out to Morrison. "You'll see."

Morrison took it and offered his to my mother, who flushed cotton-candy pink as Crixus grabbed her other hand to close the loop.

I glanced back at Mark one last time, a surge of love and worry for him coursing through me. He nodded reassuringly, his brown eyes filled with a promise I dearly needed to believe.

I love you, I mouthed.

I know, he mouthed back.

"Ready?" Crixus asked, his expression uncharacteristically serious.

"Ready," I lied.

"Then we're off."

Terrific pressure invaded my every pore until, with a deafening *pop*, the world ceased to exist.

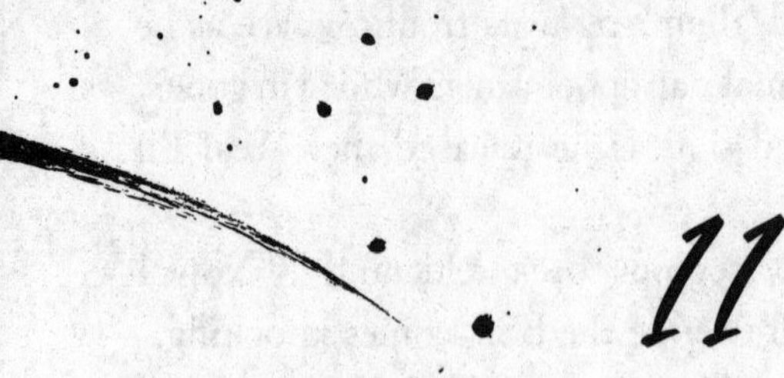

11

"Momma's home!"

The manic scrabbling of claws on hardwood echoed through the foyer as the pack of Boston terriers came yapping and sliding around the corner. Their tiny bodies and bulging eyes darted around us, their tails wagging so fast they seemed to be vibrating with excitement.

"Down!" I shouted over their shrill barks. The three little gremlins just wagged their nubby tails harder and jumped on my knees, their nails gouging me even through my jeans.

"Come on in and make yourselves comfortable," Mom said, herding us farther into the house.

After hearing the sounds she'd just made, I wasn't sure I'd ever be comfortable again.

I hadn't exactly taken the ecstatic explosions that sometimes occurred when traveling by physics-defying demigod dematerialization into consideration when agreeing to let Crixus zap us to Abilene.

Morrison showed no signs of ecstatic aftershocks.

I had gotten only the faintest feminine twinge.

But Helga Harvey had hollered like an operatic porn star, complete with postorgasmic purrs.

I did my level best to scrub the audio loop from my memory as I took in the familiar landmarks of my childhood.

The bookshelves with the sets of Time-Life art history tomes, encyclopedias with gilt-edged pages thin as onionskin.

The china cabinet displaying Oma's antique German flatware collection, quaint Hummel figurines, and naughty knickknacks she'd collected over the years. My eyes misted as they landed on the delicate rose chintz Victorian teacups she'd set out for our tea parties.

But the warm nostalgia quickly faded when I noticed just how much clutter had taken over since my last visit. Balls of yarn, empty Amazon boxes, stacks of papers, and unopened mail accumulated next to my mother's recliner. Reusable shopping bags hung from every doorknob. Tumbleweeds of fur and dust formed drifts in the corners and under tables.

Meanwhile, every available square inch of wall real estate and shelf space had been co-opted by Mom's new aesthetic.

Kitschy crosses.

Not necessarily an unusual theme for a retired schoolteacher in a town frequently referred to as *the buckle of the Bible belt*, but certainly unusual for my mother, who—like Oma—had been a self-professed lazy Lutheran, Midnight Mass and Easter Sunday being the extent of our attendance growing up.

"Wow," I said, leaning in to examine a rhinestone monstrosity above the TV that winked like a disco ball.

"Isn't that precious?" Mom asked, flicking on lamps as the three barrel-shaped Boston terrier bodies wove through her legs. "I picked it up at an estate sale."

"From Liberace?" I asked under my breath, earning me a snort from Morrison.

"Very funny," Mom said, setting down her cavernous purse and hanging her keys on the cross-shaped key rack. "I just feel safer with them around. They may not actually keep out the—"

A gasp snapped off her sentence so abruptly that I cracked my neck whirling to look over my shoulder.

Morrison stood there, an expression of polite confusion on his face.

"I'm so sorry!" Mom's hand covered her mouth. "I didn't even think!"

He offered her a reassuring smile. "One of the many regrettable inaccuracies that plague popular vampire lore." He lifted a floral embroidered Coptic cross off the wall and touched it to his forehead. "Look, Ma. No smoke!"

"Oh, thank God." She wheezed out an exhale.

Was it my imagination, or did she look a little disappointed?

"Come on downstairs. I'll show you where you'll be sleeping." Mom led us into the basement, ducking cobwebs and stepping over fire hazard piles of dust-filmed magazines as she breezily mentioned that she intended to donate everything to her church's rummage sale.

"Here's the guest room," Mom announced, opening the door to reveal a small, dimly lit space. A futon sat in the center of the room, surrounded by more bags and box piles. "I know it's not fancy, but—"

"Thanks, Mom," I replied, trying to sound appreciative despite the cramped quarters. "This will be great."

We all stood there for thirty of the most awkward seconds in my entire existence.

"Well, I know it's late. I'll let you two get settled in." Mom shuffled over to me and planted a wet kiss on my cheek. "Good night, sweetie."

"Night, Mom," I said, patting her back.

"Good night, James."

"Good night, Mrs. Harvey."

Morrison mimed collapsing against the wall as the door closed behind her.

"Don't get too comfortable." Toeing out of my sneakers, I pawed through my purse for makeup wipes. "We've got at least three more drive-bys coming our way."

Sure enough, nary five minutes elapsed before three sharp raps came at the door. "Hanna?"

I mouthed a *told you so* to Morrison. "Yeah?" I asked without rising.

The door opened a crack, my mother's pale, fretful face floating on the open slice of basement darkness beyond like the heroine of a V. C. Andrews keyhole cover.

"I brought you some towels," she said at an amplified volume clearly meant for Morrison to overhear. And then, in hushed, conspiratorial tones, "Are you okay to be alone with him down here?"

A jet of defensiveness scalded through me at the implication. "Just because we dated once upon a time and becoming a vampire has made him unreasonably good-looking doesn't mean I can't control myself, Mother," I whispered.

Her gingery brows drew toward each other, deepening the well-etched lines I was probably 99.999 percent responsible for. "I mean because he's a vampire," she whispered back.

"Oh." Heat flooded up my neck like the mercury in a thermometer, the result of embarrassment and guilt. Embarrassment at having revealed the true terrain of my thoughts. Guilt at having assumed my mother's thoughts were of a similar flavor. *I'll be fine*, I mouthed. *Promise.*

Our eyes briefly met, and she gave me a quick nod.

"Do you need washrags or anything?" Mom asked in her Outside Voice, pushing the stack of fluffy towels scented of fabric softener through the door.

"Thanks," I said, hugging them to my chest. "But I think we're okay."

"If you're sure." She held my gaze for an extra beat, the intent crackling behind her eyes.

"I'm sure," I said.

"Good night," she said again.

"Night," I echoed.

Hearing her slippers scuff away, I glanced at Morrison and held my hand up to count down from five. I had one finger left when the scuffing changed direction. "Sweetie?"

"Yes?" I called through the door.

"There's coffee in the pantry if you wake up before I do. Just make sure you don't push the Delay Start button, or you'll have to unplug the coffee maker and—"

"Wait another ten minutes before it will start again," I finished for her. "Seriously, Mom. How have you not gotten a new coffee maker in all this time?"

"Well, not all of us are lucky enough to have billionaire boyfriends with fancy espresso makers," she said in a voice that was meant to be teasing but came much closer to the truth.

My laugh sounded brittle as last season's leaves. "I guess not."

Several beats of silence. "Good night!"

"Good night."

Scuff. Scuff. Scuff. Pause.

"Oh, Hanna?"

I pressed a finger against my twitching eyelid. "Yeah?"

"If you use the toilet down here, make sure—"

"To hold the handle down after I flush so it won't get clogged?"

"I was going to say close the lid, because Zeppy has a habit of helping himself to poop punch at every available opportunity."

Morrison stifled a laugh while I contemplated exactly how much force it would require to lobotomize myself with the creepy crucifix above the futon.

"Got it!" I shouted through the door. "Good night."

This time, I waited until I'd tracked her steps back up the stairs, down the hallway, and over to her room before hauling my carry-on onto an old futon. In a wildly optimistic gesture, I unzipped the main compartment and pulled out my laptop and the burner phone Crixus had provided me, but elected not to unpack.

"Well, I'm officially in hell," I announced, mining the contents for comfy pants. "How about you?"

Morrison was silent for a moment as he looked around the room. "It's not so bad," he diagnosed. "I've definitely spent nights in worse accommodations."

Whether because of the day's draining events or the miraculous guilt-magnifying powers of my mother's home, I felt a heavy lump form in my throat.

My tolerance for everyday discomfort really was embarrassingly low.

"Like a coffin?" I asked.

"Like the Motel 6 outside of Gunnison."

Morrison wandered through the maze as I first let Abernathy know we'd arrived safely, then VPNed into the encrypted connection Crixus had set up for me to check my email and search the web for any mention of a murdered Sasquatch on Reddit threads and conspiracy blogs.

The results remained blessedly bland.

"Hey," Morrison called from the other side of the room. "What's this?"

I hopped up from the futon to find him crouched near an old army trunk. Inside was a treasure trove of my childhood sketchbooks, paint sets, and half-finished canvases.

"Oh, wow," I said, looking over his shoulder. "I haven't seen this stuff in years." My fingers trailed over the dried-out paint tubes. "I can't believe she kept all this."

Morrison smoothed out a damp-warped watercolor of a wispy-haired girl eating a strawberry, studying it with a critical eye. "You did this?"

Looking at the bold washes of color, I could remember not only *that* I'd done it but where and when. Mr. Millar's fifth-period art class. A stormy, steamy afternoon just before spring break. I'd stared at the composition so hard to get the strawberry's red just right that I'd seen a green halo every time I blinked for the next several hours.

"Yep," I said.

"You were really talented, Hanna. You know that, right?"

I shrugged.

"Why did you stop?"

"Reality," I answered.

"Meaning?" Morrison flipped through a sketchbook filled with pet portraits and still lifes.

I hesitated, feeling a familiar sting of embarrassment. "During a formal critique by my basic drawing professor, I burst into tears in front of the whole class." The memory still made my cheeks burn. "So, I figured maybe fine arts should stay a hobby and switched majors after that."

"That bad?" Morrison asked.

"I believe the words *visual vomit* were used."

"Sounds like a dickhole with zero taste." Morrison loosened his tie and draped it over the desk chair. "I'll bet he's doing web design for an MLM start-up now."

"Actually, he just received a lifetime achievement award from the Guild of Berkshire Artists." Not that I was bitter.

Morrison fixed me with one of those looks that long-jumped straight past my defenses. "You ever regret it?"

I shrugged, but his words sparked an ember inside me. Maybe I had given up too easily.

I quickly shut the trunk, wishing I could just bury those old dreams along with it.

Walking roads left untraveled could be a dangerous prospect, especially when one of them led to the beautiful immortal looking at me with kindness and keen interest.

"Sorry if I salted a wound." He stood up and dusted off his hands. "I'd selfishly love to see what you'd create if you picked up a brush now."

The thought made me smile genuinely for a moment, despite the yawning chaos swirling around us. But there simply wasn't any room for daydreams right now.

"Probably something no one wants to buy on Etsy." I braced myself on the cluttered desk and stripped off my socks.

Morrison stepped out of his dress shoes and reached for his belt.

The clink of its buckle coming unlatched triggered a Pavlovian response that finally brought me face-to-face with the facts.

Morrison and I were getting undressed.

In a room with one bed.

It would be kind of hilarious if it weren't a completely and cripplingly terrible idea.

"Well," I said, studying the futon. "This is unfortunate."

"I could always sleep on the couch," Morrison offered.

"Only if you want to wake up to my mom standing over you in her flimsiest fuck-me muumuu."

Morrison cracked his knuckles and unfolded the futon frame. "At least it's not a twin."

He turned his back to me as he unbuttoned his dress shirt and flung it on top of his tie.

Peeling my eyes away from the sight of his muscular back in a clean white undershirt, I picked up his discarded dress shirt and smoothed it over the backrest. I couldn't put my finger on what felt so unsettling about it until I realized that the fabric harbored not a hint of body heat.

Here, I faced a dilemma.

Asking Morrison to keep his undershirt on would be tantamount to admitting my attraction. And while Morrison didn't have Abernathy's uncanny and frequently inconvenient ability to detect the subtle hormonal shift of arousal, confirming its existence struck me as distinctly counterproductive to our current circumstances.

"Nothing you haven't seen before." Morrison winked at me, untucking his undershirt and stripping it over his head.

Blood boiled in my cheeks as my eyes fixated on the hard, smooth planes of his torso. The chiseled pectorals, angular ladder of his ribs and abdominals, the dangerous clefts above his hip bones disappearing into the waistband of his dark trousers.

"I'm just going to step into the bathroom." I grabbed my oversize pajama pants, their oxytocin-inducing print of kittens in various states of repose held up like a shield.

"Nothing *I* haven't seen before."

When I returned from the bathroom in my baggy sleepwear, my face completely scrubbed clean of makeup, I was relieved to find him sitting at the desk, still wearing his slacks. "Did you know that your mother donated twenty thousand dollars to some preacher in Missouri last year?"

"*What?*" I took the paper he held out, quickly scanning the small print.

"Fellowship of the Resurrected Eternal King Inc.," I read aloud. "It's not even a nonprofit."

Morrison rose from the chair and peeled back the quilt. "If I were you, I'd get to the bottom of your mom's religious reform real quick."

"I intend to." Concerned though I was, I'd never been so grateful for the lady boner–wilting power of maternal irritation in all my life.

"Left or right?" Morrison asked.

At home, mine was whichever side was farther from the door.

"Doesn't matter," I said.

Morrison stretched out on top of the covers on the side closest to the door.

I gathered my hair into a messy bun atop my head, climbed into bed, and switched off the bedside lamp.

And we were alone in the dark.

Just as we had been before.

Details from those few but memorable occasions washed over me in a sudden rush.

The possessive way his hands had roamed over my body. The hungry heat of his lips on mine. The sensation of being completely and utterly *consumed* by him.

Stop, I commanded my mutinous mind, trying to focus on the metal bar making an unwelcome introduction to my lower back.

Sidenote: This *never* works.

Rather than relinquishing the dangerous toy of my erstwhile ecstasy, my super helpful memory treated me to a vivid audio highlight reel of every filthy thing Morrison had ever panted, groaned, growled, or demanded in my ear.

Because Morrison was a moaner. As in, could easily have his own ASMR Twitch stream. As in, would make a fortune as a ladies' erotica audiobook narrator.

God, I've missed you.

That's it, baby.

Oh yeah. Take it. Take my cock.

Fuck, you're so wet.

Goddamn, I'm so deep.

Do you have any idea what you do to me?

I can't stop.

Why do you feel so fucking good?

Fuck, Hanna, you're going to make me come.

Good girl.

The entire barrage boiled down to these two words, quickening in time with my heart.

Good girl. Good girl. Good girl.

"Are you all right?" Morrison asked, his voice tinged with concern.

"Fine," I said, desperately trying to banish the erotic images from my mind. "Why?"

"Because your breathing is—" Morrison's guttural cry subsumed the sudden pained shriek of the futon's frame.

Feeling the abrupt shift in the lackluster mattress, I bolted upright, and I spotted his dark silhouette against the dim glow of the streetlamp filtering through the small basement window.

All the way across the room.

"What the hell?" I asked, clutching the blanket to my galloping heart.

"Sorry." Morrison braced himself against the wall. "I just realized it's been over a day since I fed. I can hear your blood pumping. The sound of your pulse is driving me mad."

"I don't understand," I said. "I thought you were used to it."

"Not *this* pulse."

Oh God, did he mean he could hear the blood rushing to my . . . feminine region?

The thought released a fresh wave of heat that only amplified the throbbing between my thighs.

Morrison groaned, his fangs lengthening as his eyes flared red in the gloom. A thrill of desire and fear shuddered through me.

To be wanted.

With a final snarl, Morrison smashed the tiny basement window and disappeared into the night.

I let out a shaky breath, flipped on the lamp, and whipped back the covers to search for a broom.

This wasn't even the first time a man had resorted to autodefenestration to be free of me.

I thought back to that rainy night in London when, juiced on the lifesaving transfusion of werewolf blood from Allan Ede, I'd attempted to relieve Abernathy of his pants and his virtue—such as it was. Rather than take advantage of me in my ferally frenzied state, he'd hurled himself from an fourth-story window into the Thames.

As if on cue, my phone chimed, and I glanced down to see a message from Abernathy. *Miss you*, it read. My chest tightened as guilt knotted itself around my heart. Here I was, reading this sweet, simple expression while lathered like a horse who'd been ridden hard and put away wet.

Very wet.

Miss you more!! I texted back, adding a few heart emojis for good measure. I placed my phone back on the cluttered table and tried to regain some semblance of composure as I began sweeping up the shards.

—

"Rise and shine, sleepyhead!" Mom stood at the end of the bed in a bathrobe the exact pale green of an after-dinner mint, a pink bakery box in one hand.

My nostrils flared, the tantalizing aroma of smoky sausage and buttery dough weaving a tantalizing tango that made my stomach growl on contact.

Kolaches.

A savory bakery delicacy introduced by Czech immigrants that represented one of my home state's only redeeming qualities.

"Did your little friend leave already?" Mom asked.

I rubbed the sleep from my eyes and looked around the room, spotting Morrison asleep on the floor near the broken window. "Over there," I said.

"Oh, James! What are you doing on the floor?" Mom leveled me with a scolding look I recognized from my days in elementary school, when I'd proved to be a somewhat lackluster sleepover hostess.

Which, I supposed, was still true.

After propping a piece of cardboard up to block the window, I'd dropped into sleep like a shot bird.

"It was my choice." A strange shadow on Morrison's throat caught my eye as he yawned and stretched. "Good for my back."

"You know, I think I'd read that same thing somewhere," Mom said, touching her free hand to her chin. "Now does it have to be cement, or would hardwood work too?"

"Um—"

"We'll be right up, Mom," I said, effectively dismissing her.

And had it not been for a crash and the skidding of claws followed by a muffled growl, she might have fought it harder.

"Oh, shit—shoot. They're fighting over the garbage again!" She hurried toward the stairs, and moments later, I heard the familiar patter of her slippers overhead followed by a string of colorful admonishments.

"Zeppy. *Zeppy.* Drop it. Drop it. *Drop. It.*" A silence ensued during which I could imagine her wrestling whatever it was from his jaws and putting it back in the trash. "We talked about this."

Peeling back the covers, I swung my legs over the side of the bed. "Thanks for not saying anything."

Morrison rolled onto his side. "About what?"

My back lodged a detailed complaint as I shuffled over to my carry-on to gather my pre-shower necessaries. "About my mother being absolutely insane."

A slow grin unfurled across Morrison's face as he propped himself up on one elbow. "You don't talk to your cats?"

"Sir," I said, pointing my toothbrush at him, "that is not the way to live through this."

"Good thing I'm not alive."

Shit. I'd walked right into that one.

"Is that why you slept on the floor?" I asked, turning my attention to the econo-size elephant in the room. "Because you were afraid I might end up the same?"

Morrison pushed himself up to a seated position, the movement rippling through his perfectly sculpted torso.

"Actually, it's because you kept trying to karate-chop my neck while making animal noises."

Oh.

"What kind of animal?" I asked.

"I'm not really sure," he said. "But whatever it was, it suffered."

"Why didn't you wake me up?" I asked.

"I tried. But every time I touched you, you threatened to make a bridle from my infernal intestines and ride me back to hell."

Demon donkey dream.

Had to be.

"Huh," I said, tracing one of the rug's fleur-de-lis embellishments with my toe. "That's odd."

"You have those kinds of nightmares often?"

"Only every night."

"What does Abernathy say about them?" Morrison asked, not exactly casually.

I debated for all of two seconds. "That I'm working too hard."

"For once, I agree with him."

"You need the restroom before I get in the shower?" I asked, blatantly changing the subject.

"If this is another attempt on your part to uncover the digestive particulars of my condition, it's not going to work." Morrison cocked his head, and I noticed that the mark on his neck wasn't a smudge *or* a shadow.

It was a *hickey*.

"Busy night?" I asked.

Catching the direction of my gaze, Morrison's fingers lifted to graze the mark. "I, uh . . . Yeah."

"Well, at least you didn't eat me in my sleep. Silver linings and all that," I said, unable to keep the sarcasm from my voice. "Where did you find her?"

"What makes you sure it's a her?"

"Because that's a hickey, not a hemato*ohhh*."

I felt so provincial, so completely prudish that I wanted to slink beneath the Aubusson rug.

Morrison, a bisexual?

How had I swapped countless sexual fantasies with him during our couple of sweaty postcoital pillow talk sessions, and somehow never uncovered this particular nugget?

Because you were too busy letting him uncover your nuggets.

I banished the thought before it could reproduce the complication that had been responsible for Morrison's impromptu hunt.

"Still," I said, pawing through my hastily packed clothing. "Abilene is a pretty small town. You might want to be a little more selective about your snacks."

"Interesting." Morrison met my eyes then as he stood. "I've never read that book."

"What book?"

"Things jealous people say." He smirked, eyes glinting.

I glared at him, irritation rising like the tide. "I'm not jealous. I'm concerned."

"About?"

"About your nocturnal activities resulting in a string of mysterious disappearances that could set the Texas Rangers on our trail."

Morrison moved closer to me, his hazel eyes boring into mine. "The only thing that routinely disappears is my companions' inhibitions. Besides"—his lips curved into a sinful smirk—"I take less blood volume than they'd lose at a Red Cross donation and make sure to take *very good* care of them afterward." He paused for effect before elaborating, and after each seductive word he spoke. "Betadine. Bandages. Breakfast."

The mental image of Morrison tending to his "victims" after feeding from them stirred something deep within me, causing warmth to pool in my cavernously empty belly.

Remembering the box of kolaches, something clicked.

As earthy as Mom could be, even she wouldn't make a pilgrimage to Jack 'n' Jill Donuts in her bathrobe.

Morrison must have brought them back from his . . . encounter.

And if the idea of his having hooked up with some big-haired barfly from the Blu Barrel bothered me, the concept of his having seduced a sweet-natured pastry pusher made me inexplicably and violently angry.

Especially since a passionate devotion to doughnuts had been primarily responsible for our having hooked up in the first place.

"Right, well, I shouldn't keep my mother waiting." I turned on my heel and pushed past him, heading up the stairs.

But when I reached the top, I heard an unfamiliar female voice coming from the proximity of the landline phone Mom still maintained.

"—sure missed you at our Let There Be Light Lunch." Despite being filtered through the receiver of a phone that my mom had had since I was in third grade, the syrupy Southern-accented voice reached my ears with perfect clarity.

"I'm so sorry, Maureen," my mother said in her singsongy Company Voice. "I know I said I'd be back by then, but I did send a text message—"

"And we covered far too much to put in a reply. But I could come over and catch you up."

"I appreciate that, Maureen, but it's really not a good time."

"But you said we'd get to meet this daughter of yours we've been hearing so much about."

Exactly *what* they'd been hearing, I wouldn't like to guess. Mom had, on occasion, attempted to make mutual acquaintances of ours like her more by liking me less.

A habit I found uniquely vexing.

"Actually, I don't think they're even up yet. Maybe I could check in with you this afternoon?"

The basement stairs creaked, and I held a finger to my lips as Morrison came up behind me.

"Nonsense," Maureen said. "I saw that handsome husband of hers come in with a bakery box not half an hour ago."

Husband?

Morrison waggled his eyebrows at me.

The index finger I still held at my lips curled into a fist.

"If you won't let me and the ladies come over to meet them, I'll just have to invite them over to my house for supper." Like many of the women in my hometown, Maureen was apparently an expert at issuing a threat disguised as a kindness.

That she apparently knew my mother well enough to leverage both her culinary insecurity and her competitive nature in one go, I found myself a little in awe.

"I'll see what I can do," Mom whispered and hung up the phone.

"See what you can do about what?" Okay, it was kind of a dick move on my part to engage my shifter stealth to sneak up on her, but I couldn't resist.

Mom jumped and shrieked, pressing a hand to her chest. "Hanna," she said. "You startled me."

Busted me, more like.

"Who's Maureen?" I asked, leaning back against the counter.

Mom cocked her head at me, looking like I'd just asked her what color lemons were.

"Maureen," she repeated. "My best friend?"

I stared at her for the space of an entire Life Alert commercial from the ever-blatting TV in the living room.

"Mom," I said, "you one hundred percent have never mentioned Maureen to me."

"Hanna, I have so. We met at the Friday-night Bible bingo club?" she said as if this was meant to stir up a memory.

"Since when do you go to a Friday-night Bible bingo club?" I asked.

Mom shook her head, pulling coffee mugs and plates out of the cupboard. "I know my life isn't as exciting or glamorous as yours, but it just hurts my feelings that you can't even be bothered to listen when I tell you about it."

I glanced at Morrison, who shrugged at my confusion.

"In any case, you understand that there's absolutely no way that she or the ladies who I'm assuming you'll also claimed to have told me about can stop by for a visit?" I reached in the fridge for the spicy brown mustard and squeezed a fat dollop on my plate.

Mom sniffed and looked down at her slippers.

"Mom?" I asked again.

"I just thought that maybe if they got to meet you, if they saw how smart, and pretty, and successful you are, the ladies might see how much we have in common and invite me to join some of their other activities too."

I was fully aware that women of a certain age in Abilene's close-knit community tended to wield their offspring like men measure appendages. But that my mother's standing within the group of ladies whose friendship she was courting would be solely dependent on me because she couldn't very well mention her long-lost son or newly discovered grandkids?

Talk about a donkey kick straight to the heart.

"Fine," I said, heaving a defeated sigh. "But only a quick stop by, okay? And not a word about Abernathy, or the gallery, or pretty much anything you saw or heard the entire time you were in Georgetown."

Mom mimed locking her lips and throwing away the key. "You won't be sorry, Hanna. I promise."

Somehow I deeply doubted this.

12

"All right," Morrison sighed, inspecting his properties. "It's come down to this—Baltic Avenue or bust."

Punchy, avarice-addled, and locked in a real estate stalemate, we were now on hour five of the Monopoly tournament we'd embarked on while waiting for an update from Crixus.

"Never," I declared dramatically, clutching my precious stack of Technicolor bills to my chest. "You'll have to pry this wad out of my cold, dead hands!"

Morrison's smile wilted.

"Sorry. I didn't mean—"

The doorbell rang, followed by a chorus of frenzied barks.

Morrison and I locked eyes. I unfolded myself from the futon and tiptoed over to the window, where I scooted the cardboard panel out of the way so I could peek at the front porch.

Six sets of blue-veined, knobby ankles in a variety of sensible strappy sandals were stationed on the stairs.

"They're *here*," I intoned in my best *Poltergeist* moppet impression.

"Yoo-hoo," came a warbly voice. "We brought y'all some peach cobbler."

Mom appeared at the top of the basement stairs, looking like a convict on the wrong side of the razor wire. "They're here."

"I know," I said.

"And they may have brought the bingo equipment."

"Mom, no!" I insisted.

But overhead, I heard the processional begin.

The screen door creaking open and slamming shut. The metallic rasp of hangers in the coat closet receiving windbreakers and women's activewear separates. Kitchen chairs scraping back. The cluck and cackle of crone conversation.

I looked at Morrison, panic written all over my face.

"Relax," Morrison reassured me, placing a hand on my shoulder. "Let the master work."

"The master had better work me a big alcoholic beverage," I grumbled, begrudgingly following him up the stairs.

We ascended into a sinus-assaulting bulb of overly assertive scents.

Perfume, prosecco, and pimento cheese. Moscato, melon, and mentholated ointment.

"Well, here she is." A tall, stately woman with a complicated silver coif and pinched patrician features swept forward to hug me like we were old friends. "I'm Maureen. It's such a pleasure."

Her body was all angles through her floral-print church dress, bony and birdlike.

"That's Linda," Maureen began, pointing to the apricot-haired woman at the head of the table. "And this is Gail, Martha, and Margaret."

They all nodded in turn, their magnified eyes scanning us specimens under a microscope.

"Hi, everyone," I said, forcing a smile onto my face. "It's so nice to meet you all."

Because other than Gail, whose motorized scooter was parked on the side of the table closest to the dining room door, I hadn't a crème brûlée's chance in Hades of remembering which lady belonged to which name.

"Likewise, dear," Gail replied, her gaze lingering on Morrison a beat too long for my liking. "Why don't you two sit yourselves down and visit with us?" She patted the seat next to her scooter.

I sank into it as gingerly as if a pincushion waited on the seat.

Morrison, on the other hand, remained standing. "May I offer you ladies something to drink?"

"Isn't he polite," Linda(?) said, unzipping a case and rolling bingo markers down the table. The eager hands that shot out to grab them reminded me of nothing so much as arthritis-afflicted Hungry, Hungry Hippos.

Blame it on the Milton Bradley marathon.

"So polite," Martha(?) agreed, dealing out bingo cards from a zippered pouch. "Bring me a glass of bubbly, young man."

"White wine for me." Margaret (the only other name I was reasonably sure of because I noticed her cardigan was red and thought of *The Handmaid's Tale* at the precise second she was introduced) held up a finger.

"Got mine right here," Mom called from the kitchen, lifting a purple insulated mug adorned with the swoopy cursive words *Be still and know*, surrounded by a proliferation of painted pink blossoms and butterflies. As much as the presence of yet another religious artifact in my mother's possession filled me with unease, her insistence on saving a dedicated—and superior—vessel for herself while everyone else was relegated to the chipped stemware she'd earned by saving reward vouchers from the local Albertsons totally tracked.

"And for my beautiful wife?" Morrison asked, coming around behind my chair and planting a kiss atop my head.

The chorus of *aww*s from the women around the table did little to help the sudden heat baking the surface of my skin.

Despite the fact that he was unabashedly leveraging the subterfuge my mother had created to torture me for his own selfish means, I found myself oddly touched.

Because in a vivid flash, I knew that this was exactly what it would be like if I really *were* Morrison's wife.

Coming home from a long day at the gallery to find him in the kitchen with a tea towel slung over his shoulder, Sinatra on the record player, the heady aroma of garlic and onion on the air, a bottle of cabernet already opened to breathe.

"G&T?" I asked, telepathically directing Morrison to go heavy on the *G* and light on the *T*.

The gathering fell silent so quickly, I half expected to hear a record scratch.

From the horrified looks being leveled at me, you'd have thought I dropped a deuce in the dip, as Steve might say.

"It's Water-to-Wine-Down Wednesday," Maureen said crisply. "That's why we drink the *wine*."

"Oh. Gotcha. Uh, cabernet, I guess?" Because it had the highest alcohol content.

"Coming right up." Morrison slung a dish towel over his shoulder and busied himself at the counter.

"So," Margaret said, arranging the contents of her crocheted bingo bag in an orderly row on the table. "How did you two meet?"

I glanced at Morrison, who pulled the cork from the bottle of red with a friendly squeak.

"Hanna rear-ended me on her way to a job interview at an art gallery," he said, placing a glass before me whose healthy pour made my heart leap with gratitude. "As soon as she burst into tears and told me she was uninsured, I knew she was the one for me."

Morrison's affectionate squeeze traveled down the back of my neck and lodged itself just north of my belly button.

"Don't you be embarrassed, honey," Margaret said, probably noticing my hectic color. "I've used the lady lubrication to get me out of a jam on more than one occasion."

Atomized particles of wine had already invaded my alveoli before I realized she was most likely talking about tears.

"So you got the man," Linda(?) said, pushing a pair of rhinestone-crusted readers up her nose. "But did you get the job?"

The second swallow of wine went down much smoother, coating my belly in velvet. "I sure did."

"And what do *you* do?" Linda(?) asked, accepting a glass of white wine from Morrison.

"I was a police officer when we met," Morrison said. "But I've since moved into the private sector."

"A man in uniform." Gail(?) sighed. "That right there melts my butter."

"With your cholesterol, you ought to be using avocado oil, Gail," Linda(?) said, giving her friend a good-natured nudge.

"Oh, go suck an oxygen hose," Gail retorted, shoveling a healthy wad of pimento cheese onto her Ritz cracker.

The ladies laughed uproariously, and I felt myself beginning to relax.

Maureen might look like someone had pissed in her peanut butter Cap'n Crunch, but the rest of my mother's entourage seemed relatively normal.

For a bunch of Bible-theme-obsessed septuagenarian social butterflies.

"All right, ladies," Maureen announced, returning to the table with an honest-to-God (or whomever) bingo ball cage in hand. "Shall we begin?"

"Coming!" Mom called from the kitchen.

"So's the Rapture," Linda muttered under her breath.

"Here we are!" Mom breezed up to the table, landing an exceedingly retro offering of chips and dip on the lazy Susan in the center of the table.

"About time." Martha—I was sure now because I noted the marked resemblance between her marshmallowy coif and George Washington's iconic dollar bill bouffant when Margaret had addressed her by name—accepted her glass of golden fizz from Morrison. "I'm drier than the Desert of Paran."

"The first number is B12," Maureen called. "B12."

"Amen!" Margaret stamped her bingo marker into the appropriate square with a satisfying squish and sat back in her chair, thoughtfully stroking her chin. "Hmm. Twelve, twelve, twelve."

Glancing up from my card, I caught my mom's eye across the table. "The first person who finds that number on their card picks a Bible verse with the same number to share."

Because of course they did.

Five turns and four Bible verses, and my one covert trip to the pantry to guzzle directly from the cabernet bottle later, Margaret took the win.

"Well, this has been fun." I stretched my arms, gratified when the wine in my belly produced a real yawn. "It's a shame we have to get up so early tomorrow. We just have *so* much to do."

"Really? Like what?" Maureen looked me square in the eye and fixed me with a smug smile as she parroted my earlier small-talk snare.

Like your bony ass.

"Like cleaning out the basement and replacing the water heater." Morrison, who had kept himself busy topping up the ladies' glasses and elaborately wiping down the counters, took my cue and came over to help pull out my chair. "But we'll definitely have to do it again sometime."

Like never.

"You can't leave yet!" Martha clutched my arm with something like desperation. "Not before our double Deuteronomy round."

"All the Bible verses have to come from Deuteronomy," Margaret explained.

"Who are we kidding?" Gail drained the last of her prosecco and set the glass down with a decisive clink. "These poor kids would probably rather eat wallpaper paste than listen to us old biddies quote from the good book."

"*No*," my mother insisted, stabbing me with a pleading look.

Yes, my brain resoundingly answered.

"I know." Gail toggled the knob on her motorized chair to swivel it toward me. "What do you say we head on over to Ambler and get in the game for real?"

Though I hadn't called Abilene home in over a decade, I associated the street name with a notable local scandal wherein the bingo hall's street-facing illuminated block letter marquis had caused consternation among the town's more conservative residents (see: most of them) with quasi-risqué sayings like "Come to Big Bucks Bingo, you'll love our balls."

"Now *there's* an idea," Martha agreed.

"I could turn on Animal Planet for the boys," Mom said, her use of the conditional filled with a quiet hope that I found heartbreaking. Why she viewed this crew of parsimonious pew pigeons like a sorority she wanted to pledge, I couldn't quite conceive.

"The holy spirit goes to bed after nine o'clock, you know," Maureen clucked, clearly not a fan of this idea.

Which turned out to be all the incentive I needed.

"I'm in," I said.

One by one, the ladies echoed my vote until only Maureen remained. Everyone seemed to hold their breath as they awaited her answer.

"I'll go," she said primly. "If only to keep you all on the straight and narrow."

"You can try." Martha and Gail gave each other a fist bump and pushed back from the table.

Morrison took me aside in the foyer as everyone was collecting their purses, umbrellas, light jackets, plastic rain ponchos, and waterproof hair scarves.

"So remember how we're supposed to be lying low?"

Peering at myself in the hallway mirror, I began gathering my unruly mane into a high ponytail. "Uh-huh," I said around the elastic clenched in my teeth.

"And willingly walking into a hall full of humans looking to escape their suburban ennui by competitively marking laminated grids with a paint marker fits into this plan how exactly?" he asked.

"By blending in," I said.

"Is the median age of bingo bunnies any lower than your mom's AARP apostles? Because if not, a bifocals and a Life Alert bracelet couldn't make you blend in."

Finished reapplying my matte liquid lipstick, I rubbed my lips together and patted his cheek. "I'll take that as a compliment."

"I'm serious, Hanna," he said, stepping into the center of the hallway to block my path. "I have a bad feeling about this."

I exhaled a harried breath. "Look, I used to go there with Oma sometimes, and trust me, Big Bucks Bingo is not exactly a repository of sharp-minded citizens. It's dark, it's smoky, and pretty much everyone spends the entire evening staring at their cards, guzzling beer by the gallon, and fistfighting over Frisbee golf vouchers in the parking lot."

"Remind me why you want to go again?"

In truth, I'd been asking myself the same question while the ladies wrangled over seat assignments in Gail's tricked-out paratransit minivan.

And then my brain flashed back to the proud, hopeful look on my mother's face as she put out her bowl of painstakingly made ranch dip. Flashed back to all the times when I'd watched her smile at her cliquish fellow teachers when we happened upon one of their after-hours gatherings at the coffee shop, then listened to her cry behind her bedroom door when we got home.

All my life, I'd been inoculated by her loneliness, and I'd be damned if I'd bypass the chance to eradicate the condition.

"Because I'm going to make my mom popular if it kills me."

"I just hope you're not provided with an opportunity to find how literally you mean that."

—

New Year's forecast bets I 100 percent would have lost when the ball dropped at the stroke of midnight: bumping Tom Jones on my way to a bingo after-party with my mother and her cadre of crazy church ladies in a minivan piloted by Morrison, the vampire designated driver.

"Ho-lee shit."

My hand clamped onto Morrison's wrist as the sliding doors of the bingo hall whooshed open before us, and we stepped into a parallel universe. One where elaborately decorated visors replaced the traditional mantles of authority. The cacophony of chattering voices, the clatter of bingo balls, and the rustle of cardstock, this strange kingdom's national anthem.

"Keep your peepers peeled for an open table." Gail motored up to us, her stack of ten cards secured on her chair's arm tray.

"There's one right there!" Mom announced proudly, charging toward the table closest to the bingo callers at the front of the room like a general leading her troops to battle. Maureen, Gail, Linda, Martha, and Margaret descended like a flock of birds, Mom practically hurtling herself into the chair on Maureen's right.

"Here goes nothing." I pulled the one measly card the desk attendant seemed exasperated to have to give me from my purse and set it on the table before me. Despite not giving a rip whether I marked a single box, my stomach was doing somersaults. Not because of the game itself—though the thought of shouting, "Bingo!" in front of this crowd was terrifying—but because something felt . . . *off.*

An odd thing to think in a roomful of grown adults spending hundreds of dollars on numbered cards in hopes of winning a set of mediocre steak knives, but here we were.

"Remember, Hanna, Granny's Quilt pays the most," Mom instructed, her voice all business. "Unless you can get a blackout."

Oh, I'd like to get a blackout, all right, I thought, gazing longingly at the condensation-kissed pitcher of pilsner at the next table over.

"Granny's Quilt," I repeated dutifully, though I doubted luck would let me anywhere near it. "May the odds be ever in our favor."

Real talk? The casual round that had unfolded around my mother's kitchen table had made me entirely overconfident about my prospects.

Not only did the caller pluck the balls from the cage with alarming speed, but he also announced them using a singsongy rhyme scheme that I'd never heard before in my entire life.

I perched on the edge of the chair, trying to make sense of the lingo that ricocheted around the hall like a hyperactive pinball.

"What's duck and dive?" I whispered, squinting at my card as if it held the secrets of the universe.

"Twenty-five," Mom said testily.

And she had every right.

Of the last fifteen numbers they'd called, I'd had to inquire about fourteen of them. But then—miracle of miracles—I won.

I stared at my card for a good thirty seconds before opening my mouth.

My shout of "Bingo!" came out more surprised than triumphant, drawing a murmured chorus from the colorful crowd.

"Go on up and get you your prize," Martha said, sounding almost as proud of me as I was of myself.

Which was to say, very.

Luckily, I didn't have to go far.

"Pick anything from this area, little lady." The number caller—there's got to be a better title for this, yes—paused in his labors to wave a hand over a section labeled *Basic*.

An indictment that cut a little closer to the bone than I would have liked.

"How about these?" I asked, pointing to a wooden charcuterie board and matching cheese knives that sparkled like treasure.

"All yours, darlin'."

"Beginner's luck." Maureen cast a gimlet eye over my winnings before returning her attention to the dozen cards fanned out in front of her. Stamping the appropriate boxes with a marker clutched in each fist, she looked like hell's own train conductor.

"Anyone want anything from the snack bar?" I asked, desperate to escape the thickening awkwardness.

Whether out of concentration or saltiness over my win, no one answered.

No one but Morrison, that is.

"I'll take a beer."

It was a kindness on his part, and purchased at great cost. In asking for it, he'd have to think about it, and in thinking about it, he'd have to confront his inability to ever enjoy it all over again.

A process he'd described as the most difficult part of his transition to vampire life.

I mean, imagine going cold turkey off everything you've ever enjoyed all at once.

Be that as it may, I caved to the temptation of an extra-large Frito pie with extra cheese and extra chili once I'd bellied up to the snack bar's brushed steel counter. One of the regions many snack-chip-based delicacies, it had never failed to improve diplomatic relations among the tensest of crowds.

"Soup's on," I announced, sliding the red-and-white-checked cardboard boat into the center of the table.

"Watch it!" Maureen snapped, setting down the cell phone she'd been tapping at intermittently throughout the game. "You'll get chili on my card."

I resisted the urge to point out that at least *some* of her squares would be filled that way, and moved my prize out of the way to clear more space.

Morrison gazed at the basket with a longing bordering on reverence, the serene blanket of cheese dotted with a confetti of green onions reflected in the gleaming surface of his hungry eyes.

"I'm so sorry," I said. "I know you can't have . . . uh, dairy, but I was so hungry, and it looked so good, and I'm weak." I held my hands out in supplication.

"It's fine," he said. "I'm just going to run to the restroom for a moment."

Or for as long as he estimated it would take me to eat my snack bar score, I suspected.

"Well, give it here if he's not going to have any." Maureen jerked the basket closer to her side of the table once Morrison was out of sight.

Without availing herself of either napkin or spork, she snatched bites from the platter with a ferocity that made me think twice about extending any appendages into the line of fire.

"Easy there, Mo," I teased. "It's not the Last Supper."

She slapped the table so hard, several bingo markers tipped over and rolled off the edge. "You dare compare the trash served in this den of sin to the bread broken in our Savior's presence?"

Trash or not, Maureen seemed to have no problem shoveling it into her mouth.

"No, not at all," I said, aware of my backslide into the accent I'd tried desperately to lose. "I just thought—everything y'all plan has a biblical theme, so—"

"So you thought you could mock us with impunity?"

I couldn't tear my eyes away from the carnage despite the cringe-inducing globs of cheese accumulating at the corners of her mouth.

"I'm sure that's not what Hanna meant," Mom said. "She can be a little snarky, but she'd never deliberately make fun of something sacred."

Wouldn't I?

Hadn't I?

An unsettling cracking sound came from Maureen's neck as she turned to look at my mother.

"Is that so?" In the jaundiced light of the faded overhead fluorescents, Maureen's yellowed teeth seemed unnaturally long, her mouth a little too wide for her face when stretched into an angry smile.

"Absolutely." Mom swallowed nervously.

"Because *I* seem to remember you saying that her lack of faith was part of the reason she'd disowned you and moved to Colorado once your mother had passed."

A dull ache woke in my chest.

There it was. The old song whose tune I knew by broken heart.

Mom looked like she was going to faint. "I think you may be misremembering our conversation. I said—"

"I seem to remember you saying that your daughter was selfish, and greedy, and had traded in a good man just because he didn't want to spend his hard-earned money on the glamorous European vacations she wanted so she could be surrounded by her precious art."

Now Mom didn't look like she was going to faint. She looked like she was going to die.

The skin around her mouth had turned gray, her forehead waxy and cheeks hollowed gaunt. "You're taking that out of context. I would never—"

But she would.

She had.

"She's right," I said.

Maureen wrested her attention from Mom and met my gaze. "How's that?"

"She's right," I repeated. "That's exactly what I did. I left my boring, average, lazy, neglectful husband and ran off with a rich, ruthless, charismatic millionaire who gives me absolutely everything I want."

Maureen's mouth withered into an ugly frown. Her lips began to move, but I couldn't make out the words at first.

"—will come forth out of poverty, despised of those that begat her."

"He's taken me to Germany and England and Scotland," I continued.

"The red harlot will spread her guile across the nations, and they will call her name misery."

"He built me a beautiful château in the woods."

"Her castle will be exceedingly fine in the eyes of men, but will come to dust on the shoes of the faithful." Maureen was really picking up steam now, spouting words with the cadence of a pulpit-pounding preacher. Only, the passages tumbling from her lips didn't sound like any Bible verses I'd ever encountered. "For she will be as a curse upon the land, a canker in the hearts of those that esteem her. Ye will know her by the suffering that follows her as the night follows the day."

"That's pretty," I said, twirling a lock of hair around my finger. "Tennyson?"

Maureen's lip-curling sneer revealed a broken canine as she horked and spit in my Frito pie. A translucent strand of spittle hung from her chin, but she made no attempt to blot it.

"Well, that was completely uncalled for," I said, already reaching beneath my seat for the tissues in my purse. Unable to locate them by feel, I ducked beneath the table and caught sight of something that made my intestines cramp themselves into a knot that would have rivaled one of Steve's balloon animals.

Had Morrison not returned at that moment, I might have simply stayed low and hamster-crawled my way right back out the sliding doors.

Waiting until he'd seated himself, I cleared my throat.

"Uh, James?"

"Yeah?"

"Can you help with something down here for a moment?"

"Sure." He leaned down, and I nodded in the direction of Maureen's chair.

The second he saw what I saw, he jerked and cracked his head on the underside of the table.

"That seem at all odd to you?" I whispered.

In the pocket of shadow, Morrison's eyes glowed a subtle blue. He torqued his neck as if to get a better look. "Maybe it's a thyroid thing? Or maybe she just prefers to let Mother Nature take her course?"

"I mean, I'm all for letting Mother Nature do her thing," I reasoned sotto voce, "but I'm pretty sure the thing she's doing is something she doesn't normally do except to creatures that walk on all fours."

Above the table, a low, rumbling *Moooooooooh* rose above the festive din.

Morrison and I locked eyes, and I read in his the same growing unease I felt.

"Oh, dear," I heard Margaret say. "Did the Frito pie not agree with you?"

I so badly wanted this to be true that I sat back up in my chair, prepared to offer effusive consolations and apologies for my terrible choice in snack despite not having enjoyed a single sodium-laden bite myself.

"I knew I shouldn't have asked for extra onions—" The words snapped off as I spotted the same thick, matted hair that had first caught my eye above Maureen's circulation support stockings now sprouting from her arms and hands.

She bared her strangely simian teeth, moaning the same phrase over and over again until it became a bone-chilling chant. *Mo. Mo. Mo. Mo. MoMo.*

A cold shiver slithered down my spine as I connected the dots.

The Missouri Monster—MoMo—as she's affectionately known

by the locals, was a Sasquatch-like creature straight out of (very) rural Midwestern legend.

And somehow, one of them had apparently ended up right here in Bumfuck, Texas, eyeing me like my innards owed her money.

"Thyroid, my ass," I retorted.

"Right." Morrison's tone shifted as realization dawned on him. "Well, this complicates the evening."

"Listen, Mo," I started, trying to keep my voice steady as I slowly stood. "I don't know what's got your wool in a wad, but if we could just talk this out like—"

"Talk?" MoMo snapped. "You think you can just 'talk' after all you've done?"

"If you could just be a smidge more specific about your complaint," I said, pinching my index finger and thumb together. "I would be delighted to address your concerns at length."

It took absolutely every scrap of self-restraint not to flinch as Maureen leaned across the table, ribbons of torn cloth from her floral-print dress fluttering in the icy blast of the industrial air conditioning units overhead.

"How dare you ask *me* such a question when *you* presume to rule!"

Irritation flickered like a pilot light at the base of my skull.

I'd faced all manner of baddie in my brief tenure, but having one bent on my destruction while also maintaining the *If you don't already know, I'm not going to tell you* mantra of her age and sociocultural programming was just a kick in the ham hocks.

"At least give me a chance to redeem myself. If you just get to know me—"

"Blasphemer!" MoMo roared. "*Freki* is our Redeemer!"

Hearing that name uttered in Maureen's guttural rasp made the hair on my everything stand on end.

And I do mean *everything*.

"Forgive me," I said, trying to keep my voice even. "I didn't mean to offend you. I would love to know more about Freki. To learn of her ways."

Because if my upbringing in a town where churches outnumbered stoplights had taught me anything, it was that committed congregants couldn't resist a missionary opportunity.

"Deceiver!" Mo hissed, pointing a claw-tipped finger at me. "You think I am so easily fooled? I know the tricks and snares of the Adversary."

"Just so I'm clear, am I the Adversary?"

MoMo's eyes took on a fevered gleam. "You would take credit for hell itself?"

"No, it's just, those verses you mentioned earlier kind of made it sound like the Adversary and I were at least in League, if not aligned in some kind of evil overlord situation." Slowly, and by degrees I hoped were too small for MoMo to notice behind the wire-rimmed librarian glasses still perched atop the broad bridge of her nose, my fingers crawled toward the bundle of cheese knives next to my winning bingo card. "I just want to make sure I understand so I can share the truth with my followers."

"*Followers*," Mo spat. "You have no followers. You have mindless sheep deceived by the lies of wicked men."

"Deceived how?" My fingernail grazed the cartoon cheese wedge–shaped polymer handle. "You have to remember, I wasn't raised in the faith."

MoMo's cracked lips curled into a sinister smile. "But you were, child. You were raised in *their* faith."

"*Their faith.*" Hearing these words repeated in unison by each of the women seated at the table momentarily snatched my attention from Mo.

Martha, Margaret, Linda, Gail, *and my mother* all stared straight ahead, their eyes glassy and unfocused.

"When you say *their faith . . .*" I led off, hoping to draw out additional details. "Whose faith are you referring to, exactly?"

"Wicked men," MoMo said.

"Wicked men," the Bible bingo ladies Greek-chorused.

"Weak, idle, self-glorifying pretenders who wrested power through violence and fear."

"Violence and fear," her backup singers murmured.

"But violence is exactly what I've tried to avoid," I said. This, at least, seemed a promising angle.

"You see? She lays claim to peace." A sanctimonious look I cared for not at all stiffened MoMo's feral features as she glanced around the table. "Yet she smote Morg."

A frisson of shock lanced through me.

Though it sounds ridiculous, not until that very second had I connected my current weird-ass confrontation in Abilene with the exceedingly bizarre circumstances in Colorado.

"Morg," MoMo said again. The word echoed around the table, bouncing off each of the ladies like a chorus of affirmation.

"Morg," they chimed, an unsettling chant that left me more alarmed than ever.

"For your information, I *didn't* smite Morg." My pinkie and ring finger were anchored around the knife now.

"But he perished in your home."

"How did you . . ."

But I hadn't even finished the question when the answer arrived whole and complete in my mind.

My mother.

And suddenly everything made sense.

Her impromptu visit. Her altered memory. Her blind devotion.

Whatever the fuck MoMo and her posse were, they'd targeted my mother on purpose. To what end, I couldn't yet comprehend, but I had a feeling I wasn't going to like it one bit.

"I don't suppose that you'll believe any explanation I can offer."

"Would you believe the words of one who came to power by deceiving the weak-minded?"

"I sure wouldn't."

I hadn't even noticed that a man at the table next to ours had turned his chair around, his cowboy hat propped on one knee. His hand digging through a bowl of the Big Bucks house-made chicharrons as he watched us with keen interest.

"Sir," I said, "I don't believe anyone asked you."

"As a neutral third party, I gotta say that so far, that ol' gal is making a pretty good case." A murmur of agreement rippled through the table's other occupants.

MoMo's eyes slitted in snakelike glare, her neck releasing a series of creaks and pops as she slowly turned toward the speaker. "Old?"

I hazarded a glance at Morrison while she was distracted. Having studied him quite closely on occasion(s), I recognized the sharp set of his jaw. The coiled tension in his lean limbs. Ready to unleash a Lone Star–size beatdown at a moment's notice.

"Beggin' your pardon, ma'am. I didn't mean to upset you." The man nervously fingered the pointy pheasant feather in the band of his hat brim. "My momma taught me to respect my elders."

"Elders?" MoMo spat.

"I mean, no offense, but what are you, sixty-five? Seventy?" The man's nervous chuckle was met with the discordant scrape of Maureen's chair sliding backward for what felt like a very, very long time.

She stood, and when she did, she towered at a height that definitely wasn't listed in the church's punny "Meet the Flockers" congregant bios.

"I am two thousand years old!" Mo's unearthly roar rattled the stack of plastic chairs against the wall. "And you are not worthy to lick the sweat from my sandals."

The bingo hall had fallen silent. Ladies sat frozen in their seats, their hair-sprayed curls the only parts of them not quivering with fear. Men sat open-mouthed, their hands already twitching toward the lumps beneath pearl-snap shirts where concealed carry weapons were holstered against beer bellies.

Any second, someone would scream.

Then the stampede would start.

Unless I did something to stop it.

"Hot flashes," I said, concealing the cheese knife in my palm as I rose from my chair. "We're working on getting her hormones adjusted."

Several of the women from the surrounding tables murmured their understanding and gave me sympathetic looks.

"When Freki comes, she will punish those who have persecuted us!" Mo jabbered.

I nodded to Morrison, who stood and began approaching Mo from the opposite side.

"She is the unburnt one. The rightful heir. Preserved by the Mother for these final days. And she *will* have her revenge."

"Vengeance for the fallen!" the ladies parroted.

Nope. I didn't like the sound of this *at all*.

"It's all right, Aunt Maureen," I crooned. "Let's just step outside and get some air, shall we?"

With a snarl that would put any horror movie sound effect to shame, MoMo lunged toward me, her massive hands outstretched like claws. Instinct kicked in, and I brandished the cheese knife, hoping it might make her reconsider her maiming plans.

Instead, the knife's blunt-tipped blade plunged right through her palm.

I gasped. "I'm *so* sorry. I didn't mean to—how did that even—oh Jesu—err, geeze!"

Mo only stared at the metal poking out between her knuckles before grabbing the bright yellow cheese wedge–shaped handle and yanking. The stubby serving utensil clattered to the floor.

Blood sprayed in an arterial arc, raining down on the number caller and bingo cage in rhythmic spurts.

For a moment, I could only stare at it, mesmerized by the bright spatters garlanding the laminated cardstock, soaking into the white tablecloths.

A sound brought me back to my senses.

Low, guttural, and greedy.

Morrison.

I watched as his eyes went dark and dead as a shark's, the whites turning black as tar as the bloodlust took him. His jaw tensed, a vein throbbing at his temple—a ticking time bomb in a trench coat.

The tension was thicker than the layer of dust on my treadmill back home, and I couldn't help but think of my poor cats, oblivious to the fact that their mom was currently starring in a messed-up episode of *National Geographic Meets Supernatural*.

"Can we please not do this here?" I begged, eyeing the exit and calculating the odds of making a run for it.

But it was too late.

Morrison lunged.

Mo caught him midair with a sweep of her arm, sending him flying into the bingo caller and his cage.

The bingo caller went down with a startled yelp, and someone shrieked as the crimson-spattered plastic orbs came rivering down over the table's edge, bouncing off the stage and across the floor like ball bearings.

Morrison scampered after them on all fours, shoving as many as he could into his mouth, cheeks puffed like a chipmunk, his lips a bloodied red smear.

"James, no!" I tried, but as fast as he was, Morrison would already have another bloody ball in his hands before I could finish wrenching the last away.

Until only one remained.

We both scrambled for it, but Morrison got there first. In his enthusiasm or desperation, he sucked it into his mouth.

The momentum carried it straight down his throat, where it made a hollow *thock* as it lodged in his esophagus.

He clutched at his throat, his eyes bugged out like obsidian marbles.

"You've got to be kidding me."

"He's choking!" someone cried out, not quite grasping the reality-defying absurdity of the situation. "Call 911!"

Right. Because *that* would end well.

I received an exceedingly detailed flash of me, attempting to explain to the paramedics why, despite having no pulse, no respiratory activity, and a basal body temperature of whatever the bingo hall's thermostat was set at, Morrison was perfectly fine and didn't actually need their assistance.

"Stand back!" The man from the next table who'd gotten MoMo all riled tossed his hat onto his chair. "I was a volunteer firefighter!"

About forty years ago, by the look of it.

"I've got it!" I shouted, butting my way in front of him.

I positioned myself behind Morrison, dragging my memory for the few tidbits gleaned from memories of my Red Cross babysitting course and episodes of *Grey's Anatomy*, one of my frequently rewatched emotional support shows.

Wrapping my arms around his rib cage, I balled a fist just below his sternum and clutched it with the opposite hand.

"Brace yourself," I muttered just loudly enough for him to hear.

With a deep breath, I jerked my fists upward with everything I had. Morrison's body convulsed with the force of it, a rattling wheeze erupting from his throat, but the bingo ball remained firmly lodged.

"Come on, Morrison, don't you dare die on me."

Inside joke, since he technically *couldn't* die, and there was no danger of suffocating on account of the fact that he didn't breathe. But the bingoers looking on in horror didn't know that.

I reset my grip and gave it another thrust.

With a sound remarkably like a champagne cork popping, the bingo ball exited Morrison's mouth at warp speed, narrowly missing MoMo's head by an inch.

The crowd gasped, and began clapping.

I resisted the urge to bow.

A sea of cell phones rose like flowers to the sun, all pointed at me.

"Really, no pictures necessary." I tried to bat away the cameras without actually slapping anyone.

"But you're a hero, honey!"

"Yeah! Let us get a picture for the paper."

"Please, everyone, put the phones away!" I pleaded, my frustration bubbling into my words. But my request fell on deaf ears—or rather, ears whose sound amplification apparatuses were firmly tuning me out.

"PUT. YOUR. PHONES. DOWN!" My alpha voice, demonic in its depth and power, thundered through the bingo hall unintentionally. It echoed off the walls, reverberating through bones and bingo bags alike. The effect was immediate. The room stilled, phones clattered onto tables, and wide-eyed stares fixed on me.

My mother's scream ripped a jagged hole in the silence.

I followed her frozen stare and instantly located the source.

Maureen sat slumped forward on the table, her face buried in the half-consumed Frito pie, her slackened arms returned to their spindly size.

From her neck jutted the yellow handle of the cheese knife.

"Who did this?" I asked, scanning my mother and her church chums only to be met with blank stares.

"Who did this?" I demanded.

Mom blinked at me, not quite present behind her eyes. "Why, you did, honey."

"You did," the ladies repeated.

"Mom, you *know* I didn't do this. I was over there helping Morrison."

Glancing at the vampire in question, I was relieved to see that the frenzy had passed and his eyes had returned to something like their normal hue.

"Speaking of slipping out," Morrison murmured, his gaze fixating on something beyond my shoulder, "we've got company."

I turned to see two men standing in the foyer, their stern faces, dark glasses, and equally dark suits a stark contrast to the colorful country couture of my hometown. In that moment, I knew with a cold, certain dread exactly who they were and why they'd come.

BSA agents.

And here I was, standing in the direct proximity of yet another dead Sasquatch creature, my hands smeared with her blood.

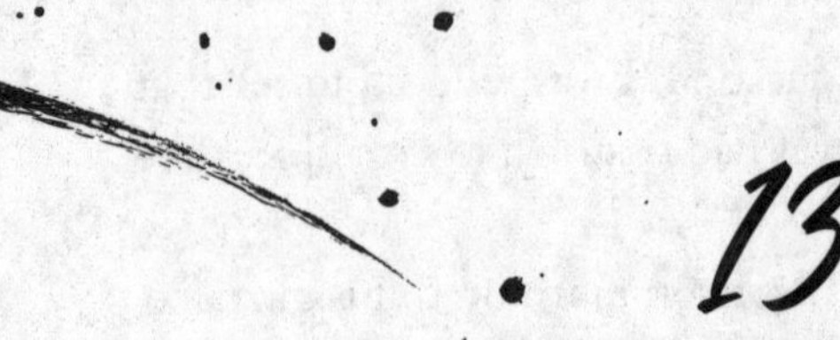

13

"Fire exit?" Morrison muttered without moving his lips.

"Yep," I said through my teeth. "Come on, Mom. We've gotta go."

She looked at me blankly. "Go where?"

"Somewhere safe."

"Hanna," Morrison warned.

The agents were halfway across the hall now and closing fast.

"But I'm safe here," Mom said, looking at me like I'd just said something mildly amusing.

"Safe here," Margaret, Martha, Linda, and Gail echoed.

"*Hanna*," Morrison said.

Ten yards now.

"I can't just leave her here," I insisted.

Morrison was already grabbing my purse and slinging it across his body. "Maybe they can join us for a nightcap at your mother's house and you can just explain that this was all a huge misunderstanding."

"Good point."

After all, my mother was human, and the BSA's policy of strict separation when it came to our worlds would incline them toward minimal interaction where she was concerned. If anything, they'd want to contain the MoMo mess with all due haste and expediency before getting the fuck out of Dodge.

It was long past time for me to do the same.

"I've got to go, Mom." I dropped a kiss on her head. "I'll be in touch as soon as I can."

Morrison and I hustled out the fire exit and sprinted toward the scrubby field behind the building. I heard the door bang open about three Louisianas after we'd exited.

Glancing over my shoulder, I saw that they were gaining.

I cursed every cheese platter I'd ever devoured as my ears flicked toward the sound of approaching footsteps.

"Faster," Morrison barked.

But we both knew there was only one way I could go faster, and it was a serious risk. If I shifted, my clothes would be a goner, and I'd be ten times more likely to get a butt full of buckshot from some farmer who assumed I was there to pick off his livestock.

My lungs ached, my muscles screamed, and a cramp like a hot blade dug itself into my side.

"Sorry about this."

And before I could process what Morrison meant by that, I was suddenly lifted off my feet and tossed over a broad, surprisingly sturdy shoulder.

"Hey, I'm not a sack of—OOF!" The sudden hoisting motion cut off my protests as the alfalfa field began to blur past in a kaleidoscope of colors.

Tall stalks of grass whipped my face, his shoulder jamming into my guts with every swift stride.

"Okay, fuck this."

Shifting had never ceased to be a wildly unpleasant sensation, like shedding my skin and growing another while being turned inside out. Doing it *while* being slung over someone's shoulder and sprinting at warp speed did nothing to improve the experience.

My bones creaked, then snapped, my human form resisting the transformation before finally giving way to the beast within.

My legs shortened, my muscles thickened, my skin itching as if infested before erupting in a layer of thick, soft fur.

Morrison grunted as I launched myself off his back.

I collided with the BSA agents, and we went down in a tangle of limbs and curses. They righted themselves with surprising agility, getting to their hands and knees.

And . . . staying there?

Only when I saw them patting around on the ground did I noticed they'd lost their sunglasses on impact.

Which was when I noticed another very odd thing.

The agents' faces were blank.

Not as in *expressionless.*

As in *nonexistent.*

"Hanna!" Morrison shouted. "What are you doing?"

"Having a small existential crisis," I said. "Run!"

Morrison needed no further encouragement.

He sprinted off in the direction of a decrepit farmhouse, its silhouette just visible between an overgrown windbreak of poplars.

I followed, a flurry of fur and feral energy, bounding toward Morrison's dwindling form in the distance.

My claws dug into the soft earth beneath me, propelling me forward as my ears picked up a sound that made the fur prickle down the length of my back and tail.

Giggling.

Sardonic, sinister snickering as the grass parted on either side of me, disturbed by someone—or something—I couldn't see.

Not good.

"Morrison!"

"I know," he called back. "I hear it too."

I poured on the speed and finally caught up to Morrison just as the sound amplified, seeming to come from everywhere at once.

"Look out!"

We skidded to a stop, narrowly avoiding a tumble into a concealed gully.

"Which way?" I panted.

Glancing back at the field, we saw a radius of paths being blazed toward us through the tall, yellowed grass, the beings causing them still concealed.

Suddenly, a shrill whistle pierced the night. For a moment, I feared some new supernatural horror but then spotted a familiar silhouette against the abandoned barn.

Broad-shouldered. Barrel-chested. Bristly.

Hank.

"You comin' or not?" He plucked a toothpick from the corner of his lips and flicked it before stepping into the barn.

Seconds later, I heard the ripping of an engine starting up.

Morrison and I took off toward the barn, the unearthly laughter growing louder as we ran.

We reached the building just as a crop duster rumbled into view from the dilapidated structure, its propeller spinning like a buzz saw. Hank was in the cockpit, an old-fashioned aviator hat and round goggles strapped to his ruddy face.

The wheels had already begun to roll, the engine's acrid blast flattening the grass and my fur as I loped alongside.

"Get in!" Hank hollered over the engine's roar.

My first leap missed entirely.

I caught the edge of the cockpit on the second, claws scrabbling on the plane's metal body before Morrison shoved hard against my haunches. With a grunt, we tumbled into the belly of the beast, the plane jerking forward as Hank gunned the engine.

The ancient, rusted fuselage groaned in protest as we shuddered into the air, the ground dropping away beneath us with a lurch. Morrison and I careened around the cargo compartment, bouncing off crates and narrowly ducking a lumpy burlap sack containing what I sincerely hoped was a taxidermy deer.

"Might wanna buckle up," Hank said, switching knobs and turning dials. "We're fixin' to make like a bread truck and haul ass."

Morrison staggered forward and into the copilot's seat behind Hank's, reaching out a hand to help me.

"I'm good," I said, still humiliated from having to be boosted into a cargo hold like one of those heart-tugging dog-in-a-ditch rescue reels.

A sudden tilt of the wings sent me skidding across the floor, claws scoring the corrugated metal as I fought for purchase.

So maybe I did need a hand. Or seven.

Without another word, Morrison reached over and grabbed me by the scruff of my neck, hauling me unceremoniously into his lap before buckling the seat belt around both of us.

"Well, this is awkward," I muttered under my breath, my haunches pressing against his khaki-clad thighs.

Glancing back down, I saw that whatever it was that had been chasing must have stopped short of the clearing.

The agents, on the other hand, stood perfectly still in the center of it, faceless heads angled up to us, their bodies shrinking to two black dots glaring upward like malevolent eyes.

I was still staring at them when a sudden drop in altitude nearly floated my stomach right out of my nostrils.

"Hold on!" Hank shouted from the cockpit, steering with one hand while adjusting his goggles with the other. "It's about to get a little bumpy!"

"About to?" I growled.

The plane lurched again, and if not for Morrison's grip around my waist, I'm pretty sure I would have been introduced cranium-first to the cockpit's ceiling. My claws dug into Morrison's thighs through his khakis, and he let out a hiss that was swallowed by the engine's relentless roar.

"*Chepasse*, you dusty bastards!"

I had assumed Hank's invective was aimed at the world at large until the buff-colored blur in my peripheral vision made me whip around fast enough to accidentally headbutt Morrison.

"Fuck!" he swore, the word muffled by the hand he brought to his nose.

The iron-rich aroma of blood filled the cockpit.

Apparently, there was enough of doughnut dude's donation from this morning left for the injury to bleed.

"There's wet wipes in the seat back pocket," Hank called, the tassels of his sweat-stained pilot's scarf flapping over his shoulder as he glanced at us.

"How about barf bags?" I asked as another sharp altitude change brought us close enough to the treetops to hear the branches scraping the plane's belly.

"Suck my exhaust, *bon de rien*!" Hank bellowed gleefully, wrenching the controls to veer the plane toward a clearing. He tipped the wings and raced just above the earth as if playing a game of chicken with gravity itself.

"Hank—" I said, noting the giant West Texas scrub oak looming ahead.

"How about a little care package, *boo doo*?" Hank lobbed something out of the cockpit window, and a bright flash of orange preceded a percussive *boom* that echoed through the open air. The sound seemed to delight Hank, judging by the cascade of manic laughter that sounded eerily like a bullfrog being throttled.

"Hank!" I shouted. "The tree!"

"*Mon Dieu!*" He jerked the wheel hard. The plane heaved upward, its engine emitting a pained whine followed by a sickening metallic crunch. I thought we might have hit the tree after all until I glanced at the windshield and saw the source of the sound.

Or rather . . . didn't see.

Where there had once been at least a foggy snapshot of the rapidly shifting horizon, there was now an opaque gray-brown screen completely obscuring the view.

"*Merde!*" Hank thumped the instrument panel.

"What the hell is that?" I blurted as I squinted at it.

And then it moved.

A distorted Rorschach test of rust-colored wings and gnarled appendages, one of its feathery antennae bent at a painful angle, yellowish green goo leaking from one corner of its mouth. It clung to the windshield, a Lovecraftian nightmare that seemed to pulsate with an otherworldly energy.

And we've discussed my nightmares, yes?

"You hit a mothman!" I cried.

"I didn't either!" Hank yanked the steering wheel, and Morrison and I were jerked sideways, his grip around my waist tightening in response. "That sumbitch hit *us*."

The ruined thing slid farther down the plane's nose, and a sliver of the night sky returned.

"Just a little more . . ." The plane tipped to the left, and the mothman let out a sound so eerily human, an icy tendril of fear wrapped around my heart. A low moan, full of pain and terror that echoed in my soul.

"We are so going to die," I said.

We were going down by the nose now, rotating in an accelerating spiral like aeronautical football.

"Have . . . a . . . little . . . faith . . . in . . . ol' Hank." Whether the g-force was compressing his vocal cords or Hank had practiced this dramatic staccato bequest for just such an occasion, I wasn't sure, but the effect was the same.

Pure, mortal terror.

All the times I had dutifully paid attention to the flight attendants guiding us through the rote rehearsal of what to do in the event of a crash while my fellow passengers donned noise-canceling headphones or tuned them out entirely, and now I didn't even have a human body to fold into the proper impact position.

It just didn't seem fair.

James's vampiric body was just as vulnerable, if not more, considering what remained of him would continue to be sentient in perpetuity even once smeared across the Texas landscape.

I felt his arms slide around me, his face bury itself in the fur between my shoulder blades, and I *knew*.

This wasn't merely bracing for impact.

He was *holding me*. Folding his form around mine like it was the last embrace either of us would ever experience. Which, considering the rapidly approaching ground, it very well might be.

"I love you," he whispered.

And in that moment with impending death shaving away all extraneous noise, I offered him the only response that remained. "I love you too."

Because I had. I did. And maybe I always would.

"Suck it, you scaly, overgrown skeeter!" Hank yelled over the roar of the engine and the rush of the wind outside.

I felt a shift in the plane's weight distribution and blinked at the goo-smeared windshield as Hank angled the plane back to a less vomit-inducing trajectory. Across the vast expanse of darkness below, I caught sight of a fluttering, hulking figure plummeting down into the inky wilderness.

With a similarly sinking feeling, I scraped another notch in my mental death toll column.

This would not end well.

—

"Ain't she a beaut?" Hank's voice was filled with a paternal pride as he patted the plane's claw-mark-gouged and mothman-dented side. "This here is *Brunhilde*."

I might have thought twice about naming a contraption that seemed primarily held together by duct tape and bayou mud after a mythical Valkyrie, but what did I know?

"She's something, all right," I said. Leaping down from the cockpit, rich, rotting loam squelched beneath my paws, the potent bouquet of decay and life commingling in a way that was uniquely bayou. I took a deep breath, drawing in the damp scent of moss-draped cypress combined with the faint tang of brackish water farther away, all underscored with a bass note of primordial earth.

"Why don't y'all come inside the house and get cleaned up?"

The "house" was a vintage Airstream trailer on a lot housing a rudimentary radio tower and bordered by dogwood trees. Scrap metal littered the yard like so much landscaping, interspersed with plastic flamingos, garden gnomes, and about a thousand glowing blue electric bug-zapping lights.

I glanced up at Morrison, who shrugged his deference.

Inside, the trailer was a symphony of kitsch, complete with a neon beer sign flickering in the window, loops of Christmas lights, and a grass skirt–wearing hula girl glued to the dashboard's center console.

"Shower's back that way." Hank hooked a thumb toward the rear of the trailer. "Help yourself."

My paws were still caked with mud from my romp through the field, and I was 99.9 percent certain that I'd find a small army of burrs stuck in my fur. Both problems that could be solved by my shifting back to my human form, but not without creating another very pressing one.

Namely, my being buckety bare-ass naked.

"I'd love to take you up on that," I said. "But . . . uh . . ."

"Oh!" Hank thumped a forehead featuring a prodigious hat tan. "My bad. Lemme get you something to change into."

"Can't wait to see what he picks out," I whispered to Morrison once he was gone.

Hank returned from the bedroom nook at the far end of the trailer with a stack of folded towels and a surprisingly white, fluffy bathrobe.

"Used to belong to my ol' lady." Hank scratched the back of his neck with his fingertips. "I burned most her stuff in the barrel out back when she ran off with one of them fox shifters, but this is better than nothin', I'd guess."

"Much better," I said, padding after him toward the bathroom.

Like "house," "bathroom" was somewhat of a misleading term for the facilities, which consisted of a small pedestal sink, an even smaller toothpaste-flecked shaving mirror, and a wall-mounted hose ending in a showerhead anchored over the toilet.

When I emerged from the bathroom freshly scrubbed and fully human, I found Morrison perched on the sagging couch while Hank lounged in his recliner like a king surveying his less-than-opulent domain, the silence between them thicker than day-old gumbo.

"Your turn," I announced.

"Thanks," Morrison said, "but I'll wait for the next stop."

"You know where that next stop is, buddy boy?" Hank opened the arm of his recliner and withdrew a cigar. Reaching over to a cluttered side table, he produced a lighter shaped like a miniature rifle and pulled the trigger to shoot flame from the tip. His stubbly cheeks puffed as he lit it.

"He has a point," I said.

"So do pencils," Morrison muttered. "Pass."

In a way, I was grateful for his refusal. It fostered my feverish if unreasonable hope that we wouldn't need to be here for long.

I'd texted Abernathy from the bathroom once I'd reverted to a form with fingers, letting him know where I was and that I would call him later to explain.

I'd received a heart-bruisingly brief *ok* in response.

"Somethin' to drink? I got beer, sweet tea, kombucha—"

"Kombucha?" I repeated.

"Brew it myself. My ol' lady turned me onto it. Helps with my digestion." Hank patted his distended globe of a belly. "Or I got some stronger stuff, if you've a mind."

"Did you brew *that* yourself?" I asked, infinitely able to envision a secret still tucked away somewhere in the junkyard ramble of his property.

"Naw," he said. "Just plain old Gentleman Jack, I'm afraid."

"Perfect," I said, perhaps a hair too enthusiastically.

Of the available options, something commercially manufactured in a facility with triple-distilling capacity seemed the safest.

Cigar perched in the corner of his mouth, Hank rose from his recliner and shuffled into the kitchen. My salivary glands contracted painfully as I watched him pull the brand-new bottle out of the paper bag and crack the safety seal.

He poured a goodly measure into a mug and handed it to me.

Seeing the pointy pair of tits bouncing on its ceramic surface, I felt a punch of nostalgia.

Oma had had a souvenir mug from Las Vegas just like it.

"I got some meat pigeons in the coops out back," Hank said to Morrison as he settled back in his recliner. "You can help yerself to a coupla them to tide you over if you want to."

Morrison's eyes flared briefly crimson, but he remained seated. "Thanks," he said.

The recliner rocked.

Hank puffed his cigar.

I slurped my whiskey.

The bug lights hummed.

Something screamed.

"Sneaky bastards," Hank muttered. "Think they can just fly wherever their pecker leads 'em."

"Speaking of." I crossed one leg over the other and re-tucked the borrowed bathrobe. "Want to tell me what you were doing parked in a barn outside a bingo hall in my hometown?"

Hank blew out an elaborate smoke ring and watched as it billowed up to the yellowed ceiling. "Same thing I's doin' at your gallery show."

"Stalking her?" Morrison suggested sourly.

"More like . . . strategic surveillance," Hank corrected with a grin that showed off more enthusiasm than teeth.

"Is that what you'd call the Sasquatch talk I overheard you having with Dan Davis?" I asked.

"Oh, that." A fine pillar of ashes sifted down to Hank's stained T-shirt. "I's just yankin' his chain. Tryin' to throw him off the scent, if you know what I mean."

"What scent would that be, exactly?" I asked.

"So you *don't* know what I mean?" Hank looked crestfallen.

"Let's just say that I'd like to hear you explain it," I said.

Hank scratched his stubbled chin, looking momentarily uncomfortable before motioning us to follow him.

"Come see for yourself."

We trailed after him through a door that creaked ominously, across a half-finished deck, and down through a set of storm doors that led to a concrete bunker.

On one wall, an assortment of dried goods and MRE packets sat on metal shelves rusted in the constant coastal humidity.

On all three of the others, photos, newspaper clippings, and maps had been plastered, all interconnected by a rainbow of yarn like a schizophrenic spider's web.

"Welcome to the command center," Hank announced with a flourish that only accentuated the absurdity of it all.

"I see," I said, scanning the images. "What do all these colors mean?"

Hank cleared his throat and spat a tobacco-brown glob into a nearby coffee can.

"The red yarn, that's for the fox shifter sightings." He moved his cigar like a laser pointer over the first radius of threads. "Purple, all the places where the coyote shifters showed up. Brown—" He tucked the cigar back into his mouth as he rooted through *another* old coffee can. "That's for them mothmen," Hank said, decisively pushing the brown-tipped pin into the quadrant covering Texas. "Green is for Sasquatch, naturally."

"Naturally," I echoed, trying not to let my skepticism show too much.

"Yellow indicates paranormal activity," Hank continued, "weird stuff that can't be immediately chalked up to shifters or cryptids. Ghosts, unexplained lights, that sort of thing."

"And what about the blue?" I asked curiously.

Hank paused and pulled on his scruffy beard, his mouth tightening into a serious line. "Blue's for Venusians."

"Venusians?" I repeated.

"Aliens from Venus, Alpha Harvey," Hank clarified, his eyes wide as saucers.

"Of course they are," I said, pressing my hand to my mouth to pretend I was coughing instead of stifling a laugh. "How could I have missed that connection?"

"*Right?*" Hank's eyes took on an intense gleam as he started pointing out the various intersections between the threads. "The mothman sightings and Sasquatch disappearances, the fox and coyote incursions, the alien abductions . . ."

"*What* alien abductions?" Morrison asked.

Hank sucked his teeth and tapped ash from his cigar into one of the red Solo cups gathered in a lazy herd on his desk. "The alien abductions are what's been causing all the disappearances and incursions."

I felt a mix of pity and irritation.

"As you know, I get a report from every faction of shifters each week. More often if there are emergencies. In all that time, not a single one of them has mentioned a disappearance that wasn't solved before I'd finished typing up an incident report for investigation."

"Exactly!" Hank stabbed a finger toward the low ceiling. "There are never any disappearances on account of they send back a clone to take their place!"

"A clone."

"Yes, ma'am." Hank nodded gravely. "Looks like 'em, talks like 'em, even smells like 'em, but they're just a shell. A meatsuit with a mainframe command line linked to the matrix."

"What happens to the real abductee?"

"Brainwashed. Memory programs wiped aboard the mother ship. Merged with the motherboard."

"Riiight," I said.

"I oughta know. It happened to my old lady." Hank pointed his wet cigar stub toward the bunker stairs. "Right there in my own backyard. One minute we were enjoyin' some of my special moonshine, preparin' for a romantic evenin' together, and then—" Hank clapped his hands together. "*Pow!* She's gone."

"Oh no," I said, leaning in to study the prodigious knot of green threads surrounding Abilene, Texas.

"I'd barely gone inside to get my shotgun and flashlight and *pow*!" He clapped his hands again. "She's back! Only it wasn't *her*."

"How do you mean?" I asked, my curiosity only mildly piqued.

"Well," Hank dawdled, scratching the side of his grizzled cheek, "she started acting real strange-like. Almost like she'd forgotten how to be my Delilah." He stared at an invisible point in the distance, lost in haunting memories. "She couldn't remember how I liked my coffee. Stopped packin' me lunches. Said she didn't even recall what went into a crawfish boil."

Hank knocked back a swig of his beer. "After that, she went cold on me. Got kinda distant. Didn't laugh anymore. Not even when I did my famous greased hog imitation. Nothing got through to her. Everything about her felt . . . hollow."

Hollow.

I hugged the robe tighter against a chill.

Something about this description seemed more than a little familiar. The memory lapses. The chilly affect.

"One day, I woke up and she's just gone," Hank said. "Didn't even take none of her stuff with her. I ain't seen nor heard from her since."

"I'm sorry," I said, noting the almost solar pattern of red and purple thread surrounding the New Orleans and Baton Rouge areas. "That must have been hard."

"Sure was." Hank pulled an oil-streaked bandanna from his overalls pocket and honked his nose into it. "Especially once they started sending them fox and coyote shifters to shut me up."

"And who are *they*, exactly?" I asked, taking another sip of my whiskey.

"The Venusians!" Hank mopped his damp brow with the same handkerchief he'd used to blow his nose, tempting the whiskey to inch back up my throat. "Don't you see? They're targeting me because I *know*. They know that *I* know that they came back and took Delilah, and they don't want me spreadin' the truth."

"I see," I said, shifting my attention to the spaghetti bowl of blue threads surrounding Los Angeles—duh—and following them eastward. "Are all these incidents ones you've witnessed personally?"

"Some of 'em," Hank said, plucking one of the blue threads like a guitar string. "The rest is from my listeners."

"Listeners?" I asked.

"Check this out." Hank's eyes gleamed like oiled ball bearings in the gloom of his bunker as he walked over to the food storage shelves.

Casually, he reached beneath a faded poster of *Charlotte's Web* and fiddled with something that produced a heavy *click*.

The metal shelves rolled away on concealed castors, revealing a panel of brushed steel. Hank punched a combination into the keypad, and the steel wall slid open with a smooth hiss of compressed air.

Behind it, there was a small alcove containing an upholstered booth and an array of sound equipment with an impressive assortment of dials, switches, buttons, and knobs blinking back at me.

"This here's my station," Hank proclaimed, puffing out his camo-clad chest. He flicked several switches, and the hum of electricity filled the room as various screens lit up with scrolling numbers and crackling static. "Broadcasting across the ether to concerned citizens across the country."

"Gives all new meaning to the term *ham radio*," Morrison breathed into my ear, nearly making me aspirate my whiskey.

"Twice a week, every week, my subscribers tune in to radio FREKI for the truth about what's really going on out there in the wide world."

I blinked at him. "What did you say?"

"I said, twice a week, every week—"

"The name," I said, grabbing Hank's wrist.

"FREKI. It's one of them acronyms. Stands for *Fur Friends Ethical Kinship Initiative*."

"But there's two *f*'s and no *r*," I pointed out.

Hank stubbed his cigar out on a plate with a moldering sandwich crust left on a shelf in the recording booth. "Yeah, well, Delilah said since we already had an *F*, we could just count the second letter. You know, like poetical license?"

I nodded slowly, my mind racing.

"So Delilah helped you start the broadcast?"

"Yes'm."

"And the name was her idea?"

"Yes'm."

"And twice a week, every week, you broadcast about . . . all of this?" I said, gesturing around the bunker by way of summary.

Hank rocked backward on his boots. "Yes'm. Delilah too, before she got her mind matrixed by the Venusians and lit on outta here."

"And since this is a public podcast where you discuss topics forbidden by the Bureau of Supernatural Affairs, how do you keep humans from tuning in?"

Hank's bushy brows gathered toward the center of his forehead. "I guess I hadn't really thought about that."

Behind me, Morrison gave a stifled groan.

This explained one possible source whereby Dan Davis and even the furries might have gleaned some of the information they'd mentioned, but I'd be damned if the name made any sense in connection to the mysterious former alpha who'd signed an agreement with the Sasquatch.

"What do your listeners have to say about the cryptid uprising?" Morrison asked, as if picking up my mental breadcrumb trail.

Hank chuckled grimly, running a hand over his scruffy beard. "Well, some of 'em think it's a distraction organized by the US government to hide the fact that they've been in cahoots with the Bigfoot clans out west for years, but I know better."

"How's that?" Morrison's expression was unreadable, but I could feel a tension radiating off him like heat waves.

"Because." The corner of Hank's mouth twisted up into a sly grin as he poked a fresh cigar into it. "The cryptid uprising ain't real."

Morrison stiffened alongside me. "Not real?"

"Nope." Reaching into the pocket of his camo vest, Hank withdrew the rifle lighter. "That there is just a cover."

"For what?" Morrison and I asked simultaneously.

The lighter's flame cast an eerie orange glow over Hank's grizzled features, dropping his eye sockets into shadow as he puffed sweet tobacco smoke from his thick lips.

"For the great extermination," Hank said slowly, tasting the words.

"The great . . . extermination?" I repeated.

Hank grinned, smoke billowing out from his nose like a cartoon dragon. "Oh yeah. The cryptids are just the start. They're testing the waters. See how we react."

"And then what?" Morrison asked, his hands folded over his chest, his expression hardened as if preparing himself to reject whatever Hank had to say.

"Then," Hank said, taking a pull off a bottle of beer he'd found on his desk, "they go for their real target."

"Which is?" I took another sip of whiskey in hopes of dislodging the lump from my throat, afraid I already knew the answer to this question.

"Shifters," Hank said.

Bingo.

"Why do you think they've been makin' so many visits to your neck of the woods?"

I blinked at him, my mind a swirling suckhole of conflicting questions. "So many—I'm sorry?"

"See fer yerself." He tipped his malodorous head toward the opposite side of the room.

Even from this distance, I could see the color concentration. The cement floor was cool beneath my bare feet as I floated over to it, carried by a craven curiosity.

Gooseflesh rose on my scalp and swarmed down my neck and arms.

There, dead center of the cobalt thread supernova, was Georgetown.

"I been puttin' out feelers," Hank said. "Tryin' to recruit some of my followers to keep an eye on you. But after what happened to Morg, I figured I'd just better come myself." Hank puffed out his chest. "I may be rough around the edges, but nobody messes with my kin."

"Kin?" I snorted. "Since when are we family?"

"Since you became alpha," he replied. "That's what FREKI's all about. Bringin' all kinds of supernatural creatures together for the greater good."

"Family or not, we'll need more than a bunker and your Pepe Silvia wall to accomplish that," I said, folding my arms. A dull, radiating ache began to throb at the base of my skull. I massaged it with the tips of my fingers, wincing at the lump I found there. "Also, I think some of your listeners might have gotten the wrong idea."

"What makes you say that?" Hank asked.

"Only the fact that not even two hours ago, one of them called me the red harlot and vowed vengeance against me in Freki's name."

"Huh." Hank scratched his balding pate. "That's real weird."

"*Weird* doesn't begin to cut it." Yanking the stogie from Hank's mouth, Morrison snapped it in two and dropped it to the ground. "Hanna's life is in danger, and all because you accidentally started a cult from your pathetic prepper pod."

Stumbling into a pile of old beer bottles, Hank clutched his chest as if Morrison's words physically wounded him. "I didn't mean no harm. Honest. I just . . ."

"You just what?" An uncharacteristic impatience grated Morrison's usually even voice. He prowled forward, a predator cornering its prey.

Hank swallowed hard, his Adam's apple bobbing. "I just wanted to protect Alpha Harvey. Warn her 'bout the Venusian-Human League."

"And how do you suggest we fix this situation, Hank?" I

asked, trying to break up the tension and redirect the conversation back toward problem-solving. If I've learned anything as an alpha, it's that macho power struggles are about as useful as a chocolate slow cooker.

"Well . . ." He backed toward his recording booth. "For starters, I can do *this*."

With a flourish that belied his earlier agitation, Hank threw back a tattered old tarp, covering what I'd assumed was a pile of junk in the corner.

In fact, it was not.

I shrieked and leaped back, colliding with Morrison as a mothman blinked its enormous, round eyes in the sudden light. Its feathery antennae twitched with mild irritation, its velvety gray wings ruffling against the ropes binding it to a desk chair.

Seeing my startled expression, Hank grinned proudly. "This here's Marv," he said, patting the mothman affectionately on one furry shoulder. "Marv's going to help me with an emergency broadcast tonight. Aren't you, Marv?"

Marv—if indeed that was his real name—gave an indignant squeak, his curled proboscis unfurling like a paper party blower.

Suddenly, I saw it.

The lumpy burlap sack in *Brunhilde*'s cargo bay.

"No wonder we were getting dive-bombed!" I said. "What the hell were you thinking?"

"I was thinking that this feller's got some explaining to do," Hank said, kicking Marv's chair. "Don't ya?"

"Explaining *how*?" I asked. "He doesn't even talk."

Hank raised one bushy eyebrow at me, tutting like a schoolteacher. "Well now, that's where you're wrong, Alpha Harvey," he said with a smug grin. "Mothmen talk plenty; you just gotta know how to listen. Show her."

Marv's antennae began to move, furiously flicking and swishing above his oversize eyes.

"Don't you use that kind of language in front of Alpha Harvey." Hank pointed a thick finger at Marv.

The swishing grew more urgent.

"Do what now?" Hank squinted and leaned in, face fixed in rapt concentration. "That's not a bad idea."

"What did he say?" I demanded.

"You really think that could work?" Hank asked, ignoring my question.

The feathery antennae began to vibrate, filling the room with a hushed, lulling hum.

Hank nodded slowly. "Roger that."

With slow, methodical movements, he seated himself in the desk chair and reached up to adjust the microphone. Without warning, a metal gate slammed down, sealing Hank and Marv in the booth before the entire setup pivoted back to the side bearing the metal shelves.

A clanging echoed from the top of the stairs, Morrison and I locking eyes the second recognition hit home.

The bunker door.

Morrison thundered up the stairs, pounding on the reinforced metal with the flat of his hand. Only in watching him did I understand the grim reality.

There was no handle on our side of the door.

It wasn't a bunker at all.

It was a trap.

"Hank!" Morrison roared, the whites of his eyes filling with bloodred rage. "Open this door right now or I will tear your throat out and bathe in your blood, so help me God!"

In the eerie silence that followed, a softly sinister voice crooned through the door.

"So help me . . . *Freki*."

14

"On the count of three." My voice wavered with a mix of determination and exhaustion. And okay, probably delusion. We'd been stuck in Hank's bunker for two days, watching the hours pass on an old analog Busch Light–branded clock, and our escape attempts had become increasingly desperate.

"One . . . two . . . three!" We both heaved against the door, but it didn't budge. I sighed, disappointed but not surprised.

Like the hope for rescue, our strength was waning.

"It's useless," I muttered, brushing flakes of rust from my hands. "We're never going to budge that thing."

"Got to . . . think positive." The words came out of Morrison at slower intervals that felt weakening and winded.

I glanced over at him, propped against the door, his eyes half-closed, his skin chalk pale and clammy.

"You look as bad as I probably smell," I said.

He snorted. "Doubt it."

"Which part?"

"Your smell."

"Yeah, well, I don't recall our having hung out after two days in an underground bunker on a steady diet of reconstituted beef stroganoff and Natty Light." I kicked one of the cans in the pile that represented the only available source of hydration in Hank's fallout shelter.

Because he believed bottled water was but one source of alien mind control, according to one of the many notes scribbled around the Technicolor web on his walls.

"Last scent . . . I remember is gun smoke, blood, and your fear sweat." Morrison rolled his head toward me on the wall as if the effort of turning his neck was too great. "Sell my . . . soul for even a second of it." His eyelids fell closed again. "If I still have one."

I nudged him with an elbow. "Of course you still have one."

"How would you know?" he asked.

"How many vampires do you know that would willingly subject themselves to my mother's basement followed by a bingo hall brawl, and a flight in Hank's hunk-of-junk jalopy that ends in a backwoods bunker bastille all to protect their cheese-addicted crazy cat lady of an ex-girlfriend?"

Morrison opened his eyes, revealing irises the mottled orange of cooling magma. "How do you know it's to protect you?"

"What do you mean?"

"What if the only reason I did it is because I get to spend every minute of every day with you? What if every minute I spent with you, I was quietly delighted thinking about Abernathy marinating in his own bitter brew of jealousy and self-pity? What if I secretly hoped that we never get out of this bunker, because at my core, I'm a selfish bastard who would rather be entombed with your corpse for eternity than spend a single moment of my life without you?"

I sat there stunned, feeling like I'd just been bitch-slapped with a frozen trout.

"That's . . . that's a lot to process," I said, my mind frantically ping-ponging between shock, confusion, and a probably deeply unhealthy sense of flattery.

"Try," he rasped, his words barely a whisper as he slumped farther against the door.

We fell into a silence punctuated only by the hum of the beer-sponsored clock, each tick echoing the eventuality of the fate

Morrison had just described. His face seemed to grow gaunter by the second, his cheeks hollower, his eyes more sunken, his lips more cracked and painful.

"James?"

"Mmm?"

"What if you fed from me?" I asked. "Like, just a little bit. Kind of like you said about the 'less than a Red Cross donation' kind of deal."

Morrison shook his head. "Not worth the risk."

"How am I any riskier than the doughnut dude?" I asked, knowing it was ridiculous to feel rejected but feeling it all the same.

"Because I didn't lo—" Morrison stopped abruptly. "Because it hadn't been as long since I fed."

"What if I make my blood less appealing to you?"

"How?" he asked skeptically.

"What I eat affects the flavor of the blood, right?"

"Yes."

"So what if I pounded something really gross?"

"Like what?"

"Uh . . ." I scanned the sparse shelves of the bunker, my eyes landing on a tin of smoked oysters. "How about these?"

Morrison grimaced, which I took as a positive sign. "You're sure?"

Sure?

Absolutely not.

Harboring a metric shit ton of guilt and punchy enough to hope that this might not end disastrously?

Definitely.

"I'm sure," I said, pushing myself up off the floor and crossing to the shelves. "Maybe if you had some of your strength back, we might have a better shot of getting out of here."

Taking a deep breath, I peeled back the lid of the tin, trying not to gag. I quickly downed half the can, shuddering with disgust as they slid into my stomach.

"Okay," I said, wiping my oily fingers on Hank's robe. "How long should we wait for this to take effect?"

Morrison managed a weak shrug. "Ten minutes?"

And lo, what followed was the longest ten minutes of my life.

"Ready?" I asked, holding out my hands to tug him to his feet.

Morrison nodded and slowly sat upright, running a hand through his disheveled hair. His eyes were still ablaze, but now they seemed less like the fury of a volcano and more like the slow burn of embers. His gaze was sharp, predatory, but also so deeply pained that it made my heart twinge in sympathy.

My breath froze in my lungs as Morrison lifted the wild tangle of my air-dried hair from my neck, exposing my jugular. His fingers were cold on my cheek as they gently tilted my head. A strange prickling numbness kissed the tips of my fingers and crawled up my wrists. The rasp of his lips on the sensitive skin of my neck made me shudder in an admittedly not-altogether-unpleasant way. I heard the discreet *schwick* of his fangs emerging, felt the twin points begin to dimple the vein throbbing like a beacon beneath his grip.

Pop.

For an absurd second, I imagined my head popping like a balloon at the puncture point, my busy brain painting the walls a bubble gum pink.

But the intense and sudden compression against my still-intact eardrums informed me that something else altogether had happened.

Crixus, demigod, womanizer, unlikely agent of rescue, stood before us in all his Thor-meets-bad-boy glory.

"Whoa," he said, holding up his hands. "Am I interrupting?"

"*Yesss.*" Morrison's guttural growl startled me so badly that I accidentally headbutted him for the second time since our unlikely escape from the mothman and whatever the fuck had been chasing us through the field.

"Oh shit! Sorry!" I said, whirling around to find him staggering backward. "I'm so, *so* sorry. At least I didn't make you bleed this time."

"Speaking of." Crixus rooted through his bag and tossed a sack at Morrison. "Here."

"What is it?" I asked just in time to see Morrison tear away the brown paper to reveal one of the oblong translucent sacks commonly associated with the blood bank.

"It's not warm, but desperate times and all that," Crixus said.

Morrison moaned in ecstasy as he brought the bag to his lips and punctured it with his fangs like a macabre Capri-Sun. Almost immediately, color came rushing into his skin, his face reinflating like a watered plant.

"Don't suppose you have a double cheeseburger in there," I said.

"Nope," Crixus said, reaching back into his bag. "But I do have these."

To my everlasting astonishment, he produced the pair of boots I'd been wearing when I'd shifted while fleeing through the field, the soles still crusted with the red Texas mud.

"How did you—"

"Picked up the BSA report on my scanner," Crixus said. "But by the time I got there, you were already gone."

"Then how did you find us?" I asked.

"Standard emotional tracker," Crixus replied nonchalantly. "Only your buddy Hank has a signal scrambler, so I had to call in a couple of favors to bypass it."

"I see," I said.

"Luckily, there was a spike in your emotional amplitude just now that made you easier to locate."

I swallowed sand. "I see," I said again.

"I have a safe house arranged for you, but we need to go now."

The slurping sound of Morrison draining the last few drops from the bag proved to be exceedingly effective punctuation.

"Fine," I said. "But can you materialize us outside first?"

"Why?" Crixus asked.

I grabbed the purse Morrison had had the foresight to keep on his person and began lacing up my boots. "Because there's something I need to do."

"As much as Hank deserves to have his intestines made into suspenders, the sooner we get out of here, the sooner I can dispatch the BSA to bring him in for questioning."

"I solemnly swear that I won't harm a hair on his sebum-afflicted scapulas," I promised, getting to my feet.

"Fine," Crixus said. "But it had better be fast."

With a percussive *pop*, we were out in Hank's yard. Even scented of the bayou, the cool breeze was a sweet relief on my fevered skin as I took in several lungfuls.

Thirty seconds later, we were on our way.

But not before I'd opened the coops and watched every single one of Hank's "meat pigeons" climb the night sky.

We arrived at our next destination with a thunderous crack, and the transition was so sudden, so intense yet seamless, I felt like I had just blinked and opened my eyes in a different world.

Mostly because I had.

Before me, a floor-to-ceiling window offered a panoramic view of the Las Vegas strip, the iconic lights and glittering signs momentarily mesmerizing me.

"Whoa," I whispered. "Where are we?"

"Las Vegas," Crixus said, walking around to flip on several lights that bathed the lushly appointed penthouse suite in an expensively ambient glow.

“That part I got,” I said. “*Where* in Las Vegas?”

“I told you.” Crixus pressed a button on a touch screen panel that made blackout curtains whir across the window. “A safe house.”

“And how do you know that it’s safe?” I asked.

“Because it’s mine.”

“You live here?”

“Sometimes,” he said.

I took in the surroundings through this new filter of information. It was half the size of a football field and looked like the kind of place where a movie star or millionaire might bring an illicit lover. All low lights, expensive-looking furniture in dark woods and rich leathers, and museum-quality artwork on the walls. There was even a baby grand piano tucked into one corner.

“You play the piano?” I asked.

Crixus fixed me with one of his trademark wicked grins. “I play everything.”

He gave us a brief walking tour while I filled him in on everything we’d learned from Hank, pointing out the kitchen—wall-to-wall marble and high-end appliances, the bathroom—a travertine tile and a bathtub I fully planned to dog-paddle around in the second he left, the bedroom—a giant four-poster bed that could sleep eight humans wide and three humans deep and probably had.

“Anyway,” I said as we circled back to the foyer, “there’s got to be something to this Freki thing. My gut says that aliens are not involved, but my gut has also been deprived quality carbs for a couple of days, so there’s really no telling.”

“Leave that to me,” Crixus replied, his expression serious. “I’ll follow up with my sources. You two just stay put, and try not to get abducted by any more rogue shifters while I’m gone. I’ll be back later.”

“Fine, fine.” I sighed, already itching to snoop through his pantry. A small, albeit fabulous incentive for lying low.

Crixus paused in the entryway, turning back to face me. "If you check in with Abernathy, I think it would be best if you didn't mention you're here. Or at least, not where *here* is located."

"Why?" I asked, my mind immediately leaping to scenarios involving phone tapping.

"Abernathy's been a little . . . emotionally dysregulated since you left," he said. A term that was clearly flavored by his psychologist situationship and probably a vast understatement. "I've already had to talk him out of coming to find you a couple times and I've got a lot of nice things here I don't want broken."

"Understood," I said. I knew the purpose for said sojourns probably had more to do with breaking *Morrison*, but the idea of being hunted down by a frothing, frantic Abernathy conjured a bubble of warmth in my middle nonetheless.

The front door swung closed, a series of locks automatically sealing us in.

"You want the shower first?" Morrison asked.

"You go ahead," I said, noting the smears of greenish moth guts and darkened blood droplets on his trench coat. I, at least, had had the opportunity to hose myself down after we arrived at Hank's. And anyway, I could use the privacy to make the call I'd been dreading since we'd returned to the realm of cell phone service.

Morrison closed the door to Crixus's bedroom suite, and seconds later, I heard the hush of water coming on.

My palms were already slicked with sweat as I fished my phone from my purse and dialed Abernathy.

In the seconds between hitting the Send button and waiting for his voice to appear on the other end, I dearly wished I had grilled Crixus about what, if anything, Abernathy knew.

It rang somewhere between two and eleventy-seven times before he picked up.

"Where the fuck are you?" Abernathy asked, his voice tense.

"Some way to greet your mate," I said, trying to keep my tone casual.

"Three days, and not a single word from you. Do you have any idea how worried I was?"

"Not really," I said. "The last text I got from you was exactly two letters long."

"How did you wind up in Hank's bunker?"

"It's kind of a long story."

"Summarize."

I launched into what I hoped would be a compelling tale, focusing on the parts he'd hopefully be proud of, glossing over the ones most likely to raise his blood pressure. "—but luckily, I hopped in and gave Morrison the Heimlich before that Chuck Norris wannabe could, or we'd have been a whole other kettle of kippers."

"You *what*?"

Well, shit.

"I couldn't just let him walk around with O22 stuck in his esophagus for all eternity, could I?" I asked. "Just be glad I didn't have to give him CPR."

"He's not even alive!" Abernathy bellowed through the line.

"*They* didn't know that!" I insisted. "You know what would happen if I got a reputation for just leaving a fellow citizen in peril in my own hometown?"

"Someone else will have to sucker punch the chunk of fried catfish out of the applicable gullet at the Cluck n' Fins Corral?" he suggested dryly.

"How very dare you!" I gasped.

And not just because the idea of a post–bingo dinner at the Cluck n' Fins Corral had been floated during our game.

"Where are you now?" Abernathy asked.

"I . . . uh, I can't tell you that," I said, remembering Crixus's earlier admonition.

"Can't or *won't*?" Abernathy shot back, clearly annoyed.

I was silent for a beat too long.

"So be it." The sound of the phone disconnecting seemed to echo through the penthouse suite.

"Ugh," I growled, tossing my phone onto the couch. My anger simmered just below the surface, threatening to boil over.

"Everything okay?" Morrison stood in the door to Crixus's suite, wrapped in a clean white bathrobe and toweling his hair.

"Peachy." Peeling myself from the couch, I padded into the kitchen, where I located the liquor cabinet after only two tries. I selected a mid-shelf whiskey, poured two fingers, dropped in a handful of ice, and marched toward the bathroom. "I'm going to go boil myself in the bathtub."

Whoever Crixus's previous conquests had been, I admired their taste in toiletries.

The bathroom cabinet was an aromatic treasure trove of high-end products. Bottles of Amarige de Givenchy, sandalwood-scented oils, and bars of luxury African black soap with shea butter, rose petal–infused bars from France, even a bar claiming to be made from Swiss Alpine herbs lined the well-organized shelves.

I reached for a jeweled glass decanter full of pink Himalayan bath salts, hoping they were up to the task of unknotting the tension that two days in a bunker followed by a disastrous call with Abernathy had knotted into my muscles.

I eagerly slipped into the steaming tub, relishing the heat as I sank up to my neck and draped a wet washcloth over my face.

Just as I was starting to relax, there was a knock on the door.

"Yeah?"

"Want me to order you some room service?"

Have more seductive syllables been uttered in all the English language?

"Sure," I said. "That'd be great."

"Craving anything in particular?"

This was not the safest question to be asked by an ex-lover while naked and luxuriating in a deliciously scented tub.

"Surprise me," I said.

But exiting the bathroom to find Morrison with his fangs sunk into the neck of the white-coated room service delivery dude wasn't exactly what I'd meant.

I stood welded to the spot, mouth open, breath frozen, and . . . nipples hard?

I'd imagined this exact scenario dozens of times. But *watching* it? Holding eye contact with Morrison as his mouth and tongue worked on the man's smooth, clean-shaven neck?

That was a whole-ass other thing.

And not just because his donor seemed to be enjoying it.

I mean, *really* enjoying it, if his tented trousers were any indication.

Because I remembered.

I remembered the intense, searing connection I'd felt in the castle dungeon before my heart slowed, then stopped. I remembered the sensation of a man I had loved swimming through my bloodstream. I remembered the relief of yielding myself up fully and completely. Of being consumed.

Talk about your unexpected kinks.

Vampire voyeurism.

Who knew?

Morrison suddenly pulled away from the attendant's neck, the wounds sealing over almost instantly.

"—and of course, the complimentary bread basket with creamery butter," the attendant said, picking up the sentence he'd obviously been speaking before falling under Morrison's spell. "Is there anything else I can get you?"

"Not at the moment." Accepting the leather folder and pen,

Morrison wrote in a tip that made the attendant's eyes bug out of his head and run into the wall twice before successfully exiting the door.

"Sorry," he said with a sheepish grin. "I love Peruvian."

I cleared my throat and sat down at the table, lifting off the largest metal dome to find a plate of beautiful eggs Benedict. Peeling off the plastic seal of the miniature Tabasco, I added a healthy sprinkle to the plate of eggs.

"Do you think there could be any truth to what Hank said?"

"Which part?" Morrison asked, raising an eyebrow.

"About the abductions," I said, sticking my fork into the sunny yolk. "The clones."

"You can't be serious."

I shrugged. "Haven't you ever known anyone whose personality underwent an abrupt and inexplicable shift?"

Morrison looked thoughtful for a moment. "Yes. But I'm pretty sure it was the result of a midlife crisis, not because she was actually an alien pod person in disguise."

"Well, when you say it like *that*," I said.

Raising another forkful of eggs to my mouth, I noticed my stomach coiling in protest. A wave of nausea swept over me—a side effect of my lingering ickiness I felt over my call with Abernathy. I tried to swallow the food, anyway, but as the eggs landed in my already churning belly, it felt like I had just consumed a bite of brick instead of a breakfast.

"Are you okay?" Morrison asked, eyeing my mostly untouched eggs.

"Fine." Collecting the miniature jars of jelly and remaining Tabasco, I rose to stash it in my purse. "I think I'm still decompressing from the stress of the last couple of days."

He appeared unconvinced. "When has stress ever made you skip a meal?"

He had a point, I supposed.

A point I elected to ignore altogether, opting instead to investigate the other dishes on the tray.

Additional domes revealed a green salad, a decadent-looking wedge of chocolate cake, and . . . a small creamy card.

Assuming it was either a receipt or tip request, I opened it.

When I read the looping cursive script, my blood turned to ice water.

If you want answers about Freki, follow the Red Fox.

"What in Alice in Wonderland hell?" I handed the note to Morrison, who scanned it quickly.

"Huh," he said, his brow furrowing. "Clue or trap?"

"Knowing my luck, probably the latter." I sighed, my curiosity piqued. "I wish Crixus were here to weigh in."

"No, you don't," Morrison said. "He'd forbid you from investigating."

"True," I admitted.

"So, what's the plan?"

Before I could answer, an eardrum-bloodying alarm began to peal outside the door. Clapping my hands to my ridiculously sensitive ears, I sprinted to the peephole. People were rushing down the corridor, some of them clutching coats and pets.

"I don't think it's a drill," I said.

"Then we'd better move."

"What if it really is a fire?" I asked. "We'll be trapped outside in our bathrobes."

Morrison was a blur of whitewash on the air, rushing into Crixus's closet and coming back fully dressed in the standard Crixus uniform of jeans, a black T-shirt, and boots, all of them just a little baggy on his non-beefcake frame.

To me, he handed a black T-shirt, black drawstring sweats, and a pair of black rubber slides.

"He didn't have one pair of panties in there?" I asked, already unbelting the robe behind Morrison's turned back.

Morrison's scalp shifted on his skull. "Not the kind you'd find especially useful in a fleeing-from-danger situation."

Typical.

Yanking up the pants and tugging the drawstring, I grabbed my purse and phone, and we hustled into the hallway, merging into the stream of humans stampeding to escape. As we neared the emergency exit, a flash of crimson caught my eye.

"Look!" I tugged on Morrison's arm. "That's the same fox furry I saw at Costco!"

This way.

The otherworldly voice echoed inside my head, freezing me in my tracks. Several residents jostled by me, causing Morrison to bare his fangs and hiss at a woman holding a bichon frise who only rolled her eyes at him.

Vegas.

I looked up just in time to see the bushy red tail disappearing through the stairwell door.

"Hurry!" I made it about five steps before I took off the oversize slides and elected to hoof it barefoot.

Finally, after what felt like an eternity of running, we reached the bottom of the staircase and burst into a casino.

But not just any casino.

All the usual accoutrements were present and accounted for.

A sea of slot machines winked and blinked like gaudy Christmas trees, their electronic jingles creating a maddening symphony of sound. Roulette tables and blackjack setups filled with high-rolling hopefuls jostling for elbow room. Poker tables buzzing with an uneasy mix of bravado and desperation. The air was thick with a heady cocktail of disinfectant, perfume, cigar smoke, spilled drinks, and desperation.

Waitresses in skimpy getups sashayed about navigating gamblers hunched over craps tables, clutching dice in sweaty palms like talismans against the fickle goddess of luck. And there were the obligatory high rollers in tables offset from the main action.

There, all similarities ceased.

The entire population seemed to be comprised of supernatural beings, from centaurs playing poker to sirens dealing blackjack. In one corner, an octopus-like creature was manipulating three slot machines at once. A werewolf in a tuxedo manned the roulette wheel, while a group of water nymphs giggled and sipped cocktails at the bar. Ghosts floated above blackjack tables, placing bets and uttering horror movie moans when they lost.

"Toto, I don't think we're in Kansas anymore," I whispered, watching as a trio of goblins hopped onto stools at the craps table.

"Over there!" Morrison pointed toward a shadowy corner of the lobby. Sure enough, the red fox was standing there, her steampunk corset glinting in the dim light.

We darted through the various amusements, my eyes fixed on the sight of that retreating puffy tail.

At last, we approached a dimly lit corridor filled with the hypnotic pulsing of trance music. The atmosphere was electric, shimmering the close air like a palpable current.

I watched as the fox's tail disappeared between a pair of black velvet curtains, the music swelling for a single second as they parted.

Morrison and I stopped, giving each other a prolonged look.

"Anything happens, you shift and run, got it?"

I nodded, too full of adrenaline to disagree.

Morrison moved in front of me, parting the curtains.

What I saw on the other side stole my breath.

A cathedral.

Of the gothic variety. Soaring arches crested overhead, ribbed pillars reaching up to the heavens, intricate stone carvings of gargoyles lining the walls, and giant stained glass windows depicting scenes of myth and folklore painted everything in shades of violet and cobalt blue. Delicate, ethereal, and otherworldly, it shimmered in the dim night light like a mirage, illuminated by the soft glow of hundreds of candles.

A cavernous dance floor draped in shadows, where bodies moved in a writhing mass, fluorescing in the blacklight saturated air.

Crowds of vampires lounged on velvet sofas nestled between the pillars, sipping blood from delicate crystal glasses as if it were fine wine. Others floated effortlessly in cages midair, their white skin and black clothes a dizzying contrast.

"Welcome to the Blood Moon Lounge," purred the goth-styled vampire door attendant, his voice honeyed but with a dangerous edge. He eyed me up and down, his silvery gaze lingering on my baggy, borrowed clothing. "There's a dress code for entry, darling."

"Dress code?" Morrison repeated.

"Relax, love," he replied, smirking at Morrison. "The dress code isn't for you. It's for her. We've got rentals, if you didn't bring your own."

"My own what?" I asked.

"Leather, love," he replied, his smirk deepening. "We don't allow jeans and flannel here, unless you're part of a lumbersnack-themed night, and that's not until next week."

I frowned at him, my brows knotting together.

"Wait. You're not . . . first timers, are you?"

"Uh . . . yeah?" I said.

"Why didn't you say so!" He clapped his hands with glee, revealing a pair of black leather gloves that increased my anxiety by a factor of ten. "First timers need to know the house rules. Rule number one: No biting without consent. Rule number two: No blood play in the dance floor area. It's been seven months since our last fall-related lawsuit, and we're trying to keep it that way. Rule number three: Humans must be leashed unless in the designated off-leash play area." He pointed into the crowd where I saw a roped-off section with scantily clad bodies cavorting beneath a crimson spray.

"Got it," I said. "Where can I find these 'rentals'?"

"Right this way, darling," he said, beckoning me to follow him into a small side room filled with racks of clothing that left little to the imagination. As I reluctantly picked out a skimpy leather bra and panties, a harness, and thigh-high platform boots, I couldn't help but wonder how I'd gotten myself into this mess.

"Ready or not," I called out as I stepped out of the dressing room, feeling absurdly exposed and off-balance in the heels. My cheeks burned as I met Morrison's gaze.

"Fuck," he breathed, his eyes shamelessly roaming my body. "You look . . . incredible."

"Thanks, I feel ridiculous," I muttered, trying to ignore the heat pooling between my legs at the intense heat baking from his gaze. "Let's just find the fox and get some answers."

"Agreed." He offered me his arm, and I gratefully took it, steadying myself as we approached the entrance once more.

"Very nice," the vampire attendant purred as he appraised my new ensemble.

Just as we were about to step through the doorway, the attendant raised a hand, stopping us in our tracks. "One more thing," he said, pointing to a sign mounted on the wall.

The fine print listed an assortment of rules and regulations, but one bullet point stood out above all others: "All human guests must consume Ecstasy and be accompanied by a vampire who will drink from them."

"Wait, what?" My heart raced as I looked back at the attendant, hoping against hope that I'd misunderstood. But his knowing smirk told me everything I needed to know.

"Club policy," he said with a shrug. "It's for your own safety, really. Humans have a tendency to freak out when they see vampires feeding, and it can ruin the vibe." He opened a small silver box and held out a small red pill. "Take this, darling."

I looked at the pill, back at the vampire, then over to Morrison.

"Is there any way we can, you know, *not* do that?" I asked hesitantly, glancing over at Morrison. He looked uncomfortable, his hazel eyes flicking between me and the host. "Seeing as I'm not strictly hu—"

A sudden stinging pain in my left butt cheek made me suck the rest of the sentence down on a gasp. Morrison gave me a pointed look.

"Not strictly . . . uh . . . hubric enough to think anyone would even want to drink my blood."

"Sorry, love," the attendant replied, his tone dripping with insincerity. "Rules are rules."

I sighed, weighing my options. On one hand, letting Morrison feed on me while under the influence of Ecstasy sounded like a recipe for disaster—not to mention incredibly intimate. On the other hand, the red fox might be our only lead to unraveling the mystery of FREKI.

Morrison frowned, glancing down at the pill, then back to me. "You don't have to do this, you know. We can leave right now."

Looking past the host, I spotted the fox climbing a set of spiral stairs.

"No," I said. "I'm going in."

I closed my eyes, opened my mouth, and felt the nearly weightless pressure on my tongue.

"Enjoy your time at the Blood Moon Lounge." He clipped the leash around my neck and handed the loop to Morrison. "I hope you find what you're looking for."

As the bitter pill dissolved on my tongue, I couldn't help but wonder if what I was looking for would be worth the price we were about to pay.

15

The pulsating bass throbbed through the room like the heartbeat that so many of its occupants lacked as Morrison led me through the crush of bodies and into a long corridor. The rooms on either side offered vignettes of an all-you-can-drink buffet of hedonism, with vampires and humans alike indulging in all manner of blood-related kinks.

In one, a completely nude woman sat spread-eagle atop a piano, the vampire maestro's hands masterfully flying over the keys as he drank from her femoral vein.

In another, a burlesque dancer twirled in midair on a crescent moon–shaped lyra, feathered fans fluttering around her as a vamp clamped down on her ankle spun above the mesmerized crowd.

"Every now and then, it occurs to me just how vanilla I really am," I said, tearing my eyes away from the sight of a man stretched into an *X*, vampires with their mouths fastened to each of the silver suspension hooks sunk into his skin.

"Maybe you've just never been presented with the right opportunity," Morrison said.

I swallowed hard as we approached an ornate gilt door that the red fox had disappeared through at the end of the hallway.

"Ready?" Morrison asked, his hazel eyes searching mine.

"As I'll ever be," I replied, trying to sound braver than I felt.

Morrison turned the oversize handle and pushed the door open, revealing a space that could only be described as *Eyes Wide Shut* meets *Bram Stoker's Dracula*.

Thousands of candles bathed the room in flickering amber light, catching shards of the giant crystal chandeliers sparkling overhead. Plush velvet couches lined the walls and alcoves, occupied by vampires engaging in various carnal acts with their human pets. In the center of the gleaming marble floor, a group of humans wearing outfits similar to mine gathered around a raised dais. Disciples worshiping at the altar of some depraved god.

Then they parted, and my jaw dropped.

Lounging on a chaise lounge on the platform was none other than Oscar Wilde.

Dressed in flamboyant eggplant-purple pajamas that looked like they might have been lifted from Prince's closet, Oscar's face was much as I remembered it, save for a few not-so-minor details.

Like the scars.

A thick, silvery worm of skin bisected one heavy-lidded eye, the color of his iris an eerie white-blue. On the opposite side of his face, a puckered cavern below his prominent cheekbone tugged one corner of his over-sensuous lips into a perma-smirk.

Reminders of the London brawl with Abernathy that had changed all our lives.

"Dearest Hanna," Oscar said, his voice melodious and languid, like honey dripping off a spoon. "What a delightful surprise."

"Surprise?" I questioned, feeling the hairs on the back of my neck stand up. "But weren't you the one who sent me that note?"

"Note?" His curious expression was authentic enough to wake me to the staggering leap of assumption I'd made.

Encountering Wilde again in this context had all the hallmarks of their first nearly-fatal meeting. The showdown. The moment when all the latches and levers his clever, cunning mind had engineered to deliver me into his hands had clicked into place. In the thrall of that strange echo, I'd been willing to assign him credit for all.

Once a megalomaniacal, machinating master puppeteer, and all that.

"Never mind," I said.

"I never do," he replied, flashing a mischievous smile. "I must say, your taste has certainly improved since our last encounter." His eyes moved over Morrison in a languid leer. "Come, let us celebrate your arrival."

He gestured to a muscular man wearing only a bejeweled bunny mask and matching banana hammock. He stepped forward, proffering a tray packed with a mouthwatering assortment of energy-restoring delights, from miniature lobster truffle mac and cheese to ever-so-tempting Brie and raspberry en croûte.

"Thanks," I said, actively swallowing saliva, "but I already had dinner. Couldn't eat another bite."

"I don't suppose you'd like to describe it to me," Oscar said, toying with the tassels of the brocade pillow he was propped on. "For old times' sake."

"If memory serves, you tried to murder me after the old time in question."

"*Experience* is simply the name we give to our mistakes," he said with a sheepish shrug. "A libation instead, perhaps?"

He waved a hand toward the opposite side of the dais, where an equally ripped man in a similarly blinged-out thong and cat mask held a tray with a bottle and several green glass goblets.

"Pass," I said, raising an eyebrow. "I had whiskey earlier, and mixing liquors gives me a terrible hangover these days."

"Ah, but this is no ordinary vintage, my dear." Oscar swung his silk-clad legs over the side of the chaise. "It's a special blend designed to enhance one's experience of the senses."

"I'm pretty sure I already took something that's designed to do that," I said. "Besides, my mother taught me never to accept strange beverages from undead playwrights."

Disco Cat knelt beside the chaise with his tray.

"Ah, but you and your charming mother have already partaken of this particular beverage, my dear." Oscar pulled the cork from the bottle with a flourish and began pouring. The scent wafted toward me, strangely familiar.

Sun-warmed honeysuckle. Summer meadows.

Recognition arrived with a synaptic snap as my eyes fixed on the liquid sunset filling the goblet.

Morg's elderberry mead. The odd, disembodying draft.

"But . . . how?" I stammered.

"To drink deeply of the mysteries before us, one must first be prepared to taste them." Oscar studied the glass as he swirled it, meeting my eyes above the thick rim. "Morg wasn't prepared."

"You mean, you poisoned him?"

"How delightfully dramatic!" Oscar chuckled, his eyes sparkling with amusement. "Yes, he was poisoned, but not by me."

"Then who did?" I pressed.

"Dear Hanna." Oscar sighed and rose from the chaise. "Always so inquisitive."

The candlelight caught the gold thread on his monogrammed slippers as he descended the few steps and began to circle me like a shark. "I might be willing to share that information with you. Provided you're willing to share something with me in return."

"What's that?" I asked.

Wilde stopped his circuit directly in front of me. "Your blood."

"Absolutely not," Morrison interjected, stepping protectively between us. "We can't trust him, Hanna."

"Perhaps not," Oscar conceded with a smirk. "But you can trust my self-interest."

"Keep talking," Morrison said.

"As you know, I rather enjoy the company of earnest-appearing gentlemen such as yourself."

"And?" Morrison asked.

"Provided you can trust yourself as much as you mistrust me, perhaps *you* could be the vessel," Oscar suggested. "Seeing as you and I are afflicted with the same quixotic quirk of nature, you're amply capable of extracting what I seek, but far less likely to succumb to my appetites. Unless, of course, you'd *like* to succumb to my appetites." He winked at Morrison. "Which I'm not at all opposed to."

Morrison stiffened.

"Sounds good to me," I said.

Because all of a sudden, it *did* sound good. In fact, *everything* sounded good.

Like, *really* good. Like *every cell of my body brimming with boundless love for all creation* good.

"Splendid," Oscar purred, his eyes gleaming with anticipation.

"Are you sure about this, Hanna?" Morrison asked, concern etched on his face.

"See, that's the thing." I held up a finger for emphasis, then noticed just how exquisitely beautiful the rhinestones on the winebearer's cat mask were and promptly lost track of what that "thing" was supposed to be. "What was the question?"

"Are you sure that you want me to feed from you and let a vampire who once tried to kill you drink your blood from me in exchange for answers about a mysterious entity who poisoned the duly elected leader of the Sasquatch during your surprise birthday party for Abernathy?"

"Oh, right! Thing is, everything in the universe is, like, experience. And even experiences that might seem bad at the time can bring us truths we wouldn't have learned otherwise. And those truths end up enriching our lives in ways that not only benefit us but everyone around us. So when you think about it, there's really no such thing as a wrong choice. Whether you're a werewolf or a vampire or . . . or whatever the hell that thing is," I said, pointing to Rave Rabbit. "It's like a choose-your-own-adventure book, but life-size and in 3D."

I looked around the room for approval and was pleased when a knot of copulating humans and vampires was nodding along with me. Confident that I was making perfect sense, I continued.

"When you think about it, letting you drink from me and Oscar drink from you is really the most natural thing in the world. Since our consciousness is really the universe experiencing itself, separation is really just an illusion, anyway, you know?"

Morrison's eyes narrowed. "You're totally fucked up right now."

"But I'm not," I insisted. "For the first time in my life, I feel totally *un*-fucked. I want you to feel that too."

I lifted the hair from my neck and tilted my head to provide him with easier access.

With a nod of acceptance, Morrison approached me. The entire room seemed to fall silent, all eyes on us. In that pocket of pin-drop stillness, the deep and abiding sense of well-being continued to course through my veins, making every nerve ending tingle with anticipation.

"God help me," Morrison whispered, sending shivers down my spine. His lips brushed against the curve of my neck, teasing the sensitive skin there before his fangs sank into me.

A gasp escaped me, followed by a surge of pleasure that washed over my body like a tidal wave. My entire being seemed to vibrate with a primal need, and I couldn't help but lean in to him, craving more. It felt as if our souls were intertwining, connecting on a level deeper than physical touch.

With a soul-deep groan, Morrison pulled away, a single trickle of blood darkening the corner of his lips. He looked at me with a mix of such acute longing that, for a moment, I almost forgot we had an audience.

"Come here, Wilde," he said, tearing his gaze from mine. There was a feral, dangerous edge to his voice that sent another shiver down my spine.

"Gladly," Oscar declared, kissing Morrison's offered wrist before sinking his fangs into the flesh.

The room seemed to hold its collective breath as he drank, and I felt an odd, vicarious thrill course through me at the sight.

Morrison's face contorted with mingled pain and pleasure, his body tensing as though fighting to maintain control.

Meanwhile, I'd utterly surrendered mine.

Hunger stormed through me like dragon fire, igniting my most sensitive places with its purifying breath. And it felt so good. So good, to simply let my body feel what it felt, want what it wanted, crave what it craved.

"Stop," Morrison choked out.

But Oscar didn't stop.

"Enough," Morrison repeated, more forcefully this time, and the sound of his voice seemed to snap Oscar out of his trance. He released Morrison's wrist, but remained exactly where he was, eyes fastened shut as he began to speak.

"Her blood as sweet as honeyed wine,
It sets my senses all a-twirl,
One taste enough to make me pine,
For this enchanting lycan girl."

"You said it, brother." Morrison clapped Oscar on the back. "That is some sweet shit."

I wondered if he, too, wasn't feeling the effects of what I'd consumed.

"Right, well, it's your turn now," I reminded him, struggling to focus. "You promised me answers."

"That I did." Oscar dabbed the remaining blood from his lips with a handkerchief and returned to his chaise. "Ask away, my dear."

"Who killed Morg?"

"Morg killed . . . himself."

My mouth dropped open, the liquid warmth shrinking farther toward my center. "What?"

"Took the poison he was supposed to give to you," Oscar continued.

"Why would he do that?" I asked.

"Because they'd have killed him otherwise." Oscar's hand floated up to pet Disco Cat's muscular thigh. "And likely in a far more painful way."

"Who are *they*?" I demanded.

"Freki," Oscar said.

"Wait, so Freki is more than one person?" I asked, growing more confused by the second.

"Freki is many people."

I massaged my temples, hoping to rub some IQ points back in. "You're not making any sense."

"What's your connection to Freki?" This question came courtesy of Morrison, whose eyes seemed to have sharpened over the last several seconds.

"The same as all of Freki's followers," Oscar said, finally peeling his eyes open to look at me. "Freki despises you as much as we do."

The iridescent bubble of my mood popped, leaving me feeling naked, and foolish.

There were so many parts of his sentence that bothered me that I didn't even know where to start.

Freki despised me. Freki had many followers who also despised me. Freki, and Freki's many followers who despised me, despised me enough to want me dead. Some of those followers who despised me enough to want me dead had obviously volunteered to un-alive me. At least one of those followers had allegedly un-alived himself so as not to be torn to bits by the fanatical legion whose unifying credo involved my violent and/or exceedingly unpleasant death.

This wealth of data gathered in my brain, but only two choked words emerged as a result. "But . . . why?"

"Hmm?" Oscar grunted.

"Why do they despise me so much?"

"Well," Oscar began.

"I mean, I know that I interrupt people, and that I talk about cheese way too much, and say 'like' more often than a circa 1990s Valley girl, and sometimes I get that popping sound in my jaw when it's damp outside, and should probably stop showing pictures of my cats to total strangers, but I also almost always let people with fewer items cut me in the grocery store line, and I hold the door for strollers, and I've been sponsoring a horse with dwarfism named Munchie for the last five years!"

"Actually," Oscar said. "It's more—"

"Not to mention the birds I feed, and the grocery carts I return, and the carry-on luggage I always have arranged for maximum efficiency in the screening line."

"Yes, well—"

"And this is to say *nothing* of the fact that I took on a completely unpaid position that requires me to donate my time and energy to establish peace and plenty among a group of wildly ungrateful nonhumans who do nothing but complain about everything I could do better without making a single shred of effort to be of actual assistance. So, come to think of it, you, Hank, Maureen, Freki, and all their followers can kiss my furry fanny—and I mean that in the strictly American linguistic usage, because *I* am a goddamn delight!"

Oscar was silent for an extended beat.

When he spoke, his answer was so far removed from what I'd expected to hear that it took me a full minute to process it.

"In this life, perhaps."

"Excuse me?" I finally said.

"In this life," he repeated. Disco Cat had surrendered his tray and was now draped over Oscar's lap emitting an alarming purring noise as Oscar stroked behind his ear.

"Perhaps part of the reason you seem to be so obsessed with people liking you is that, on some level, you're aware that they've had good reason not to."

The room spun. Maybe it was the Ecstasy, or maybe it was the shock of the revelation, but suddenly, I found myself doubled over, fighting a wave of nausea.

"As for me, when Freki approached me about assisting with their little project because of my connections in the cryptid community, I was all too happy to lend my efforts to the cause. Just as I'll be happy to lend them to yours . . ." He trailed off, running a lazy finger over one of the bejeweled ears. "If the price is right."

"You're offering to betray Freki in exchange for a bribe?" Morrison asked.

I found myself immeasurably grateful for Morrison's brass tacks tendency to summarize in the least flowery way possible.

"Quite," Oscar said.

"And why should I believe you?" I asked. "Seeing as you apparently also despise me and have been secretly plotting against me?"

"A true friend stabs you in the front," Oscar said, quoting himself yet again. "I am here, showing you my hand, offering my wares rather than hiding behind a thousand faces."

"A thousand?" I repeated. "Is there really—"

"What do you want?" Morrison asked, once again cutting to the quick.

"Nothing much." Oscar leaned back and pillowed his arms behind his head. "Shall we say, dinner and a show?"

"I don't follow," I said.

Oscar sat up with a harried sigh, causing his boy toy to slide off to the floor. "I'd like to watch the two of you fuck each other and sample more of your sanguine sangria after you're through. Betrayal for betrayal. Seems fair enough to me."

"In exchange for what?" Morrison asked.

"In exchange for information." Oscar leaned forward conspiratorially, his voice dropping to a whisper. "I'll tell you what they want. What they have planned. In fact, as an act of good faith, I'll even tell you their true name. It's—"

A brief red blur sliced across my hazy vision.

Oscar Wilde blinked, glanced down at the blood gushing from his neck and darkening his smoking jacket, and uttered a "That's odd," before his head slid from his shoulders and bounced down the dais steps.

Time seemed to slow as the head rolled end over end like a bowling ball, coming to rest near my feet.

"Bugger," Oscar said, lifting his eyes to mine. "This is going to be quite the inconvenience."

Having finally digested what had just happened, I glanced back to the dais where Oscar's beefcake boy toys were hissing and snarling at the red fox, who still brandished a silver blade.

At first, I assumed the loud crash and shouted commands echoed from outside the room were from some kind of security who must have witnessed Oscar's decapitation through a video feed.

But as the shouts and screams filtered through my still-somewhat impaired consciousness, three letters sifted to the surface.

BSA.

"It's a raid!" someone shouted.

Chaos erupted around us as vampires and humans alike scrambled for cover or escape routes.

"Fuck," Morrison growled, grabbing my hand. "We need to get out of here."

"Agreed," I said, casting one last glance at Oscar's decapitated head. "But where?"

Follow me.

The red fox's voice filled my head, drowning out all else.

As much as I feared getting nabbed by the BSA, I also couldn't summon much enthusiasm for a furry who had recently decapitated an immortal.

"Quickly!" The red fox grabbed me by the arm and yanked me behind the curtains, Morrison following close behind. I could hear the BSA agents entering the VIV room, their radios quacking a staticky "Is she there?" as the echoes of their boots on the marble grew closer.

Inexplicably, they marched right by us, the breeze from their flight cooling the sweat blooming on my forehead and cheeks.

I hadn't even completed my epic exhale when the fox grabbed me. One padded paw muffling my mouth, the other anchored around my waist as she hip-checked open a hidden door.

We half lunged and half tumbled through it and went down hard in a tangled heap.

I was still trying to extract myself when I heard the instantly recognizable *click*.

Morrison was already moving, putting himself between me and the unmistakable sound of a gun safety being disengaged.

Dan Davis.

Emerging from the shadows, his gun cocked directly between my eyes. "Well done, Vada," he said, a smug smile stretching his lips.

Vada?

My nostrils flared, sifting the air for any trace of the smoky sandalwood aroma I'd come to associate with that name.

"Don't bother," Dan said. "Your pathetic powers are no match for ours."

As if in demonstration, the fox's faux fur began to bristle, the oversize anime eyes and pointy ears shrinking until they formed the familiar features of Sasquatch Sips' leonine ladydom barista.

"I thought we were saving the big reveal for *after* the kidnapping," she said tersely.

"Apologies," Dan said, his eyes briefly flashing a reptilian yellow with elongated vertical pupils. "I've just been waiting for this moment for so long."

"What the furry fuck *are* you?" My Ecstasy-addled mind scrambled to untangle the mess of information that had just been dumped into my lap. Vada. Dan. Oscar Wilde. Sasquatch.

Vada grabbed me by the upper arm and roughly turned me to face Dan. "You'll find out soon enough."

"Come," Dan said, pointing our way with the gun's muzzle. "The Guild awaits."

16

Pain.

Acres and acres of it, throbbing behind my eyes, gnawing at my fingertips, burrowing into my lower back.

I blinked my gritty lids against the dim light, hoping for a brief, strange interval that this was only a horrific new nightmare.

At any moment, I'd hear Abernathy grunt beside me. Feel the warm, reassuring weight of his hand on my cheek. See the familiar shapes of our darkened bedroom assembling around me.

None of that happened.

But even as my surroundings swam into focus, I struggled to make sense of them.

A circular stone floor painted with runes I recognized from my random encounters of them in the wild.

A platform in the center of the circle.

My feet on the platform.

Rope around my ankles.

Rope around my wrists.

My wrists above my head.

My head resting against something blunt but hard.

The same blunt, hard thing between my shoulder blades.

A pole?

My wrists chafed against the rough rope as I struggled to free myself, each movement sending waves of hot, searing agony through my stiff muscles. Fear began to creep in, replacing my initial disorientation with icy tendrils that wrapped around my heart.

My eyes darted around the room, desperate for any sign of help or familiarity.

Which was when I discovered that I wasn't alone.

Morrison stood with his back to me, his posture ramrod straight, his nose pressed to a wall like a naughty schoolboy.

Peeling my tongue from the roof of my mouth, I hissed a "Psst!" that Morrison either didn't hear or wouldn't acknowledge.

"He's in time-out." The smooth, sonorous male voice brought everything back to me in an unwelcome flood.

Dan.

The gun. The kidnapping. The Guild.

The . . . robe?

Crushed velvet and a little too short for his lanky frame, the robe's hem fluttered against his calves as he dropped a pile of wood near the platform's base.

"For what?" The words came out as a harsh whisper.

"For being a disingenuous, deceitful swine," Dan said crisply.

"Got your boxers in a bunch because your bro-crush was really just mining you for information?" I guessed.

"No," Dan insisted a little too quickly. "Just deeply disappointed that a gentlemen's agreement means so little to a self-professed cryptid sympathizer."

Looking at Morrison's stiff form, I felt a stab of gratitude. For the man he was. For all he'd done on my behalf just to end up in yet another sticky snarl of circumstance.

"Still," Dan continued. "This momentous occasion wouldn't have been possible without him."

"Momentous?" I asked, my fear momentarily eclipsed by irritation. "I mean, I get that a LARP gathering requires a lot of coordination, but that's overstating it a hair, don't you think?"

His smug smile slipped from its moorings. "You dare compare our sacred ritual to a *game*?"

"What other choice do I have?" I asked, wriggling my foot in increments I hoped he wouldn't notice. "It's not like you've been very forthcoming with the details."

He chuckled darkly. "If you really were the rightful alpha, you would know them already. I'll bet you haven't even read the prophecy."

"If I did, I must have missed the part where the chosen one would be a coffee simp with a dino porn fetish."

"Your mockery is beneath me," he sneered. "Freki's power is far beyond your comprehension."

"Speaking of things beyond comprehension," I said, trying to keep my voice steady as I attempted to distract myself from the fact that I was still very much tied up and very much panicking, "how did a man of science such as yourself abandon your empirical principles in favor of superstition?"

Dan's dark eyes narrowed. "It was *I* who was abandoned. By my academic advisor. By my colleagues. Laughed out of symposia because I dared speak the truth that's been staring science in the face for millennia. That Homo sapiens share the planet with beings older and far more sophisticated than they can begin to imagine. That they owe us their allegiance."

Oddly, it was the *they* that caught me.

"So, uh, weird question," I said. "But aren't *you* Homo sapiens?"

Dan lifted his chin a notch. "Freki has promised to make me in their image. As a reward for my faith."

"Gotcha," I said. "You do remember what happened to Renfield, right?" I asked, already mentally reviewing the short list of supernatural species capable of expanding their numbers via corporeal conversion.

"Scorn if you will," Dan said. "But paranormal beings *will* take their place as the rightful rulers of the earth as Freki has prophesied. And as one who's studied the extinction of some of this planet's most remarkable species, I believe that time can't come quickly enough. Every day that humans are allowed to retain the belief that this planet belongs to them is one day closer to catastrophic planetary holocaust."

As much as I hated to admit it, I didn't necessarily disagree with Dan's evaluation, if not his species-driven genocidal game plan.

"Would you stop boring poor Hanna with your heat-death-of-the-universe spiel and finish bringing in the firewood?" If Dan's cloak was Spirit Halloween store, Vada's beautifully cut floor-length garment was bespoke Burberry. She brushed splinters from the crimson velvet as she set a large leather tome on an ornate stand directly opposite me. "And what's with the overhead half hitch?" she asked, gracefully leaping up to the platform behind me. "Just because Freki wants her as a sacrifice doesn't mean the last moments of her life need to be uncomfortable."

A sentence that didn't exactly fill me with optimism.

"Sorry about that," Vada said as my arms dropped to my sides, numb and limp as noodles.

My hands felt alternately hot and cold as blood rushed back into them, my fingertips prickling as she gently guided them behind my back. "New recruits tend to be a little evangelical," she said. "I personally think Shibari should be part of the required curriculum."

I wasn't certain what role the art of Japanese rope bondage played in Freki's congregation, but I found myself immeasurably grateful for this small courtesy.

Last moments of my life or no.

"Better?" she asked.

"Much," I said, flexing my fingers against the silky wood. "How long have you been part of the faith?"

Vada's cape billowed out like a sail as she stooped to grab several logs and returned to stack them around the platform's base. "Since there *was* a faith, pretty much."

"No way," I said, injecting my voice with as much enthusiasm as my reduced lung capacity would allow. "Really?"

"Really. In fact—"

"You're stacking those wrong, you know." Dan bustled over and set down his log load, several inches of pale, hairy ankle visible as he knelt to rearrange the pile. "To cultivate a suitable combustion, it is imperative that one increase the convective flow of gases to sustain an optimal fuel-to-oxygen ratio as dictated by the first and second laws of thermodynamics."

"I'm sorry, did you just mansplain *fire* to me?" Vada's eyes narrowed dangerously as she turned to face him. "In case you've forgotten, only one of us actually lived through the Salem witch trials, and last time I checked, it wasn't you, bone boy."

"Wait, you were at the Salem witch trials?" I asked Vada, my curiosity momentarily overriding my fear. "What was that like?"

"Terrible food and even worse hygiene," she replied, rolling her eyes. "I wouldn't want to be part of the sequel."

"So, are you?" I asked.

Vada's eyes flicked upward. "Am I what?"

"A witch?"

The fetching dimple in Vada's cheek winked as she smirked.

"You don't have to answer if you don't want to," I said. "But if I'm mathing right, that would make you at least three hundred and thirty, and you look kind of amazing, so—"

"*Sycophant*," Dan coughed.

"Says the guy who traded details about the local wolf pack to Freki in exchange for a business loan," muttered Vada.

Suddenly, all kinds of things were making sense.

Dan's sniffing around the gallery. His inviting Steve to join this mysterious "guild."

"At least I didn't stage a fake furry fight at a suburban big-box retailer so one of my minions could poison some pastry," Dan spat, his ears reddening.

"It wasn't poison, it was *potion*," Vada argued. "And you try distracting a legendarily violent and volatile male werewolf in broad daylight long enough to lace four dozen goat cheese tartlets with an obedience draft."

"Obedience draft?" I asked, ignoring the ache in my middle that had nothing at all to do with the giant wooden pole at my back.

"Basically renders anyone who consumes it unable to act in a manner counter to Vada's will," Dan explained. "We figured the gallery show was a perfect opportunity to dose everyone associated with the Crossing just in case."

"But did you *have* to kill the caterer?" Vada asked, stooping to rearrange the logs Dan had just finished propping up. "His black truffle buckwheat blintzes were *bomb* as fuck."

"You . . . killed Jacques?" I asked, experiencing a stab of guilt for all the unkind thoughts I'd had about the flamboyant Frenchman.

"Technically, *you* killed Jacques." Dan's cape toss would have been far more dramatic had the sewn-in care instructions tag not flashed from the seam.

"How do you figure?" I asked.

"I had him trapped in a closet and called you to refuse the job, but you never picked up," Dan said with a shrug. "I couldn't take the risk."

"So is that why Morrison's not moving?" I asked, feeling icy tendrils of panic begin to slither through my veins. "The obedience draft?"

"Affirmative," Dan said.

"But Morrison couldn't eat any of the gallery show snacks or drink the coffee that I'm guessing you also dosed. How could you have given him any of the potion?"

"We didn't," Dan interrupted, looking rather pleased with himself. "*You* did."

"Bullshit," I said. "I would never—"

But I hadn't even finished the sentence before the images came to me, complete and clear.

Me, drinking the only available hydration source in Hank's bunker. Crixus interrupting the moment when I'd nearly let Morrison feed from me.

Me, taking the little red pill, obediently offering my neck at Oscar Wilde's insistence.

"Why don't you come on out and join us, Detective Morrison?" Dan invited.

Morrison's body lurched away from the wall, and with jerky, zombielike steps, he turned to face us. Despite the naked fury blazing in his eyes, the sight of him so utterly powerless only heightened my growing sense of dread.

"Why can't he speak?" I asked.

"Oh, he can," Vada said. "Dan was experiencing auditory overstimulation from all the threats and whatnot, so I put him on mute for a bit." She waved a gloved hand at Morrison, who apparently picked up right where he'd left off.

"—touch her, and I'll break you in half and shove your own head so far up your ass, you'll be tasting what you ate last week."

"Puh-lease," Dan scoffed. "Even if that were physiologically possible, efficient digestion is one of the many benefits of a raw vegan diet. Try again, troglodyte."

Without warning, Morrison surged forward, fist raised to strike. His arm froze mid-swing, his breath coming in ragged gasps as he battled to finish the blow.

"What the eff, V?" Dan, who had nearly tripped over his own cape cartoonish scramble backward, turned prolapse purple.

"Oops," Vada said. "I guess I forgot not to want you to get punched in the face for a second."

"And did you also forget that I am the Chosen One?" Dan demanded.

"How the hell have you not zapped him with anal warts?" I asked Vada, tilting my head toward Dan. "He'd be insufferable even if you were an entry-level barista as opposed to a clearly powerful and infinitely creative sorceress."

"Dude." She heaved a long-suffering sigh. "You have no idea."

"Meanwhile, what is it with men and the whole villain monologue thing?" I asked.

"Oh, I *know*," Vada said, setting an ornate silver dagger on top of the stand with the grimoire. "Can't even carry out a simple coup without needing to bloviate about their brilliance."

"I wasn't bloviating," Dan pouted petulantly. "Hanna *asked* me."

"Of course she did," Vada said. "She probably knew that the longer she kept you talking, the more likely you were to let something vital slip. It's a wonder you didn't give her the recipe for the potion antidote."

I felt my heart beat a little faster in my chest.

Guilty as charged.

Worse, the little hamster in my brain was already jogging on the How to Get the Recipe for the Antidote wheel.

Vada scrubbed her hands together, stepping back to assess the setup. "Well, I think we're about ready for the guest of honor."

"Freki?" I asked, the pit in my stomach deepening into a cavern.

"Not quite."

Two syllables of that deep, smoky voice were sufficient to reorganize the entirety of my inner landscape.

Fear into faith. Despair into delight. Rage into relief.

Abernathy's eyes glowed a menacing reddish gold as he stepped from the shadows, his entire body a hulking knot of barely restrained wrath. He didn't look at me. Didn't even acknowledge my presence.

And though I knew it was ridiculous under my present circumstances, I felt a dull ache in my chest.

Abernathy's muscles rippled beneath his shirt, the telltale sign that he was seconds away from shifting into the giant, dark wolf that made its den in my soul.

"Ah, ah, ah," Dan chided, wagging a finger at him. "I wouldn't do that if I were you."

"Why not?" Abernathy snarled, his bones already beginning to crack and pop.

With a flick of Dan's wrist, the curtains at the back of the room were flung aside, and several figures in hooded black cloaks marched mechanically into view, their movements eerily synchronized as they surrounded the circle of runes where I stood staked like some kind of kinky rotisserie chicken.

"Meet our new acolytes," Dan announced, gesturing grandly toward the procession. "They'll be making sure you don't interfere with our little ceremony here."

In unison, they pulled back their hoods, and my heart sputtered and died within my chest.

Steve.

Shayla.

Helena.

Kirkpatrick.

My mother.

They all stared straight forward, their eyes dull, their faces blank.

"You know what to do," Dan instructed them coldly. "If Abernathy tries anything, kill him."

Despair settled over me like a lead blanket, smothering whatever hope had been kindled by Abernathy's arrival.

Abernathy could do nothing to save me without having to harm someone I loved.

Okay, well, didn't exactly despise, in Helena and Kirkpatrick's case.

It was brilliant.

It was diabolical.

It was—

"*Freki*," came the eerie chant from all around me at once.

Another crimson-cloaked figure had appeared next to Vada.

Tall and slender. Most assuredly feminine.

Long, elegant hands rose to the cloth, drawing back the hood.

Our eyes met, and I fell backward in time. To the restroom doorway where we'd first crossed paths, then to the hotel lobby in Germany.

Then further.

Flashes of places, of faces, of flames, of fury.

Of *her*.

Abernathy's sister, Katherine.

It was strangely unsettling to see such virulent hatred directed at me from a face whose features reminded me so much of the one I loved.

Katherine was as beautiful as I remembered.

More so, maybe.

Long waves of hair a slightly more reddish variation of Abernathy's chocolate brown fell down around her shoulders. A more delicate version of Abernathy's angular jaw and prominent cheekbones. The kind of flawless complexion that typically only filters could produce. A beauty mark above lips that influencers would screenshot and flash at their aestheticians before going under the needle.

Her eyes, however, were where the similarities ended. Wider than Abernathy's, they were the color of arctic ice and twice as cold. They harbored a ferocity, a bleak intensity that instantly communicated what she looked like as a wolf.

Sleek, dark, ruthlessly stunning.

"Well done, my love," Katherine purred, her eyes sliding to Vada with something akin to admiration.

My love?

I blinked rapidly, trying to process this new piece of information.

Katherine and Vada? Together? Romantically? For how long?

"Anything for you, Kat." Vada's hand tangled in Katherine's dark hair, the lean muscles in her forearms flexing as she drew her in for a kiss that made it feel like someone had already lit the logs at my feet.

It was raw. Real. Passionate in a way that made my stomach feel heavy and my head feel light.

Right up until Dan conspicuously cleared his throat.

Katherine pulled away from Vada slowly, her face tight with irritation as she turned to look at him.

"Apologies for interrupting, Dark Mistress," he said, ducking his head deferentially. "I just wanted to see if there was anything else we needed before we begin. I drew the runes, and got the wood, and set up the stake just like you said, but if there's anything about my preparations that you'd like to change, I'd be honored to be of further service."

Emphasis on *I*.

Katherine and Vada shared a knowing look.

"Everything is fine, Dan," Katherine said coolly. "Thank you."

With that, she glided forward to the podium and flipped open the ornate cover of a large leather book before looking up at me with a slow, sinister smile.

"Let the ritual begin."

17

"So, contextually, I can pretty much guess what this ritual entails," I said, trying to keep my voice light despite my fizzing adrenaline. "But I would definitely appreciate a little more insight as to the goal."

"My goal," Katherine said, flipping through the book's thick vellum pages, "is to be free of you."

"Is that all?" I asked. "Because if that's the case, I can make you free of me right now."

"I sincerely doubt that," she said, lifting a thick red ribbon from the book's spine to mark her place.

"And I completely understand why," I said. "Despite your having arranged several elaborate murder plots against me, we don't actually know each other all that well."

"I know you." Her pale eyes glowed with malicious fire as she lifted them from the elaborate calligraphic text. "I know you better than you know yourself."

"If that's true, then you'd also know that my willingness to leave . . . uh, wherever this is and never come back is sincere and earnest."

"You'd come back," she said idly, touching a thumb to her tongue and flipping to another section. "You always do."

You'd come back. You always do.

The words rang through my head, an echo of something Allan Ede had once told me.

This isn't your first time around.

Supposedly, in all those previous times, I'd rejected Abernathy and his attempts to acquaint me with my heir status, causing him enormous amounts of pain and heartache.

But as far as what else those lives entailed, I hadn't a single clue.

"Look, if this is about something I might have done before I got stuck with my current incarnation, please know that, while I have no idea what it was, I profoundly regret it and will do my utmost to make amends."

She raised an eyebrow, disbelief etched on her face. "You really don't remember?"

"Unfortunately, no," I admitted. "But if you'd care to give me a hint, you have my word that I will seek out a mental health professional and/or topically appropriate podcast to address it."

Katherine's hand paused mid–page flip. A smile I didn't care for at all curled the corners of her lips. "Did my brother ever tell you that I left our ancestral home to help him search for you?"

"Kat, don't." Abernathy, who had remained eerily silent up to this point, held up a supplicating hand.

"It's true," she said, stepping out from behind the book stand. "From the time I was a wee bairn, he'd tell me how someday, the two of us would restore the rightful heir to the shifter kingdom. Put things back the way they were meant to be. And do you know the crazy thing? I believed him. I believed him *so* much, that I let him drag me all over the continent," she said, climbing up onto the platform with me.

"And the misery you put us through. If I hadn't idolized my big brother the way I did, I probably would have quit after the first time you lit me on fire. Or hired a cat shifter to chew my face off. Or sicced your demon donkey on me."

A silky lock of Katherine's hair tickled my fingers as she paced around behind me.

"But no. For fifty years, I chased that dream. *His* dream."

Fifty.

Fifty years.

For longer than I'd been alive, Katherine had endured the kind of soul-sucking chaos I had fanatically fantasized about escaping for only the last year.

"What made you decide to stop?" I asked, desperate to keep her talking in hopes of delaying the inevitable.

"Would you like me to show you?" Katherine asked.

"Kat, *no.*" Abernathy's entreaty held such a tender, earnest note that it pierced the miasma of my growing dread.

"Sal?" Katherine said, glancing over her shoulder at Vada.

"Sal?" Struggling against my ties, I craned my neck to meet her leonine eyes.

"I kind of lied to you about my name," she said. "Or at least about how I got it. It's Salvation. So I've used both Sal and Vada depending on—"

"Sal," Katherine said again, this time with a flinty edge.

"Sorry," Sal/Vada said, looking sheepish. She waved a hand, and Abernathy's mouth snapped shut with an audible *click*.

So they'd managed to dose him too.

The small, sputtering flame of my hope guttered to the barest ember as Katherine leaned in and pressed her lips against mine.

The world around me vanished, replaced by an overwhelming flood of sensory input.

A crimson cloak. A cottage. A fire. A curse. An explosion. Blinding pain.

The flashes came faster then. Sights, sounds, smells, the faces of those I'd hurt—friends, allies, even family—all flashing in front of me like a macabre slideshow. Waves of scalding guilt and shame washed over me as I realized how much pain I'd caused throughout my many existences.

As the torrent of memories slowed to a trickle, I was struck with an epiphany.

My nightmares, those torturous visions.

I had died the way I had lived.

And some part of me remembered.

"Please," I choked out against her mouth, my tears wetting both our cheeks. "No more."

She pulled away, leaving me gasping and reeling, my streaming eyes searching for Abernathy, whose gaze remained firmly fixed on the floor. I felt sick to my stomach, crushed by the weight of centuries' worth of mistakes.

I could hardly breathe through the knot of shame lodged in my throat.

"Do you see?" Katherine asked.

I nodded.

I did.

Like my favorite part of the games of solitaire Oma used to play with me whenever I stayed home sick from school, the cards were rapidly falling into place.

"I tried to steal your souls," I said. "You discovered your powers saving Abernathy . . . from me."

"Yes," Katherine said.

"The daughter of a witch and a werewolf, more powerful than the men who had declared themselves the masters of your kind."

"Yes," Dan echoed.

"You should have been the alpha," I said.

The rightful heir. Preserved by the Mother for these final days.

"You were robbed of your birthright. Forced to flee your ancestral home."

Mindless sheep deceived by the lies of wicked men.

"You came to the colonies seeking freedom, but you and Salvation were tried as witches."

She is the unburnt one.

"They tried to hang you both, and when you didn't die, they tried burning you instead."

"Yes," Sal chimed in.

"The real witches of the colony intervened. They . . . sacrificed themselves so you could get away, and you've lived in the shadows ever since, forming alliances with those who believed you were the rightful heir."

She will punish those who have persecuted us.

"Yes," Katherine said.

"And now Abernathy will watch me burn the way you and Sal did before the women helped you escape."

And she will have her revenge.

"Yes," Katherine, Dan, and Sal said in unison.

I took a moment to gather my thoughts despite the awkward silence that followed.

"I can totally understand why you'd want to start a cult and gather devotees who share your common goal of a shifter-friendly world with you as its supreme leader," I said. "I can even empathize with wanting to make me look like a murderous psychopath so I'd die alone in infamy and you'd be lauded as the beloved savior of the supernatural realm."

Katherine smirked, clearly pleased with herself.

"But," I continued. "Have you ever thought that maybe, just maybe, my being the alpha *is* my punishment?"

A fine crease appeared between her dark brows. "What do you mean?"

"I mean that being the alpha totally blows. And if you're volunteering, lady, I'll step down right the fuck now."

Abernathy made a strangled sound from behind his forcibly sealed lips.

"Step down?" she sneered, her face twisting into a mask of disgust. "You think I want your pity, your scraps? You truly believe that will atone for centuries of torment?"

"Actually, no. Becoming the alpha will pretty much *guarantee* you centuries of additional torment. But since you seem so hell-bent on it, I just felt like it was only fair to give you a heads-up."

"Duly noted," Katherine said dryly. "Dan, Sal, it's time."

Dan cleared his throat. "My Exalted Priestess?"

"What is it?" Katherine snapped.

"About the ritual . . ." he led off hesitantly.

Katherine's wickedly pointy boot tapped beneath the hem of her cloak.

"It's just, you said that I would get a real cloak once I had delivered the Usurper. And I delivered the Usurper, so . . ."

"I said you would get a real cloak. I didn't say *when*," Katherine said, turning her back to him to return to the grimoire stand.

"True, Your Magnificence. It's just, I was kind of hoping to have it for the ritual. Since you and Vada—er, Sal, have yours—"

"I'm not going to say I told you so," Sal sang beneath her breath.

"Then don't," Katherine said, testily flipping through the pages. "It's not like I've had infinite options in terms of accomplices."

"As witnessed by Hank," Sal said breezily.

Hank.

Hank?

My ol' lady . . . she ran off with one of them fox shifters.

I couldn't quite stifle my gasp when it finally clicked.

"You? And *Hank*?"

"I know, right?" Sal muttered.

Katherine's nostrils flared. "Look, he had a still where we could brew potions in bulk, and he was gullible enough to believe it was kombucha. And anyway, it wasn't like the puritanical pricks were exactly lining up to hide us when we had to flee from Salem."

From the way Hank had spoken about his lost lady love, I had simply assumed theirs had been a relatively recent relationship. It hadn't occurred to me to care how old Hank was, nor how long he'd been haunting the sultry swampland.

Rich irony indeed that he'd been dead right about the mind control, but not about its source.

Witches instead of aliens.

"So, is that a no on the cloak?" Dan asked, bouncing the tips of his index fingers together.

"Daniel—" Katherine began.

"Darklord Doomwhisperer, My Infernal Queen." Dan quickly averted his eyes. "That's my warlock name, remember?"

Sal gave her partner a "your project" shrug.

"Enough!" Katherine roared, her rage boiling over. Her eyes locked onto mine with a ferocity that made me shudder. "We do this now."

Something passed between Katherine and Sal, who blew out an exhale and turned to Abernathy.

I watched, awestruck, as he took several lurching, labored steps toward an honest-to-Goddess torch anchored on one of the old stone walls.

In a moment, I saw it all.

Katherine was going to force her brother to set me ablaze.

My heart punched against my rib cage as Abernathy's hand closed over the hilt. The veins in the forearms I had worshiped with my eyes, my hands, my mouth strained against his skin.

"It's not like you haven't watched her die before, big brother," Katherine taunted. "What's one more time?"

Flames trailed from the torch like a comet's tail as he swung around to face me. Sweat stood out on Abernathy's brow, his teeth bared, the tendons of his neck bunched like iron cables.

For the first time since I'd left the home we shared, our eyes met.

The world seemed to hold its breath, and a very strange thing happened.

I saw Mark Abernathy for the first time.

As he had been at the top of his stairs the first time I'd set foot in the gallery, his shoulders filling the doorway to his office, that strange, secret smile on his lips.

As he had been at a smoky speakeasy in the Roaring Twenties, his dark hair slicked back, taking solace in jazz and gin.

As he had been in a gritty, seventeenth-century Scottish pub, his tartan kilt dull with road dust, his hulking form as weary as his eyes were alive.

As he yet would be, dark hair silvered at the temples, grooves carved into his kingly brow as we shook hands in dappled light beneath an indigo sky.

In the midst of this surreal montage, it was my own words I heard. A question I had once asked him in a bower of standing stones on the cool, damp grass.

How do I know I'm not going to lose you again?

Then, as now, his answer fell like cool rain on my fevered skin.

Because that's what love is, Hanna. You lose each other a thousand times, but you find each other a thousand and one.

I felt my body go slack and peaceful, my mind absurdly calm.

I could fall. I could drown. I could break. I could burn.

Always, he would find me.

"Why isn't it working?" Flames danced across in the lenses of Dan's black-framed glasses, folds of his not-real cloak clutched in either hand.

"Because Vada's will isn't strong enough," Katherine said coolly.

"Yes . . . it . . . is." Sal's voice came in labored grunts, and for the first time, I noticed that she, too, showed signs of struggle. Sweat saturated the fringe of her coal-black pixie cut. Her eyes were red-rimmed and glassy.

"Think of everything we've suffered!" Katherine shouted above the chanting. "How long we've waited for our vengeance."

"For *her* vengeance," I said, noticing that the torch was making a modicum of progress downward. "This isn't your fight, Sal."

Abernathy's grip on the torch tightened, his knuckles going bone white as he began to pull it *away* from the pile.

Katherine screamed, her voice ragged with rage. She raised her arms, sparks pinwheeling from her fingertips and gathering in a glowing ball between her palm.

The sudden burst of heat and light was so intense I could feel it tightening the skin on my cheeks, temporarily clouding the surface of my eyes.

Katherine reared back, arms poised to hurl the mini-inferno, but stopped abruptly, her eyes widening in shock. Her chin tipped down toward her chest, a look of puzzlement overtaking her features. She sank to her knees, then crumpled onto her side, the knitting needle protruding from her back beating in time with her heart.

And there, behind her, stood my mother, her eyes gleaming with triumph. "No one throws a fireball at my baby girl."

"Mom?" I gasped, my mind struggling to comprehend what had just happened.

"Kat!" Sal skidded to her knees and gathered Katherine in her arms. Trying to staunch the flow of blood with one hand, she waved the other over her lover's wounded body while muttering an incantation in a language I didn't recognize.

"Finish . . . her," Katherine whispered. "Please."

The anguish in her voice was so desperate that I felt a pang of sympathy for her despite being the target of her death wish by proxy.

But Sal shook her head, tears streaming down her face. "I don't give a fuck about vengeance, Kat. I never have. I only ever wanted what we'd talked about from the beginning. To wrest control from the patriarchy and restore the world to its natural matriarchal state. I'm done with this heir obsession. I'm done watching you suffer."

Abernathy was gaining momentum now, the torch juddering from side to side as the muscles in his biceps bunched.

Sal glanced upward, seeing, as I did, the black-cloaked figures surrounding her beginning to twitch and jerk.

And with a deep, guttural shout that made the air shiver, Sal and Katherine disappeared in a shower of orange sparks.

The air itself seemed to lighten and cool. One by one, Steve, Shayla, Kirkpatrick, and Helena pushed their hoods back and glanced around, confusion writ large on their faces.

"Wh-what just happened?" Steve stammered, his eyes darting back and forth between the now-empty space where Katherine had been and the knitting needle that had saved us all.

"I think Mom just saved me from having my soul banished into oblivion," I said. "Could someone . . . uh, you know?" I angled my chin down toward the ropes still binding my ankles.

Morrison and Abernathy both moved forward before James caught himself and hung back.

The ropes slackened first around my wrists, then my ankles. Which, unfortunately, were still encased in the six-inch black platform dominatrix boots I'd worn to the vampire rave. I might have taken a header off the platform if Abernathy hadn't been there to steady me. Caught in those strong, familiar arms, I let myself soak up the smell of him, the feel of his body bracing mine. It was enough to make me forget about the crowd of hooded figures looking on.

"How come Hanna got that outfit and I had to wear this stupid sackcloth?" Helena asked, plucking at the belled wizard sleeve of her cloak.

"Never mind that," Scott Kirkpatrick said. "How the devil did we get here?"

In my all-consuming gratitude not to have been roasted like a six-foot bratwurst—okay, weisswurst if we're being true to complexion—I actually felt a twinge of affection for Kirkpatrick's Teddy Roosevelt–esque adventurer speak.

"How about, where the fuck *is* here?" asked Shayla, ever the pack's voice of practicality. "Last thing I remembered, we were on a double date at the Puttin' Place."

Which meant their respective broods were likely under the care of a sitter. Something I'd felt a momentary ripple of worry about.

Steve scratched his soul patch. "Despite the conspicuous lack of a dungeon master's table and Wes Anderson posters," he said, surveying the room with a critical eye, "I'd say we're in Dan Davis's basement."

At which point, seven pairs of eyes swiveled to the only remaining crimson-cloaked figure left in the room.

Dan—aka Darklord Doomwhisperer—took a step backward. "Look," he said, his voice shaking as badly as his hands. "None of this was my idea. I just wanted to be part of something, to belong somewhere."

"I know exactly where you belong." Abernathy rolled his neck and licked his chops.

"Wait!" Dan insisted. "Just hear me out."

Abernathy advanced another step. "Save your breath for screaming."

"But I can be useful," Dan babbled, patting his pockets beneath the cape. "Really."

"There won't be enough of you left," Abernathy said.

Dan held his phone up like a shield. "I have the Guild's WhatsApp group thread receipts. I'll send them to you right now. Just please, don't eat me."

"You want the leg or the thigh?" I said, glancing at Abernathy.

"Neither," he said, sniffing Dan's sideburn. "I like the cheeks."

"Helena?" I asked, glancing over my shoulder.

"Depends," Helena said. "Is he organic?"

"Vegan," I said.

"Ugh." Helena rolled her eyes. "They're so . . . grassy. What do you think, baby?" She trailed a long, vampy nail down the front of Kirkpatrick's fisherman's vest. "Anything whet your appetite?"

"You know what my grandsire always said." Scott plucked Helena's hand from his chest and kissed his way up her arm like Gomez Addams. "The best parts are the least used."

"Which'd be his balls, I'm guessing," Mom said, shrugging off her robe to reveal . . . another robe. Mint green instead of black.

"Never been a fan of Rocky Mountain oysters myself," Steve said, whipping off his cloak like a toreador. "But I'd eat his liver with some fava beans and a nice chianti." At which, he sucked air through his teeth in the iconic *ffff-ffff-ffft* of Hannibal Lecter, complete with creep-tastic tongue flick.

"If you'd read the book, you'd know it was 'a big amarone,'" Dan recited, pushing his glasses up his nose.

"I've read it," Shayla chimed in. "But I've always thought *Hannibal* was superior. Especially the part where Dr. Lecter sautés a certain stool pigeon's sweetbreads with butter sauce and shallots."

Dan's Adam's apple bobbed on a conspicuous swallow. "I don't suppose it would make any difference if I told you that I can clear Hanna with the Bureau of Supernatural Affairs."

My heart began to beat a little faster in my chest. "How?"

"I know who killed Morg," Dan said.

"Morg killed himself," I said. "Oscar Wilde said so."

"And you believed him?" Dan snorted. "The same Oscar Wilde who's been spouting flippant aphorisms since the Age of Enlightenment?"

"Don't you dare condescend to me, you obsequious fuckstick," I said, poking a finger into his sternum. "I have a mostly useless master's degree in art history, I'll have you know. I was scribbling his flippant aphorisms on my recyclable book covers when you were still leaving skid marks in your skivvies."

"Who killed him?" Shayla asked, once again blazing the shortest path to useful information.

Dan took a deep breath. "It was . . . Marv."

"Who's Marv?" Steve whispered to Morrison.

"Mothman," Morrison said.

"Marv?" I repeated. "Why would Marv kill Morg? I thought they were friends."

"Friends?" Dan looked at me as if I'd just confessed to putting ketchup on my filet mignon. "What on earth would give you that idea?"

"Wallis said that the mothmen were part of Morg's gift for Abernathy's surprise party," I said. "I assumed—"

"That a foul-mouthed unicorn who was so hard up for cash that he agreed to schlep bottles around a sketchy celebration in exchange for non-fungible tokens was a reliable source of information?"

"As opposed to an aging hipster who mortgaged his coffee shop to a vengeful vulpine witch in exchange for a polyester cape and a basement full of broken promises?"

"*Burn*," Steve said, wriggling his hand as if he'd touched a hot stove.

"To answer your question, the mothmen hate Sasquatch," Dan said, adopting the tones of a graduate student lecturer. "Honestly, do you know anything about the cryptid kingdom at all?"

Suddenly, the frantic beating of wings once Morg had caught fire made so much more sense.

"But one of the mothmen dive-bombed us as we were trying to escape from Big Bucks Bingo," Morrison said.

"Dive-bombed *you*?" Dan folded his arms across his chest.

Hank.

Knowing that I might have had an unlikely ally didn't really change anything at this point, but it did make me feel slightly less salty about the whole situation.

I made a mental note to send a fruit basket once I figured out exactly where Marv and the other mothmen might live.

"So Marv the mothman killed Morg," I said, ticking homicide number one off on my index finger. "What about Maureen?"

Mom cleared her throat, her eyes taking on a shifty quality I recognized from when she'd raid my Halloween candy and replace her ill-gotten gains with far less palate-pleasing fare.

Like I wouldn't notice a sudden infestation of stale Tootsie Rolls.

"*You?*" I gaped at her.

Mom nodded, her fingers twisting nervously at her waist. "Everyone was distracted with Mr. Morrison choking and all, so I figured it was as good a time as any."

Beside me, Abernathy stiffened.

I really wished she hadn't mentioned that.

"But why?" I asked. "I mean, I get that she was a passive-aggressive, parsimonious zealot, and I personally wanted to give her an atomic granny-panty wedgie, but homicide seems a little extreme, no?"

Mom squared her shoulders. "Pretending to want me as part of her little clique so she could get information about you was one thing. Trying to gain favor with this Freki person by volunteering to help kidnap you was another."

I felt my jaw unhinge itself. "Wait . . . what?"

Rooting around in her bathrobe pocket, Mom came back with a crumpled tissue. "Forty years I live in that community, and not a single soul invites me to their ladies' lunches, their shopping dates, then all the sudden it's 'Helga, you should come to our Bible brunch. Helga, how about a game of pickleball? Helga, can we host our Scentsy party at your house?' Then I show up, and all they want to talk about is you."

"That must have been terrible," I said, struggling to inject a modicum of consolation into my voice.

Mom sniffed and dabbed her nose. "The sheer audacity. That

they actually thought they could use me as their little spy just because my daughter was the alpha."

"You . . . *knew* that Hanna was the alpha?" This was perhaps the first question Abernathy had willingly asked my mother.

She gave him an incredulous look. "Of course I knew Hanna was the alpha. You don't carry an heir in your womb for nine months and push her from your own loins without sensing when she's finally fulfilled the promise of your family's ancient lineage."

"I was a C-section," I reminded her, lest she be tempted to embellish upon the graphic anatomical details as she almost always did when she insisted upon telling me the story of my birth on my birthday every year. "So what was with the amnesia bit?"

"My point is, I knew Hanna was the alpha, and I knew Maureen was only including me in her little club so she could mine me for information about her. I just didn't know why, until—" Her voice choked up. "Until I got a peek at her phone while we were at Big Bucks."

I flashed back to Mom insisting that she be on Mo's right at the table, and the realization crystallized. What I had assumed was a quasi-religious sycophantic seating request was actually a snooping-related ploy.

Totally on brand.

"What exactly did you see?" I asked.

"It looked like part of a group text," Mom said. "I didn't get to look at it long, but I saw the part that said, 'Keep Tiger Swo there, they're on their way.'"

"Tiger Swo?" I repeated.

"An acronym that incorporates the acronym for *The Great Red She-Whore*." Dan, who had somehow inched himself closer to the door during our discussion, apparently couldn't resist pontificating even now.

"How the hell did you get that Hanna was in danger just from that?" Helena asked.

Mom bit her lower lip. "Mostly from the GIFs that followed."

"What kind of GIFs?" Shayla asked.

"Well, there was one of a flying pig, which I thought was really cute until I saw the one where an old-fashioned Mickey Mouse was reading a book titled *How to Kill*, and then one where Stephen Colbert was at his desk that said *Someone's getting murdered*, and then one where a little girl was dragging her finger across her throat, and one where there was a floating dumpster on fire, which I didn't really understand at the time, but that makes a lot more sense now, actually."

I arched an eyebrow at Dan, whose cheeks flamed a crimson not at all dissimilar from his robe. "The dumpster one was Katherine's."

A low, ripping growl issued from Abernathy's chest.

"I don't understand," I said, trying to sift through the maelstrom of information in this new context. "When I asked you who had stabbed Maureen, why did you say that I'd done it?"

"Well, I had to, didn't I?" Mom said defensively. "Otherwise, the ladies would have known that I wasn't under the influence of Maureen's spiked sauvignon blanc."

Additional flashes of insight followed the revelation.

Maureen's insistence that everyone drink the wine she'd brought.

Mom's stubborn refusal to use anything but her own kitschy vessel.

Mom's slapstick self-deprecating performance of klutzy court jester at my expense.

Pretty much every one of her vexing habits had actually been a protective measure.

Which just annoyed me to no end.

"*Madre*," Steve said, holding up his hand for a high five. "You're like a Lone Star state Beatrix Kiddo."

Mom flushed, visibly pleased with herself as she slapped his palm.

"Morg, Maureen," I said, simultaneously summing up the

current tally and changing the subject. "That just leaves us with Oscar Wilde. Was he part of the Guild too?"

"Not initially," Dan said. "But after Maureen elected to go agro and Hank decided to go rogue, we needed someone who could assist us with the final phase of the plan."

"Which was?" I asked.

"To ignite the spark of rebellion within the remaining shifter community and rally them to our cause," Dan revealed, a glint of maniacal pride flashing in his eyes. "And who better to incite a revolution than the author of *The Soul of Man Under Socialism*?"

"I'm not following," I said.

Dan issued an impatient sigh. "We needed a plausible suspect to blame for your and Abernathy's deaths following the ritual so the cryptid and shifter communities would unite behind Katherine's rule. Who better than a vampire who had ample reason to want vengeance against both of you?"

Who indeed.

And, added bonus, Oscar's club was peopled with the two species she intended to target once she rose to power.

Humans and vampires.

The brilliance of her plan left me a little breathless.

"Then why did Vada cut his head off?" I asked.

"Because he betrayed Katherine. He was supposed to drink from you directly so Vada could get it on video. Not play a game of Ecstasy-laced vampire-human centipede with you and Morrison."

My stomach somersaulted in my sternum.

"You let him drink from you?" Abernathy's question slid between my ribs like an ice pick, cold and sharp.

"A little," I admitted. "But only because—"

"Maybe now is not the best time to discuss this," Morrison pointed out.

But judging by the sounds coming from Abernathy, the time when anything could be discussed was officially over.

"You know what?" Shayla said, clapping her hands together. "I think I'm going to call Crixus to pick up this dickweasel."

"Splendid idea," Steve agreed, picking up a length of the frayed rope from the base of the stake. "Little help, Scotto?"

"Happy to."

Before Dan could even squeak out another protest, Scott lunged and, with a swift, practiced grace surprising for one of his size and build, flipped him face down on the ground.

"You should use that modified Somerville bowline we tried the other night," Helena said, her lips curved in a dreamy smile. "It certainly stood up to a lot of . . . *friction*."

I felt a strange mix of gladness and jealousy.

At least someone's relationship wasn't on a collision course with conflict.

Together, Steve and Scott hog-tied Dan, giving the rope connecting his wrists and ankles a sharp tug to test the hold.

Dan grunted in protest.

"Looks pretty solid to me," Steve assessed.

"Ditto," Scott said. "Should we leave him down here until Crixus comes?"

"I think we should go ahead and drag him upstairs," Shayla suggested. "Save Crixus the trip."

"I'll second that motion," Helena said, raising her hand.

"On the count of heave," Steve said. "One, two, *heave*."

And so it was that Dan made his exit to a soundtrack of *Whump*. "Oof." *Whump*. "Oof." *Whump*. "Oof."

I turned to my mom, whom I noticed had hung back, probably hoping to spectate the inevitable dustup brewing above our heads like a storm cloud.

"You're welcome to wait for us at our place," I said, putting my hand on her arm. "Unless you wanted to head over to Steve's and hang out with the grandkiddos."

"Actually, I need to get back to the boys," she said, scuffing a slipper on the concrete floor. "I put out some extra kibble for them before I let Vada kidnap me for leverage and pretended to be under her spell, but knowing Zeppy, he's probably eaten all of it already."

"I understand." I squeezed her arm, feeling a jolt of surprise at just how soft it was. How fragile. And perhaps for the first time, it registered that my having mated with Abernathy meant I would lose her long before I drew my last breath.

All my life, we'd struggled so hard to understand each other. To know each other and be known.

The same way she and Oma had.

Oma, to whom I'd always given the unfiltered adoration that my mother had craved.

Never once realizing that I was cheating us both in the process.

"You ever thought about changing your mind?" I asked.

"About what, sweetie?"

"Becoming a werewolf," I said. "I know plenty of shifters who would be more than happy to do you the favor."

Her smile was small, but sad. "Oh, honey. I've always known this life wasn't for me."

"How come?" I asked.

She reached up to tuck a tendril of red hair a slightly deeper shade of her same auburn behind my ear. "I'm not as brave as you."

I hugged her then, filling my lungs with her signature cocktail of Dove soap, fabric softener, and hand lotion. The scent of sick days in front of *Judge Judy* and *The People's Court*. The scent of a thousand Friday-night scary movie marathons on the couch, the cushions stuffed with concealed snacks.

"Yes, you are," I said, and kissed her cheek.

We were both dabbing at our eyes when we broke the embrace.

Mom stopped at the base of the stairs.

"Do you think that Crixus fellow might be willing to zap me back to Abilene?" Mom looked at me from beneath shyly lowered lashes. "I completely understand if not," she quickly added. "I just thought it would be faster and all."

"I'm sure he would be happy to," I said, fully intending to make sure Crixus gave her the first-class package.

Then, there was only Abernathy and Morrison and me.

My nails dug into my clammy palms, my throat aching with dangerously sharp words.

"What happened at Oscar's club—" I began.

"I don't want to know." Abernathy's jaw flexed, his lips a flat, tight line. "What's done is done. Let's just get this cleaned up and get out of here."

By "cleaned up," I assumed Abernathy meant summoning the crack team of miraculous magical restoration specialists who somehow managed to conceal and contain the catastrophic aftermath of our many scrapes with disaster and destruction.

And there had been many.

"You go ahead," Abernathy said, already pulling his phone from his pocket. "I'll follow you when it's finished."

I glanced at Morrison, his cheekbone still smudged with soot from Katherine's fireball, his borrowed jeans still spattered with dark flecks of Oscar's dried blood.

"I guess I'm going to head home," I said, feeling strangely fragile. My bones brittle. My heart bruised.

"Are you sure?" Morrison asked.

I nodded, already dreaming about boiling myself in the shower. "I think I'm okay with delegating this time. Are you going to stick around?"

Morrison took a step closer, his face creased with an emotion I couldn't identify. "I meant, are you sure you want to go home with *him*?"

His question hung in the air between us, his hazel eyes holding mine, pooling with a silent concern that vacuumed my head hollow.

I had no words. No answers. No breath. No thoughts.

In my peripheral vision, Abernathy went completely still, his body vibrating with the silent, violent promise of a detonator.

"Who the fuck do you think you are?"

Morrison's eyes blazed a brilliant violet as he squared his shoulders to Abernathy. "I'm a man who loves her."

The world tilted on its axis as the implications of what had just happened took root, wrapped around my brain stem, and squeezed.

"How fucking *dare* you." Abernathy's voice shook with barely restrained rage. "How dare you stand there with *my* mate's blood in *your* veins and ask her if she's sure she wants to come home with me."

Morrison took one step, two steps, stopping only when he put himself within striking distance of Abernathy's huge, white-knuckled fist. "*Is* she your mate?"

"You're lucky I don't rip your throat out and piss down your neck hole."

"*Fuck* your luck." The words ripped from Morrison's mouth with a fine spray of spit that landed on Abernathy's cheeks. "You stand there, pouting like a goddamn toddler about *thirty seconds* I shared with Hanna when those thirty seconds are the only time I can feel anything at all. The only time when I can taste anything, smell anything. The only time I can bear to remember what it's like to be alive. When *you*, who have lived four hundred and thirty-two years already and will probably live for four hundred more, waste your time with an emotion as selfish and pathetic as jealousy instead of falling to your knees with gratitude that the woman you love is alive, and you're alive, and she chose you despite the hell that her life has become since you entered it.

"*That's* how I fucking dare. I dare because when I die, if I *can* even die now that I'm this thing, and I meet my creator, if there's a being sadistic enough to have made this shithole world on purpose, I fully intend to account for the choices I made and atone for my mistakes. And the biggest one I ever made was letting Hanna get on that plane after you fucked off to London and left her alone with the fucking fiend who wanted her dead. You've done a dog-shit job of protecting her, and you've done an even worse job of making her happy. So no, I don't give a flying *fuck* what bullshit laws of nature or man or science say she belongs to you, and you can bet your ass I'm going to ask her if she's sure. And not just tonight. I'm going to ask her every single time she looks like she looks right now. And if by some incalculable chance she ever says no, I will take her the fuck away from you, Abernathy. I will take her away, and I will love her until you're not even a memory of a memory."

"It's not," I blurted. Both men whirled around to look at me as if surprised to find I was still in the room.

"Hell," I quickly added, realizing simultaneously how much time had passed since that bit of Morrison's monologue and how ridiculous the assertion was in my present circumstances. "Not all the time, anyway."

Neither man spoke.

"Sorry," I said, waving Morrison on. "I just wanted to put that out there."

For an interminable length of time, I watched them glare at each other, afraid they would erupt in a brutal tangle of claws and teeth.

What happened instead was somehow worse.

Morrison simply turned and left.

Abernathy said nothing.

18

"And that's why I had no choice but to take recreational party drugs in a roomful of humans and vampires committing unspeakable sexual acts and allow Morrison to put his mouth on my neck and suck the life blood from my jugular while Oscar Wilde watched."

The eyes boring into mine remained distant, his gaze cool and unmoved. His expression, implacable.

"You're right," I said to Gilbert, who was watching me lather my hair from his new favorite perch on the towel rack by the shower—recently reinforced to hold his bulk. "Too submissive."

Tilting my head back, I let the steaming water sluice over my back and shoulders, rinsing the grime and sweat of a night spent navigating the supernatural underworld in rental PVC bondage gear. Relieved as I was to be back in the comfort of my own home, the dread I felt about the tense conversation looming on the horizon left my stomach in a tight, cold ball.

My decision to request a formal meeting to hash things out with Abernathy rather than just getting it over with right there in Dan Davis's basement while still wearing clothes borrowed from Oscar Wilde's Las Vegas vampire sex club was seeming less inspired by the second.

"You think I should leave out the part about the unspeakable acts? I mean, Abernathy is probably going to assume that, anyway, right?"

Gilbert hunkered down into loaf mode, sending an avalanche of clean washrags to the floor. This seemed like a bad omen.

"I'm sure it's going to be fine," I said, my hands trembling as I squeezed body wash onto my loofah. "Abernathy is a reasonable man. He'll understand."

Flopping onto his side, Gilbert's feline fupa billowed nearly to the edge of the shelf. My reflection in the steam-fogged glass looked equally unconvinced.

"Either way, it's not like I haven't faced scarier creatures. I mean, shit. That time I woke up on the couch in Abernathy's office and Mrs. Kass transformed into that half-wolf, half-naked geriatric ghoul thing?"

But thinking of that made me think of Abernathy in wolf form crashing through the chimney, his daggerlike teeth dripping with saliva in anticipation of the kill.

Which was less than helpful.

Once out of the shower, I wrapped my hair in a towel and pulled on some comfy sweats.

"All right, guys," I said, sitting down at my vanity. "Momma's gotta put on her face."

I'd gotten to the final phase of applying a bold red lip when I heard the whir of the garage door opening, and my chest tightened.

Abernathy was home.

He'd gone for a drive through the canyon, undoubtedly brooding as I was over all that happened.

Over all that it meant.

I tracked the sound of his footsteps, bracing myself for their inevitable ascension of the stairs.

But they didn't.

I heard him cross the kitchen, a cupboard open and close, the back door to our deck open.

"Okay," I whispered, looking at my cats. "Let's do this."

I made my way downstairs, feeling like I had lead leg warmers puddled around my ankles. I spotted Abernathy on the back deck, lost in thought as he sipped a glass of scotch. The breeze ruffled his dark hair, and his broad shoulders were tense.

My heart ached with longing as I watched him, wishing I could just come up behind him, wrap my arms around him, and have everything go back to the way it was before my newfound responsibilities as alpha and all its unanticipated consequences threatened to pull us apart.

Taking a deep breath, I was about to join him on the deck when the doorbell rang. I felt a stab of irritation, not needing yet another delay to our dreaded conversation.

But when I swung the door open, I was surprised to see Crixus standing on the other side.

"Hey, Hanna," Crixus greeted. "Got a minute?"

"Not much more than that," I said, completely thrown off by his unexpected arrival.

"This won't take long," he assured me, sauntering inside. "Just here to share a few updates. You don't mind if I grab a beer, do you?"

"Help yourself," I said, gesturing toward the kitchen.

Crixus snagged a beer from the fridge and popped the cap off with a flick of his wrist. He leaned against the counter, taking a swig before turning his attention back to me. "So what's up?" he asked. "You look like you're about to face a firing squad."

"Nothing much," I said evasively. "Just . . . stuff."

"Stuff," he said, clearly not mollified but, thankfully, not pushing it any further.

"Yep," I said, attempting to change the subject. "What's this news you came to share?"

Crixus took another swig of his beer. "I just got word from the Bureau of Supernatural Affairs. You've been officially cleared."

"Really?" I heaved an epic sigh of relief.

"Really," he said. "Between Dan's and Hank's testimonies, there was more than enough evidence to clear you of all charges."

"That's great," I said. "So they're both in custody?"

"Both in custody," Crixus confirmed.

"How about Katherine and Vada?" I asked.

Crixus picked at the beer bottle label. "Still at large, I'm afraid."

My stomach clenched, remembering the burning hatred in Katherine's eyes as she'd leaned in to kiss me. If she survived her stab wound, and I assumed she would, it was only a matter of time before she found her way back to my doorstep.

I glanced at Abernathy through the wide window off the dining room.

"How did he like Dr. Schmidt?" Crixus asked, having noticed the direction of my gaze.

"What's that?" I asked.

"Dr. Schmidt. They had a video consultation."

My eyes widened in surprise. "Wait, really? How do you know that?"

"Dr. Schmidt's assistant, Julie. She mentioned they had a new patient that was a 'total zaddy of a werewolf from Colorado,'" he said, mimicking an obviously bubbly young woman's voice with surprising skill.

"When was that?" I asked.

"Couple of days ago, I think."

"Before or after you rescued us from Hank's bunker?" I asked, wanting to determine just how guilty I needed to feel about Abernathy's carrying through on a promise for therapeutic self-betterment.

Crixus's broad, tanned brow furrowed. "Before I *what*?"

I plucked the beer bottle from his hands and placed it on the counter. "Had a few of these already, have we?"

"Actually, no." He lifted the bottle to his lips again. "Have you?"

"*Noooo*," I drawled. "But unless you have a pretty convincing doppelgänger out there, you absolutely rescued Morrison and me from Hank's bunker and zapped us to Vegas."

"The only person I've zapped lately is your mother. Which, by the way, *wow*," he said, chuckling under his breath. "By the time she remembered her actual address, we'd stopped in at least three different neighborhoods in your hometown. You might want to get her to a neurologist."

I felt a gust of warmth at my mother's capacity for capricious machination despite my growing concern about Crixus's memory.

"If you know of a good one, you might want to grab yourself an appointment," I said. "There's bound to be a decent one near your Vegas time-share."

He raised an eyebrow, looking at me like I was the one in need of a neurologist. "Vegas time-share?"

"You know." I shrugged. "the swanky penthouse suite with black satin sheets and a view of the Strip?"

Crixus set his beer down on the counter with a decisive thud.

"Hanna," he managed between chuckles, "I don't own a time-share. Not in Vegas or anywhere else. But if I happened to own one in any proximity to an underground vampire sex dungeon owned by Oscar Wilde, I sure has fuck wouldn't have stashed you there."

An excellent point that hadn't even occurred to me in all the chaos.

But if not Crixus, then—

An image flashed into my mind.

Vada, right outside the kink chamber where she'd lopped off Oscar Wilde's head. What had looked like a furry costume had simply vanished right back into her skin.

At the time, I'd been so focused on the *why* that I hadn't given much mental bandwidth to considering the *how*.

If it was the same kind of magic that enabled her to brew compulsion compounds and disapparate a wounded Katherine out of Dan's basement, might not that magic also be used to take on different forms? As in, a blue-eyed demigod with a startling resemblance to Johnny Bravo?

"You okay?" Crixus asked. "You're looking a little chalky."

"I think I need to lie down," I said.

"You want me to get Abernathy?" he asked.

"It's fine," I said, padding toward our overstuffed leather couch and plopping down. "I just need a minute."

Crixus perched on the arm, the roasted grain sweetness of beer on his breath as he studied me. "Dr. Schmidt has warned me against giving out unsolicited advice, but as a being whose been around for a few thousand years longer than you, may I throw some facts out there that you're welcome to use or disregard as you so choose?"

No doubt about it, I liked this Dr. Schmidt already.

"Bestow upon me your wisdom, oh ancient one," I said sarcastically.

"Emperor Nero was a megalomaniacal, murderous man baby, but he had Klaud to arrange his ridiculous entertainments. Klaud was a conniving, obsequious fuckstick of the first order, but he used a soul bond to force me to feed his penchant for craven curiosities. Dr. Schmidt is an uptight, perfectionistic control freak in desperate need of a dirty weekend with me on the Basque coast, but she has Julie pack her calendar so full, she almost never sees daylight."

The fondness with which Crixus pronounced this last part produced a flicker of warmth in my aching heart.

"You're saying that the thing all these beings have in common is good help so they can balance their responsibilities while maintaining balance in their chosen lifestyle?" I asked.

"I'm not saying a word," he said, and mimed locking his lips and throwing away the key. "But hypothetically, if I were, it might also include something about none of the beings I mentioned feeling a need to prove their worthiness to occupy the various roles within their realm by taking on herculean amounts of responsibility solo."

Okay, I really, *really* liked this Dr. Schmidt.

"Non-message non-received," I said with a little salute.

"Good." He rose from the arm of the couch and downed the last of his beer. "You guys recycle?" he asked.

"It's the blue bin under the sink."

Hearing a crash, I peeled myself off the couch. "Was that the dining room table?" I asked. "It's never been the same since Morg—"

The words died in my throat.

Crixus lay on the kitchen floor, his big body racked by convulsions. Foam bubbling from his mouth, eyes wide, pupils dilated.

"Mark!" I screamed. "Come quick! It's Crixus!"

Abernathy came strolling in at a pace that defied all logic, his drink still cradled in his hand.

"I don't know what happened," I blathered, cradling Crixus's head so it didn't bounce against the floor like his juddering motorcycle boots. "One minute he was drinking a beer and talking to me and the next—"

Crixus made a terrible gurgling sound and coughed a mouthful of foam onto his chest.

"He just collapsed," I said, panicked tears washing my eyes.

Time took on a surreal stretched quality as Abernathy lifted the glass to his mouth and took a long swallow. I watched in rapt horror as the hand holding the glass began to shrink, the fingernails darkening to a vampy purple. The cuffs of his dark blue dress shirt gapped away from his dwindling wrist, the dark hairs sprinkled over his skin vanishing. My gaze moved up his arm, shriveling beneath the fabric as the shoulders above it narrowed.

By the time I reached his neck, I knew, but I finished the circuit, anyway.

The angular chin, the sharp cheekbones, the leonine eyes.

Sal smirked at me above the glass's rim and shot the rest of the contents. "Fucking *finally*. I thought he'd never shut up."

I looked at her in shock. "What did you do to Crixus?"

Sal set her empty glass on the counter and shrugged nonchalantly. "I had some poison left over from taking care of Morg, so I went ahead and laced the beer," she said. "He'll be fine, though," she said, nudging Crixus with the toe of Abernathy's shoe. "Demigods don't die. Unfortunately."

Crixus was now convulsing less dramatically but still clearly in some distress.

"So, hold on," I said, processing her sentence at a significant delay. "I thought Dan said that Marv the mothman killed Morg?"

"He did," Sal said. "Well, *I* did, but I was technically using his body at the time."

If my brain were an engine, it would have just dropped the transmission right out of its undercarriage.

"Tell you what." Sal boosted herself up onto the kitchen island and crossed one leg over the other. "I'm sure you'll have lots more questions. Let's see how many of them I can answer to save us some time. My full name is Salvation, no surname since I was left on the steps of a medieval convent that belonged to the Order of the Crimson Cloak in Tossa de Mar on the Catalan Coast until I left to become an independent contractor specializing in unaliving entities my clients found problematic, noisome, or otherwise vexing in some way. Met Kat in Scotland in the seventeenth century when I was hired to find her by a sketchy witch who lived in a cottage made of cheese."

Here, she paused to give me a look that made the back of my neck go hot. With all that had happened in the past forty-eight hours, I hadn't quite made peace with the whole *trying to eat people's souls in a past life* thing.

"I'm a Gemini kitsune," Sal continued, "do part-time possessions and full-time shape-shifting, love long walks on the beach, hate new country music, and unfortunately, I have to kill you." She shot me a dimple-flashing grin. "How'd I do?"

"Pretty good," I said, rapidly scanning my memory for any additional kitsune-related details.

Typically female fox Fae trickster spirits, known to be capricious at best, malevolent and/or malicious at worst. Capable of assuming a human form of their own.

Like the one swinging her legs from my Carrara marble countertop.

"As far as the Morg thing, though—"

"Right." She snapped her fingers. "He and Kat go way back. When we fled from Salem after the whole attempted burning thing, we had to take refuge in the wild. That's where we met Morg. He gave us food and shelter, reached out to the shifter community to gather support—"

"Where did the name *Freki* come from?" I asked.

Sal flicked a crumb off the counter. "The Vargyr were part of the shifter community Morg contacted. The first ones who swore to back Kat's claim. They came to visit us. Called us *Geri* and *Freki* after the two wolves who accompanied Odin. The greedy and the ravenous, respectively. I didn't have the heart to tell them I'm not actually a werewolf."

"Understandable," I said.

"Anyway, Kat gave him the scoop about Abernathy, the hunt for the heir, and they signed a pact basically stating that along with the cryptids, they would be loyal to Katherine as the true alpha."

My throat ached with a dry swallow. "But they didn't keep up their part of the pact."

"No," Sal said, her eyes darkening. "No one did. Not then. Not now. Not ever."

For reasons I would never understand given just how much fuckery Katherine had brought into my life, I felt a deep and abiding sadness yawn open in my chest.

"When she got word from Dan that Morg was coming to meet

with you," Sal continued, "she was *pissed.* Of course, Morg backpedaled hard and fed us some story about only accepting the invite so he could officially denounce you in person, but neither of us bought it."

"I see," I said. "But how did Dan know what Morg was going to do?"

Sal heaved a disgusted sigh. "That fucking guy. Practically blew a load in his boxer briefs when Kat introduced him to Morg. Dan was supposed to infiltrate Morg's colony and report back to Kat; instead, he only opened a goddamn Sasquatch-themed coffee shop. I mean, I've heard of fanboys, but how pathetic can you get?"

"And you were working there because Katherine didn't trust Dan?"

"That, and we were supposed to befriend your brother and convert him to the cause."

"Just like Maureen with my mom," I reasoned.

"Exactly," she said. "Basically, it was kind of a *turn everyone in Hanna's immediate circle against her to break her heart and slowly crush her spirit before banishing her soul to oblivion while making Abernathy watch* kind of thing. Failing that, it was poison them one by one."

And oh the rich and abundant irony that, had my brother's gastrointestinal constitution been less temperamental and my mother's relationship been healthier, Katherine's plan might have worked.

Which led me to her next target.

"May I assume Abernathy is one of your part-time possessions?" I asked. "Or did you just shape-shift his form?"

"Great question," she said. "I've been borrowing Abernathy's body on and off for a few months now."

"Define *borrowing*," I said.

Sal looked thoughtful for a moment. "I guess the closest example

I can think of would be renting a car, only Abernathy *is* the car. And it's my mind and not my body driving him."

"Buuut I'm looking at your body right now," I said.

"Aha," she said, holding up a finger. "That's where the shape-shifting comes in."

"Wait. You can shape-shift bodies that only your mind—or whatever—is occupying?"

"Yup." Her full lips curled into a self-satisfied smile.

"So your body—your *real* body—isn't even here right now?"

"Nope," she said, brushing a flake of sea salt from Abernathy's pants. "Just Abernathy's cells conveniently glamoured into my chosen form."

My heart sank.

This complicated things considerably. Were she merely an Abernathy doppelgänger, killing her would at least be a possibility. But as long as she was inhabiting my mate's physical being, there was no way to hurt her without hurting him.

Which reminded me of another question. "While you're driving Abernathy, where exactly *is* Abernathy?"

"Oh, he's in here," she said. "His consciousness is just sort of on screen saver mode while I'm behind the wheel."

"Gotcha," I said, suddenly wondering how often I'd been speaking not to my mate but to the ancient fox Fae spirit capering around his corporeal form.

"On a related note, I'm solidly sapphic, but . . . damn, lady." Her golden eyes lowered to the crotch of Abernathy's too-large trousers.

"Mm-hmm," I drawled, dismayed to find that I liked her even now. "But let's be honest, both Abernathys are kind of ridiculously hot."

"You're not wrong," she agreed.

"How's Kat doing, by the way?" I asked.

Sal's face darkened. "Not great."

"I'm so sorry to hear that." Remembering the way my mother's knitting needle pulsed from Katherine's back, I knew it had to have pierced some vital anatomy. "Hearts are hard to heal in all the ways. Even for a werewolf."

"Oh, no," Sal said. "Her heart is fine. She's just super depressed ever since the ritual went sideways. She's kind of a perfectionist. Super self-critical, you know?"

"How could you not be, with a dad like theirs?"

"*Dude*," Sal said. "You *met* him?"

"Not only did I meet him, I was there when he tried to sell his son to Emperor Nero in exchange for a spot as king of the shifters after their would-be coup."

Sal shook her head. "That's so fucked up."

"I mean, it's no wonder things ended up like this with all the ancestral trauma they must have."

"Kinda makes me glad someone left me on the steps of a convent." Sal sighed.

"I hear that," I said.

Sal scooted forward on the countertop, planting her hands on her knees. "I've just gotta say, I'm really bummed I have to kill you, you know? If we'd met under different circumstances—"

"Totally," I said. "But for what it's worth, I think it's really romantic that you'd do this for Kat. Acts of service is one of Abernathy's love languages too. Not that I know what to do for him lately. I can't even tell what he's thinking, much less what he needs."

"Um, hello," she said, pointing a finger at her own chest. "You're talking to someone who's spent *months* inside his head."

"No shit," I whispered. "You can see his thoughts?"

"I saw yours too, for the couple of seconds I was in there."

"In . . . where?" I asked, somewhat confused.

"You," she said.

"You mean, while Abernathy and I were . . . uh, you know?"

"Dude, *no*," Sal insisted. "That would be all kinds of wrong."

I snorted, somewhat amused by the idea that murder was perfectly fine, but squatting in someone's head during a romantic encounter was crossing a line.

"Then what did you mean by—"

Shazam!

Sal's voice echoed inside my head as it had both at Costco and during our red fox casino chase, accompanied by the wave of nausea.

"Ohhhh," I said, steadying myself at the counter. "And here I thought you were telepathic or something."

"I wish," Sal said. "But no. As for Abernathy, he thinks he ruined your life."

A cold, hard knot formed beneath my rib cage. "*What?*"

"Yup." Sal swung her legs up and folded them beneath her on the counter. "Wondering if he should have left you alone to lead a happy human life is his Roman Empire. Especially after Morrison's speech in Dan's dungeon the other day—which, *wow*—Abernathy thinks you picked the wrong man."

My heart wheezed to a stop. "He does?"

Sal's nose scrunched as she searched for the right words. "He's kinda wishing he'd stayed a lone wolf. He thinks about what it would have been like if you married Morrison. Whether you might have been able to have kids if you'd stayed human. He's even imagined watching from a distance as you and James chased your kids around in a big backyard. Vegetable garden. Lots of dogs. Rescue goats. Very *Casablanca* meets *Sliding Doors*."

It felt as if the floor beneath me had given way and I was pitching into an abyss.

"But if it hadn't been for Abernathy, I might never have even met Morrison," I said.

"Well, sure, but you know how men are. Their fantasies are either action hero or victim of fate."

If I lived through this, and I sincerely hoped I would, I resolved to heed Crixus's advice. Hire some help. Hire an entire staff, goddamn it. Take Abernathy somewhere warm where the rain could water us like flowers. Never stop telling him how grateful I am that I'd chosen him. Tell him a thousand times how much I wished I'd chosen him in every lifetime.

"Thanks for that," I said. "It kind of sucks that I won't get to do anything about it now, but it still helps to know."

"You're welcome," Sal said. "As hosts go, he's actually been one of my favorites."

"Aww," I said, surprised that I found this genuinely touching. "That's really nice of you to say."

At my feet, Crixus groaned and twitched.

"Well." Sal's sigh was heavy, laden with the weight of inevitability. "How do you want to do this? I don't want it to be painful for you or anything, but I also don't want you to feel like you didn't get a chance to fight or whatever. I've never done a murder-suicide before. I'm open to input."

Murder-suicide.

She intended to take Abernathy out in the process.

A breeze widened the gap of the deck door, carrying the scent of rain on its back. I looked out the bank of windows, goose bumps rising at the restless gray thunderheads rolling in over the pines.

"Have you ever been inside Abernathy when he was a wolf?" I asked.

"Actually, no," Sal said.

"The very first time I ever shifted, Abernathy and I ran through that forest under a full moon." Hugging my arms around my middle, I walked toward the windows, gazing into the thick wall of pines. "If you go far enough up that rise, there's a cliff."

Glancing over my shoulder, I met her eyes to make sure she took my meaning.

She did.

"Want to go for a run?" I asked.

"Love to," Sal said.

I headed toward the door, relishing the silky wooden boards beneath my bare feet. I took a deep breath and shifted into my wolf form, feeling the quick rush of energy as fur sprouted from my skin and my bones rearranged themselves into something fleet and deadly.

Sal watched, her eyes bright with curiosity. "In all these centuries, I've never possessed a shifter during a transformation."

"Just like riding a bike," I said. "If the bike is on fire and missing a seat."

Sal barked out a warm, uproarious laugh. "Fair enough."

With that, she followed suit. It was a shockingly swift process, her glamoured human form melting away like a sandcastle under a relentless wave. In her place stood a large, formidable wolf, mirroring Abernathy's lycan form save for two small details.

The eyes—pale gold rather than Abernathy's deep amber.

And the tails.

Sidenote: This is not a typo.

Where normally Abernathy had a single swishy dark garland, there now were three. Just like the furry I'd seen at Costco. An event that seemed like it had taken place in another lifetime.

"Ready?" I asked.

"Lead the way." Hearing Sal's voice come from the powerful wolf whose every feature had been branded on my brain proved deeply disjointing.

The rain was a misty curtain by the time we neared the top of the steep hill behind our house. The trees bowed under the waterlogged weight of it, their drooping boughs like a mournful farewell wave.

"It's beautiful here," Sal said, taking in the rocky face jutting out like a precipice at the world's end. I watched as the rain collected in its crevices, forming tiny rivulets that cascaded over the edge and disappeared into the forest below.

"It is, isn't it?" I gazed out over the familiar dollhouse village of Georgetown nestled snugly in the valley below. Its redbrick buildings and tree-lined streets. The scar the railroad tracks cut into the canyon.

"There's the Crossing," I said, aiming my muzzle toward Main Street, a strip of stars within the encroaching dusk, the tiny windows winking with friendly golden lights that made my heart ache with a rush of nostalgia.

"And Sasquatch Sips," Sal said.

"Can I ask just one more question?" I said, settling my haunches on a cool patch of moss.

"Shoot."

"You seemed like you really liked working at Sasquatch Sips," I said. "Was that all part of the act?"

Sal's vulpine face cut tipped toward the rough-hewn rock. "It wasn't," she said. The thunderheads rumbled, stirring a chilly breeze heavy with petrichor. "It was kinda nice to have something to do that didn't involve constantly plotting the pain and suffering of others."

"It's funny," I said.

"What is?"

"All this time, Kat resented Mark's obsessive hunt for the heir. But she chased her vengeance the same way."

Sal was silent, staring out at the horizon.

The wind picked up, hushing through the trees and sending ripples across my fur. I tried to memorize each sensation as I steeled myself.

"How does this work, exactly?" I asked.

Sal blinked and turned to me. "How does what work?"

"I mean, when Abernathy's body goes over the cliff, do you go over too, or . . ." I trailed off, unable to imagine what other alternative might exist.

"As long as I leave his body before it hits the ground, I'm golden," she said.

"Gotcha." I padded back into the trees far enough to get a running start. "Race you?"

"Thema and Louise–style?" Sal asked.

I nodded.

"You're on." Sal loped back to me, bringing her much larger paws in line with mine on the lichen-kissed rock.

"On your mark, get set . . . penis!"

I took off, Sal shouting an indignant "Hey!" before galloping to catch up with me.

Which was exactly as I'd hoped.

The trees blurred by as we raced across the rain-soaked ground, my heart thrumming in my chest like an ancient drum line.

I was winning.

A whole body length ahead, the wind whistling past my ears, the cliff five paces away. Four. Three.

At the very last second, I veered to the left, bolted up a tree, and swung from a branch by my teeth before dropping back down behind Sal like a four-legged Cirque du Soleil gymnast.

Her powerful paws skidded on the rock face, her snout already over the abyss when I lunged, clamping my jaws down on her tail and wrenching my neck hard to the side.

The great, dark wolf's body hovered in midair for a split second before momentum overtook gravity, and it was yanked backward and sideways, hurtling away from the cliff.

I felt a pop, heard a terrible ripping sound followed by a demonically cacophonic howl of rage.

A sudden supernova of red-orange light sent me skidding backward as Sal's spirit separated from Abernathy's body. An ethereal form shimmering with every shade of sun-burnt orange before winking out like the last falling crumbs of Fourth of July fireworks.

Abernathy's canine body bounced and rolled away from me.

His tails . . . stayed clenched in my teeth.

I spat them out like so many sticks of lit dynamite, emitting a high-pitched yelp of revulsion that drew an answering barks and howls from the valley below.

"Mark!"

I reached his side in a wild skid, eyes darting over his body to assess the damage.

His big body stretched and contracted in spasmodic jerks as though still trying to run, his breath a labored panting. His eyes, deepening from Sal's pale gold to Abernathy's earthy bronze, had the half-pained, half-bewildered look of one waking from a nightmare.

"Hanna," he whispered, his voice raspy and hoarse.

"Abernathy," I said, nudging him with my nose. "Is it really you?"

The soft chuff from his chest blew bits of moss away from his muzzle. "Who else would it be?"

"Your sister's kitsune lover occupying your body and mind in hopes of vengeance," I said.

"Oh," he said. And then, "Are you okay?"

"Me?" I settled my haunches down next to him. "I'm fine."

Abernathy's onyx nose twitched. "Then why do I smell blood?"

"Well—"

A crash resonated from the tangle of trees, saving me from the uncomfortable answer.

My hackles rose as I instinctively leaped between Abernathy and the growing commotion, a worried whine escaping me as the fur on my spine formed a spiky line of alarm.

Had Katherine returned for round two?

Were we hosting a surprise Sasquatch tea party?

Or maybe we'd accidentally interrupted a family of bad-tempered wolverines.

Take your pick, none of the options seemed positive.

Until the underbrush parted and James Morrison broke through, a panting, heaving mess. His normally wet-combed hair was in disarray, a branch stuck to one side. Mud caked his oxford shoes, the hem of his button-up shirt untucked and torn, revealing a flash of marble-pale abs.

"What the fuck?" he gasped, bending at the waist and pressing a hand to his side as if experiencing a cramp.

Which ought to be an impossibility seeing as he didn't breathe.

"Crixus," he panted. "The door—the tracks—"

"Sal," I said by way of explanation. "She's a kitsune. She's been driving Abernathy like a rental car."

Morrison assessed the scene, his eyes widening when they reached the red-tipped dark garland of Abernathy's tail still spasming among the rocks. "I don't want to be the bearer of bad news, but I think the rental car is missing its bumper."

Hearing his use of the singular, I glanced over, surprised to see that the three fluffy appendages had melded into one.

Abernathy's great dark head lifted from the ground, but I quickly moved to block his view. "The important thing is, Sal's gone, you're alive, and everything is going to be okay."

"Hanna . . ." Abernathy's voice was weak, but insistent as he looked up at me with enough love to make my heart swell in my rib cage.

"What is it, baby?" I asked.

The ragged, red, degloved stump at the base of Abernathy's spine twitched. "Why can't I feel my tail?"

"Because it's over here," Morrison said, pointing at the ground from a good ten feet away.

I closed my eyes and indulged in a long exhale as Abernathy began to pant. "Sal?"

"Not exactly," I said.

"What, exactly?" Abernathy's eyes narrowed.

"When I saw that you had three of them instead of one, I remembered that the Costco furry form that Sal had been occupying did too," I explained. "Then I remembered that Braxton kid saying that the way to kill a kitsune was to tear its tails off, so I—"

"What if he was wrong?" The fevered look in Abernathy's eyes felt contagious, leaving me hot and buzzed.

"That was a risk I was willing to take?" I posited, curling the russet ruff of my own tail around my paws.

"Why are we up by the cliff?" Abernathy asked, rolling onto his belly.

"It's a long story. Maybe we should talk about it at home?" I said, feeling a stab of guilt at the pine needles stuck to the sticky, silver-white stump at the base of his spine. "Preferably in direct proximity to Band-Aids and antibiotic ointment?"

"Home," Abernathy echoed, wincing as he tried to push himself up onto his paws. His massive wolf body collapsed back onto the cold ground with a pained yelp that cut through the still forest.

Morrison, who had been examining his torn shirt and grumbling about needing a drink, rushed to Abernathy's side. "Hold still," he said, dipping with arms extended.

"Fuck that." Abernathy scrambled backward with a guttural growl, his teeth bared at Morrison.

"Fuck your pride," Morrison snapped, exasperated. "You're bleeding like a stuck pig and you can't walk. Unless you're suddenly planning on sprouting wings, I need to get you home so you can heal."

Abernathy growled, but didn't fight, emitting a single yelp of pain when Morrison slung him over one shoulder.

"It's funny," Morrison said, glancing back at me as we picked our way down the mountain.

"What is?"

Morrison ducked under a branch, supporting Abernathy's haunches as he bent at the waist. "I went to your place because I couldn't shake the feeling that something was wrong."

"What's funny about that?" I asked.

Morrison paused on the path, dappled moonlight splashing his face with swatches of silver. "I *felt*."

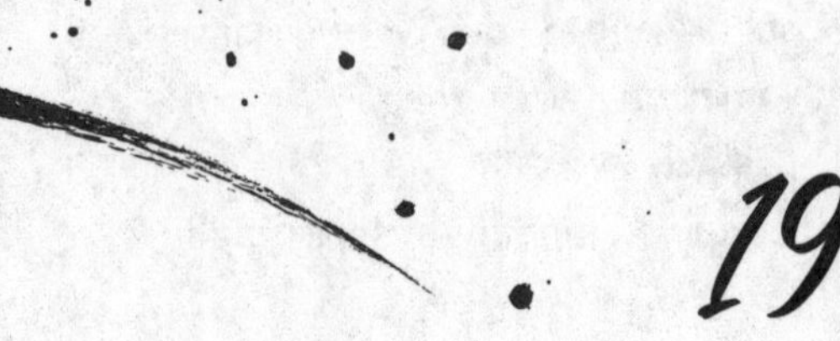

19

The rising sun painted the room in hues of blush and coral as I sat beside Abernathy on the bed, mesmerized by the savage beauty of his unconscious form.

A muscular monolith beneath the cotton sheets, his chiseled chest rose and fell in a deep, steady rhythm, his dark hair tousled over his furrowed brow. Troubled, even in dreams.

I reached out, trailing my fingers along the rough stubble on his jaw, my heart throbbing with an ache that was as much his as it was mine. A knot tightened in my belly, a tangle of gratitude and guilt. Longing and loss and love.

I wanted to reach inside his stubborn skull and unspool every last regret. I wanted to sift out his worries and scrape away his sorrow.

In the wake of Vada's revelation about Abernathy believing he had ruined my life, I deeply doubted that would be possible.

As if sensing my would-be intrusion into his psyche, Abernathy stirred, his eyelids fluttering open, his lips curling in a sleepy, sexy smile.

"Hey," I said.

"Hey," he said. "How long was I out?"

"About twelve hours," I reported.

"Have you been sitting there watching me the entire time?" he asked, his voice still smoky from sleep.

"No," I lied.

Abernathy lifted an eyebrow at me.

"Maybe," I said.

His smile deepened.

"Crixus okay?" he asked.

My mind flicked back to our having arrived back at the house with a profusely bleeding Abernathy to find the hulking demigod stretched out on our couch, a rapidly melting ice pack balanced precariously atop his head.

"Dude," he'd groaned. "What happened? I haven't had a headache like this since Octavian's Saturnalia festival."

Then he'd noticed Abernathy and launched into action, helping Morrison schlep him into the bathroom. I had cleaned and bandaged the wound the best I could, putting extra towels down on the bed before tucking Abernathy into it, praying sleep would do for him what it had always done for Steve.

"He's fine," I said. "Feels like he has a pretty wicked hangover, but that's about it."

"Good." Abernathy's hand slid from beneath the covers and found mine. "You okay?"

The answer to that, alas, was far more complicated.

"Actually," I said, sandwiching my palm atop his roughened knuckles, "there's something I want to talk to you about."

"Is it related to the discussion we were supposed to have yesterday?" he asked.

"Kind of," I admitted.

While I had regaled him with everything I'd learned from Vada until he'd nodded off last night, I'd sort of skimmed over the part where she'd given me a direct download from Abernathy's cerebral database. I'd spent the hours Not Watching him sleep embroiled in a mental wrestling match of my own, debating how best to say what needed to be said.

In the end, I'd decided that direct was best, cobbling together an argument that addressed his concerns a point by point.

And rehearsing it in front of the cats about eighty-seven times.

Taking a deep breath, I launched.

"I know you've been going through some difficulties lately, and those difficulties are mostly because of me. Because you wonder whether you made a mistake making me a werewolf."

My throat tightened, coming to the part I'd struggled with in all my rehearsals.

"The thing is, I *do* regret choosing to be a werewolf sometimes. But I also regret choosing to wear a turtleneck, or staying up until 2:30 in the morning watching TikToks, or eating dairy and gluten in the same meal," I hurried on, desperate to smooth the tension that the first part of my statement had injected into his features. "But what I have never and will never regret is choosing *you*."

Abernathy looked at me, his expression inscrutable. I hurried ahead, not wanting to lose my nerve.

"Even if you'd just been an art gallery owner and I'd just been an unemployed art history grad student. Or if you were a bootlegger and I was a flapper. Or if you were lord and I was a tavern wench, I know that the life we'd have built together would be as beautiful as this one. And it *is*, Mark." I squeezed his hand for emphasis. "It's more beautiful than anything I ever imagined I'd get to experience, even when I'm mopping mothman guts from my muzzle or pressure-spraying Tommyknocker penis pudding from my planters."

Abernathy's predictable wince at my choice in terminology only spurred me on.

"*Ruith ri mo thaobh*," I said, repeating the silky Gaelic syllables he'd spoken to me on the night we had mated. Extending the invitation to him that he had to me. "Run by my side."

Abernathy bent his arm to press our clasped hands against his chest. "Morrison was right. I have done a dog-shit job of protecting you. Of making you happy."

"One, Morrison needs to deeply evaluate his ideals of masculinity," I pointed out. "And two, I don't think that being happy is the point of being alive."

"What is?" he asked, his dark, world-weary eyes searching my face.

"Experience," I said. "Making breakfast and messes and homes and mistakes. Tasting snowflakes and burnt toast and birthday cake and tears. Having sex and chicken pox and fun and dessert. Feeling bored and heartbroken and sick and amazed. Being exhilarated and angry and lazy and free, and loved. And you are, Mark Andrew Abernathy. You are loved. By the pack you built. By the community you chose. By the artists you support. But most especially by me."

Abernathy blinked rapidly, his jaw flexing. "I love you too, Hannalore Harvey."

"Even though I bit your tail off to exorcise a vengeful fox demon?"

"Especially because of that," he said, pushing himself up in the bed.

"On a related topic, I need to check your wound," I said, whipping back the covers. "Wanna roll over so I can take a peek?"

Abernathy complied, rolling onto his hip to expose his lower back and rear end. "You can check me from scalp to soles if you'd like."

"I would definitely like," I said. "Just as soon as Morrison heads home."

I saw the muscles of his lower back tense. "He's still here?"

"Yes, sir," I said. "Spent all night outside, patrolling the perimeter of the house so I could focus on you and you could focus on healing. Which it looks like you did a pretty bang-up job of, by the way." I traced a finger over the bright pink patch just over the cleft of his ridiculously perfect behind.

Abernathy rolled onto his back beneath the covers.

"What if my tail doesn't grow back next time I shift?"

"That doesn't make you any less of a wolf," I assured him. "Anyway, cropped tails are totally a thing. Just think how tough you'd look. Like a—"

"Boston terrier?" Abernathy drawled.

"Doberman," I corrected. "Or a rottweiler."

"You need the shower?" he asked, stretching his arms in an expansive yawn.

"All yours," I said.

I bit my lip, feeling a flicker of desire as I stole a glance at him sauntering stark naked into the bathroom.

After making the bed, I went downstairs to start coffee and feed the cats.

"Come and get it, guys!" I called, setting out three bowls of Fancy Feast pâté nuked for exactly ten seconds. Three furry bodies raced into the kitchen, led by Gilbert, who always managed to move surprisingly fast when victuals were on the line.

Wrapping my hands around my warm mug, I gazed out the dining room windows onto the deck and felt my heart give a painful squeeze. Morrison sitting in an Adirondack chair propped against the back door, his eyes closed, his arms folded across his chest.

I gently tapped on the glass, not wanting to startle him.

But startle him I did.

In an explosion of movement that had my cats scattering for cover, Morrison lurched to his feet, his eyes glowing crimson, fangs bared, body braced for violence.

Oops, I mouthed through the glass.

Sliding the door open, I stepped out onto the deck, hugging my steaming mug close to my chest. "Sorry about that," I said, trying to hide a grin. "But if it's any consolation, I'd be scared shitless if I were an actual threat."

His irises returned a less alarming hue as his limbs slackened. "How's he doing?"

"Nearly good as new," I reported. "A little worried about the logistics once he shifts, but remarkably normal in human form, at least."

"Glad to hear it." Shoving his hands in his pockets, Morrison gazed out over a sky turning from pale yellow to blue. "How are you doing?"

"I'm okay, I think."

"You *think*?" Morrison shifted his eyes to me. "Or you *know*?"

It was a seemingly innocuous question, or would have been, if I didn't know what he was really asking.

I could simply say *I know*, and this discussion would be over. He would leave, and I would step right back into the life I'd built as if nothing had ever happened.

But I owed him more than that. So much more, and for so long.

"What you said, in Dan's basement—"

"Don't," he said. "We don't have to do this. Not you and me."

"We do," I said. "I wish we didn't, but we do."

He nodded slowly, turning to the sound of a rooster crowing from a neighbor somewhere down the valley.

"When we were going down in Hank's plane and I said that I love you, it's because I do."

"But not like you love him." Bitterness hardened his words.

"Did you love your ex-wife like you love me?" I asked.

"I've never loved anyone like I've loved you."

Talk about your epic backfires.

"But you would have." I regretted the words the instant I'd spoken them, but it was too late to call them back.

A crease appeared in the center of his forehead. "What do you mean?"

"Nothing," I said.

"Tell me."

My coffee mug's enamel handle slipped in my clammy grip, sloshing tawny liquid over the rim. "*If* your ex-wife hadn't lost her baby, *if* you had a daughter, you would love that little girl even more than you love me."

In my peripheral vision, I saw his eyes close for an extended beat.

"Yes," he said.

"Imagining her right now, you can feel that love. How real it is. How true?"

"Yes," he repeated.

I gave his answer the moment it deserved, then angled my shoulders to face him. "James, you're my *if*."

Gilbert chose that exact moment to nudge through the open door, padding out onto the deck. Turning his round green eyes up to Morrison, he obliterated the tense moment by headbutting his khaki-clad calf.

Morrison bent to scratch behind his ear, but I had to say it, anyway. Had to say the thing that would hurt this man who loved me.

"What we could have had, what we could have been, it's no less real because it didn't happen. But the difference is, you're still trying to live in that reality, and I can't."

Morrison stood and took my hand, his skin cool from the summer morning mountain air.

"For me, it's still happening. For me, it will never *not* be happening. Even if—"

Gilbert's throaty yowl effectively hijacked of the remainder of the sentence, his tail puffed like a feather duster as he stared out at something unseen in the forest.

Morrison followed his gaze, eyes narrowed.

"Probably just a hawk or something," I said. "This guy would hiss at an envelope if it folded wrong."

With an explosion of locomotion that left me gaping, Gilbert sprinted down the deck stairs.

"No!" I shouted. Strictly an indoor cat since I'd adopted him from Denver's Dumb Friends League—a heart-tugging name if ever there was one—my kibble-motivated big boy had never so much as climbed a tree.

I sprinted after him, panic making my heart hammer.

Morrison vaulted over me, gaining on Gilbert as they raced across the lawn and toward the trees.

"Gilbert! Come back!" I shouted, fully aware that the only words the elder statesman of my feline roommates knew were food-related.

They disappeared into the forest, my mind already churning out a highlight reel of all the terrible fates that might befall my docile, dopey, emotional support tabby.

I thundered through the foliage, scenting the air but finding nothing.

Not surprising, considering Morrison's scent-suppressing self was hot on Gilbert's trail.

Five minutes passed.

Then ten, panic rising within me like the mercury in a thermometer.

I backtracked to the yard, wanting to be there in case he derped his way back home.

I squatted by the edge of the deck, hugging my knees and waiting. And waiting. And waiting.

Time stretched out before me, an immovable object bowing under the weight of my fear.

My vastly unhelpful mind conjured up images of Gilbert being whipped about in the ravening maw of a bear. Or cowering before a cougar. Huddled in the hollow of a tree, a bag of fur and bones, wondering where his safe, warm home had gone.

So immersed was I in my catastrophic fantasies that I didn't even notice Abernathy until his shadow fell across the deck stairs.

"Hanna?" he asked. "What's wrong?"

"It's Gilbert," I managed, my voice shaky.

With those words, the floodgates opened, and a hot, concentrated brew of every awful thing that had happened to me in the past year shook itself free via the sobs racking my rib cage and squirting out of my eyes in a hot, salty stream.

Abernathy crouched beside me, curling an arm around my shoulders, pulling me into his chest, his dark hair still damp from the shower.

"He got out, and Morrison . . . went . . . after . . . him—" I bawled, two wet, shuddery breaths for every word. "But . . . it's been . . . ten . . . minutes and . . . they're . . . still . . . not . . . *back*."

The last word got away from me, tearing from my throat in a choked whine.

Petting my hair, Abernathy gently rocked me back and forth. "Morrison will find him," he said. "He's a detective, remember? It's kind of his thing."

I was on the point of telling him that Morrison's detecting usually involved digital evidence trails, when a rustle caught my attention.

I was on my feet before my next blink, hope floating my heart into my esophagus.

"Gilbert?" My ridiculously syrupy warble sounded pathetic even to me.

Morrison emerged from the trees, his cheek scored by a staff of thin red lines, his arm held aloft in a *Lion King*–esque Circle of Life presentation.

With a bulky tabby bundle balanced on his elevated palm.

I remain surprised that the grass didn't catch fire in my race across it.

"Oh, my baby," I crooned, burying my nose in the warm, slightly dusty scent of his fur. "My baby boy. Don't ever scare Mommy like that again."

I kissed his head and fluffy cheeks before being rewarded with a bunny kick to the wrists. Nevertheless, I held on until we were safely back inside with a door closed behind us.

We all stood around the kitchen island, awkwardness thickening the air. I, with my tear-clumped lashes. Abernathy, shirtless in a pair of gray sweatpants. Morrison, rumpled from his night of patrol, bits of the forest still decorating his hair and khakis.

"Well, I guess I'm going to head out," Morrison said, catching my eye.

"Okay," I said, hugging my torso. "Thank you. For everything."

Morrison gave a stiff little nod and turned to go.

"Wait." Abernathy's word surprised me as much as it had Morrison, who was slow to halt on his way toward the door.

Another exceedingly awkward stretch of time elapsed, during which I struggled to figure out just what Abernathy's pained, uneasy expression reminded me of until I remembered the seconds immediately after James had sucked the bingo ball down his windpipe.

"I owe you . . . an apology."

My fingers flexed against the marble countertop as the floor seemed to skate beneath my feet, not at all certain I'd heard him correctly.

Not often surprised, Morrison's face briefly flashed annoyance before lifting in amazement. "You? Why?"

"In Dan's basement," Abernathy said. "I should have thanked you."

Now, I wasn't just confused, I was completely and utterly confounded. *Thank him? For ripping Abernathy several new orifices before threatening to make off with his mate? In what universe was that a thing?*

Morrison must have been embroiled in a similar contemplation if his stunned silence was any indication.

"What you said. You were . . ." Abernathy's jaw bunched. He swallowed. Swallowed again. "Right."

If, at that moment, the Kool-Aid man had come bursting through the breakfast nook, showering us with chunks of drywall and insulation fluff while delivering his interjectory catchphrase, I would have been less surprised.

"I haven't done a good job of protecting her. But you did when I couldn't. You saw what she needed when I didn't. And you care enough about her happiness to call me on my shit. Even when doing that might decrease your odds of getting what you want."

The truth of these words registered in Morrison's eyes as sadness, the pain immediately evident by their darkening.

"You think she made a mistake when she chose me. And the truth is"—Abernathy's bare chest inflated on a deep inhale—"sometimes I think that too."

The instant denial bubbled up in me, but for once in my mostly chaotic life, I kept my mouth shut.

Abernathy splayed his hands on the counter, the muscles in his forearms and shoulders bunching as he stared down at the veined surface like a road map.

"But the more I think about it, the more I wonder if the real mistake was making her choose at all."

The kitchen fell into a silence so profound I wondered if some cosmic power had just hit Mute on the universe.

I shot a glance toward Morrison, who looked as flummoxed as I felt.

Abernathy lifted his head and looked me straight in the eye. His gaze brimmed with an open vulnerability so raw and real that it stole my breath. "My question is, what if you didn't have to?"

I blinked, certain I'd heard him wrong. Then I blinked again. "Didn't have to what?"

Abernathy didn't look away. Didn't move or shift or do anything that would provide me the opportunity to escape the intensity of his question. "Choose."

20

Outside the windows of my sunny kitchen, the world went on exactly as it always had. Birds sang. Trees rustled. Bees hummed through their busy morning work. And yet, none of it seemed real.

How was it possible that Abernathy's proposition hadn't altered the external landscape the way it had my inner one?

My hand shook as I took a sip of my now-cold coffee, desperately needing to dampen my parched throat.

"Is this a trap?" I asked. "Because this feels like a trap."

"It's no trap," Abernathy said. "It's a question."

I set down the mug and folded my arms across my chest.

"What exactly *is* the question?" I asked. "Because I feel like it's very important to define our terms here so no one ends up making any incorrect assumptions."

Abernathy folded his hands behind his back and paced over to the windows. "While you were gone, I broke a lot of things. I also chopped enough wood to last us for the next five winters. Anything I could do to keep my jealousy from eating me alive."

I tried to catch Morrison's eye, remembering what he'd so accurately forecasted while we were still in Hank's bunker.

"But," Abernathy continued, "I was also relieved that you were with him. Because I knew. I knew he would protect you at all costs. And, as much as I hate to admit it, I'll never be enough to protect you from all the threats out there now that you're the alpha."

Morrison cleared his throat. "It's not like it's the easiest job."

"Being the alpha?" I asked.

"Protecting you," Morrison said.

Abernathy gave him half a smile. "Right?"

"Then, when we were in Dan's basement, and you crawled up my ass for being jealous, it finally hit me. The way I felt while you were gone is how Morrison must feel all the time."

I bit my cheek to stifle a snort.

This just in! Local lycanthrope discovers empathy, join Live Five News *at nine for further details!*

"And again this morning, when—uh—the striped one who always looks like he has TV static happening behind his eyes got out—"

"*Gilbert*," I said.

"Gilbert," Abernathy said. "My first thought was how grateful I was that I didn't have to chase that bastard through the trees, knowing how devastated she would be if I failed and something happened to him. My second was that I couldn't wait for you to get the fuck out of here so I could drag her back to bed."

It's a good thing I hadn't fully finished sipping my coffee, or I might have inhaled what remained of my French roast. My cheeks felt like they'd been blowtorched.

Morrison's lips tightened into a line.

"My third thought was how fucking unfair it was that you'd spent all night protecting us, all morning chasing her goddamn cat, but I'd be spending all afternoon fucking the woman you love enough to help even though you'd probably be spending yours alone."

Mixed hungers warred on Morrison's face, and for a moment, I couldn't tell whether he wanted to crush Abernathy's skull with his bare hands or put those hands somewhere else entirely.

"I can't promise I won't want to disembowel you every time I look at you," Abernathy said, fingers clenching into fists. "But for Hanna's sake, I'm willing to try."

Abernathy's gaze swiveled back to me then, eyes blazing my favorite shade of burnt-sugar amber. "So, my question is, is that something you'd like to *experience*?"

My heart beat so hard, I was afraid it might tear free of my rib cage.

"I-I don't know," I stammered. "I've never thought about it."

Abernathy raised an eyebrow at me. "*Never?*"

"*Well*," I said, tracing a finger along a vein in the marble countertop. "It's not something I ever thought about as a possible option in real life."

"And if it were?" This time, the question wasn't Abernathy's, but Morrison's.

Which, I realized, was tantamount to his admitting that he was at least considering it.

"I guess that would depend on what kind of experience we're talking about," I said. Heat had already begun to bake from beneath the collar of my blouse, a fine film of sweat misting the back of my neck.

I glanced at Abernathy, wondering if he'd gotten that far along in his considerations.

Judging by the murderous look in his eyes, he had.

"I don't think I can handle the thought of the two of you alone together," he admitted. "Before we'd mated, it nearly killed me."

I gave him a querulous look.

"Okay," Abernathy said. "It nearly killed other people. Mostly Morrison."

"Understandable," Morrison grunted. "I've pictured your violent death more times than there are grains of sand on the French Riviera."

Abernathy nodded. "Only fair."

"So we're talking you . . ." I pointed to Abernathy. "And him." I gestured to Morrison. "*And* me?"

"More like you and me, *and* you and him."

I couldn't quite tell if the shadow that passed behind Morrison's eyes was desire . . . or disappointment.

An idea I bookmarked, highlighted, and cataloged in my mental spank for a long, cold winter.

Or, you know, a Tuesday.

"I'm in," Morrison said.

Woe betide me to realize that the instant jolt of adrenaline I felt course through my system wasn't excitement but panic.

I'd spent so much of the conversation trying to determine if these two men who'd openly loathed each other with a vibrant and burning passion could possibly arrive an agreement about this proposed arrangement that I hadn't actually considered whether *I* could.

Me, naked, with Abernathy *and* Morrison.

Which led me to an even more terror-inducing thought.

Abernathy *and* Morrison, naked with *me*.

At which point, my keen deductive powers delivered me to the most alarming prospect still: Abernathy *and* Morrison naked *with each other.*

Or *near* each other, at least.

"We're all consenting adults," I said. "I think, given time to lay out some ground rules and discuss some healthy boundaries, we could potentially put together an equitable and mutually satisfactory arrangement, don't you?"

And then I fainted.

I awoke in my very own giant four-poster bed, fully clothed, and deeply confused. Abernathy perched on the edge of the mattress, his handsome features creased with concern.

"I just had the *weirdest* dream," I said.

"What's that?" he asked, brushing a lock of hair away from my cheek.

"Well, we were in the kitchen, and Morrison was there, and you said—" I giggled, feeling my face heat. "You said that you, and he, and I should—" I shook my head, unable to even speak the rest. "Can you even imagine?" I asked, cackling uproariously.

Abernathy didn't join me. "So you've changed your mind?"

As the last wisps of unconsciousness drifted away, I looked up into Abernathy's earnest gaze, and I remembered.

It hadn't been a dream at all.

Just a development dramatic enough to feel like one.

"Look, you know how much it means to me that you were willing to consider this," I said, lacing my fingers with his. "But I just don't think I'm cut out for that kind of thing, you know? I can barely handle an in-person conversation with more than one human, let alone a—"

And then Morrison walked out of our bathroom wearing only a towel, and my mouth snapped shut with an audible *click*.

His sandy hair still wet across his forehead, droplets the towel had missed gliding into the sharp shelf of the deep *V* cut into either side of his hips, and I completely forgot what I'd been saying.

Forgot what words were entirely, pretty much.

"You guys have great water pressure," he said.

"It's actually the showerhead," Abernathy said. "Our contractor used to be a Swedish engineer."

"You'll have to give me his name." Morrison re-tucked the fold of his towel, the light pouring in from our bedroom windows providing the briefest hint of the anatomy beneath. "I've been meaning to redo the bathrooms in my townhome for a while now."

This mundane snatch of conversation somehow made everything that much more bizarre.

"How are you feeling?" Morrison asked. "Better?"

So, of course, I burst into an insane fit of giggles.

"My vampire ex-boyfriend is standing in the bedroom I share with my mate, wearing nothing but a towel and asking me how I'm feeling while the aforementioned mate sits there like he doesn't want to tear his arms off and beat his cranium like a snare drum." I wiped a tear of mirth from my cheek. "I'm totally fine. Everything is totally fine. This is all completely normal."

Abernathy and Morrison traded a look.

"What are you most afraid of?" Abernathy asked.

I pushed myself up, propping my back on the pillows. "I just don't want this to change anything. Between us."

Gazing deep into my eyes, Abernathy scooted closer to me on the bed. "I do," he said.

My eyes must have betrayed the instant surge of anxiety I felt, because Abernathy leaned in, taking my face in his hands.

"I don't want to be like Kat," he said, his voice raw with sincerity. "I don't want to be fossilized by jealousy and bitterness."

He touched my cheek lightly, his fingers brushing the corners of my lips. "I want something different for myself. For us. But whatever happens, there's one thing that will never change."

"What's that?" I asked.

Abernathy's eyes darkened. "You are *mine*, Hanna." He rubbed the pad of his thumb over my cheekbone. "You belonged to me before you ever set foot in my gallery. You belonged to me before you rear-ended Morrison's car. You belonged to me before he ever kissed you. You belonged to me while he was inside you." He swiped my lower lip. "And you will belong to me while I watch him make you come. If you want that."

I lifted my eyes to Morrison, leaning against the dresser, awaiting my answer.

As I was.

Did I want this?

How could I even know, when the rules of the patriarchal

culture I'd been raised in and Abernathy's legendary territorial jealousy had made any connection with Morrison—platonic or otherwise—a total impossibility?

"I could want that," I said. "Hypothetically speaking."

"What would it take to make it *not* hypothetical?" Abernathy asked, pushing a lock of hair back from my face.

I thought for a moment, meeting his eyes. "Proof that you can handle it. That no matter what happens, or how you end up feeling about it, you won't shut me out."

"What proof can I offer you?" he asked.

Scooting up in bed, I held out my hand. Abernathy took it, his large, rough palm warm against mine.

"A vow," I said.

His dark brows punched together. "What kind of vow?"

"Repeat after me. I, Mark Andrew Abernathy—" I began.

"I, Mark Andrew Abernathy . . ." he echoed.

"Do solemnly swear—"

"Do solemnly swear . . ."

"That no matter how irritating, mentally taxing, or emotionally uncomfortable I might become—"

"No matter how irritating, mentally taxing, or emotionally uncomfortable I might become . . ."

"I will not brood, scowl, break things, or shut myself in my den for days on end with cured meats and a detailed list of my grudges."

Abernathy's eyes widened.

"I literally found the list the first week I was working for you," I said. "Just say the words."

Abernathy's nostrils flared, but he did as ordered.

"I will do my best to verbally communicate my thoughts and feelings at all times so my mate can act accordingly."

Once again, he dutifully parroted my words.

"Especially if naked," I added.

Despite his flattened lips, Abernathy managed the last phrase.

I released his hand. "Do you accept those terms?"

"I do," he said.

Such a short phrase, this vow spoken by countless lovers over countless generations. The formal declaration tasked with twining two lives.

Today, it would join three.

So many of the stories that ended this way began with a drunken whirl, lowered inhibitions, a chance encounter, flirtation catching fire.

It seemed right somehow that ours wouldn't.

Not a dance in the dark but a fight by daylight.

The opening punch thrown by me in the form of a giggle that only grew more manic the harder I tried to banish it.

Because I had never been a sultry siren. Had never mastered the seductress's art.

"Sorry," I said, fighting to keep a straight face as Abernathy closed the door to keep the cats out and Morrison approached the bed.

I drew in a deep breath and blew out a "Whew" as I passed my hand in front of my face like I'd seen so many actors do when trying to shift characters.

"At least you guys will finally be able to answer whose is bigger*ohhh* my God I am *so* bad at this!" I buried my face in my pillow to stifled a teakettle squeak. "I'm so sorry," I mumbled through the layers of cotton batting. "I can do this. I promise."

"I don't know if I can." Hearing the stricken note in Morrison's voice, I felt an immediate pang of regret.

I shot up in the bed, snatching the pillow away from my face. "James, *no*. I was totally kidding. You're both—I mean, neither of you have anything to—"

"It's not that," he said. "At least, it wasn't until you just said that."

"What is it?" I asked, my voice suddenly softer, more tentative.

Morrison, still leaning against the dresser, blew out a long breath before answering. His hazel eyes held a far-off look that made me worry. "I just . . . haven't been with anyone since . . ." He broke off, looking frustrated with himself.

Silence descended upon the room as his confession hung in the air.

Seeing his wicked hickey after the doughnut shop encounter and hearing about his process, so to speak, I had just kind of assumed he'd been tapping asses left, right, and center.

Abernathy cleared his throat. "It's not mechanically impossible, you know. As long as you've fed recently, you should be able to—"

"I know that," Morrison said, rolling his eyes in disgust at Abernathy's attempted undead birds and bees talk. "Jesus, Mark."

"Ohhhh," I said. "You're not worried about my comparing you to Abernathy. You're worried about my comparing you . . . to you."

By the sullen set of his jaw, I knew I'd hit the mark.

I patted the bed, and Morrison walked over and sat down. "Thing is, we're all kind of in uncharted territory here," I said. "You haven't been with me since I turned into a werewolf. I could be completely different from how you remember too."

"But your completely different doesn't involve cold skin and a tendency to bite."

"You're half-right." I winked at him and was gratified that it won me a smile, however strained. "Let's just take it slowly, okay? No expectations. No regrets."

He nodded.

"Would it help if you fed now?" Hearing Abernathy ask this made my heart skip double Dutch.

"Probably," Morrison said.

Abernathy tipped his head to one side. "Help yourself."

I wasn't sure who was more surprised by this development—Morrison or me.

"Look, I know you're on this whole experience kick," I said, "but—"

"I want to know how it feels," Abernathy said.

"But you've been bitten by a vampire before," I reminded him.

"I haven't been bitten by *him*."

And he had a point. Having been bitten by exactly two vampires, I could attest to the vastly varying quality of the experience, even though both of them had ended in near death.

"Are you sure that's a good idea?" I asked. "You did lose a lot of blood yesterday."

"I don't think lack of blood flow is a problem." Following Abernathy's quick downward glance, I made a remarkable discovery.

He was already hard.

"If you're sure," Morrison said, his eyes lingering on the sizable bulge in Abernathy's sweats. Because it was, of course, filled with blood.

"I'm sure. With one stipulation?"

"Which is?" Morrison asked.

"Do it to me like you did it to her."

Morrison's eyes began to darken, the whites disappearing as if filling with spilled ink. "Gladly."

He stalked over to the bed with the lethal grace only the undead could possess. In a flash, Morrison was straddling my knees, grabbing Abernathy's nape from behind without a moment's hesitation and turning his head to expose the long line of his throat. Abernathy inhaled sharply as if all the air in the room had been sucked into his lungs.

Both men were looking at me as Morrison's fangs sank into the smooth, tanned flesh of Abernathy's neck.

They groaned at exactly the same time.

Mark's pain.

James's pleasure.

It was savage.

It was beautiful.

It was without question the most erotic thing I'd ever witnessed.

Yet.

The towel swathed around Morrison's hips tented as his arousal became apparent, and a sympathetic ache unfurled in my abdomen.

Mark suddenly grabbed my wrist, yanking me over to him with a primal growl. His lips crashed into mine, frantic, his hand tangling in my hair to keep me close. It was as if he was trying to drink from me the way Morrison drank from him, his tongue sweeping over mine in long, wet, possessive strokes.

Claiming me. Branding me as his own. Sealing his vow.

His hand beneath my skirt, pressing against the seam of my sex, already damp through the lace.

"Christ," Abernathy breathed.

The bed shifted as Morrison wrenched his mouth away, his teeth coated crimson as he exhaled an ecstatic breath to the heavens.

"What does it feel like?" I asked, slipping a finger beneath the lace edge of my panties. "To have his blood inside you?"

Morrison's eyes fell closed, rapture radiating from his features.

"Like fire." His hand moved toward his chest as if he needed to physically feel the words he was uttering. "Like lightning in my veins."

The rough pad of Abernathy's finger brushed the hot bundle of nerves at my core, and I was unable to contain my moan.

"*Fuck*," Morrison panted. "I can smell it. I can *feel* it. I can feel your need." His nostrils flared, his face contorted in a heartrending echo of one of my favorite Baroque statues, *The Ecstasy of St. Theresa*.

Agony and ecstasy.

His eyes flew open, golden as the dawn.

"Please," he begged. "Please can I taste you? I don't know how long this will last."

I looked to Abernathy, his dark gaze as solemn as a priest's, offering absolution.

"Yes," I said.

Morrison crawled toward me on his hands and knees, his eyes wild and primal, blazing with a fierce intensity that made me shiver. Hands on the back of my knees, he pulled me down the covers and pushed my thighs apart, not even bothering to pull my panties to the side before he pressed his tongue against the lace.

"Gods, Hanna. You have no idea how I've missed you. Missed this." He pushed his mouth against me, the words vibrating against my already sensitive flesh.

But I did.

Because I remembered.

I remembered, because—unlike Abernathy—Morrison and I hadn't been together long enough for me to stop counting.

The first time, when he'd touched me with the gentleness of a saint and worshiped me with the reverence of a sinner.

The last time, when he'd clutched me like I was his salvation and drove into me like I was his damnation all at once.

Desperation only served to amplify the intensity of his passion.

His mouth was hot and unyielding, his tongue stroking against my cotton-clad center, sending shivers rocketing down my spine. I gasped as the first wave of pleasure radiated from my core, tensing and arching under his artful ministrations.

"I used to imagine this." Abernathy spoke as one in a trance, moved like it too. His eyes distant, his fingers slow and methodical as he slipped open the buttons of my blouse.

"When I knew you were with him, and I was alone. I'd think about the two of you, together." Abernathy's finger circled my stiff nipple, a distracted echo of Morrison's tongue flicking and rolling around my clit. "It almost drove me mad."

I bucked as Abernathy lightly pinched a stiff peak.

"I hated knowing that he'd been inside you." Flicking open my bra, Abernathy uttered an appreciative grunt as my breasts tumbled free. "I hated that he knew something about you that I didn't. Because even after all the lifetimes when I'd found you, courted you, begged you, I still didn't know what it would feel like to fuck you. What it was like to sink into you. Inch. By. Inch."

Abernathy punctuated his words with flicks of his tongue, fastening onto the hard bud on the last. Electricity arced through me, a frisson between the hot, wet points of pleasure.

"I *hated* him for knowing what you sounded like when you came."

A ragged *unh* tore from me as Abernathy tested the sensitive flesh with his teeth.

"So why don't you show me?" Lifting his head from my breast, Abernathy glared at Morrison beneath hooded lids. "Why don't you show me how you made her come?"

My fingers threaded through Morrison's silky hair. I gasped in surprise, arching my back, offering him more. His mouth fastened onto my clit, making me squirm and writhe. Gasp and moan.

I could feel it, building. A storm within me, spurred on by the sensations assaulting my body. The tension coiled tighter, a spring wound near to breaking. My fingers twisted in the sheets, clutching at the rumpled fabric as if it were a lifeline.

Abernathy's gaze met mine, an intensity burning within their depths that seemed to rival the sun.

And then, Armageddon.

Cataclysm.

I convulsed with a thunderclap of pleasure that left me breathless and aching. Morrison rode out the storm with me, his fingers circling my center through wave after wave of ecstasy. Abernathy didn't break eye contact through it all, watching me, studying me.

I lay slack and boneless, wet and wrung out.

As I lay there, my chest heaving and my body still trembling with the aftershocks of pleasure, Abernathy moved. He slid his fingers along the length of me, tracing the path Morrison had taken moments before. I let out a soft groan, rolling my hips against his hand. Desire flamed back to life within me like a phoenix reborn from its ashes.

"On your knees," Abernathy ordered, his voice low and seductive.

Not in a million years would it have occurred to me to disobey.

Abernathy gathered my hair in one hand, his fingers a comforting weight against the back of my head as he guided me onto all fours.

"That's it," he murmured, the tender tone of his voice in stark contrast to the pressing hunger I could sense in him. In one swift motion, Abernathy pushed down the waistband of his sweats, his erection springing free. His gaze moved from me to Morrison. "Now you're going to watch her suck my cock."

Abernathy looked at me with a satisfaction that was terrifying and thrilling all at once. I shifted my gaze to his cock, thick and heavy in his hand, the sight of it making my mouth water with anticipation. Then he turned me toward Morrison, who had risen to his knees, his eyes a hot mix of desire and curiosity.

He watched as Abernathy pushed my head down toward his groin, our eyes locked on each other's as if daring the other to look away first. I could almost taste the crisp saltiness of Abernathy's skin on my tongue before I'd even wrapped my lips around him.

My fingers curled around his base, stroking him lightly as I leaned in. I heard Morrison's sharp intake of breath but didn't break eye contact. Abernathy shuddered beneath my touch, his hand flexing in my hair. He was already hard, throbbing against my palm, a pearly drop glistening at his swollen head.

"How do I like it?" Abernathy growled.

"Like this," I murmured to Morrison, running the flat of my tongue up Abernathy's length before flicking it against the slit at the top.

"That's right," Abernathy groaned, the sound deep and guttural as he tightened his grip on my hair. "Now suck it."

I obeyed. Closing my eyes, I took him into my mouth, sliding my lips down his length. I could taste him now, his flavor overtaking all senses.

"Jesus, Hanna . . ." Abernathy gasped, his breath hitching.

I moved my head, taking him in and out, the rhythm growing faster and harsher. My hands cupped around his base while my tongue swirled him inside my mouth. His reactions were addicting; the way his body jerked, the low groan that sounded in his throat.

Abernathy's fingers twitched in my hair, a wordless plea as his body tensed. "Easy, baby," he warned, his voice choked with imminent release. He pulled away abruptly, leaving me gasping and blinking up at him. Sweat glistened on his brow, making his dark eyes appear almost feverish. "I'm not ready to come yet."

Abernathy gripped the base of his cock, squeezing hard. "Morrison," his voice was gruff and full of strained desire, "come here."

Morrison rose to his knees, scooting behind me on the bed.

"Let him see, baby," Abernathy said as he slowly moved his hands over my back. His touch was soft but commanding, creating goose bumps over my skin as he traced the curve of my spine to the swell of my ass. "Let him see how wet you are for me."

My breath hitched as Abernathy nudged my legs apart, exposing me fully to Morrison's gaze. I could feel his eyes on me, burning and intense, and it ignited a new wave of arousal that left my knees weak. Abernathy's fingers trailed along the slick folds between my thighs, collecting the wetness that had accumulated there.

"You want to feel this?" he asked Morrison.

"Yes," Morrison growled.

Abernathy slipped a finger inside me, then two, stretching and stroking before he pulled them out, wet with arousal. "Then taste her first."

Something flickered in Morrison's eyes, but he didn't hesitate to lean forward, capturing Abernathy's fingers in his mouth. His actions were rougher than I'd expected, intense and hungry as he had been when fastening his mouth to Abernathy's throat.

Abernathy's cock twitched as if in experience.

"What do you think, Hanna?" Abernathy asked, beginning to move his fist up and down his own length. "Should I let him fuck you?"

Far beyond trying to decipher motives at this point, I gave my answer by wrapping my lips around the head of Abernathy's cock.

He jerked, his hips driving forward before snapping back.

"I think she wants you to fuck her, *Detective Morrison*."

How devastatingly erotic the reminder of their initial enmity was with Abernathy looking at him over my sweat-kissed back.

I felt Morrison's body behind me, warmed by Abernathy's blood, his taut abdomen pressed against my bare buttocks. His fingers danced across my spine, following the path of my vertebrae down to the curve of my bottom.

His hands were shaking as he guided himself to my entrance. I gasped at the sensation of him pressing against me, the tip of his cock teasing my wetness. I released Abernathy's length from my mouth, looking up at him with hunger in my eyes.

"Do you want us both to fuck you?" Abernathy asked, tipping a finger beneath my chin.

I nodded.

They did.

Morrison groaned as he thrust forward, filling me in one swift movement. Abernathy grunted as he sank himself into my mouth. The mutual pleasure was piercing, making me arch my back and cry out in divine satisfaction.

My body was a living, breathing conduit of pleasure, lit up with the feel of them both. Every nerve ending seemed magnified, every touch amplified, every sensation meteoric.

Abernathy's hand tangled in my hair, gripping it tight like reins as he deepened his thrusts into my mouth. His groans were low, guttural, punctuated by hisses of breath as I used my tongue to stroke him. The taste of him was heady and intoxicating—raw masculinity, carnal need.

Behind me, Morrison matched his rhythm. Slick, slow, and deliberate, each thrust pushing me farther onto Abernathy. A delicious tension coiled within me, the sensations too much and not enough all at once.

"Good girl," Morrison murmured, his voice thick with pleasure. "Oh, fuck, are you a good girl."

I could feel them escalating, driving each other onward through me.

"Should we let him come inside you?" Abernathy asked, knowing full well I couldn't answer. "Or make him come on your back?"

A wicked thrill coursed through me at Abernathy's words, and I sent him a heated look from beneath my lashes. His eyes were feral with desire, the pupils dilated almost to the point of swallowing the earthy color whole. The sight only heightened my own arousal, making me clench around Morrison.

Morrison groaned against my skin, his hips jerking as he thrust deeper inside me. A shiver rocked through me, a precursor to the climax building inside me like an incoming storm. I tightened around Morrison involuntarily, causing him to buck forward and slam his cock into me.

The sudden sharp pleasure was too much, and I felt myself losing my breath, my control, my sanity.

Morrison's hands settled on my hips, gripping me tightly as he pounded me from behind. His body was molded against mine, moving with the same brutal rhythm that had my mind reeling and my senses swimming. I could feel the strength in his arm as he held me in place, the tenderness in his touch as he kneaded my flesh.

Abernathy watched, his eyes glazed with lust as he enjoyed the spectacle we made. His cock throbbed in my mouth, hot and hard as I sucked him eagerly, doing my best to match Morrison's tempo.

A low, guttural growl rumbled in his chest as he stared down at me, eyes blazing with dark, primal lust. Then, with a swift motion, he pulled me toward him, and away from Morrison, who uttered a single sob before losing himself in hot pulses on the small of my back.

Abernathy lasted a full ten seconds longer, pumping his hips into my mouth before letting out a growl that was more wolf than man. He spilled himself into me, the taste of him as familiar and known as my own heartbeat. I swallowed instinctively, taking all of him in until he stilled, spent.

We collapsed into a messy, sweaty heap on the bed. Abernathy was panting, his chest rising and falling against my back, still cupping my breasts lazily as if he just couldn't bear to let go. Morrison lay sprawled behind me, his fingers tracing absent circles on my hips. The room hummed with satisfaction and half-told secrets.

I wasn't sure when or how we'd fallen asleep, or how many times we'd woken to create a shifting collage of passion and pleasure. The first light of dawn crept through the curtains, casting a warm glow on the tangled limbs and tousled sheets.

Carefully, and with patience I never would have guessed myself capable of, I disentangled myself from not one but two men who had altered my life, and now each other's for all eternity.

As I walked into the bathroom, I caught a glimpse of the wanton in the mirror—wild hair, flushed cheeks, body a map of passion.

Meeting her glowing green eyes, I smiled.

I had never looked more like myself.

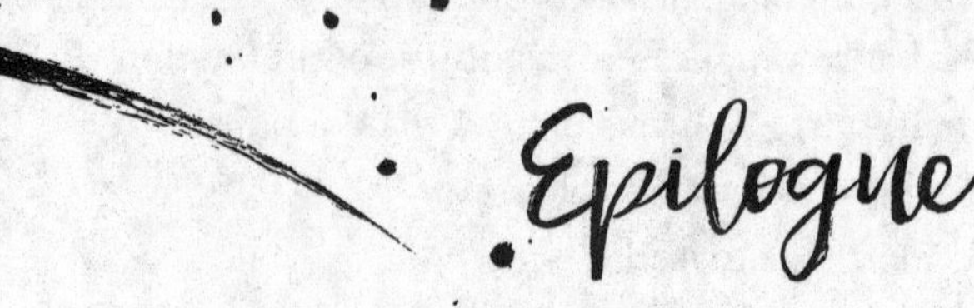

Epilogue

"I told you it would grow back!"

Morrison and I stood on the immaculate green bolt of pristinely manicured lawn cloistered by cypress trees, the historic Italian villa in the quaint seaside town of Castiglione della Pescaia stretching skyward behind us. In front of us, a view—a slice of ocean so hypnotically blue it could've been swiped from a postcard. And against that improbable perfection, a large, dark wolf sat, its elegant muzzle aimed toward his tail.

Here, on the first vacation we'd taken together as a throuple, a full two months after our first shared encounter, Abernathy had finally mustered the gumption to shift so he could assess the damage.

"Does it look smaller to you?" Abernathy asked, his features conveying worry despite their brutal, canine grace.

Morrison, who had been lounging against an ancient olive tree, squinted at Abernathy's backside with the seriousness of an American Kennel Club judge.

"I mean, I'd only ever seen you in your . . . uh, alternate form a handful of times before—"

"Before Hanna ripped it off."

"To save your life from a vengeance-driven fox Fae spirit, thank you very much," I pointed out. Folding my arms across my chest. "And what's with you asking Morrison? Now that there's a male in your immediate vicinity, it's automatically his opinion that matters?" I said with mostly feigned irritation.

Abernathy's golden eyes flicked to mine. "Okay, does it look smaller to you?"

Rolling my eyes, I strolled closer to inspect the appendage in question. "Looks like the same old tail to me," I said, trying to keep a straight face. "Fluffy, expressive, and with that cute little kink at the end."

"Gee, thanks," Abernathy said, curling it around his paws.

As I watched him, with the last rays of Mediterranean sunlight glancing off his fur, I couldn't help but think about the twisted road we'd traveled to get here. My first order of business—after having an existential crisis about how inviting Morrison into our bed would affect my life in general—was to hire help to run the gallery.

In addition to the shifter community.

By slow degrees, I'd been able to take more and more off my plate.

Leaving treasured pockets of time for me to begin asking myself a radical question.

What would I *like* to do today?

Sometimes the answer was splurging on a sheep's milk cheese from the Pontic Alps. Sometimes, it was suggesting that my mate and my vampire lover take a spontaneous Tuscan vacation.

And slowly, our new normal had begun to take shape.

"Hey," I said suddenly, an idea sparking. "How about we test that tail in a more dynamic environment? Like, I don't know . . . racing to the cliff? It's almost sunset. I'll bet it's going to be gorgeous."

The sun was flirting with the horizon, casting a warm glow over the sprawling villa grounds as if nature herself had swiped right. The mature trees stood like silent sentinels, witnessing our every sigh, and the ocean view was so breathtaking it should've come with an inhaler.

"I'm in if Mark is," Morrison said, the corner of his mouth tilting up in that devil-may-care smile.

"You're on," Abernathy agreed, his voice a low rumble that promised trouble of the most entertaining kind.

I grinned, shucking my sundress and stripping off my bikini before tapping into the wild, willful wolf within. "Last one to the cliff is a rotten egg!"

I took off, my heart pounding with excitement, Morrison's laughter and Abernathy's growl intertwining in a symphony of delicious male rivalry behind me.

Bolting through the villa's garden, my paws pounded against the earth—a symphony of thuds that sent soil and the scent of rosemary and wildflowers into the air.

The world blurred into a verdant green as I zigzagged through the thickets.

"Are we hiking or auditioning for *The Fast and the Furriest*?" Abernathy quipped from somewhere behind me, his voice laced with amusement.

"Jesus, you're old!" I shouted back with utmost fondness.

As we ascended, the air grew cooler, tinged with the salty kiss of the ocean mingling with the earthy musk of damp, cool foliage.

My calves began to protest, but I pushed on, spurred by the exhilarating rush of the chase and the promise of a sunset. The ground leveled out just as I caught sight of a khaki blur blowing by me to the cliff ahead.

Morrison.

He reached the top first, followed by Abernathy a split second later.

"Show-offs," I wheezed, trying to slow my heart as I approached the cliff.

The view was nothing short of breathtaking. Below us, the ocean stretched endlessly, its surface growing silver scales as the full moon asserted its presence.

"Wow," was all I could muster, wit failing me in the face of such majesty.

"Pretty impressive," Abernathy agreed, seating himself next to me.

"I'll say," Morrison said, plopping down on my other side.

Later, after we'd exhausted ourselves once again, I stirred from sleep, gently extricating myself from the tangled mess of sheets and limbs. The villa was silent except for the gentle lullaby of the sea outside.

Wrapping my naked body in a throw blanket, I slipped through the open French doors onto the balcony, feeling the balmy night air against my naked skin.

The full moon silvered the restless sea, and damn if those waves weren't the exact luminous shade of Katherine Abernathy's eyes.

A shiver ran down my spine that had nothing to do with the night air and everything to do with the thought of her out there, plotting her next move in our centuries-old game of cat and mouse. Or in our case, wolf and . . . well, other wolf.

"Katherine," I whispered. "I'm not afraid of you." The wind stirred, caressing my naked skin. "I'm not afraid of anyone."

And for the first time in my strange life, I knew it was true.

Just as I knew that Katherine would find me again.

Just as I knew that when she did, I'd be ready.

Acknowledgments

My undying gratitude to Kerrigan Byrne, my first reader, Emotional Support Human, and friend. You are the Gutter Bear to my Trash Panda. Me and thee.

My enthusiastic adoration for my brother, Stephen, and his wife, Shayla, who continue to let me borrow them from real life to make Hanna's world a friendlier, funnier, and infinitely more fabulous place.

My thanks and huge hugs to Susan Barnes, for her exceptional editing prowess, and to the entire team at Tor Books. Thank you for helping me bring my silly stories to the world.

And finally, for the lovely readers who've (mostly) patiently waited for Hanna and the pack's ongoing tale. Here's hoping it will be worth the while . . . and then some. <winky face emoji because, damn it, I'm a Xennial and you'll have to pry them from my cold, dead, arthritic fingers.>

About the Author

USA Today bestselling author Cynthia St. Aubin is the author of the Case Files of Dr. Matilda Schmidt, Paranormal Psychologist series and the Jane Avery mysteries, *Private Lies* and *Lying Low*. She wrote her first play at age eight and made her brothers perform it for the admission price of gum wrappers. A steal, considering she provided the wrappers in advance. Though her early work debuted to mixed reviews, she never quite gave up on the writing thing, even while earning a mostly useless master's degree in art history and taking her turn as a cube monkey in the corporate warren. Because the voices in her head kept talking to her, and they discourage drinking at work, she started writing instead.